"Hard A'starboa
Hands to Hea
Haul, You Bit
Haul!

I caught the rail as the ship surged suddenly beneath me, heeled slightly and leaped forward, urgent as a living thing.

Ahead of us, the clouds opened, wider and wider, revealing a blazing expanse of blue that hurt the eye to look at. Purest, infinite azure above us and below, the depthless blueness of a perfect sky. I stood rapt. It was in light we rode, light that filled our sails and rippled beneath our timbers, light we breathed, light that filled our veins and quickened our pulses.

As a boy I'd lain on the lawn, looking up at the clouds passing over the rooftop, imagining they were standing still and that I and the roof were surging upward among them. Now it was happening.

Over us great sea birds wheeled and cried. In Jyp's voice I heard the same wild exultation, limitless as the horizonless blue beyond.

"Over the dawn! Over the airs of the earth! We're under way!"

"Remarkable... A very good and very powerful writer"

Anne McCaffrey,
author of *NERILKA'S STORY*

Other Avon Books by
Michael Scott Rohan

THE WINTER OF THE WORLD *Trilogy*
THE ANVIL OF ICE
THE FORGE IN THE FOREST
THE HAMMER OF THE SUN

CHASE
~THE~
MORNING

MICHAEL SCOTT ROHAN

AVON BOOKS • NEW YORK

AVON BOOKS
A division of
The Hearst Corporation
1350 Avenue of the Americas
New York, New York 10019

Published in hardcover by William Morrow and Company, Inc.; for information address Permissions Department, William Morrow and Company, Inc., 1350 Avenue of the Americas, New York, New York 10019.

First AvoNova Printing: May 1992

AVONOVA TRADEMARK REG. U.S. PAT. OFF. AND IN OTHER COUNTRIES, MARCA REGISTRADA, HECHO EN U.S.A.

Printed in the U.S.A.

RA   10 9 8 7 6 5 4 3 2 1

Dedication

To John Jarrold

CHASE

~THE~

MORNING

The hour that dreams are brighter and winds colder,
The hour that young love wakes on a white shoulder ...
That hour, O Master, shall be bright for thee:
Thy merchants chase the morning down the sea ...

Flecker, *Hassan*

CHASE

~THE~

MORNING

CHAPTER ONE

I BRAKED HARD and pulled up; but the car in front of me shot through the lights just as they changed. I sat cursing myself as I watched those tail-lights dwindle away into the gathering gloom, and the other endless lanes of traffic come swarming out after them. The idiot in the flash German sport behind me beeped his horn, but I was too irritated with myself to pay any attention to him. There had been time, the half-second or so before the other lights changed; I could have put my foot flat down and raced through. I'd been close enough to the lights to get away with it, but this was a difficult, twisty junction, with lousy visibility on all four sides. All it would need was somebody else as impatient as me ... Damn it to hell, I'd done the safe thing! But then that was me all over, wasn't it? Safe driver; safe car; safe job; safe life ...

Then why was I so furious? At work it hadn't been the sort of day that leaves you snarling; it rarely was. Momentarily, idiotically, I found myself wishing it had been, that I'd had something to snarl at, to tussle with, to put a sharper flavour into the day. I raised my eyes to the skies, and at once forgot all my irritation. The sun had already left the ground in gloom, but it was lighting up a whole new landscape among the lowering clouds, one of those rare fantastic sunset coasts of rolling hills, deep bays, stretches of tidal sands, endless archipelagoes of islands in a calm estuary of molten gold. This one was made even more convincing by the shallow slope of the road; I might have been looking down from some steeper hill onto the real estuary. Except that that was far less picturesque, a flat, grim industrial riverside first laid waste when ships and shipbuilding boomed, then stricken a second time when they collapsed. None of the goods I dealt with passed through the docks here now; they were as dead as that skyscape was alive.

1

A horrible blaring discord of horns jolted me out of my dream. The lights had changed again, and I was holding up the queue. With a touch of malice I stabbed my foot down and shot across the gap so fast the glittering brute behind me was left standing. But the ring-road opened out into two lanes here, and in seconds he'd over-hauled me and gone purring past with ruthless ease. I had a terrible urge to chase him, to dice and duel with him for pride of place, but I refused to give in to it. What was the matter with me? I'd always loathed the kind of moron who played stock-car on overcrowded commuter routes; I still did, come to that. No question of cowardice – it was other people that sort put at risk. Anyway, we were coming back into speed limits again. Another car whined past me, the same make, model, year as mine, the same colour even. I had to look closely to be sure it really wasn't mine – and swore at myself again. Was I feeling the strain, or something? It had leopard-skin seats, anyway, and a nodding dog on the parcel shelf. At least mine didn't; but right then it might as well have had, the way I felt about it, and about myself. Christ, I ought to be driving a Porsche too! Or something less crass – a Range Rover, a vintage MG even, something to stir cold blood a bit more than my neat sports saloon. It wasn't as if I couldn't afford to. If I was the real high-flyer everyone said I was, the wonder boy, shouldn't I at least be getting a little more fun out of it – instead of stashing all my cash away in gilt-edge and blue-chip and just a little under-the-counter gold?

I pulled off at the exit – the same, the usual exit, the fastest way home. Home to what? The prospect of my flat loomed up at me, my neat, empty, expensive little designer garret, warming up as the heating came on. The idea of cooking dinner suddenly sickened me, the prospect of eating something heated up from the freezer even more so; I changed gear sharply, signalled only just in time that I was changing lanes. I was going to eat out; and not in any of my usual places. I might regret it in the morning, but I was going to find somewhere more exotic, even if it wasn't as well-scrubbed. Thinking of the docks

2

had started me on that tack; I remembered there'd been lots of crazy little places there, when I'd last passed through – and lord, how long ago was that? I'd been in my teens; it might have been ten years ago, even. And that was just on a bus, looking out on my way to somewhere else. I'd been a child when last I'd trodden those pavements, the times when my father had taken me down to see the ships unloading. I'd loved the ships; but the docks themselves had always seemed rather sad to me, with weeds growing up between the worn flagstones and the crane rails rusting. Even then they'd been dying. I remembered dimly that there'd been attempts recently to tart up parts of them for tourism, as somewhere picturesque; but how, or with what success, escaped me.

Why had I never been back? There'd been no time, not with the job, not with the social life and the sport, all the other excitements and ambitions. Things that got me somewhere. I hadn't actually set out to bury my taste for useless mooching about, but I'd had to let it slip away. Like a lot of other things. There was no choice, really, if I wanted to keep on the ball, to get ahead. And yet those trips to the docks, the sight of all those cases and containers with their mysterious foreign labels – they'd sparked off something in me, hadn't they?

Not exactly steered me into my career; I'd thought that choice out very carefully, back at college. But they'd added something extra, a touch of living colour other likely jobs didn't quite have. That hadn't lasted, of course. You wouldn't expect it to survive the rigours of routine, the dry daily round of forms and bills and credits. I hadn't missed it much. Other satisfactions had taken its place, more realistic ones. But thinking about the docks just now, when I was feeling a bit adventurous, a bit rebellious, had woken a queer, nagging sort of regret. Maybe that was what had really sparked off this craving to go and eat there – the urge to rediscover the original excitement, the inspiration, of what I was doing. I did feel rather empty without it – hollow, almost.

I frowned. That brought back a less comfortable memory, something Jacquie had thrown at me years ago, in those last sullen rows. Typical; one of those daft images she was always coming up with, something about the delicate Singapore painted eggs on her mantelpiece. How they'd drained the yolk to make the paint ... 'You'd be good at that! You should take it up! Suck out the heart to paint up the shell! All nice an' bright on the outside, never mind it's empty inside! Never mind it won't hatch! Appearances, they're what you're so fond of –'

I snorted. I shouldn't have expected her to see things the way they were. But all the same ... The turn-off wasn't far, just at the bottom of the hill here was – what was it called? I knew the turn, I didn't need the name, but I saw it on the wall as I turned off the roundabout. Danube Street.

All the street names were like that round here, as far as I remembered. Danube Street; Baltic Street; Norway Street – all the far-off places which had once seemed as familiar as home to the people who lived and worked here, even if they never saw them. It was from them their prosperity came, from them the money that paid for these looming walls of stone, once imposing in light sandstone, now blackened with caked grime. Herring and spices and timber, amber and furs and silks, all manner of strange and exotic stuffs had paid for the cobbles that drummed beneath my tyres now, at a time when the town's prime street was a rutted wallow of mud and horse-dung. Some of the smaller side-streets had really arcane names – Sereth Street, Penobscot Lane; it was in Tampere Street I stopped finally and parked.

I hoped the name didn't reflect the local habits, and that the car would be all right; but I couldn't face being shut in it any longer. I wanted to explore on foot, smelling the sea in the wind. I felt a few drops of rain in it instead, turned back a moment, then looked up at the sky and caught my breath. Over the warehouse rooftop opposite blazed the last streaks of the glorious sunset; and against them, stark and black as trees in winter, loomed a network of mastheads. Not the simple mastheads of modern yachts, nor the glorified radar rigs of the larger ships; these were the mastheads of a square-rigged sailing ship, and a huge one at that, the sort of things you would expect on the *Victory* or the *Cutty Sark*. The last time I'd seen anything like them was when a Tall Ships rally had put in, and that only on local TV. Had the tourist bods moored one here, or something really old? This I had to see. I pulled my light anorak closer about me and walked on into the deep shadows between the wide-set street-lights. The hell with the weather, the hell with every-thing! I was a bit surprised at myself. No doubt about it, rebellion had me in its grip.

An hour and a half later, of course, I was regretting it bitterly. My hair was plastered flat to my wind-chilled scalp, my soaking collar was sawing at my neck, and I was desperate for my dinner. All those odd little places I remembered were just boarded holes in the high walls now, or seedy little cafés with fading pop posters and plastic tables barely visible through the grimy glass; and every one of them was closed, and might have been for years. The sea was within earshot, but never in sight; and there was no trace of masts, or of the signs you'd expect to a tourist attraction either. I would have been happy enough now with something microwaved at home, if I could only get back to my car; but just to cap everything, I'd lost my way, taken a wrong turn somewhere around those featureless warehouse walls, and now everywhere was strange. Or simply invisible; either some of the streets had no lighting, or it had failed. And there wasn't a soul about, nor even a sound except my own footsteps on the cobbles and the distant breath of the ocean. I felt like a lost child.

Then I heard voices. They seemed to be echoing out around the corner of the street ahead, and so desperate was I that I'd gone rushing round before I'd realized that they didn't sound at all friendly; more like a brawl. And that, in fact, was what was going on. At the street's end was the sea, with only a dim glimmer to distinguish it from the sky above; but I hardly noticed it. There was a single light in the street, over the arched doorway of a large warehouse, now half-open; and before it, on a weed-grown forecourt, a tight knot of men were struggling this way and that. One tore himself loose and staggered free, and I saw that the remaining three – all huge – were after him. One swung at him, he ducked back, stumbling among the weeds and litter, and with a twinge of horror I saw metal gleam in the fist as it swung, and in the others as they feinted at him. They had knives, long ones; and that slash, if it had connected, would have opened his throat from ear to ear. They were out to kill.

I stood horrified, hesitant, unable to link up what I was seeing with reality, with the need to act. I had a mad urge to run away, to shout for the police; it was their business, after all, not my fight. If I hadn't baulked at that stop light, perhaps, I might have done just that, and probably suffered for it. But something inside me – that spirit of rebellion I'd raised – knew better; it wasn't seeking help I was after, it was an excuse to run away, to avoid getting involved, to pass by on the other side. And this was a life at stake, far more important than a stupid trick like running a light – far more important even than any question of courage or cowardice. I had to help ... but how?

I took a hesitant step forward. Maybe just running at them, shouting, would scare them enough; but what if it didn't? I hadn't hit anybody since I had left school, and there were three of them. Then in the faint gleam my eyes lit on a pile of metal tubes lying at the roadside, beside a builder's sign, remnants of dismantled scaffolding. They were slippery with filth and rain, but with a heave that made my shoulders crack I got one about seven feet long loose, heaved it over my head and ran down the slippery cobbles.

None of them saw me at first; the victim slipped and fell, and they were on him. I meant to shout, but at first only a ridiculous strangulated *hey!* came out; in the middle it cracked and became a banshee howl. Then they noticed me, all right. And to my horror they didn't run, but rounded on me all three. I was past turning back now; I swung the tube at the first one, and missed by a mile. He leapt at me, and in a fit of panic I just clipped his outstretched arm on the backswing. He fell with a howl,

6

and I saw a knife fly up glittering into the air. Another feinted at me, jumped back as I swung the tube, then flung himself forward as it passed. But it was slippery enough to slide through my hands; the end poked him in the belly and stretched him on his back on the cobbles. Hardly believing what I was doing, I swung on the third — and my feet skidded from under me on the wet smooth stones, and I sat down with an agonizing jar. He loomed up, a hulking shadow against the halo of light; I glimpsed white teeth in a contorted snarl, the knife lifting and slashing down.

Then something flashed over me, feet crashed on the cobbles, and the shadow drew back. It was the man they'd been attacking, a hunched, taut figure with a shock of red-brown hair, bounding and bouncing forward, dodging the clumsy slashes the bigger man aimed at him with an ease that looked effortless. Suddenly his own arms lashed out; there was a gleam of metal and a terrible tearing sound. They whirled into the light for a moment, and I saw long slashes in the tall man's rough coat, and blood spurting from them. I struggled up, then flinched back in fright as the darkness seemed to burst out at me; I flung out a punch, and felt a stab of agony in my upper arm. I yelled with the sudden pain, and louder with the anger that hissed up like a rocket in my head. A leering, slobbbering face, greyish and sickly in the dim light, shone out suddenly in front of me, capped by a cockatoo crest of green, a mass of gold ear-rings jangling. I smashed at it with my good arm, felt the blow connect and exulted — till the rocket burst, or so it felt, and my teeth slammed together with the force of the impact. I doubled over, clutching my head, unable to see or even think straight, my mind crazed across like a mirror by the blow. I heard a yell beside me, a burst of noise and expected the worst, the sharp agony of the knife or the blunt bite of boots. But my back bumped against a wall and I straightened up, grateful for its support, and forced my eyes open in time to see the three shadows go clattering away for their lives down the street towards the sea, one limping badly, another clutching his chest; the third they were dragging

7

between them, his feet scrabbling helplessly at the rounded stones. A black trail like a snail's glistened where he had passed.

The man they'd been after was crouched down against the wall to my right, by the doorpost, clutching his ribs and breathing heavily. I thought at first he was injured, but he looked up and grinned. An ordinary enough grin, on a lean, mobile face. 'Now that's what I call timing!' he said, and chuckled.

'Who were they?' I managed to croak out.

'Them? Just Wolves, as usual. Out for anything that's not nailed down, and a good few things that are – *you* know!' He looked up suddenly. 'Hey – you don't know, do you? You're not from this side of town, are you?'

I shook my head, forgetting, and dissolved the world into needles of blinding pain. I swayed, stunned and sick, and he sprang up and caught me. 'What's the matter? Didn't stop one, did you? Ach ... not from this side.' The questioning in his voice had turned to certainty without any answer from me. 'Not a local. Might've known, the way you came barreling in like that.' He propped me against the doorpost and searched my scalp with blunt fingers, causing me more bouts of agony. 'Well, that's nothing!' he concluded, with infuriating briskness.

'You try it awhile and say that!' I croaked at him, and he grinned again.

'No offense, friend. Just relieved your dome's not cracked, that's all. A bump and a little blood, no sweat. But that arm of yours, that's different.'

'Doesn't hurt as much –'

'Aye, maybe; but it's a blade in the muscle. Could be dirty, if no worse. Hold on a moment ...' The blade he himself had used to such effect flashed in his hand, and I was astonished to see it was no knife, but a fully-fledged sword, a sabre of some kind; he twitched it adroitly into a scabbard on his belt, unhooked from beside it a ring of huge old-fashioned keys and locked the warehouse door behind him with one of them, muttering to himself the while. 'C'mon now, nothing to worry about; I'll see you right. Just lean on your old mate Jyp – that's it! Just round

8

the corner a few steps – lean on me if you like!'

That seemed a daft idea – he was such a short man. But as he bore me up by my good arm I was astonished to realize he was hardly any shorter than me, and I am over six feet. It was next to the others he'd looked unusually small; so how tall were they?

This close, too, he didn't look so ordinary. His face was bony, hard-jawed, but his features were open and regular; a bit Scandinavian, maybe, except that expressions played across them like shifting light. Lines appeared and disappeared, making his age hard to guess; early forties, maybe, by the lines about the eyes. Below them the remains of a tan welded together a great blaze of freckles across his cheekbones. His eyes were calm, wide and intelligent. The look in them seemed remote and far-seeing, till I caught the twinkle that matched the mercurial expressions and the wry smile. I rarely take to people on sight, men especially; but there was something instantly likeable about him. Which was pretty damn surprising, as I couldn't have placed him in any way. Liking, of course, doesn't have to mean trusting; but right then I'd very little choice in the matter.

Together, like a pair of companionable drunks, we staggered down towards the seaward end of the lane; but before we reached it my old mate Jyp, whoever he was, manoeuvred us across the road and down a dank and evil-smelling back alley to emerge into a much wider street, like all too many I had tramped down that night. In this one, though, was what I'd been looking for all along; a single building bright with lights, and the unmistakeable look of a pub, or perhaps even a proper restaurant, about it. Grimy diamond-leaded windows glowed a warm gold between peeling shutters, and above them a sign spanned the building, brightly painted even in the dim light of the flickering lamps on the wall below. My head was clearing in the cold air, and I stared at it, fascinated; this must be one of the little specialty places. The sign read *TVERNA ILLYRIKO* in tall letters, red upon black, and beneath them *Illyrian Tavern – Old Style Delicacies – Dravic Myrko, Prop.* On a board above the door I saw repeated

Taverne Illyrique, Illyrisches Gasthof, the name in every language I could recognize, and a good few I couldn't.

'Come along, we'll get you fixed up here!' said Jyp cheerfully, and added something else I wasn't sure I'd heard.

'What was that?'

'Not a bad place, I was saying, so long as you steer clear of the sea-slugs.'

I closed my eyes. 'I'll try to. Where are they? On the floor?'

'On the menu.'

'Christ!'

That did it; I had to stop and retch, painfully and unproductively, while Jyp watched with sympathetic amusement. 'Guts empty?' he enquired. 'Pity; a good puke can help, when you've had a dunt on the head. Like with seasickness; if you're going to throw up, at least get something inside you to throw, that's what I always tell 'em. Ammunition, as it were.'

'I'll remember that,' I promised, and he chuckled.

'All right now? Mind the steps, they're worn.' He kicked open the faded red door with a ringing crash. 'Hoi, Myrko! Malinka! Katjka!' he shouted, and bundled me inside.

Half an hour earlier I might have welcomed the gust of smells that came boiling out. There were a hundred I couldn't put a name to and a few I didn't care to, but there was also garlic and paprika and beer and frying onions. Now, though, the mix made my aching stomach shrivel.

'It's you, is it, *pylot?*' came a hoarse answer from inside. There was the sound of somebody shovelling coal into a stove. 'Malinka's out, you'll just have to make do with me.'

'Got a friend here, Myrko,' Jyp shouted. 'Hey, what's your name, friend? Stephen? Myrko, this here's Steve, he pulled some Wolves off my back and stopped a knock or two while he was about it. Needs something to set him up. *Katjka!* You're in demand! And bring your puncture repair kit! Now, me old mate, just you sit down there ...'

I slumped onto a high-backed wooden settle, trying hard not to jolt my head or my arm, and stared around at the room. I'd seen touristy Greek bars trying for this kind of look. Now I realized what they'd been imitating. Here, though, the bunches of dried herbs and sausages dangling from the rafters, hams in sacking, huge slabs of salt cod, octopi looking like mummified hands, bloat-bellied wine-flasks with crude labels of dancing peasants, and shapes less identifiable, weren't plastic; their fragrance hung heavy on the air, and the faintly trembling light of the lanterns that hung between them gave their shadows a strange animation. They were real lanterns, oil lanterns; you could smell them, too. I glanced around, and saw no sign of switches or power points anywhere on the walls; and come to that, the outside lights had been lanterns too. Their light was strictly local, and bright only in the centre of the room; the tables there were empty, but from the more shadowed ones in the corners I could hear the low buzz of voices, male and female, and the music of glasses and cutlery well wielded.

A tray clattered on the table in front of me, a bottle full of some pale liquid and a little narrow-necked flask of the same, no glass. A squat, rounded little man with the face of an amiable toad leaned over me and grunted. 'On the house, friend! Anyone who takes a crack at Volfes does us all a favourrr!' He had an accent as heavy as the spices in the air, heavy and guttural. There was a rumble of agreement from the shadowy depths of the room, and I was astonished to see the glint of glasses being lifted.

'You should've seen him, Myrko!' enthused Jyp. 'They'd got me down, got my little sticker away, and he comes for 'em with a goddamn great iron bar! Three of 'em, and he fells two, the third gets a crack in before I get my blade back and open him up a bit! Went for 'em bald-headed, he did, just like that!'

Myrko nodded soberly. 'Wish I had ssseen it! That was bravely done, my lad. Now get that down you, it's for drrrinking, isn't it? Sovereign rrremedy!' I grasped the little flask gingerly, and tilted it to my lips. There was a trick to the shape of it; it shot the whole lot at the back of

11

my throat. If you want to know what it felt like, tie a plum to a rocket and fire it down your gullet, preferably during an earthquake. I breathed out heavily, expecting to see the air glow, and Myrko poured me another while the flask was still in my hand. Suddenly the chill inside me lessened, my shivering stopped; I felt the blood pulsating in my veins, and the pounding in my head became bearable. I downed the second flaskful, and let him fill another before I held the bottle to see the label. '*Tujika*,' I said, with sudden understanding. '*Slivovitz*. But about three times as strong as any I've tasted before!'

Myrko grinned, looking ready to catch a fly any moment. '*Shliwowitch*, yess, if that's what you want to call it. Rrreal upland stuff, best this side of the *Karrpatny*. Hoi, here's Katjka!' I blinked. Out of the aromatic gloom a girl appeared – quite a girl. In that gaudy costume she went with the décor of the place; she might have stepped down off one of the wine labels, a picturebook peasant girl from somewhere on the upper Danube. Perhaps not a girl; a second glance put her in her late twenties. And perhaps not a peasant either; the embroidery on the flared red skirt and black stomacher was just too gilt and gaudy, the cut of the white blouse over her full breasts just a little too low, too strained. Her blonde hair looked natural, but the face beneath it was lean and foxy, not quite pretty, and the deep hard grooves either side of her mouth betrayed the kind of experience peasants don't usually come by. Apart from that astonishing cleavage her eyes were the best of her, wide and grey and anxious.

'What is it?' she demanded urgently, her voice startlingly deep, her accent less noticeable than Myrko's. 'Who's hurt, Jyp? Oh –' Before anyone could answer she had swooped on me, clucking like a mother-hen and cursing the others for not calling her sooner. She had my anorak off my shoulders so swiftly and gently I hardly felt a twinge, and the buttons of my shirt seemed to fly apart as her nimble fingers flew down my chest; she slid that off too, leaving me shrivelling with embarrassment. But if anyone was staring I couldn't see them, and there was no change in the buzz of voices; anyway, it didn't seem to worry this Katjka girl. She pulled my head down to rest between her breasts without the least inhibition, and when Myrko came puffing up with the hot water she'd sent him for she began to clean and search my throbbing scalp with incredibly delicate fingers, and smooth on something pungent and seaweedy from a jar. 'Relax ...' she crooned, but on that particular pillow it was both difficult and only too easy; in the end I just accepted the situation, and sagged.

It seemed to please her, but I wasn't quite so sure; nice creature though she was, from my vantage I couldn't help but notice one thing about her. It wasn't that unpleasant, not the kind of rank stink you associate with squash-court changing rooms, but all the same it was there, and pretty strong. No worse than our ancestors, our great-grandparents even must have been, or folk in countries where baths were still a luxury. I remembered an Eastern Bloc coal export official complaining that girls back home never bathed enough because of constant fuel shortages; he should've talked. But in our enlightened land of Lifebuoy and hot water on tap there wasn't any excuse; it wasn't necessary, that was why it put me off. Or wasn't it? I glanced up at the lights again. Maybe they weren't just decoration, atmosphere; maybe this place genuinely didn't have electricity or even gas. In which case she might well have the same problem. But what sort of place didn't have one or the other, these days? Even Highland crofts could get bottled gas. And how could any kind of eating-house survive the hygiene inspectors without them?

With slivovitz and other things I was still a bit light-headed, thoughts like that buzzing aimlessly around, getting nowhere. But gradually I found my head was clearing, and, wonder of wonders, that it was hardly throbbing any more. Katjka seemed to sense this, because she pushed me gently upright and with careful fingers set to work on my punctured arm. I glanced at it once, then away; it looked worse than I'd guessed, a fearful mess of clotted blood. Besides, I preferred looking at her; beautiful or not, she was a nice-looking creature. And now she was

13

clasping my arm to that bosom of hers, and leaving my hand dangling loose in her lap; quite a distraction. Beside us I heard Jyp and Myrko talking, but what they were saying only filtered through to me gradually.

'So say to me, *pylot*, how's this all happen, then? How'd a fly lad like you let a few mangy Volfs get you down, anyhow?'

'Just careless, I guess. Decoyed me to the door and jumped me. Kind of subtle, by their lights.'

'*Daj*. Let's hope they not learrning brains. But why so much trouble? What's in that warrehouse, anyhow?'

'Just the usual.' Jyp sounded puzzled. 'A few old loads that've lain there months now, and the stuff out of the *Iskander*, docked this morning from out West. Nothing unusual in that. Black lotus for Patchie's, a couple of gross merhorse skins that Mendoza's shipped up from Te Arahoa on spec and died on the market. A load of flamewood planks for the trade, indigo, peppers and coffee from Huy Brazeal, auk down – twenty bales of it! – and a few tons of dried Conqueror Root and Nighteye for the shops on Damballah Alley. Not the sort of stuff a man can pilfer to any profit; it'd take more'n three to carry off any worthwhile pickings. There *was* a load of black-devil rum, fifty hogsheads, but Sutler Dick picked that up not four hours after it come in.'

'Maybe nobody tells the Volfs,' puffed Myrko.

'Maybe ...' echoed Jyp, but he didn't sound convinced. I was just about to ask him what all those daft-sounding commodities were meant to be when Katjka distracted me – with a vengeance. I jerked rigid with agony, and all but kicked over the table. It felt exactly as if, having cleaned the wound off gently, she'd suddenly pulled it sharply open, sunk her teeth in it and sucked hard. I looked down and saw that that was exactly what she had done. What's more, she was still doing it. I sank back trembling, unable to speak, and saw Jyp grinning at me.

'Could be dirt in the wound, remember? Filthy things, Wolf blades, you never know. That's how Katjka's folk deal with it, and I can vouch for it working, b'lieve me. Mind you, they're all vampires in her corner of the world, anyhow!'

Katjka looked up, and spat my blood accurately onto his trousers, which looked like glossy leather; he wiped it off with a snort.

'The company you keep, you shouldn't be so high and mighty, *pylot!* Not too painful now, no, my Stefan?'

I managed a grin of sorts, as she picked up the slivovitz bottle and began to wash the wound with the blazing spirit. 'Can't think of anyone I'd rather be eaten by,' I managed, and she giggled.

'Especially *marinado*? Okay! Then I put a little more salve on this, so, and bandage it up, and in a day or so you are right as rain – all right, *daj*?'

I breathed out hard, and managed half a smile. Jyp handed me the bottle, but I shook my head. 'Thanks, but I've had enough. Got to drive home.'

'With that arm? Think you'll be all right? Better you doss down here for the night. Try Myrko's robber steak, with french fries and a demi of old Vara Orsino – put hair on your chest and lead in your pencil, that! And for your afters a tumble with Katjka – set you up a wonder, she will! And you give him the very best, you hear, lass, the real sailor's holiday! My treat, right? It's Wolf-meat I'd be if it wasn't for my old mate Steve –'.

I blinked a bit and stole a glance at Katjka. Jyp's casually commercial attitude didn't seem to bother her, if anything it flattered her. 'Well ...' I said, and she turned those large grey eyes on me. I had a suspicion they'd stripped many a seaman of his inhibitions, if nothing worse. But I reached for my shirt.

'You're not *goink*?' she enquired in hurt disbelief. It was obviously a routine line, but she seemed to mean it. Or was that the routine as well? But Jyp and Myrko were looking just as crestfallen.

'Hey, c'mon,' protested Jyp, creasing up his young-old face. 'I was goin' to give you a party – I owe you, remember? Can't leave me feeling like an ungrateful louse, can you? And Katjka all limbering up for it, too! Sit down! Stay! You're among friends!'

That almost got me, that last word. Among friends — I was, I felt it, as I hardly ever had all my life. I faltered. Ahead of me that light was changing again, and all of me longed to put my foot down and race through it — away, out, into that dreaming sunset, chasing some new dream of my own. Some kind of fulfilment I couldn't imagine — something to fill up the shell ...

But I felt the twinge in my arm as I drew on my shirt, and my own blood stuck it clammily against my skin. I stamped on the brake. No more rushing in, not tonight. 'I know. I'm sorry. Another time, maybe, but — I've got to go. If I can find my car, that is. I parked it in Tampere Street, wherever that is from here.'

For a moment I was horribly afraid they would all ask what a car was. But Jyp, though he was obviously hurt and disappointed, said casually, 'Okay, Steve. I understand. Another time it is. Suppose I should be getting back to the warehouse myself. Tampere, right, that's back behind here, round the corner ahead, past the big old bonded store, first left then right, right again and straight down; at the end you'll see it. Got that? I'll come show you the way.'

'If it's that simple, I'll manage, thanks. You get back to your work. I don't want to make things hard for you. And thanks — thanks for the puncture repair, Katjka. And — and the drink, Myrko ... Thanks, all of you —' I was sounding like an idiot. I was nervous, I didn't want to offend these weird, warm people. Myrko just grunted, but Katjka smiled.

'All right, Stefan. Make it soon, hah?'

'Yah,' laughed Jyp, 'while I've still got some dough!'

'Whether he has or not,' said Katjka calmly.

Jyp turned on her with his bony jaw dropping; she menaced him with her fist, and he turned back to me. He looked me up and down a moment, as if sizing me up anew. 'Yah, you come back, you hear? One way or t'other I'll bet you will. And hey, be you looking for me, you can't find me, you ask for Jyp the Pilot, right? Just that. Jyp the Pilot. Ask anyone, they all know me. Anyone, right! Be seeing you, Steve.' He leaped up and wrung my hand with startling strength. 'And thanks, man; *thanks!*'

I stopped at the door, and looked back, reluctant. It seemed dark and cold out there, and I didn't want to let this fragile shred of life and colour go so easily forever. What chance is there you'll ever come back to a dream? Myrko had vanished into the shadows, Jyp had his head in Katjka's lap, but it was me she was watching. She smiled, and inhaled slowly. I looked down, and lifted the latch. The door creaked twice, and I was exiled into the sea-wind, bitterly cold and heavy with harbour stenches and the last few drops of rain. Hastily I raised my collar, and it whipped the points about my ears in mockery. The cobbles glistened and glittered now under a newly clear moon, and I had no trouble seeing my way. I turned once to look back, but the wind dashed stinging salt into my eyes and hurried me on with invisible hands.

Jyp's directions were straightforward enough. Which was just as well, for there was nobody else to ask; the streets still seemed to be deserted. I saw the bonded warehouse ahead the moment I rounded the corner, a louring mountain of a place that had once been imposing; now eyepatches of rusty corrugated iron filled its lower windows, and barbed wire crawled about the broken crenellations of its outer walls. First left was obvious enough, too, but it didn't look – or smell – very pre-possessing; even as alleys went this was the dregs. I hesitated, could he have forgotten this, and meant some broader way further on? But when I stepped back to look I saw there wasn't one; the road curved around to the right. Holding my breath, I was just about to take the plunge when I heard a slight scrape, and a flicker of motion caught my eye, back at the corner I'd just turned. But when I looked around there was nothing, and I thought no more about it. The alley was as foul as I'd expected, the water that plashed around my hapless shoes awash with pale shapeless things half floating, its muddy shallows releasing a terrible stench as I disturbed them. Fortunately it wasn't long. When the puddle ended I stopped for a moment to tip the foulness out of my shoes and scrape them clean. But as I leant one-handed against the grimy bricks I heard that sound again, echoing slightly down the alley. Forgetting my squishy feet, I turned and looked suddenly back almost frozen to the spot. There came just a whisper of movement, no more than a flicker; but it seemed as if for one moment some huge bulky shadow had filled the alley's other end, blocking off the light. Though it was gone almost at once, there was no way I could deny it, search though I might for such a shadow among the broken cobbles. I swallowed. Somebody didn't want me to see them. Why? Because they were following me, that was why; it had to be. But who? Jyp, maybe, seeing his guest safe – no, hardly. But I could find out easily enough. All I had to do walk right back around that corner and confront – him? Them? Or ... what?

Except, fortunately, that I wasn't quite that stupid. I thought of Wolves; but there was no scaffolding here, hardly even an unbroken brickbat, let alone Jyp with his sword. I turned and hurried as quietly as I could out of the other end of the alley. In the street beyond, turning right, I stopped a moment, listening for the splash of that inescapable puddle. There was nothing – which meant they either weren't coming, or they were coming with greater stealth. I swallowed and strode on. Just as I reached the next corner, another right turn, I dared to glance back again. Nothing – except –

A sudden tremendous splashing erupted from the alley, as if something was charging headlong through that puddle, charging with heedless ferocity. Perhaps I yelled; certainly I fled. Down the street I pounded, noticing only that it was mercifully wide and short on shadows, and had smooth cinder pavements that scuffed muddily under my feet. My breath seemed to go shallow very suddenly, and bands of agony sprang up around my head; my injuries were beginning to tell. Where now? Where next? I couldn't even remember. I stopped, bewildered, panting, and looked up at the skies. And what I saw there drove out all other thoughts, even of what might any moment round that corner behind me.

The moon was afloat, it seemed, sailing above a sea

of cloud. By its light the clouds were transformed, spread out beneath it into a landscape of shimmering night-bound beauty, low hills and the sea beyond, the sea and islands. But that alone could not have held me, in the state I was. What bound me to the spot was the almost tangible shock of recognition. Beyond all possibility, yet equally beyond all doubt, it was the same landscape the sunset had shown me, at least three hours earlier. The same, yet — as you might expect — seen from a slightly different angle. I began to shake; had the blow affected my brain? Yet I'd never felt more sure of anything; both visions burned together in my brain, the seas of gold and silver. Bewildered, I looked down, and saw, above that landscape mirrored in a stagnant gutter, a sign on the grimy wall. Beneath the gutterings of spray paint it read, quite clearly, *Tampere Street*. I ran forward wildly, and there, not a hundred yards from the corner, was my car.

Forgetting all else, I bolted for it. But now, some-how, the wind was in my face, whirling up cinder dust to sting my eyes, buffeting me on the slippery cobbles; it felt like a hand holding me back, barring me from my refuge, my escape. A filthy rag of polythene hissed out of the gutter and tangled itself lovingly around my ankles; I kicked it free and trampled on it like some living menace. But I was there, my hand fell on the wing, its steel cold beneath the smooth paintwork. I fumbled for my keys, barely catching them as the wind sought to whisk them from my numbed fingers into the drain beneath, yanked the door open and plunged in.

It was slow to start; I almost flooded the carburettor in my impatience. I forced myself to sit still a moment while the wind buffeted the car, staring into my rear-view mirror at the darkness I'd come out of. Then I tried again, my foot light upon the pedal, and heard the blessed cough and rumble of the engine, felt its vibrations stronger than the wind. I slipped it into gear, twisted the wheel and all but threw the car out from the kerb, growl-ing across the cobbles. Only once I looked back, but the street's end was in deeper shadow still; anything or nothing might have been lurking there. Then I turned out into the main road, into Danube Street where there was lighting that worked, cold and orange though it was, and the prospect at least of the noise and colour and company, the safety of the city I knew. It came crazily into my head how for the ancient Romans the Danube was a barrier of civilization, holding barbarism at bay; but it was not a comforting thought, for at the end that barbarism had come rolling across the Danube in an overwhelming wave. I slowed, waited at the junction and turned, and there it all was. Noise, colour, company, safety – but all of it strange, all men about me strangers. Safe, but strangers. Suddenly the trade didn't seem so good, the escape less of an escape. Had that light really been red? Or had I just been afraid to see it was amber? I couldn't answer. I was tired, sore, and I hadn't eaten.

I went home, and threw something into the microwave. Hard.

CHAPTER TWO

THE OFFICE NEXT MORNING pulled me sharply back. Everything seemed solid and familiar, everything was bright and sunlit and unmysterious, from the squeak of the fake-mosaic tiles under my shoes to the sweet smile from Judy behind the switchboard. This morning, too, it was nicely flavoured with sympathy.

'Hallo, Steve – how's the arm?'

'Oh, it's okay, thanks. Settling down.'

There was nothing mysterious about these corridors, all light-flooding windows and cool daffodil-yellow walls, no dark corners, no strange atmospheres. After last night they felt businesslike, bracing, reassuring. The only smells in the conditioned air were fresh polish and coffee and the warm tang that surrounds VDUs and other office electronics, with an acetonal whiff of nail varnish and menthol cigarettes as I passed the typists' room; clean and calm and predictable, all of it. Strange, perhaps, that so many exotic commodities should pass through these offices, in a manner of speaking, and yet leave never a trace behind. Cinnamon, manganese, copra, alligator pepper, sapphires; we handled them by the tonne as readily as sheet steel or crude oil. All the trade goods of the world, and yet none ever came within miles of this place; I'd only ever seen them on rare visits to docks and airports. Only their legal identities passed through my hands, in notes of shipment and bills of lading and Customs inventories that left nothing in the air but the faint dry taint of toner ink. When I opened the door of my own office I smelt it; but there was also Clare's flowery perfume, and the girl herself shuffling little sheaves of documents on her immaculate desk.

'Steve! Hallo! I wasn't expecting you so soon! How's your poor arm? It isn't anything serious, is it? I mean, slipping in the rain like that? You might really have hurt yourself!'

I'd woken late, exhausted, with my arm swollen and stiff; I'd had to phone in with some sort of excuse. Yet now it seemed more like the truth; I could almost see it happening. A slip, a gash – far more likely than a knife in the hands of some weird dockland thug. Far easier to believe; I was close to believing it myself. 'It's not too bad, thanks. Bit stiff.'

'You're sure?' I was a little startled. Her intense blue eyes were very wide and concerned. She half rose. 'Look, just sit down a moment and I'll get the First Aid box –'

I grinned, rather uneasily. All this concern, it wasn't the sort of thing I was used to. 'Give you half a chance and you'll have me swathed up like King Tut!' Of course, she'd been the office first-aider since that course last year. She must be itching to find some use for it; she'd had nothing better so far than Barry cutting his thumb on the cap of a whisky bottle. That would account for it. 'No thanks, love, I, er, got it seen to. Any calls?'

I was allowed to pass on to my desk with a small sheaf of mail, a circular from the Brazilian *Aduana*, and instructions to sit down and take it easy. Dave Oshukwe was at his desk already, head down over his terminal, rattling keys; he lifted a limp brown hand to me, leaving a comet of expensive cigarette smoke in the air, but thankfully didn't look up. I settled down in my armchair, flicked on my terminal and settled back to let it warm up and log on. The firm leather upholstery of the chair enveloped me and bore up my sore arm, the chrome of the recline lever cool beneath my fingers. I touched the wood of the desk, solid under glassy layers of polish and varnish. I ran a finger along the terminal casing, mirror-smooth and clean and dustless, and felt the faint shiver of the current beneath. This – this was what it was all about.

I'd been half off my head last night. Hallucinating, almost. Sick and dizzy from that stab, no doubt about it, half drunk and unhappy; seeing everything through a haze. Small wonder I'd cast a romantic aura round places that were shabby or just plain squalid, over people – well, good-hearted enough, okay, but underprivileged, uneducated, simple, rough. Or since we were forgetting the euphemisms, downright crude and backward. I'd turned something utterly ordinary into a strange, feverish experience. That was the truth beneath the dream. All this was real. This was every day, this was my life. Here was Clare with a cup of coffee, just like every day; only for once she hadn't tried to slip me sweeteners instead of sugar. 'You need building up!' she said. 'If you've lost a whole lot of blood like that –'

'Hey, don't I get any?' demanded Dave.

Clare sniffed. 'Yours is coming. Steve's hurt himself!'

'Oh yah, I heard.' He peered around his terminal. 'How's you, me old massa? Can't be too bad, he's still upright, enney? Not on crutches or in a bathchair or anything!'

'Can't you see how pale he is?' Clare protested, so fervently it took me aback.

Dave crowed. 'Me you're asking that? All you pale-faces look alike to me –' He ducked as Clare swiped at his ear. 'Okay, okay, maybe he does look a bit green! That's usual – good night out, was it, Steve? Wasser name then?' Dave's real accent came from a very upmarket school, better than mine, but he would try to sound like an East End kid.

'Come on, Dave, I cut my arm, that's all.' I turned to Clare, still fussing over me, trying to find out what sort of bandage I had on and getting my eyes full of long blonde hair. 'Better get him some coffee too, love, or he'll be impossible all morning. Instead of just improbable. Oh, and ask Barry if he's spoken to Rosenblum's yet ...'

It gave me an excuse to get rid of her. I needed it. Clare in this mother-hen mode unnerved me. By the time she got back I could be comfortably sunk in my work, much too busy to let things get personal again. 'And you, Dave, anything turned up on this Kenya container mess yet?'

He lounged over to the printer and ripped off the protruding form. 'Just sorting it out when you came in, boss. Been sitting up a branch siding near the airport, getting mouldy. They're scrubbing it out now, with apologies. I've slapped on demurrages up to today, but told them to hang on to it till we see if there's some kind of return load we can get.'

'From Kenya? Should be, for a refrigerated container. That's well done, Dave.' I typed for some listings on my terminal, and peered down them. 'I'll get on to Hamilton, for a start, and see if he wants an extra half-tonne of red snapper this week. Meanwhile, could you get me those roughs on the German veg oil contract? And all that EEC crap about shipping it —'

The phone buzzed before I could pick it up. 'Barry for you,' said Clare, 'about the Rosenblum's business — urgent!'

Yes, this was real life all right.

And yet, as the day wore on, I found it wasn't quite the same. I sank myself into my work, determined not to be distracted, not to let myself maunder over weird wonderings about last night; I kept Dave and Clare too busy chasing this way and that to chaff or cluck over me. It seemed to get results. I managed to wrap up everything that could be settled that day in little more than half the normal time. And yet it left me less at ease, less satisfied than ever.

'Not feverish or anything, are we?' enquired Barry, perching elegantly on the edge of my desk and flicking through a sheaf of forms as if pulling the petals off a rose. He tapped his long blunt nose. 'I mean, you know as well as I do how bloody important every one of these contracts is, Steve. I'd far rather you took your time and went through them with your usual sharpened toothcomb than — well, skated over something significant.'

I grinned. 'Can't win, can I? You've been after me for years to speed up contracts — then today I hit one lucky streak and suddenly you're flagging me down! They're all right, Barry. Don't worry about it.'

He plucked a few more petals and ran a hand over his greying yellow curls. 'If you're really happy about them —'

'I'm happy. Dave's done his usual great job, and Clare too. And you've been through them yourself, or you wouldn't be sitting here asking! Go on, Mr Managing

24

Director, sir, get your pinstriped arse off my desk! I'm happy!'

But I wasn't. Not about the contracts I'd processed; about those I was confident. I might be twenty years younger than Barry, but I knew my job. I just wasn't enjoying it as much as usual. I hadn't wanted to go into every twist and turn of the business behind each bit of shipping, the way I normally did; I'd missed the old urge to linger and learn about every commodity we shipped, from foodstuffs to fine arts, an urge that had picked me up a lot of very useful background knowledge. I was suddenly more impatient of the whole sticky web of formalities, anxious to be rid of it. And Barry, being the canny businessman he was, had scented something of that. But as well as being a boss you could joke with, he was also sensible enough not to harass his staff. 'All right, my precocious infant! I'll go polish Bill Rouse's desk instead, see if Accounts can catch the speed bug too and push these through in record time. Probably kill all our regular clients – the shock, you know. Er – I'd suggest you push off home straightaway and rest that arm, but if you can hang on another half-hour or so – just in case anything crops up – you know how it is ...'

'Sure. No problem, Barry.' I wouldn't have gone home, anyway; something told me I wouldn't be any happier there than here. I was getting fed up with this haunting half-memory that trailed dissatisfaction shadow-fashion at my heels. I'd had a hellish, frightening time last night; serve me right for meddling with low-life. But the more I tried to think about it, the less I could remember – hardly anything now, anything clear. Faces and places were nameless blurs. As if that haze was like a conjuror's veil, lifting to reveal emptiness; as if I really had dreamed the whole thing up, from scratch. So then why was it turning my own ordinary life upside down, my own care-fully tailored slimfit Armani existence – the life I knew I could handle?

I badly wanted time to settle down and think – to remember, so I could comfortably forget. But here was Clare, bringing me one more cup of sugary coffee and hovering distractingly again. As a distraction she had natural advantages. Normally I never let them bother me; I made a point of treating her as the competent secretary she was and not as some brainless dolly. Not that she looked like one, exactly; if she fitted any stereotype, it might have been a milkmaid in a butter commercial. Her hair and eyes set you thinking of cornfields and summer skies, and the rest went with them, her slightly blunt, sensual features, all cream and freckles, her slender but heavy-breasted shape, her unselfconscious charm, bubbly but sincere. Most of the time I enjoyed it without letting it get to me, though when you are trying to think hard about something – or even harder not to – that hair on the back of your neck, that breast negligently brushing your shoulder could be damnably irritating. Now and again, naturally, it kindled fantasies, but I wasn't stupid enough to muddy office waters, chasing a casual affair. And what other kind made sense?

That struck a tiny spark. I'd stepped back from something last night – hadn't I? That girl – what was her name, then? What did she look like? I could hardly remember. As if I had conjured her up out of nothing, right enough; as if the whole crazy night were that kind of dream, vivid enough to jar you awake, yet impossible to hold onto, draining out of the memory and leaving only its emotions behind, like a hollow impression. I should have been relieved to think that; I wasn't. To think you could have some vivid, shocking, *living* experience, something strong enough to leave such nagging echoes – and yet find the details melting away like morning frost ...

What was solid? What wouldn't melt?

My fist clenched tight around my cup. Unwisely; a fierce red rocket of pain soared up my arm and burst into a glittering blossom – an image, sharp, sparkling, alive. There she was! Katjka, her teeth sunk in the wound, myself shivering with agony, only half hearing Myrko and Jyp calmly discussing –

Discussing a ship. And its cargo. Commodities. Goods. But the damndest ones a man ever heard of. And I had this business at my fingertips.

My fingertips. I had an idea daft enough to match. But after all, why not? There'd be no harm in it. Computers can't laugh at you. Idly, laughing at myself, I reached over to the keyboard and tapped in a call to the freight and docking databases. It might be amusing, at least, to see what they made of a query for the *Iskander*.

I hadn't a second to laugh. There it was, right in front of my nose, an entry in the usual file-card form, complete with a location code for dock and wharf. But what an entry!

> **SS. Iskander (500 tons)**
> **Out of:** *Tortuga, Santo Domingo and ports West*
> **Master:** *Sawyer, Jas. G.*
> **1st Mate:** *Mathews, Hezekiah I.*
> **2nd Mate:** *MacGully, 'Black' Patrick O'R.*
> **Supercargo:** *Stephanopopoulos, Spyridion*
> **Bosun:** *Radavindraban, J.J.*
> **Offladen –**
>
> *Black Lotus, 2 doz. chests (consigned, in bond)*
> *Indigo, 80 kilos approx.*
> *Peppers (dried), 1 tonne*
> *Conqueror root (in bale), 2 tonnes*
> *Coffee Bean (Grand Inca), 4 tonnes*
> *Skins – Merhorse, 2 gross (consigned)*
> *Plank flamewood, 38 tonnes*
> *Auk down, 20 bales (comp.)*
> *Proof Cane Spirits, 50 hg. (consigned)*
> *Nighteye, 1.5 tonnes*

Now loading for return Tortuga, Huy Brazeal and ports West
Capacity: spoken for, deck cargo only at shipper's risk

I was still staring at it open-mouthed when Dave came over.

'What's this, then? Still working –' He stared at the monitor. 'Well, bugger me! Where'd you get that from? It's *brill*!' He straightened up as somebody came in the

27

door. 'Hey, Barry! Clare! Come look at this!'

Barry's beak cut out the light as he leaned over above us. He stared for a moment, then began to chuckle. 'Very good, Dave, very good! I say, wouldn't it be marvellous if there was some way we could actually slip that into the database?'

Dave flapped his hands. 'Hey, I didn't have anything to do with that! Steve got it —'

Barry stared. Evidently he didn't think me capable of inventing it. 'You mean it actually was in the database? My God, nowhere's safe from those hackers these days. Next thing it'll be a virus program, mark my words —'

Clare bit gently on a knuckle and giggled. I wasn't fooled; she was generally thinking hard when she did that. 'It has to be a fake — hasn't it? I mean, five hundred tons — what kind of displacement's that for a merchant ship! And what's Conqueror Root? And a-a merhorse?'

'Might be a mistranslation,' I ventured, having had some time to think about it. 'For hippopotamus — or walrus — you know what happens when somebody sits down with a dictionary.'

'Might be,' agreed a baffled Barry. 'How come you called this up, Steve, anyhow?'

I shrugged. 'Just overheard the name of the ship then other day — you know, pub gossip ...'

I caught a very odd look from Clare, as if she'd sensed a wrong note somewhere. 'Well, there's one way to find out,' she said practically, going to my shelves and taking down one of the disc binders. 'Why don't we see if this *Iskander*'s in Lloyd's Register?' She put a hand on my shoulder as she leaned over me to slip the iridescent disc into the CD-Rom unit, and let it rest there. I typed in my query as soon as the menu came up on screen, and the unit purred for only a fraction of a second before the answer came.

'Not a bleeding sausage,' Dave said regretfully.

I pondered, carefully ignoring that light touch. 'Yes — but this is just the annual Register; it doesn't include back issues, old entries, historical ones ... I'm going to try their main database.'

It took quite a lot longer to get through, and five full minutes to access my query. We were about to give up, when suddenly the answer popped up on the screen. We stared; it wasn't at all in their usual detailed form.

Iskander, 500 tons – merchant sailing vessel, 3 mtr.
Reg. Huy Brazeal.
Ref. Register of Shipping vol. 1868

Barry cackled wildly. '1868? And what's this Huy Brazeal registry? A misprint for somewhere in Brazil, I suppose. Honestly, I wonder if they haven't started trading in certain substances down there! Or it really is hackers. There's nothing else?'

'I could go down and look up the actual 1868 lists,' suggested Clare thoughtfully.

Barry snorted. 'Well, not on the firm's time you don't! As of now I for one give up! We don't chase wild geese, we ship 'em livestock – eh, Steve? I just dropped in to say everything's in hand, you should push off now and get some rest. See you tomorrow!' He took one last look at the screen, then shook his head and grunted derisively. 'Hackers!'

But I wasn't so sure. As I drove home that night through a thin weeping drizzle I glanced uneasily at the turn-off for Danube Street. But there was no sunset banner to tempt me seaward; the sky was overcast, a featureless dome of gloomy grey cloud, and the louring buildings were wrapped in shadow, sullen and forbidding. It looked both sinister and depressingly ordinary, and thoroughly damped any desire I had to turn that way and test the truth of my strange experiences. To find they were just some kind of lunatic dream, or an overlay on ordinary things – or to find they were real and still there ... I didn't know which alternative scared me more. Inwardly I kicked myself for ever looking up all that nonsense from the files; now Clare and Dave and Barry must be wondering if I was some kind of nut. Come to that, I was wondering myself. I'd do better to go home and get some sleep.

It was as well I did, because I was shot out of God knows what dream at about four-thirty in the morning by the shrill braying of the phone. With a head like a carpentry shop – eyes full of glue, mouth of sawdust and the sawblade screeching across my brain – I struggled to make out what Barry was squawking about.

'Broken into, dammit! *And* smashed about! Badly, they say – the cops, yes! No, not yet, I'm on my way down there this minute – I want you and Rouse and Bailey and Gemma too – get hold of 'em, will you? And don't take no for an answer – this could be really fucking serious, lad!'

But it wasn't, though no wonder the cops thought so. So did I, the moment I walked in the door, and Gemma – our brass-bound and case-hardened head of Transshipment – actually burst into tears. Somebody had gone through both inner and outer back doors, shattering their central panels of wood and wired glass without opening them, and so bypassed our rather basic alarm system. There was an ominous stink in the air, a real pig-farm stench. Every office door in the place was open, and through them spilled filing cabinets and bookcases like so many prostrate corpses, strewn around with the ripped and mangled remains of the papers and books they had held. Even the beautiful Victorian bookcase in Barry's office had been thrown down, shattering a coffee-table, and its collection of antique atlases and traveller's tales ripped to shreds.

'Lovely books they were, too!' said the CID sergeant sadly, when the department heads gathered there a few hours later. 'Worth a bob, too, any idiot could see that. And yet you're sure none of them were nicked?'

'None!' said Barry between his teeth. 'Just bloody *ruined* like this!' And he hurled the shreds of a heavy old binding at the wall.

The sergeant clicked his tongue sympathetically. 'But nothing else gone – just like all the other offices. Didn't even touch your whisky bottles. Yet they wiped out every bit of paperwork in the place!' You could practically see the wheels working behind his eyes. 'Shipping business, eh? Import-export ... a high-pressure field is it? Kind of cutthroat competition? Lot of competitors?'

Barry shrugged. 'Not so many. And I know most of them – we do lunch, play squash, that sort of thing. Always friendly. We're fixers, expediters, there's plenty of elbow-room; sometimes we put business each other's way. You're not suggesting ...'

'Well, sir – I mean, all your files destroyed, all your records – even the bloody phone-books! That's bound to hold up your trading a bit, isn't it? Could even –'

Barry guffawed. 'Put us out of business? Not a chance! Paper's just one way we keep our records – and a pretty obsolete way at that. Everything that matters passes through the computer system; that gets stored on discs, discs are automatically backed up to hard disk and hard disk onto tape streamers, all day, every day. And the streamer cartridges go into that little safe over there; fire-proof, the lot. Three different levels of media – and not one of 'em's been touched, in any office. All we've got to do is print it back out again.'

The sergeant's face clouded over. 'I see ... and your competitors would know about this system?'

'Oh, they all work much the same way,' Gemma remarked. 'Not always as secure, perhaps, but that, let us face it, is their own look-out. If they really had wanted to hurt us they'd know a hundred better ways. In fact, officer, losing the papers is causing us far less trouble than all this absolutely *disgusting* smearing they've done all over the actual computers –'

'Ah yes, miss,' said the sergeant, his face resolutely rigid. 'Very nasty, that – unhygienic and all. As if it really did hit the fan ... Well, you should be able to get it cleaned up soon enough; the photographers will be through with it any time –'

'Photographers?' demanded Rouse. 'Good God, man, my terminal looks like the wall of a Lime Street lavatory! What'll a photograph of that tell you?'

The CID man met him with a superior smirk. 'Maybe quite a lot, sir. You see, it's not random, er, smearing; there's definitely patterns in it. Not writing or anything, but ... well, signs, I suppose, though we don't know what

31

they mean yet. In fact, I'd like everyone to have another look at them, all the staff, before you clean them off; they might mean something to somebody, you never know. There's one in particular, too, that has ... something else. We might start with that one – fourth door in on the left.'

All the heads turned in one direction – towards me. 'It would appear to be your week, Steve,' sighed Barry. 'Shall we go? And Gemma love, will you tell Judy to let the cleaners know they can start soon?'

We crowded into my office. Dave was already there, sitting on the overturned filing cabinet and chain-smoking to drown the stink, unsuccessfully. With assorted mutterings of disgust we all crowded round the sergeant as he gingerly turned my terminal this way and that. 'No suggestions? Ah well. How about this, then?'

The police had warned us not to touch the terminals, and we'd needed no discouraging; I hadn't looked closely at what dangled there. Even now it just seemed like more filth, a patch of matted feathers stuck together with something revolting, right in the centre of the screen. I looked at him and shook my head.

'Funny,' he said. 'You're the only one they favoured with that. And it's not more crap, that stuff; apparently it's blood, quite fresh. But mixed into a paste with something – some kind of flour, the boys think. Labs should tell us more.'

We stared at the ugly thing in uneasy silence, thinking each other's thoughts. Blood? Where from? What? Or whom? Then a new voice, soft and tentative, broke into our thoughts.

'Sah? 'scuse me, sah?' Smiles of relief broke out, and we turned away thankfully. This was the head of our cleaners, a plump cheerful creature in her fifties, all calm and motherly good nature. She seemed like the living antidote to the upheaval around us.

'Oh, Mrs Macksie,' began Barry distractedly. 'So very sorry we've had to drag you and the girls in! But you see –'

'Ah, thass' all right, sah!' she said sympathetically. 'It's terrible, ain't it? But we clean it up orright, you see!

32

Now wheah you want us to –' She stopped, or rather she choked; I thought at first it was Dave's overpriced gaspers, then that she was having a heart attack. Her eyes bulged; she made no sound but a strange little croak, one hand clutched at her coat. The other she made as if to lift, then let it fall limply. I stared at her like all the rest; but when I met her eyes it was as if a curtain had been drawn behind them.

Clare touched her arm, and she flinched. 'Mrs Macksie! Are you feeling all right?'

'What's the matter, love?' The CID man spoke softly; but it was a demand all the same. She turned her hooded eyes away, but he persisted. 'Seen something? Something you recognize? Somebody left a mark of some sort – somebody you know? Want to tell us about it, then?' Patently that was the last thing she wanted. 'C'mon, love!' His voice was taking on just that slight warning edge. 'You know you'll have to, sooner or later –'

Barry caught his eye warningly, but too late. She glared up at the policeman, and her jaw set like a rat-trap. 'What you talkin' about?' she demanded. 'You tellin' me to my face I done this? I had anythin' to do with whoevah done this?'

Barry spread his arms. 'Mrs Macksie, of course not – everyone knows you here, but –'

'I'm not havin' anybody tellin' me I done a thing like this,' she said obstinately, a little shrill. 'I'm a respectable woman, my husband was a lay preacher and I'm a deaconess! How long I've worked for you now? Five yeah, that's how long! I'm not standin' for this boy heah tellin' me I've anythin' to do with jus' plain filthy things like *obeah* –' She'd said too much. She positively tried to snap the word off, but we'd all heard it. She snorted with annoyance, then turned on her heel and stalked out. She might have looked funny on her plump little partridge legs, but she was too much in earnest. I caught Clare's eye quickly; she nodded, and hurried after the indignant woman.

'Obi-what?' demanded the policeman, of nobody in particular. We all looked at each other, and shrugged. He turned to Dave. 'Now, sir, I don't suppose you could –

with maybe something of a similar background —'

'No I fucking well can't!' snarled Dave, shedding his usual cool with startling speed. 'Background? Jesus, you were born nearer her than I was — why don't *you* bloody know? She's Trinidadian, and I'm from Nigeria. I'm an Ibo — a Biafran, *if* that means anything to you! What's common about that?'

'Nothing at all, Dave,' I said wryly. 'So slip back into lounge-lizard mode as usual, please, and go ask her. She does have a soft spot for you, after all, though there's no accounting for tastes.'

'It's the letters after my name,' he said cheerfully, his flash of temper gone as fast as it had come. He lit another cigarette. 'Mad keen on education, all these West Indians are — worse than the Scots. Okay, I'll ask.'

But when he appeared a few minutes later he was looking a little ruffled. 'She'll tell,' he said. 'I think maybe Clare persuaded her, more than me. And — well, could be we do have something like this back home, though not by that name. But city folk, educated classes — it's not something we'd ever run into. Strictly for the hicks in the stix — straight down from the trees, as you might say, sergeant, eh? *Juju*, that's what they call it.' He grimaced. 'That word — my old man'd have a fit if he'd heard me use it. Wash-your-mouth-with-soap stuff.'

'*Juju?*' Barry frowned. 'But isn't that —'

He was interrupted by the return of Mrs Macksie, leaning on Clare's arm. She launched into a speech like a diver off a high board. 'I want you, sah, to understand — about all *this* I know nothin' — nothin' at all. But there was a time I see something of the sort befoah. When my late husband he was a medical orderly back home in Trinidad, the Lord's work call us to missions often. There was a bad time then, on other island far away; all kinds of folk comin' away in feah of their lives — to Jamaica, Trinidad, anywhere they could, Cuba even. We see a lot of them round missions, we get to know their lives. Poor folk, bittah folk with bad blood an' scores to pay; Things went on — She squirmed, as if the very thought made her uncomfortable. 'Devil's work. *Obeah. Ouanga*, they call it

34

in their fear. We war against it as we could with love, but theah's some too steeped in darkness to see the light. Theah we see things done ... like this. Never so bad, though, even then. The signs I doan' remember, not at first, not till I see *that* ...'

She drew a deep shaky breath and pointed at the nasty speck of blood and feathers on my screen. 'That ... You want to know what *obeah* is? That theah's *obeah*. You take that and you burn it.'

'I'll be glad to,' said Barry, a little shakily. 'But what is it?'

'It's bad – you need to know more? Okay. It's called a *cigle don-pedro*, and I don' know what that mean any more'n you and I don't ever *want* to know. Sometimes the *Mazanxa* use it, sometime the *Zobop* or the *Vlinblindingue*. Use it with signs like these, and for nothin' good. An' thass' all I'm telling you, 'cause thass' all I know.'

'Hold on a minute,' said the policeman hastily. 'Am I to understand –'

Ignoring him, she turned to Barry. 'And now, sah, if you'll kindly excuse me, there's a heap of work heah, and I'm getting all behind.' With serene calm she turned and walked out again. The CID man gaped after her, but he didn't try to stop her. He turned to Dave instead.

'What the hell was all that about? Was she trying to tell me this was done by these – what the hell did she call them? These refugee types? Where were they refugees from, anyhow?'

'That's the kicker,' said Dave with ghoulish relish. 'You ask me – it looks like we got turned over by some of those West Indian yobs from out South Street way.'

'West Indian?' blinked Barry. 'Why so?'

'Well, I can't see there being that many Haiitians in town – can you?'

'*Haiitians?*'

'You heard the lady. That's where the refugees were coming from. Happy little Haiiti. And *obeah*'s just the local name for practices no respectable Trinidadian would be caught dead in – if you'll pardon the expression.

35

But down thataway they're a lot more common.'

The CID man shut his notebook with a snap, and twanged a rubber band into place around it. 'Good as computers, that, for me ... Yes. Well, it's a lead, I suppose. Don't suppose we've been treading on any West Indian toes lately, have we, sir? No Race Relations Board cases?'

Everyone laughed. Of course we hadn't; we were a respectable company, and our business was international. Our standards were high, but an unusual or exotic background was a positive plus; we hired people from all over, and discriminated on just about everything *except* race. It said something for our good sense, if not so much for our social conscience. The only employee who'd been caught up in any fracas at all recently seemed to be me. And no way was I about to mention that, not something I couldn't be sure had even happened. Even if it had, those huge thugs weren't West Indian, anyhow.

They'd been burglars, though. Or something illicit, anyhow, something they cared enough about to spill out lives. Some motive that wasn't immediately obvious ... any more than it was here, either. The police were visibly writing the whole thing off as the work of drunks, druggies or kids, who had just happened to descend on us, found nothing worth stealing and wrecked the place out of spite. They'd keep their ear to the ground, but ...

I couldn't accept that. The unease that was dogging me grew stronger, darker, clutched hard at my heels. It lurked there behind my thoughts, all through the rest of the day that should have banished it, hectic but reassuring. A kind of minor spring filled the office as the air grew sharp and piny with disinfectant, then heady and flowery with scented polish, and at last cool, clean and neutral as the air conditioning took hold; in the background phones trilled cheerfully and printers chattered and whizzed like bright insects, restoring our records to hard copy. Normality burst out like an impatient seedling, stiffened and blossomed into the *status quo*, sunflower-bright. The smooth speed of it was awesome, like watching a time-lapse film; we had an efficient business here, and a committed workforce. It should have reassured me. It didn't.

Two break-ins that wouldn't go away, both strangely motiveless – and with one other obvious connection, namely me. Not one little bit did I like that idea, and I couldn't make sense of it. Suppose I really had been followed, that night – but I'd got to my car, and away. No other car had followed me out of Tampere Street, not even Danube Street. They might have caught the number, but somehow I didn't see them using the police computer to trace me. And then they'd have had to follow me not only home, but to the office next day; and why bother? Why hit the office, when they could have got to me personally at home? No, it was a daft idea; but daft or not, it was getting under my skin. If I could find some way of distinguishing the two incidents, some reasonable explanation for one or the other ...

First things first. *Modus operandi.* The office raid must have been a swift and well-planned affair, to do so much damage without attracting attention. Not so the other; in fact, it could hardly have been sloppier. What were the raiders up to, muscling up to the front door like that on the flimsiest of pretexts? Why would anyone want to break into a warehouse that way – with a murder added, and out on the open street, when with an ounce more planning they could have kept everything behind closed doors? Because they wanted their victim to be found outside? As if – almost as if they were trying to establish beyond all doubt that it *was* a burglary. And ruthlessly enough to snuff out a life for corroborative evidence.

Now *that* rang a bell. I'd come across cases like that; where somebody was trying to use the break-in somehow ... to account for something. Something that wasn't there, and should have been. Or something that was, and shouldn't –

'Jesus, yes!'

I couldn't help exclaiming aloud. A chill wind of certainty blew through me. I'd found my motive.

Across the newly gleaming desks Dave, deep in checking his recovered records, looked up startled. 'Whazzat?'

'Nothing.' I wanted to be up and running. But I forced myself to be calm, act natural; and yet there might not be much time. If I really hadn't dreamed up the whole thing ... 'Just getting worked up about this raid again. So bloody senseless. Or so it seems. But sometimes there's a hidden motive to these things.'

'Gotcha.' Dave leaned back and tapped his cigarette packet. To my relief he'd run out. 'Damn! Like that tonne of hash they had to sneak out of a wool shipment before it came out of bond, and explain the hole it left — so they staged a break-in —'

'That's it. Couldn't be the same here, of course. Not a lot of pot you could slip in with bills of lading.'

'Maybe we should try it!' grinned Dave, rummaging in his blazer pocket. 'Give ol' Gemma a blast! Ah —' He popped the cellophane off another black and gold packet.

I stood up. 'If you're going to light up more of those coffin-nails, I'm off! It's late, and you've probably done me in already today. Never heard of secondary inhalation? If I get cancer, I'll sue.'

'Go ahead, man! I'll claim I was driven to it by a brutal boss who slunk off early and left me up to here in it. Literally!'

'That's no way to talk about Barry!' I said reprovingly. The banter covered up my departure nicely, and my injured arm gave me a good enough reason for leaving before the others, even on this embattled evening. The wince as Clare helped me on with my anorak was quite genuine.

'Oh, sorry — Steve, look, be sensible for once.' Those clear eyes were weighing me up with an expression I couldn't fathom, almost as if she could see right through the frantic unease I was hiding. And dammit, she was nibbling at that finger again. 'Let me drive you home. Go on —'

That was the last thing I wanted. 'Don't fuss! Just a bit tired, that's all — same as you. You get out of this, too. Tomorrow's soon enough.'

Judy's good night was even more sympathetic than before. But once through the door I had to stop myself running for the car.

I headed home, chafing at the tail end of the rush-hour traffic; I took some absurd risks lane-hopping, because home wasn't where I was going, and I might already be too late. I had to tell Jyp, and fast; but I'd already let one night slip by. By the time I turned into Danube Street the sun had already sunk behind the high buildings, and I was racing into a gulf of shadow. It had never looked more mundane; and behind the rooftops there were no masts to be seen. I writhed with doubt; but I drove on.

My tyres rumbled like urgent drums across the cobbles, echoing off the grime-crusted walls. I turned into Tampere Street, where what looked like the same filthy paper was still blowing about, but this time I didn't park. I thought I'd worked out which way the docks ought to be, but it turned out not to be so simple; a one-way street sent me careering off like a pinball through a maze of featureless back streets, and I was as lost as I had been on foot. Every so often as I passed a narrow turning I'd glimpse something at the far end; then I'd turn down the next one and find it dog-legged around and away in the wrong direction. Or I'd slow down, reverse back and into the actual turning, only to find the glimmer of light that suggested open water was a reflection from a boarded-up window, or that the flash of red that looked so much like the tavern signboard was a forgotten poster flapping ragged from a wall. When at last one such alley spat me out into the wider street I'd glimpsed, it turned out to be Danube Street again, much further along past Tampere Street. And there beneath a glaring orange streetlamp hung a gleaming new brown and white tourist sign, that I'd have seen the first night if only I'd kept on going –
< < < HARBOURSIDE

Somehow or other the sight of it only made my heart sink more. But I turned the way it pointed, and drove on. Until, quite unexpectedly, there were no more grim walls ahead, and Danube Street opened out onto a neat little roundabout with bright lights and bushes growing in concrete tubs, and blue parking signs in all directions. And beyond it, flanked by a row of buildings whose scrubbed stone and brick and new paint positively blazed in the last rays of the falling sun, was a dock pool, empty of ships and hung with the same white chains you find on suburban gardens. I pulled in beside them, at a vacant parking meter, and clambered slowly out of the car. I looked down the pool, to where it opened out onto the sunset sea; but the waters were empty. There was not a ship in sight, and the only warehouse I could see was marked with a pink neon disco sign across its upper storey. The seawind was tainted with dust from a scaffold-shrouded building behind me, and the spicy staleness emanating from an Indian restaurant nearby. I'd found only what I'd set out to look for, that night; and it seemed almost like a mockery, a judgement.

Ask, and ye shall receive; seek, and ye shall find. What had I found before? Hallucination? Delusion? In my mind I couldn't be sure it had ever existed; in my memory it was already clouded. And yet all my feelings shouted that it was there somewhere, that I had to find my way back to it before it was too late. I thrashed frantically against the doubts that ensnared me. But what could I do? I was a child again, and lost. I was shut out.

CHAPTER THREE

THAT PLACE ...

Just two days back I'd have liked it. I might even have checked out that disco, it looked stylish and upmarket. Not that that would make the cocktails less lurid, the moronic beat less numbing; but the clientele would be smoother, and there'd be no need to talk. Eye to eye, body to body, direct; no well-worn lines, no show of caring, no rite of lies. That was the way they liked it, too, the ones who went there; a short, sweaty, sleepless night, make-up smears and animal smells, and if it went well a shared breakfast. The girls who hung up their clothes first – they were the ones it went best with; I'd noticed that. Names were things we traded lightly, without obligation, between kisses; no need to call again, and these days I seldom did. All right, so it wasn't love; but love isn't for everybody. At least – unlike so much – it was honest. At least nobody got hurt.

Now, though, even the idea of the place and all that went with it made me sick. The sight of the whole petti-fied street clawed at my sanity. Its mere existence seemed to clash horribly with what I'd stumbled on that night, romanticized or not. I had to get out, or believe ... Or believe nothing, trust nothing, my senses least of all. I forgot the car; I blundered blindly across the road, lucky that it was empty. If there was anyone to see me they must have thought me drunk. I plunged gratefully into the sheltering blackness of an alley mouth like an animal injured, desperate to hide. My fingers skidded along the still fresh paintwork of a window-frame, and struck worn stone beyond it. I blinked, and looked around. The alley was narrow and dark, now the sun had gone down; but that only made it look more like the ones I'd gone weaving through that strange night. Whatever had been done to it the shadow hid; the faint glimmer of twilight, sheltered from the harsh street lighting, draped its mantle of mystery around it once more. I looked back and laughed aloud at the contrast; all that newness seemed like a façade, a thin gaudy crust over what really lay here. Suddenly it wasn't so hard to believe in myself again. Just as Jyp had predicted, I'd come back.

As Jyp had predicted – and what else had he said? '... *you ask for Jyp the Pilot, right?*' It came back to me, clear as I'd heard it. '*Ask anyone, they all know me ...*' Well, that ought to be easy enough. But somehow I didn't relish it round here, not in any of those dinky-looking little bistros, they didn't seem suitable somehow. But at the far end of the alley there was a dim yellowish gleam of windows. That ought to be something.

It turned out to be a pub, not very large and anything but restored; in fact, it looked about as run-down as any I'd seen. It stood on the alley corner, defined by a curved fascia of Edwardian glazed tiling in dark red and blue, very cracked and dirty, and stained-glass windows, equally dingy and opaque, etched with adver-tisements for the forty-shilling ales of forgotten breweries. The light that escaped was glaring, the sound of voices raucous; it looked tough, and it made me nervous. But it was somewhere to start. The warped door squealed as I stepped through into a suffocating cloud of smoke.

I'd half expected the conversation to stop; but nobody paid me a blind bit of attention. Which was just as well, because in this company, this spit-and-sawdust setting, I knew I was a sharp contrast, my white designer anorak and grey houndstooth casuals an intrusion as stark as the electronic fruit machine flickering unheeded at the back of the bar. The fluorescent light showed it up all too brutally: the cracked vinyl flooring in its faded gaudiness, the smoke-yellowed walls, the crumpled walnut faces of the old men who were most of its customers, elderly labourer types hunched and shrunken in their grubby raincoats. And deaf, probably, since the loud voices were theirs; the few younger men, mostly fiftyish versions of the same, sat glumly contemplating them like a vision of destiny. By the door a handful of teenage skinheads swilled cans of malt liquor and moaned at each other. I plucked up my nerve, and pushed past them to the bar. The beefy landlord served me my scotch in a glass clouded by scouring, and wrinkled his brow when I asked if a fellow called Jyp had been in.

'Jyp?' He stared at me a moment with great incurious ox eyes, then rounded on his regulars, leaning over the peeling varnish. 'Gentleman asking fer Jyp – anyone know him?'

'Jyp?' The old men turned their heads, muttered the name back and forth among themselves. Frowns deepened, one or two heads were shaken, others seemed less sure. But nobody said anything, and the landlord was just turning back to me with a shrug when one old fellow hunched up by the gas fire, browner and more wrinkled than the others, suddenly piped up with 'Wouldn't be Jyp the Pilot he means, eh?'

There was a moment's silence. Then cackling chorus of recognition arose, and the landlord's brow suddenly lost its furrows. 'Oh, *him!* Haven't set eyes on him in awhile! But –'

And, astonishingly, the whole place seemed to change, as if some subtle shift in the light, perhaps, transformed it. Nothing looked different; but it glowed like a gloomy painting suddenly well lit. Somehow the whole grim tableau came alive with an atmosphere that transcended its grime and depression, made it seem almost welcoming, comfortable, secure, the centre of its own small community. It was as if I was seeing it through the old men's eyes. 'Bound t'be around somewhere, he is!'

'Down Durban Walk, maybe –'

'Seen him up by old Leo's yesterday –'

They were transformed too, coming alive, chipping in cheerfully with tips and directions to places I might try. It wasn't only me who noticed; the skinheads were gaping at the old men as if they'd gone berserk – and at me as well. Finally a consensus emerged; Jyp would almost certainly be having his dinner at the Mermaid. But I'd have to run if I wanted to catch him before he went off to work. That I certainly did; and I tore out of that pub faster

43

than anyone can have in years, though not before I'd settled for the scotch.

Their directions were mercifully clear, and I had the sense not to go back for the car. I tore around alley and lane until I found myself skidding over some of the worst and filthiest cobbles ever, and saw in the narrow street before me an ancient-looking pile that could hardly be less like the pub I'd just left; its irregular three-storey frontage was genuine half-timbering, none of your stock-broker's Tudor. The sea-breeze was freshening – if that was the word to use of something which stirred up so many remarkable stenches. On the creaking signboard swung a crude painting of a mermaid, bare-breasted and long-haired as usual, but with a sharp-peaked crown and twin curving tails. No name, but who needed one?

I went to the door, found it opened outwards, and down some wooden steps into a smoky room crammed with tables, lit, it seemed, only by the marvellous open fireplace at the back. It was pretty rough-looking, but ten times more alive than the other fleapit. The long tables were crowded with drinkers, mostly arty-looking long-hairs, weirdly got up and arguing noisily, chucking dice, dealing cards and tilting what looked like earthenware mugs – a real-ale place, evidently. Not to mention haggling over mysterious heaps of leaves on the table, or stuffing long pipes with them, reading aloud to each other from handwritten pages or crudely printed sheets – all this along with, and sometimes accompanying, some pretty heavy necking and groping with the few women visible – sometimes remarkably visible, but I restrained my interest. Too many of their gentlemen friends openly wore remarkably wicked-looking knives on their belts. Just the sort of place Jyp would like, I thought, shuddering slightly; but there was no sign of him, and the only service visible was one fiery-nosed oaf in a leather apron slouching around about four tables away, deaf to louder shouts than mine. I wound my way through to the back by the fireplace, a more respectable enclave with marvellous old high-backed cushioned settles. A couple of middle-aged hippy types were monopolizing the ones nearest the fire as if they owned them. One was short, rotund and piggy, the other middle-sized and balding, with a close-trimmed moustache and goatee. I thought one might be the landlord, but heard them arguing uproariously about literature in flat yokel burrs. I put them down for Open University tutors, but asked them all the same, and was surprised when the taller one very politely directed me to the snug at the side. And there, sure enough, with his lean nose buried in a huge pot of beer, sat the man himself.

He almost dropped the jug when he saw me, and all but overturned his table leaping out. '*Steve!* Told you you'd be back, you hoot-owl! Hey, sit down, have a beer – hell, I gotta get to work, you know, we can't make tonight that party I promised you, dammit – but we've still got time for a beer – or maybe two beers, or three –' When he'd pounded what little breath I had out of me I managed to break in and let him know I'd something to tell him, something serious. He insisted on getting me beer before I started; but when he heard about the raid on the office he almost choked on his.

'*Obeah? Ouanga?* Yeah, I heard of those all right. I've sailed those waters, once or twice. And *Mazanxas* ...' His face wrinkled up as if at some disgusting smell. 'Them and the *Zobops* and the *Vlinblindingues*. They're bad news. They're secret societies, brotherhoods of cunning men, warlocks, sorcerers – *bokors*, they call them. Powerful brotherhoods. And *ouanga*'s just their style.'

'Great. And just what the hell sort of voodoo is this *ouanga*?'

He shrugged. 'You said it.'

I swallowed my mouthful very carefully. 'You mean – it really *is* voodoo?'

He spread his hands. 'Well – not exactly. Voodoo now, I can guess what you'd think about it, but truth is it's a faith like any other – still a mite rough at the edges, maybe. Worshippers dance 'emselves into a trance, call down their gods to possess them – but Christians, Jews, way I hear it is they were all doin' that once. Kind of a stage faith goes through, maybe; I'm no scholard. Only there's good and bad in any faith. S'pose ... suppose it was a stone in the ground, okay, and you turn it over? What's underneath, darkness and things crawling – that. That's *ouanga*.'

I said nothing, and he nodded to himself. 'Kind of like devil-worship is to us, I guess – only there's a lot more of it about. Plain voodoo, now, it's a little wild, maybe, but its gods or spirits – *loas*, they're called – they're mostly good guys, or neutral at least. But the worst of these *bokors*, they worship with different rites, rites of blood and wrath. They call down different *loas* – real bastards, mean, destructive, maneaters, the lot. Only – funny thing, this – they're called by pretty much the same names. As if the rites could somehow twist their natures right about. All got their good counterparts save one, and he's the one the rites are named for – a shadowy type called Don Pedro. Not a nice guy, by all accounts.'

I started; but Jyp, still thinking hard, didn't seem to notice. 'So yeah, it sounds like some kind of voodoo guys turned you over. But who – or whether it had anything to do with the other night – it's beyond me, Steve! I can't guess. If it'd been round here now, this raid, I'd have said yeah, it might've been the Wolves handing out a warning – or just their little bit of fun. It's from down that way the bastards stem, same as most of the *Iskander*'s cargo; and they'll follow any god who's as big a stinker as they are. But on the other side of town – the everyday side, the Core? Hell, no! I just can't believe it, Steve! The Pack'd never stray so far in – never! What's to make them? Greed, fear, those are the things drive their breed strongest, and they weren't satisfying either one. You – can you think of anything?'

'Not about my raid, Jyp – but about yours. And that reason for it you couldn't figure out, remember? What if you were just meant to be window-dressing?'

This time he did choke. But when he got his breath back and the beer out of his nose I told him about my idea, and he began to nod as he listened, first excitedly, then grimly. 'Dandy!' he said at last. 'Stage a burglary to cover up dirty dealings – and leave a body to make it convincing. It could be, Steve — it could well be! A bit smart for the Wolves, maybe — but even they get a rush of blood to the brain once in a while … h'mm. But if that's so, what's so hot about it? Didn't come off, did it? Thanks to you. But here you've got yourself lathered up like a trotter —'

'Don't you *see*?' I barked, so loud it momentarily halted the hubbub outside. I lowered my voice. 'I'm only surprised they waited a night! Whatever they came to do, it's still undone! Whatever was wrong with that cargo still *is* wrong. Something's not there that should be, or is there when it shouldn't be! And what's that mean? It means ten to one *they'll come back* —'

Jyp sat there a moment, silent. Then he slammed a palm against his temple making his red hair fly. 'They had to wait a night,' he mumbled. 'To put the hex on you.'

'*What*? But how'd they know anything about me?'

He snorted. 'They've ways. Maybe you were followed — though there's other things might've done that. That's the way the Wolves'd think, okay. Couldn't believe you'd just turned up out of the blue, no — not when you started pokin' round after the *Iskander*. At least I got half a brain working — jehosaphat!' He gulped at his beer, then straightened up.

'Thanks, Steve — though thanks still ain't enough. Chances are you just saved my life one more time.' He grinned. 'Getting t'be a habit, ain't it? But let's us both do some more thinking now, and quick — *will* they be back? Word got around about that raid, y'know. Next morning half the folks with stuff there showed up post-haste — and they checked through it all real careful on the spot, with me there. Nothing funny there. Now lemme see, what's left? Not much. Half the flamewood — but you can't hide things in loose planking. What else's large enough to be hoaxed easily?'

He muttered to himself, then suddenly hissed 'The roots! Damn great shapeless bales of them — could get anything in there!' He began drumming again. 'Can't just go tearing into them to look, though. Not without the consignee being there. *He's* in Damballah Alley — and that's way the other side of the docks, up behind Baltic Quay ...'

Damballah Alley? We looked at each other. Even I'd heard that name somewhere.

'Okay, so Damballah's a voodoo god,' protested Jyp uneasily, as if he didn't like where this was leading. 'He's one of the good guys, the source of life – couldn't be less like this Don P. character. And it's only natural the *Iskander* would be carrying some stuff for those Alley fellas, sailing from those waters. Doesn't prove anything. Still, sure, we ought to get the consignee and go look –' His face hardened suddenly, as a wash of anger swept away the uncertainty. 'The hell it doesn't prove anything! It's the best lead we've got. It fits; it all fits, too goddam well! And if old Frederick's been trying to pull anything I personally will make him shove every one of those roots – sideways! But there's not much time, and the far side's a couple of miles away; a boat'd be fastest – if we can find one at this hour –'

'Look, Jyp,' I suggested, rather diffidently, 'My car's not far away – I think –'

His face lit up. 'Your *car*? Wow, great! Let's go! Let's go!' He bounced up again, excited as a schoolboy; hastily I downed my beer – a shame, it was excellent – and followed. In my confusion I hadn't noted the street where I'd parked, or even the name of the dingy pub, but Jyp recognized the description and led me back there by what seemed a much shorter route. As we passed the pub he stuck his head round the door, to be greeted by a cheerful roar, and shouted his thanks; and from there I had no trouble finding my way.

As we emerged from the alley I was surprised; darkness had fallen in earnest now, with a touch of moist haze in the air, and it had transformed the place. New paint and trendy trimmings were swallowed up in a gloom the glaring pools of the streetlights only deepened. The strings of bright globes and glowing signs seemed to hang suspended in space before the solid untouchable shadows that were the buildings; their rooftops, orna-mented with gable and turret, were timeless silhouettes

48

against the lambent sky. For a moment I wondered if the car would still be there.

It was, though. When we got to it Jyp circled it, fascinated, unable to keep his hands off the smooth paint-work; and when I unlocked the door for him he got in awkwardly. 'Ain't never been in one of these fancy closed-in autos before,' he confessed with an abashed grin, and was fascinated by the sun roof. He seemed equally impressed when I turned the starter, but as I accelerated smoothly away across the cobbles I heard him suck in his breath sharply, and when I reached thirty I glanced across and saw him rigid and staring in his seat, his feet braced against the well. A little cruelly, I took it up to forty as I turned into Danube Street, but it had the opposite effect; once he realized we weren't flying out of control, he kicked and whooped 'Hey, can you get any more out of her?'

'Fifty-five suit you?'

He bounced on his seat as I accelerated, and yelled 'Twenty-three skidoo-*ooo-ooo! Faster* – hey, what're you slowin' down for?'

'There's that junction you mentioned – and such things as speed limits in this town! And traffic lights!' Though look what stopping for one of those got me into ...

'So where do we go from here, pilot?'

Jyp had slumped down in his seat, sulking, but he sat up quickly to gaze around like an excited child at the bright lights and garish shop windows of Harbour Walk. It had been a while, he claimed, since he'd been this way. Just how long, was something I should have been wondering about – but oddly enough it didn't occur to me to ask, just then. Fortunately the geography didn't seem to have changed, he picked an unlikely-looking turn-off, and gave me clear directions down a whirl of side roads. Once off the main road I took a corner or two too fast, just to cheer him up.

At last, tyres screeching, we turned into a much wider street, a smoothly curving terrace of stone build-ings with tall half-columned frontages. These were no business buildings; they must once have been the town

49

mansions of merchants, within easy reach of their wharves and counting-houses. They must have been really imposing then, with their tall windows and carved door lintels towering at the head of broad steps, all faced in fine-chiselled sandstone. Now the steps were dished with wear, the lintels cracked and chipped and bird-fouled, the windows mostly boarded and eyeless; torn posters and spray-paint slogans spattered the blackened stone. Only two or three of the street-lamps were working, but there was no sign of life to need them. I pulled in by a crumbling kerb, and almost before I could lift the handbrake Jyp bounced out. Something clattered against the door-frame. 'C'mon!'

I blinked. Somehow I hadn't noticed that particular something before. 'Jyp – hadn't you better be careful? That, uh, sword you're wearing – do you want to leave it in the car?'

He chuckled. 'Round here? Like hell I do. Bundlers, Resurrection Men – never know what you might run into. But don't worry! Nobody'll notice it, like as not. Folk only see what they want to see, most times; if it doesn't fit in, they just ignore it.' His teeth flashed in the gloom. 'How many strange things've *you* seen out of the corner of your eye? C'mon!'

I hastily locked the car and scuttled after him. He wasn't easy to keep up with, and I didn't want to get left behind in this mirk. I wondered what a Bundler was, but I hadn't the breath to ask; and it occurred to me, as the car faded from sight, that I wasn't really that crazy to know.

Jyp didn't head for any of the steps, but instead turned into a narrow and uninviting gap around the middle of the terrace, a lane that led us past what might once have been stables and carriage-houses, but were now half-crumbled hulks. At the end the old mews bent sharply to the right, and as we turned it felt as if a warmer, darker air flowed about us. There were lights ahead, though, and as we drew closer I saw they were old-fashioned street-lamps mounted on wall brackets, illuminating the frontages of a row of small shops. The light was warm and yellow, and as we passed by the first of them I heard hissing and looked up; it was a genuine gas lamp. I wondered how many of those were still in use. On the wall beneath it a Victorian nameplate, much cracked and defaced, read *Danborough Way*; I spoke it to myself as I read it, and the sound made me stop and think for a moment.

The shops themselves seemed just as peculiar; they all looked old, and one or two even had bottle-glass window-panes, though mended here and there with clear glass or painted slats of wood. Many of the windows above them were lit; odd scents hung in the still air, a murmur of soft voices, and occasionally the thud and stutter of rock music, never loud. One shop, at the far corner, had a modern illuminated newsagent's sign, cracked in one corner, and another, further along, had what looked like the original Victorian sign to proclaim it was a 'Provision Merchants to Family and Gentry', and a heap of faded cans in its window. Another, better kept, seemed to be a second-hand shop, piled high with furniture. But the others were harder to guess; they had no signs, or hand-lettered cards that read '*His Grace the Sovereign Joseph!*' or '*The Mighty Gunzwah's Emporium*', interspersed with advertisements for ginseng, hair restorer, Tarot readings, Goon Yum tea and vitality tonics for men. One immense luminous orange effort read '*Have You Got The Runs???*', as if trying to persuade me I was missing something.

Fortunately it was towards another door that Jyp turned, the shop next to the furniture store, and the best kept by any standards; its woodwork was well varnished, its brasswork gleaming, its windows an orderly riot of everything from gaudily-covered books to bunches of feathers, incense burners and what looked like very good ethnic jewellery. What really caught my eye was a painting a crazy piece of naïve imagery, gaudy as a parrot and childlike in its directness – but with anything but a childish effect. A black man in a fantastic white military uniform complete with scarlet sash, gilt buttons and plumed sun-helmet, sitting tall and proud in the saddle of a winged horse, rampant against forked lightnings crossing in a stormy sky. In his hand a curved sabre – and round his head a coruscating halo of gold leaf. A real ikon, in fact – only the style looked African, Ethiopian maybe, because it was obviously Christian. Or was it? Along the bottom I read, in neat copperplate script, *Saint-Jaques Majeur*. But that look didn't square with any saint I'd ever heard about – least of all the shower of scarlet droplets that flew from the sabre's edge. I turned to ask Jyp, but he pushed impatiently past me. A mellow bell bounced on its spring as he flung open the door.

Out of the door behind the counter, as if he had been pushed, popped a black man, middle-aged or older, with elegant white mutton-chop whiskers. He wore a neat green baize apron, like a butler cleaning the silver, over a brown corduroy waistcoat. 'Frightfully sorry, gentlemen,' he began in resonant tones, 'but we are closed for business today –' Then he saw Jyp, and beamed. 'But not to you, of course, captain! What can I –'

He was choked off as Jyp shot his long arms across the counter, caught the waistcoat and drew the man over the counter with such inexorable strength that his feet left the ground. Jyp glared at him narrow-eyed, almost nose to nose. 'That shipment of root, Frederick! The one that's gathering dust down at the warehouse right now? It's your order, isn't it, all of it? Then how come you've not been down to pick it up, huh?'

The man's eyes widened and he flapped his hands and cawed in helpless surprise. I felt suddenly ashamed, and caught Jyp's wrist; it felt like steel cable. 'Let him down, Jyp! He can't answer you if he chokes!'

Jyp said nothing, but he released the man, who almost collapsed behind the counter. 'But captain,' he wheezed, 'I haven't the slightest – I really do not understand – if I have somehow given offence, I – I am really not as young as I was, you understand, it is not as easy for me to arrange matters as – I do not presume –' Even stammering, he remained beautifully spoken.

'You couldn't get down there yourself, then?' I prompted him. He drew a deep breath, and smoothed down his ruffled whiskers.

'No indeed, sir! For smaller loads I can fit in my car, certainly – but the roots are a large vanload, and I no longer maintain one.'

Jyp tapped the marble-topped counter thoughtfully, and looked around the little shop. 'That so? Why'd you order so much, then? You mean to leave it with us, and just pick it up piecemeal as you need it?'

Frederick permitted himself a pitying smirk. 'At such rates of tonnage and floorage, sir? Hardly. No, I have a most obliging neighbour who maintains a suitable van, and has promised to go down and collect the roots when next he has a few hours free; but he has not managed it yet, and naturally in these matters one does not wish to press ...'

Jyp's lined face had gone very cold. 'Maybe it's about time one did. C'mon, Fred, you're going to introduce us. This instant.'

'Whatever you wish, captain, whatever ...' babbled the old man as Jyp drew him irresistibly out from behind the counter. 'But I assure you ... Mr Cuffee ... most pleasant and helpful fellow-tradesman ...' Jyp propelled him gently out into the street. 'So large a purchase ... the advantages of buying in, ah, bulk, if I may venture upon the vulgar phrase ... His initiative entirely –'

'Was it now?' enquired Jyp, with gentle menace. 'High time we had a word with such an enterprising guy. Now which door might his be?'

It was the furniture shop. I jabbed the plastic bell-push labelled *Cuffee*, heard the harsh shrilling echo through the place, but nothing stirred. Again, and there was nothing, and no light in the upstairs windows. Again, and the old man blinked. 'How unusual! He is most often at home at this time. And his truck is not in its customary place. Perhaps he is clearing a house somewhere –'

'Perhaps,' I said. I looked at Jyp. 'Unless he's running that little errand right now –'

Jyp whirled. 'The warehouse – c'mon!' He loped off down the street, dragging the protesting shopkeeper stumbling after him, green apron flapping in the heavy air.

'But captain – my shop – it's not locked up –'

'It won't blow away! Steve, this time can you really hit the gas?'

'If you're sure it's that im–'

'I'm sure. I'm goddam sure! Though I'd just love to be wrong.'

'Well ...' I swallowed. 'I can try.'

The tyres screeched on the cobbles as we swung around the corner, and Frederick, tumbled headlong in the back, added a note of his own.

'*Stop!*' barked Jyp, crouched pale and drawn beside me. I stamped hard on the pedal, and he braced himself stiff-armed against the dashboard; he'd had speed enough to last him awhile. The back end almost broke away, fish-tailed madly for a moment before I brought her to a snaking, slithering sideways stop. I flicked off the ignition and slumped over the wheel, fighting off the manic laughter of relief. To think I'd ever baulked at a red light ...

'We're here!' said Jyp.

Following his gaze, I saw the same dim street, all quiet, all mundane, the same pile of scaffolding, the pale light over the warehouse door, quay and ocean beyond hidden in the shadow of emptiness; not a soul in sight. But Jyp snapped his fingers and pointed; from the shadows beyond us my headlights awoke twin answering glitters, and gleamed faintly on the dark bulk of a furniture van. Then the sea-breeze sighed a little, and the dark line dividing the warehouse doors seemed to deepen for an instant.

Jyp fought the doorhandle, then he was out and running. I tumbled out more awkwardly and sprinted after him. I caught him up as he reached the doors; they were ajar, creaking slightly in the breeze. There was no other sound, and still nobody in sight. Cautiously Jyp pushed the door back. Inside it was blackness, tinged with a thousand peculiar odours. Nothing moved, and I stepped after him, saw his silhouette in the faint light from outside cast around this way and that – then trip over what looked like a sack on the floor just inside the door, grunt and stoop down to it, turn it over. Emptiness gaped up at us, a ghastly mockery of my own surprise, all wide eyes and sagging jaw. I didn't know the man; and never would, now.

'Remendado,' whispered Jyp hoarsely. 'The day man – I should have relieved him about ten minutes back –'

I stumbled back, sickened, deadly afraid, and something clattered underfoot. Jyp looked up – and then threw himself away with a yell as a long blade flashed into the light, hissed across the air where he had been. He vanished into the shadows, and suddenly they were alive with jostling forms, with trampling feet. Hands grabbed at me, a grip that slipped and instead threw me crashing back against the door – saving me, as another tongue of metal sang in front of my face.

I was free. So I ducked down, grabbed the sword I'd tripped over ...

I didn't even think of that. I didn't think of anything. Perhaps I screamed; I remember a scream, and there'd been no other voices. But what I did do was fling myself aside, away, towards that line of light and through it, an instant before heavy bodies hurled against it slammed it at my back. And then, staggering on the step, I ran away.

I just took to my heels. It wasn't blind panic, if there is such a thing; I knew what I was doing, selfish and ashamed. I wasn't going for help, or anything like that; I was running in deadly fear. It was like trying to scale the side of a collapsing pit, crumbling under me. The clutch of those hands in the dark had ripped away any self-control I might have had, laid bare the sheer animal. I was running to save *me*. It was just some mad quirk that sent me in the wrong direction, away from the car, down towards the shadows of the docks and the nightbound ocean beyond.

And even as I ran, the door crashed open again behind me. I looked back, and there was no stopping then. Three figures, huge and lanky, came bounding out in the hazy lamplight, long coats flying, and after me in an instant. And in the hand of each there gleamed no mere knife, but a great broad swordblade, dully glinting.

Then I definitely yelled; and I ran all the harder. But it seemed to me that the shadows drew back, would not touch me, refused to hide me; and my pursuers loped long-legged at my heels. Out of the street's end I bolted, chest bursting, and turned right because that was the nearer side, onto what was only half a street; on my left it fell away to a gleam of open water. I had run out onto the wharfside itself. But what I saw in that water stopped me dead as little else could, shaking with a fear far greater than any those pursuing figures could inspire. In that awed moment I forgot them completely.

Only by that starlit gleam was the water visible, a pool of blackness turned suddenly to a mirror of black glass, gently rippling. It was the image in that mirror that held me spellbound, a web of black lines, a thicket of leafless thorns. In utter amazement, all else forgotten, I lifted my eyes, knowing what the shadows had been hiding from me, what I would now see.

I knew, yet I was not ready for it. The thicket was a forest; a forest of tall masts, of tangled rigging and stern spars crossing the night. To either side they stretched before me, as far as my eyes would reach, stark against the stars, high and magnificent. The docks that only an hour or two earlier I had seen stand empty and forlorn were now thronged with many tall ships, moored clustered and close. So many they were, so high they stood, that sky and sea were all but blotted out. The pool I saw gleamed through the gap between a reaching bowsprit and a high-transomed stern. I may have heard the crash of feet behind me, but hardly noticed it. I was confronted with a wonder wider than my mind could take in, a towering glimpse of the infinite. Like the wind off the ocean it shook me, chilled me, showed me how vanishingly small I was, and all my concerns. I knew only too well it was no illusion; it was I who felt unreal. Where something like this could happen, fear seemed irrelevant.

Until the last moment, when the clatter of boots became too loud to ignore, and I heard the panting breath of my pursuers. Then, agonized at my own stupidity, I turned to bolt again; too late. A hand plucked at my sleeve. I tripped on a loose stone, spun around and crashed down on my back. Hard boots stamped painfully down on my arms as I struggled to rise. Winded, helpless, I wheezed for breath. Their long faces bent over me, silent, expressionless, leaden and grey in the faint light. A swordtip glinted, a great broad cutlass-thing, looking rusty and pitted and not very sharp. It swung idly back and forward before my eyes, so close it parted the lashes; then it went swinging up for a great slashing stroke. The animal kicked out in me again. I filled my chest with one fiery, sobbing breath, and screamed for help.

The sword did not fall; and I felt the feet that pinned me stiffen. Piercing yellow light fell across us like a net, and froze all movement. Someone had answered, a sharp voice from seaward, clear and challenging. Wood boomed hollowly, like a menacing gong. I twisted my head around and blinked. Down the lowered gangplank of one of the nearby ships another figure came bounding, tall and lithe. A shaggy mane of hair, golden in the light of the deck lantern, swung over broad shoulders and bare arms, long and muscular. 'Well, cubbies?' came the voice again, cheerful and insolent. 'What're ye nipping at tonight? Drop it, and back to your kennels! Or must I whip ye there myself? I'll have no mongrels pissing around this wharf!'

Half stunned, half dazzled, I heard something strange in that voice, something more than its slight burr. But then for the first time one of my pursuers spoke, and I could imagine no stranger voice than that. Gargling, growling, grating like feet on frosty gravel, it ran ice in my blood to hear it, wholly, horribly inhuman. *'Grudge the Wolves their honest meat, does thee? Hie thee back to thine own bounds, bitch, and mind what's thine!'*

Bitch?

A rich untroubled laugh answered him. As my eyes adjusted I gaped at the newcomer. A belt of gold plates sparkled over tight black jerkin and breeches, much like Jyp's, and a long sword swung from it. But for all their tightness it still took me a moment to realize this was a woman, and quite an attractive one at that. Her face clouded with anger as she stared down at me, and it rang in her voice. 'So ye're snapping after strangers, now, are ye? Off, away, back aboard that hulk of a *Chorazin* else I leather a lesson on your hides! That's no fit meat for puppies!'

They stood fast above me, and their laughter was ghastly. '*Then come thee, vixen! An' take it from 'em!*'

Before the words were done she swung up her scabbard and with a sharp hiss of metal she drew on them. Animal-swift they responded, snarling, shifting to a fighting stance – and forgot me. Their feet lifted from my arms. 'Up, boy!' yelled the woman. 'Up, and t'heels! Run!' And with that she charged straight at them.

Run again. Run as I'd been told to, and leave someone else in the lurch; a woman, at that, who'd saved my neck without even knowing who I was. And perhaps it was being called *boy* ...

'Like *hell!*' I said, and flung myself at the ankles of the nearest Wolf. It was like butting a lamppost, but I'd played rugby at school; he yelped with surprise and went crashing down on the stones of the wharf. His sword skittered across the paving. I meant to jump on him, but then the woman and the other Wolves collided in a clash of steel. One Wolf staggered back from the impact, but the other plunged in, his great cutlass of a sword flung high, and brought it cleaving down. It looked unstoppable, but the woman's own blade caught it; and hers was longer, and hardly any narrower, a huge straight sabre of a thing. Its hilt enclosed her hand in an intricate basket of gold-work; against that the Wolf's blade jangled and was caught. A sudden slash drove it back against him, skipped free – slid upward – and straight into his throat. The Wolf reeled, staggered, dark blood welling between his scrabbling fingers; he collapsed, kicking, she spun about to face the other –

A boot glanced off my temple and sent me sprawling, head ringing, eyes unfocusing. Rolling over, trying to clear my head, I saw the woman and the second Wolf cross blades in a flickering sequence of thrust and parry.

Her guard sagged, the Wolf lunged – and shot right by her as she danced lightly aside, and ran the sabre with ruthless ease right into his unguarded armpit. But the third Wolf, mine, had had time to retrieve his sword, and even as the woman's sword sank deep into his fellow's side he aimed a violent slash at her.

Or tried to; because, staggering up, I'd wrapped both arms around his swordarm, and hung on. He was almost strong enough to carry me along with him, but it made nothing of his cut. Then the air sang above me, like the beat of a great wing, and I felt the shock down my arms. The body jerked and bowed like a cornstalk in a reaper and I let go hastily as the head flew up on a dark fountain. I shut my eyes, and heard two distinct splashes from the water below.

When I looked up, the woman was swiftly rifling the pockets of the other two bodies, stuffing the proceeds down her cleavage. She grinned. 'Whole, are ye? That was rudely well done, for a man unarmed. How'd ye set those hyaenas on your traces?'

'Jyp –' I croaked, and she stopped.

'Jyp, ye say?' she barked. 'What of him? And where?'

'At the warehouse – got to help him –' Her hand caught me under the arm, hauled me up like a kid.

'Follow then! *Fast!*'

I only stopped to scoop up one of the fallen cutlasses, but even so she left me well behind. Sword still in hand, she was almost at the corner, her soft-topped boots slapping the stones. But I caught her up as she reached the forecourt, and together, no word spoken, we charged against the door. Nobody had locked it; it flew wide, till it juddered against another body – another Wolf, not Jyp – and the dim light flooded across the roof. From the back somewhere came the clang of metal, and a shout. The woman plunged that way, I after her, and down a long aisle between stacks of packing cases. Acrosss the far end a shadow dodged, and after him others, taller, brandishing swords and what looked like fish-spears, vicious tridents; some stopped, saw us and turned, menacing.

59

She didn't stop. Straight into the midst of them she ploughed. Her sword slashed this way and that with a noise like wind in phone lines, and there was a horrible croaking scream; one Wolf fell kicking, another crossed blades with her, but another yet ducked under her arm. He was coming for me! The cutlass felt like a ton of iron in my hand, but I stuck it out in the best imitation of her lunge I could manage. The Wolf, still straightening up, ran on the point; but I was too far away. He jumped back with a shrill curse, and hacked at me; I tried to parry, but the sheer force of the impact smashed the hilt right out of my fingers and toppled me back against a packing case. The blow smashed right into it and through, and sliced my neck hairs before the splintering wood stopped it. The Wolf snarled, ripped it free – and was felled where he stood by a slash through the back of his neck.

He slumped like a coat off a hanger. The woman swung back and stabbed at the one scrabbling on the floor, then seized me by the arm and dragged me after her, shaking my stinging fingers. Together we sped down another aisle, past another twitching body, and around again. Ahead loomed a stack of planking, the air heavy with the sweet sappiness of cut wood. A minor riot was developing round its base, with Wolves hopping up and jabbing their weapons viciously at something I couldn't see. One was clambering up like a gross spider, almost at the top, but the last board he hung on tilted suddenly, swung out and tipped him and a minor avalanche of planks right down onto the heads of his fellows.

Into the midst of the mêlée, blonde hair flying, the woman charged with a carolling war-cry. The Wolves swung to meet her with a chorus of ghastly snarls and the narrow aisle erupted in a tumult of bangs, crashes, splintering wood and shrieks. This way and that they fought her, but in the narrow way no more than two or three could reach her at once, and among the scattered planking she was far more agile then they. I saw one flung back and sag down, another run through, double up and drop, another –

Why I went after her, unarmed idiot that I was, I

don't and didn't know; maybe her sheer fury swept me up, maybe I was too scared to be left alone. I leapt up on a plank, only to fall off with a yell as a Mohawk-crested Wolf sprang up at the other end. I hadn't expected their eyes to gleam green that way in the near-dark; it damn near threw me. He lunged at me with his trident, I dropped and it hit the stack behind me and stuck, quivering. A long hand snaked out and seized me by the throat, held me pinned while he struggled to work it loose; I lashed out with my foot. He howled shrilly. He was human enough there, anyhow, but it didn't put him off one whit. Snarling seventy kinds of murder, he left the trident, plucked a massive cutlass from the folds of his coat – then dropped it and collapsed as a plank came whistling down edgewise on his skull. After it, with a wild rebel yell, flew Jyp, flinging himself down from the pile onto the remaining Wolves. Caught off-balance between him and the woman, they wavered – and she struck. One, two, it was like an explosion hurling them back, and they sprawled twitching where they fell; another folded violently as Jyp's sword slammed into his stomach, but the tall Wolf behind him seized that chance to slide past and run at the woman. Only he saw me first ...

The trident was stuck. The cutlass lay at my feet. I knelt, scooped it up and slashed at him. No nonsense playing fencer this time; I just struck out with my best squash-player's back-hand.

He must have thought I was cowering. He didn't stop to raise his guard. The impact was jarring, the sound ... horrible. The thudding chop you hear from the back of a butcher's shop, muffled by wet meat. The cutlass flew out of my hands again, and the Wolf reeled, gaped, clutched frantically at his upper arm. A slight ripping of cloth and it came away, entire, in his hand. A dark rush stained his side. Eyes glaring, foam and slaver pouring from his lips, the Wolf loomed over me like death incarnate; then suddenly his eyes wandered, he gave a high-pitched womanish shriek and staggered. Still shrieking insanely, he fell down at the feet of his fellows and died. That broke them, and they turned to run. Not far. I grabbed the trident, and this time it tore free, but I didn't need it. Only one escaped and bolted down the aisle, but Jyp launched himself like a leopard onto his back and slashed his throat as he ran.

I pressed face and stomach to the planks, shaking with fright and reaction, struggling hard not to throw up. I couldn't believe what I'd just done. The sight of death in there was revolting, the reek was worse; not even the spicy fragrance of the planks could drown it. It didn't seem to bother the woman. When I looked up eventually I saw her perched casually on a packing-case, breathing deeply. It would have been eye-catching if her top and trousers hadn't been spattered with blood, though none of it seemed to be hers. As my sickness subsided the implications sank in; this big blonde amazon had just butchered maybe a dozen strong men, or whatever, bigger than herself, and suffered no worse than a scratch or two. For a moment she seemed as inhuman as the Wolves; but I couldn't look at her that way. She'd saved me, gratis and for nothing; she'd saved Jyp ...

A hand fell on my shoulder, and the light of a lantern blossomed around me. 'Ye've no hurt?'

I blinked. She looked different, close to; and younger. She was taller than me, but not by so very much, and though her features were too large and strong to be really pretty, they were by no means rough or mannish. Her face was oval and regular, clear-skinned and creamy, her nose long but tip-tilted; full shapely lips made up somewhat for the slight trace of jowl at her jaw. The effect was slightly coarse, but sensual. Her heavy-lidded green eyes were surprisingly mild and sympathetic.

'No worse than a few bruises ... and maybe an old cut opened. But that's all thanks to you – stepping in where you'd no need –'

She waved a hand; that at least looked raw-boned and strong. 'Ach, think no more on't, boy! Always my delight to scotch that stinking Pack in their dirty businesses! And since it was to help Master Jyp here, I'm well repaid!'

'You're a friend of his, then?'

'Hey, that's right!' chuckled Jyp. He was wiping off his clothes with a Wolf's long overcoat. He bounced up and draped his arms around our shoulders. 'You two don't know each other! You made such a good team I clean forgot! Steve, this is Mall, an old drinking buddy of mine –'

'That's a stale honour!' she grunted sardonically, scratching her bare shoulder. 'So's every sot in the Ports – the more so an they're lechers also.'

'Known to her victims as Mad Mall,' continued Jyp smoothly. She tossed her mane, revealing a band of something like rich brocade around her brow, but the nickname didn't seem to displease her – rather the reverse. 'She's in the same line of work I am – everything from manning your ship to guarding your cargo! And that's her specialty! She's the best damn help you could have brought back.' He gave a wry smile. 'Hell, that's three, Steve! The other night, the warning, and now you pull me out of this. You're my lucky charm; I've *got* to see you're okay! Keep this up and I'll never get quit!'

I groaned. Disgrace came flooding back. 'Christ, Jyp – if you only knew – I just buggered off. I'm sorry – I was scared sh–'

He cut me short, chuckling. 'What else could you do? You ran in the right direction. I don't care much for coincidence, not in these parts. And you came back; and it's thanks to that I'm still here. Counts for one hell of a lot with me, does that. It's your play, pal; you chalk up the point.'

I wasn't so sure. 'Jyp, – look, I wasn't thinking of fetching help, I just –' His gesture was so sudden, so savage, it shocked me into instant silence. He listened an instant, took two soft padding steps – then sped and pounced like a panther. A frightened shriek split the air, and something heavy was knocked over. I heard Jyp chuckle, and it was not his usual open laugh. 'My, oh my!' he said. 'What've we here? Seems there's mice about as well as rats! Say, Steve – mind seeing if Frederick's okay? I've something here'll drive him wild!'

Frederick was all right. In more sense than one; for

as I got back to the warehouse door he was just tiptoeing up to it, with the jack handle from my car clasped in a pudgy fist. He leaped like a hare when I emerged, but he didn't drop it. 'Oh, my dear sir!' he said, and rolled against the wall. 'Most awfully sorry – so cowardly of me – saw you go for help – but simply lacked the nerve –'

'Oh no?' I grinned, which seemed to unnerve him all the more. I must have looked pretty ghastly, and I was thinking how I'd behaved. Courage came late to us both; to him it had come unaided. 'I left the keys,Frederick. And I know you can drive.'

He mopped his face with an enormous silk handkerchief. 'Indeed, sir! But would you believe it never once occurred to me?'

'Frankly, no. Put that thing back and come along; Jyp wants you to meet somebody ...'

The old man's face could hardly darken with anger, but it looked as if it did, his smooth brows knotting and his whiskers quivering with the strength of his feelings. Neither could his neighbour turn pale, exactly; but the fat man Jyp had hauled out of his hiding place had gone a strange shade of grey, and was quivering like a jelly. Small wonder, with his late employers lying in assorted pieces around him, and Jyp's sword resting idly on his shoulder.

'This is absolutely monstrous, sir!' puffed Frederick. 'Nay, outrageous! I demand an explanation, Cuffee! To make me a dupe, to involve my long-established business as an unwitting party to some low deceit – some common fraud –'

'Seems pretty uncommon to me!' interrupted Mall cheerfully. 'Thought I'd played the gamut of cozening and coney-catching, but this one's left me dry!'

'An explanation, Cuffee!' persisted Frederick. 'Or I shall have to take steps! Severe ones! What will you tell the Invisibles, man? Think! You can't argue with Ogoun!'

'Maybe I've a better idea,' drawled Jyp. 'Our late friends here didn't have time to get anything away, now, did they? So if there was something here, chances are there still is! So we should take a good look – get to the root of all this, if you'll pardon the expression!' Mall groaned. 'And Mr Cuffee here can do the work!' Jyp was watching the shopkeeper closely; and I was a little surprised at the man's reaction. He went even greyer and got up enough nerve to start blustering; but Jyp jabbed him with the sword, and he slouched to his feet, still protesting. I didn't like that. It suggested we'd hit on something he was more afraid of than Jyp. And that didn't make sense; for two pins Jyp would have cut Cuffee's throat there and then.

For all that, Jyp didn't goad him more than was absolutely necessary. I was glad, for a good many reasons. We herded the man, still protesting, round to the far corner of the warehouse, to where a great stack of misshapen bales stood in three rough layers against the wall. The odour of them was indescribable – not bad, exactly, just indescribable, except that some of it was dry earth, and the rest suggested medicine rather than food, and resin rather than spice. Like menthol, it seemed to numb some senses and heighten others; and it was very penetrating. As the lantern caught the shapes I saw they were enormous square-sided bundles of crude straw netting, through whose wide meshes dirty pinkish things, gnarled and knobby, stuck out in obscene-looking attitudes.

Frederick motioned Cuffee that way. 'Open the bales!' he ordered his neighbour. 'Each one now, one by one!'

Cuffee held back, glaring around at us, sweating hard. I saw now he was by no means old, and he had a weightlifter's muscles beneath his dirty t-shirt – from hauling furniture, no doubt; but his great quaggy belly put ten years on him, and fear seamed his face. He mouthed an obscenity at us all, and visibly faltered before seizing the first bale on the top row. He dug his fingers into the tough netting and effortlessly ripped it apart, then skipped sharply back. Roots exploded everywhere, tumbling down around our ankles; the heady smell billowed up about us, but there was nothing else there. 'Carefully, damn you!' growled Jyp. 'Don't go damaging Frederick's stock!'

Shaking his head and cursing frantically, Cuffee tore open the next bale more carefully, but still skipped back and let the contents flow down; and for all Jyp's curses and Frederick's puffing he did just the same with the next one, and the seven or so after that. A sloping heap of roots grew and slumped out across the floor. I leaned heavily on the trident; I was already giddy with the shock of things, and the heavy fumes seemed to make it worse. But beyond a few mouldy-looking duds, Cuffee turned up nothing at all out of place. We all watched him. He was scared, all right; so scared that when he came to the beginning of the bottom row, he baulked again. Jyp wasted no word, but simply jabbed his swordpoint against Cuffee's kidneys. The man yelped and jumped, unseamed the first bale right down the front, then as it slowly spilled its contents he flung himself away so fast he skidded on the hard round roots and crashed to the ground.

But beyond the rustling trickle of roots there was nothing – nothing at all. In idiotic puzzlement Cuffee stared at the little low heap that was left in the sagging net. He began to giggle hysterically with the reaction, and I felt like joining him. Then he reached out a tentative finger, and poked it.

Something pounced back at him. In all my life I'd never seen anything like it.

It was a hand, a huge one; but that makes it sound too human. Transparent, half-formed, fluid, it shone mistily from within, shimmering the colour of distant lightning through the dimness. It clutched at that probing finger and clenched shut. There was a crackle, a shriek, a puff of smoke – and a glare lanced down Cuffee's arm, a brightness so intense I saw all the bones shine right through the flesh as if it was smoky glass. Light flared out between the roots as if a furnace blazed there; then before we could even blink the last of the bale burst outward. A blinding corona enfolded the hapless Cuffee like an anemone snaring a fish.

'*Dupiah!*' shrieked Frederick, in a voice that shivered the air. And, clapping both hands to his bald head he bolted, still shrieking, for the door.

'*Dupiah!*' Mall echoed him. Jyp dropped the lantern with a crash. As one, before I could move, they seized hold of my arms and flung themselves after him, dragging me along bodily between them, still facing backward. Out of the shadows came the deep boom of the door as Frederick reached it. Staring helplessly as my heels skipped over the boards, I saw the glaring glow rise and come after us, shifting and changing as it moved. It was a view I could have done without. I seemed to see all sorts of things in that ghastly orb of swirling smoke and light, eerie, horrible things that set my teeth on edge. I shook with a sense of sheer immanent malice I would never have believed; devouring hatred poured out of it like an acrid stream. Just one jump ahead of it, it seemed, we raced around the corner, and reached the door.

It was shut.

In his panic the old man had slammed it behind him. Jyp and Mall dropped me like a sack and threw themselves at it. I scrambled up, half hypnotized by that glowing, seething thing bearing down on us. It was sheer loathing and revulsion, nothing like bravery, that drove me to dash back and swing out at the thing with the trident I still held.

The shaft slowed suddenly, as if the air had thickened and grown glutinous; it jarred, stopped, stuck. Then the ghastly light danced upon the three tines, and came racing and sizzling down the shaft towards my hands. I dropped the thing with a yell, barely in time, as the door creaked open. The others seized me, flung me bodily out to crash across the cobbles, and themselves after me. Jyp pulled the door closed behind him with a crash, and Mall threw her weight against the handle while he fumbled with the keys. I sat up, dizzy and sick; my arm was agony again, I had struck my head badly on the cobbles, and acquired a whole new set of bruises. I watched Jyp trace a strange symbol with his swordtip in the thick paint of the door, a weird curlicued shape like a series of interlocking arcs ringing a compass rose. Then he reversed his sword and thrust it through the twin handles like a symbolic bar.

That done, he sank to his knees with a gasping sigh. 'Damn!' he muttered, in a shaken voice quite unlike his normal confident tones. 'What a goddam crock! We'll have to get old Le Stryge to this!'

'Aye, well enough,' said Mall, hitching up her tight pants. 'But what of —' And she jerked a thumb at me.

I swallowed. Words wouldn't come, sensible words. 'What ... what was that bloody thing?' was the best I managed.

'Nothing!' barked Jyp, so savagely I hardly knew him. Anger burned off any sign of his normal friendly self. He sounded almost contemptuous. 'Nothing for you to meddle with! Nothing for an outsider!'

With astonishing strength and urgency he seized my arms, lifted me bodily and slammed me on my feet as if I was a child. Then he more or less frogmarched me out into the murky road and up to where my car stood, its doors still wide, the courtesy lights glowing yellow into the haze.

'Now go!' he barked, and thrust me roughly into the driving seat. 'Get lost! Beat it, y'hear! Come back in a week, maybe — no, a month, if you must! Better still, forget what you've seen — forget me — all of us — everything! Drive off in your fancy closed car — close your mind! Forget!' And with that he slammed the door violently shut.

Unable to speak, I stared beyond him. Mall was barely visible, a pale face watching beneath the dim warehouse light. She stepped back, and blended with the dark. Jyp spun on his heel and went off down the cobbles at a fast trot, without a backward glance, till he too was one with the night.

Slowly, shakily, I started the engine, slipped into gear and turned the car out and away. I wasn't sure I'd be able to drive, at first. But the way back seemed shorter somehow, the streets I knew eager to reclaim me. I turned out of Danube Street into the bright lights and hubbub of a cheerful city evening. But I couldn't feel at ease there, not for now; I'd looked into the heart of another light, and it writhed still inside me. Something had been scorched out of me, new fires set alight. It occurred to me then, with a slight twinge of surprise, that I'd never been what you might call sensitive to other people, adept at reading their feelings, not normally. But something had given me that gift, however briefly. I'd read Jyp like a book. And so I wasn't as bewildered as I might have been, nor any way offended by his sudden harshness. The man was terrified. It was as simple as that. Strange and formidable as this creature who'd befriended me seemed to be, he was almost out of his mind with fear. It was for my own good he'd tried to drive me away.

CHAPTER FOUR

ONLY THE NEXT MORNING brought the reality home to me. It struck as my eyes opened, a singing shock of memory that snapped me bolt upright and shaking in my bed before I was fully awake. That *light!*

My pyjama jacket clung clammily to my back. The air seemed close and stale with the stink of fear. I'd come face to face with ... Something I'd never believed in, not even as a child. Something that seemed utterly impossible here, in my own bedroom, all smooth cool greys and hi-tech decor, with bright light only the touch of a switch away. And yet – What other word was there?

With a demon.

I'd seen it gulp a man down like a mayfly. I'd seen killing done. God, I'd killed a man myself! The awful thump of the cutlass blade, the sinking, jerking impact ... Sickness bubbled up in my throat. What had I done? God, what had I done? I'd only wanted to help!

My hands were sticky. I stared down at them in horror, but of course it was only sweat, not blood. Had I really done anything? Or had it all been some kind of mad dream again? I'd had plenty of those. Awful figures had stalked through my sleep, stooping over me with leering faces; horrible images had haunted my dreams, half alluring, half menacing, visions of bizarre cruelties and lusts. Three times at least they'd woken me with titanic drumbeats roaring in my ears, shaken by gusts of fear and shame. But as my pulse subsided those nightmares had faded, leaving only shapeless shadows of fear. The wharf, the warehouse, the light – those things hadn't faded. I wished to hell they would. I sank my head in my hands – and winced as I touched the raw patch left when I hit the cobbles. That kind of confirmation I didn't need.

It proved nothing. There *was* no proof. I might be mad, or I might not; I couldn't tell. And who else was there? I was alone. Very methodically, very neatly, I'd arranged my life that way. As deliberately as I'd styled my flat, cool, spacious, uncluttered, scrupulously tidy – empty. It could have been the set for an upmarket TV commercial, though I'd never thought of it that way before; and if I had, it would probably have pleased me. It didn't, now. I was alone in a sterile melamine box, alone with my terrors and my delusions, and there was nobody to care. I ducked back under the bedclothes and buried my face in the pillow, I felt awful; I didn't want to get up and go to work, I wanted to hide.

But habit in itself is a kind of hiding place. Soon enough it had me up and in the shower, and under the hot water the horrors and tensions of the night seemed to slough gradually away. In no time I was dressed, gulping down my muesli and black coffee off the kitchen counter, clattering down the stairs to the car-park, almost eager to face the pale drizzle and the fearful rush-hour traffic. Jockeying for position in its swirling streams I sailed past Danube Street without so much as a glance. I was even a little early when I strode purposefully into the office, and when I reached my desk, freshly aromatic with polish, I sank back into my armchair with a luxurious sigh. When Clare came in with the post I was already hard at work.

She eyed me narrowly. 'You're looking tired,' she said accusingly. 'You're sure you're not pushing yourself too hard, Steve? I mean –' She shrugged. She seemed less certain, less bossy today.

I fended her off with a confident grin. 'Hey, what's all this? Still fussing? Come on, I'm in my element – you know me. Pig in clover, that's me here.'

'Well, okay,' she remarked ruefully, tugging at a lock of hair. 'I've got that general idea! But – you will be sure and take care of yourself outside work, too? Try to relax a little? I mean, you know what they say about taking stress home …'

I nodded reassuringly. She deserved to be taken seriously. 'I'll be careful,' I said, and meant it. After last night I was going to stick to my old regular life so closely you could put me on rails. Last night? Just the thought of it made me dizzy. Had I got drunk or high or something and doped the whole thing up? Or worse? Unlikely. Whatever had hit me this morning, it was no hangover. And I'd never have touched anything else capable of cooking up last night. Whatever my taste in clothes, designer drugs weren't exactly my bag. I began remembering shreds of a Sunday supplement article on schizoid fantasies – or was that paranoid? Either way I wanted no part of it. What was this, the first signs of burnout? A psychoanalyst might tell me, but no way was I ready to go running to one just yet; these things get about. But could I possibly have just dreamed up anything so fantastic? Clare was on her way to get my coffee when I called after her.

'Er – one thing,' I wasn't at all sure I wanted to ask her this – but, after all, who else was there?

'Look, I know it sounds a silly question, but ... You wouldn't ever call me the over-imaginative type, would you? Sort of fanciful? Not really?'

She stared back at me for a moment, wide-eyed. Then she seemed to quiver from head to foot, and jammed her knuckle to her lips again. Dave appeared in the doorway, gaping like a fish. His face crumpled, and he doubled up, slapping his knee and howling with laughter. That set Clare off. She shook her head violently and fled into the outer office with shaking shoulders, giggling unmercifully. Dave straightened up, tears streaking his burnished cheeks. 'Thanks very much,' I said dryly. He was about to ask something, but I discouraged him. 'Thanks a heap. That's all I wanted to know. *Absolutely* all.'

In no time I was digging back into my work again, squeezing every minute detail out of it the way I'd always enjoyed. Now, though, it was a deliberate exercise. I knew what I was doing; I was deliberately tightening my grip on normality, upon real things. Upon safe things; they were my anchors, my moorings. I was afraid of being swept away.

So went the day. But all through it memory sat at my side, tugging constantly at my elbow, rising up suddenly and scattering my thoughts. So did Clare; she still fussed

72

over me, more lightly than before, perhaps, but she seemed determined to hover. She kept coming up with all kinds of things that demanded my personal attention and sitting beside me while I ploughed through them. Every time I looked up I met those eyes of hers, contemplating me. Why do they always say dark eyes are inscrutable? Hers were as clear and cheerful as a cloudless July sky, and as unfathomable.

'Wish she'd come bouncing round me like that!' grinned Dave as he watched her saunter out.

'Don't wish too hard,' I said disapprovingly, 'or – what's his name? – Stuart the Prop will be coming to bounce *you* around!'

Dave grinned. 'Bit behind in the gossip, aren't you? Big Stu's old news. She gave him the heave-ho months back!'

'Oh? Who is it now, then?'

Dave blinked thoughtfully in his own cigarette smoke. 'Don't know there's anyone in particular, right now. Hey! Speaking of which, I met this amazing girl at a dance last weekend –'

Dave had a unique gift; he could describe any number of girls in minute detail, and still make then all sound alike. He was probably right, at that. I let the anatomy lesson chatter on; it was something else familiar, and I needed everything I could get. I couldn't drive away the night. It obstinately refused to fade; indeed, little details kept leaping back at me, bright and clear – the gleaming patch of water and its entangled masts, the heavy tang of those roots, the woman's jewellery jingling lightly as she drew sword, the hidden tremor in Jyp's voice. There was no getting away from it. Last night either something had happened, *something* had been unleashed – and I did not like to think what – or I was steadily going mad. I couldn't say which idea scared me more.

At last Dave went in search of coffee, and left me alone to face my dilemma. Faced it had to be. Why couldn't I just let this fade, he way it had the first time? Or was that only madness, too? I could run the same computer checks again, but what would that tell me? Couldn't

I remember any other solid facts but that one ship name? Then I hesitated. There was something ... The jingle of that woman's jewellery, Mall's jewellery — that voice of hers telling the Wolves to get away, get back on board that hulk ...

Pretty evidently she'd spat out the name of the Wolves' ship, or of one crewed by them. What if I —

Quickly, looking around anxiously to see if Clare or anyone was coming, I logged onto the harbour register once again, and tapped in the name as I guessed it must be spelt. *Chorazin* ...

The search screen stayed up only a second or two. Then it blinked and scrolled down into the usual file card.

Chorazin, merchantman privateer (630 tons, 24 guns)
Danziger Wharf, berth 4

Out of:	*Hispaniola, ports West*
Master:	*Rooke, Azazael*
In transit:	*repair and reprovision, indef.*
Capacity:	*spoken for*
Destination:	*the East*

I closed my eyes. What next? If I typed in *Flying Dutchman*, what was I going to find? Captain Vanderdecken, overdue at the Europoort-Scheldt with a cargo of ectoplasm?

But there the entry was, when I opened my eyes. There was no fooling myself, not this time, no writing this off as drunken romanticism or nightmares. After last night I knew the difference only too well.

I wasn't even mad. And if I wasn't, perhaps a great many other people weren't, either. Beneath the blandly obvious surface of things there must be all kinds of dark undercurrents stirring; and perhaps they, like me, had swum blindly into one and been borne away, kicking, far beyond their depth.

Jyp had been right to boot me out. I was a creature of the surface, of the shallows; I'd no resources to help me cope. Suddenly I was afraid to confront the world I knew, the world I thought I'd come to some kind of truce with. Never mind sticking to everyday life now, moving on rails – I wouldn't even dare trust that, not any more. How could I believe the blandly ordinary appearance of things now? How was I to know some other, stronger current wasn't lurking in the depths beneath, ready to sweep me away?

The telephone on my desk began to ring. It had a soft, warbling call, but I jumped and sat staring, heart pounding, as if it were the chatter of a rattlesnake. Then Dave came back in, and with a hasty snort I extinguished the screen with one hand and picked up the phone with the other.

'A Mr Peters to speak to you, Steve,' said Clare. 'About a private shipping matter, is all he says, so he wants you personally. Are you feeling up to dealing with him?'

'Oh, put him on,' I sighed. Every company in our line gets its share of private individuals wanting to ship Auntie's armchair or their bargain grandfather clock over to America, that kind of thing; we usually referred them to specialist movers. But when the smooth voice came on the line I changed my opinion.

'Mr Stephen Fisher? But of course!' The English was too impeccable, and accented. *A lawyer*, was my immediate reaction, or a broker, or some other kind of fixer. 'My name is T.J. Peters. Accept my apologies for breaking into your busy day. But I have a matter in hand of a substantial goods consignment I wish to import. The nature of it I would rather not disclose –'

'Then I'm sorry –' I began. Once in a while we also attract cagey characters wanting to exploit our reputation to ship large anonymous crates without attracting customs attention; them we fend off, hastily.

'Over the telephone, I should say. To you in person, of course, there need be no problem of commercial security. But the matter is urgent. If I might assume the liberty of calling upon you later this afternoon, say around four-thirty, would I find you in?'

Of course he would; I could hardly say anything else.

But as the afternoon wore on I wished more and more I had put him off. The sky outside had stopped drizzling, but looked heavier and greyer and more thundery as the day passed. It was stifling; but worse still was the growing sense of oppression that hung in the heavy air. The whole office seemed to feel it; people snapped at one another, made stupid slips or just gave up working and sat staring into space. Dave fell silent; Clare made me three cups of coffee in twenty minutes. Gemma went off home with a headache. There was something almost menacing about it. I longed for honest thunder and rain to break the spell. Thanks to Mr Peters I couldn't just slip off home; and I was glad of that, in a way. I didn't want to be alone right now. The thought of it kept me working, though I didn't seem to be getting very far. At last, around four-fifteen, I decided I needed some air to wake me up before my client came, and mooched out along the back corridor.

The glaziers had finished with the back door, and I swung it open and stepped out onto the balcony leading to the metal stairs. A few breaths of air were stirring here, freshened by the trees beyond the wall of the car-park; faint drops of rain sprinkled onto my face, like tears. I drew a few deep breaths, thought of climbing one floor up to the top, but decided against it. Mr Peters should be here in ten minutes, and I wanted to brush up, straighten my tie and so on. I was glad I'd put on my Cagliari suit today; these Continental types were more impressed by Italian tailoring. I went back inside, and was just passing the back of the office next to mine when I heard the first voices raised, a rising scale of protest, outrage, and sheer fright. Then the crash came.

In that sullen quiet it was appalling. It might have been thunder; but the shriek that followed froze my blood. Now there were other voices, angry shouts, cries and sounds of smashing, crashing, things falling – and more shrieks.

I froze, with every nerve in me raw and shivering. Before last night I might have gone running to see what was the matter; and who knows what might have happened then? As it was, it took all the strength of will I had to inch forward. And as I did so, I saw, blurred behind the ribbed glass partition of my office, tall shapes that strode back and forth amidst a crescendo of booming and splintering crashes. Then suddenly one stopped, loomed up with frightening speed right against the glass, and I saw a weird spiked crest bobbing, heard that harsh reptilian croak again, raised now in a crowing rasp of triumph.

Wolves.

That unfroze my limbs. I moved; I ran. As well I did; the glass exploded outwards above me. A huge fist burst through in a shower of splinters and spraying blood, clutching just where my head had been. There was no going back. I sprinted along the corridor, dived around the corner as I heard the back door of my office burst open behind me and boots come clashing out into the corridor. But I was just far enough ahead. I dashed out into the front hall, a devastated mess with nobody in sight. I skidded violently on the tiles, avoiding the over-turned bookcase, and clutched at the sagging front doors. One came away in my hand, lurched sideways and fell; I sprang through the opening and out onto the landing. There were the stairs; but in four floors they'd have me. The lift – I risked a precious instant to lunge at it, jab the button. And miracle of miracles, the doors slid open.

I plunged in, slammed against the wall and just as the first of the Wolves came crashing out of the offices, I stabbed a finger at the control panel. The sudden look of relief on my face must have puzzled the Wolf, because he and the others at his heels halted, gaping, as if expecting something to happen. But nothing did. The doors stayed open. And I remembered in a sudden flood of terror that there was always a few seconds' delay –

The look on the lumpen grey face changed suddenly to oafish triumph. Saliva gushed between the gravestone teeth, and he hurried himself forward, arms outstretched. With a soft mechanical sigh the doors clunked together in his face. Something crashed against the outside with jarring force; but the lift was moving. I sagged with relief again; but still I felt something was wrong. the lift began to slow, the extra weight lifted off my shoulders – and only then did I realize what it was.

In my panic I'd pressed the wrong button. The lift had gone *up*. There was only one floor above, and nothing to stop the Wolves running up after me. I reached for the down button, stopped myself just in time; they'd page the lift on the way back. The cage bounced gently to a halt, and the doors clunked open. I flinched back, expecting to see tall shapes waiting, or coming spilling up out of the stairwell. There was nobody, nothing except clattering from below. I dashed to the railing and – very gingerly – peered down.

The Wolves were battering at the lift doors. One huge lout with a bristly shaven head was struggling to force what looked like a crowbar between them, bracing his huge boots against the frame and slamming his heavy shoulders against the door. I goggled, and ducked back. They weren't even looking up or down the stairs. Daft as it seemed, they couldn't have the faintest idea what a lift was. They must think I was still shut in that little room there, behind the metal doors.

There was a sudden screech of metal, and then an even louder howl that seemed to echo away into the distance. Then, out of that same distance, an equally echoing crash cut it short. I had to cram the back of my hand in my mouth to stifle a whoop of hysterical laughter. The Wolves had valiantly forced the doors, and at least one of them, the crowbar boy probably, had fallen a full four storeys down the shaft. Behind me the lift alarm clanged into sudden life, with enough volume to bring the whole building running. For good measure I smashed the glass of the fire alarm – I'd always wanted to use that little hammer – and thumbed it too. From the floors below came the sound of doors slamming. I turned, to see the switchboard girl from this office peering nervously out through the doors.

'What – what's all'a noise?'

I grabbed her and ducked back in. 'Have you called the police yet? No? Christ, didn't you hear –' I heard the tinny jangle from the headphones of the walkman on the desk. 'Never mind!' I dived for the switchboard. 'Are you the only one up here?'

She made a face. 'Aye. They're all off early wi' the weather. I've gotta wait f'me boyfriend t'pick me up'.

'Worse luck for you! The back door – locked? Then find somewhere you can shut yourself in, the ladies' maybe – Operator? Police, please – *fast!*'

And fast they were. There must have been a patrol car nearby; it was only a minute after I'd put down the phone, and I was still fighting the temptation to go and lock myself in the ladies' as well, when I heard the approaching siren. It gave me enough nerve to snatch up a weighted ashtray stand and go cautiously back out. There was no one visible on this landing or ours, nothing to hear above the row except a rising hubbub from the street, where the fire alarm had decanted the lower floors. I sidled down the stairs, wishing my heart would steady up a little; still nothing. I reached our landing, dithered momentarily whether to go in, but showed some sense and fled hell-for-leather down the stairs. When I came back up a minute later it was with two policemen at my back, one huge, *and* three rugby forwards from the insurance brokerage below.

I don't know what I expected to find. I dreaded the thought. But to my great relief the first thing we came on was Barry, blood all down his expensive shirtfront, ministering to Judy from the switchboard. She was stretched out on the visitor's seating, with a black eye, and, by the looks of it, a broken arm; but at least they were both alive.

'Steve!' he said, rising and grabbing me. His nose started bleeding again, but he didn't seem to notice. 'They didn't get you? It was you set off the alarms? Christ, that was timely thinking! You saved our bloody bacon! Those bastards! Kicking us round like footballs one minute, then one ring, and off like bloody bunny rabbits! Should've seen 'em run! Bloody cowardly maniac punks –' I gave him my handkerchief. He dabbed gently at his swelling nose, and I saw it shift slightly, it was broken. '*She* tried to call,' he mumbled. 'Knocked her flat an' tipped her desk over on her ... Bastards! Utter frigging bastards ...'

He ran down into shaky swearing, and I helped him to a seat by Judy. The police and the others hadn't hung around; they'd charged swiftly through the offices, and I heard them shouting that the bastards had got out the back. Other police were arriving now, and the office staff were beginning to appear. By the looks of it they were all walking wounded, nobody actually dead or crippled, but they still made a hell of a sorry sight – a limping parade of black eyes, bloody shins, split mouths, lacerated ears and blossoming purple bruises everywhere. Some had scalp wounds, bleeding like pigs, others streaks of vomit over their clothes. It looked as if the Wolves had roughed everyone up just as a matter of course, men and women alike, especially about the head. I'd heard of muggers doing that, to disorientate their victims. Most of the typists and younger secretaries had had their clothes ripped half off, too – by the looks of it, more to humiliate than harm. Even Gemma's PA, five years off retirement, was clutching her elegant blouse closed as she helped one of her secretaries along, green with shock.

Secretaries ... There were faces I didn't see. I leaped up and ran around to my own office. When I reached it I stopped dead in the doorless frame. The other day's devastation was nothing compared to this. The place had been quite literally torn apart, every stick of furniture shattered. Even the partition between the inner and outer offices had been smashed down; and as for my terminal, my desk, my chair even, I was hard put to it to recognise them. They lay shattered and trampled, stamped into a shapeless pile. One of the rugger players was helping Dave up from the floor below his desk. 'Dave!' I shouted. He blinked confusedly at me through his unswollen right eye. 'Dave! is Clare all right?'

He only mumbled 'Uh – Clare? Take Clare –'

I seized his shoulders and shook him. '*Where is she?*'

The insurance man pulled me off. 'Leave him, Steve! Can't you see he's concussed?'

I let him go, and pushed past. She wasn't in the wreckage of her own office; nor, fortunately, was she under the mess here. If she'd been elsewhere when the attack came ... I looked in every office, but there was nobody left. With a numb, leaden feeling inside me I stalked back around through the milling, chattering crowd, peered into the typists' room, the photocopier room, the gents, even into the ladies; none of the girls mopping up their injuries there gave me a second look. And none of them was Clare.

'Clare!' I shouted above the hubbub. 'Has anyone seen Clare?'

One of the typists, gulping down water, gave a sudden squeal and dropped her glass. '*Clare!* They were carrying her –' Then she dissolved into hysterics.

That was enough. I barged out into the lobby and ploughed through the crowd, now swelled by arriving ambulance men, and down the stairs at full gallop. Down at the bottom was Barry, with a police sergeant, staring at a track of blood that led across the hallway from the liftshaft. 'Pretty tough punks, if you ask me, to drop four floors and just crawl away – and why the hell –'

Barry saw me and waved me down. 'Sergeant, it was Steve here who –'

I shook loose. 'Later, dammit, Barry! *They've taken Clare!*'

The sergeant plucked at my arm with a heavy and practised hand. I tried to pull loose, but it almost jerked me off my feet. In a sudden, desperate rush of frustrated anger I whirled around and smashed my fist into his face. Even a day earlier I would never have done it; and I would never have dreamed I could hit so hard. He literally seemed to fly backwards off his feet, and hit the wall in a crumpled heap.

I turned and ran, hearing Barry trumpet 'What the hell –' from behind me, and then, more urgently '*Steve!!*'

I owed Barry a lot, but I didn't dare listen. I'd no intention of waiting, for him or for the police; I didn't dare. I ran. Out into the street, scattering the crowds of doughy-faced gawkers; one made a tentative step into my path, thought better of it and sprang back. I reached the car-park, fumbling with my keys, flung the door wide and thumped down behind the wheel. I twisted the car back in a roaring arc, hunching it down on its suspension like a springing cat, and drove straight out. My mirror showed me blue uniforms spilling out of the door, but they didn't worry me. The mouth of the little street was so choked with ambulances and gawkers that they'd never get after me in time, and it was one-way; the far end would be clear. They'd put out an alert, of course; but all the local cars were probably here already, and once I was out of the area spotting my car among all its anonymous look-alikes in the late afternoon rush would be a matter of sheer chance.

Provided, of course, I drove sensibly and didn't draw attention to myself. I had to be careful about that. It was oddly exhilarating, playing the fugitive, for all the sick worry underneath. Oddly, because it didn't sound like the man I saw in my shaving mirror. I'd always been a law-abiding type by nature — still was, come to that. I'd no malice against the police, none at all, no wish to make a hard job harder. Sooner or later I'd have to face the consequences of what I'd done. No question what it would look like, punching the policeman, bolting from the scene like that; they'd figure I knew something — and they'd make damn sure I told them. All right, I'd try, mad as it would sound; but I just couldn't let them get in my way, not now. It was a higher, older law I was obeying now.

A law of the instincts, perhaps. The thought of anyone innocent in the hands of those creatures was bad enough — but Clare ... What was she to me? A junior colleague. Hardly even a friend. I'd been careful to keep it that way; hardly ever saw her outside work, didn't know much about her life. Yet she'd been my secretary for four years. In that time, whether or not I'd meant to, I could hardly have helped getting a pretty clear idea of her personality, the essential Clare. A better sense of what made her tick, maybe, than any of her come-and-go boyfriends. To update an old saying, nobody's a hero to his secretary. Yet she'd stuck to me; and I'd reason to know she'd taken my part fiercely when it counted. It surprised me a little how fiercely I wanted to repay that. I told myself it must be sheer guilt. I was responsible for her; yet I'd brought this on her, by my lunatic compulsion to delve into things better left alone, things I should have forgotten as Jyp told me to. But there was more to it than guilt, than the wish to help I'd have had for anybody in that plight. I could see her in my mind's eye, and it took a lot of effort to drive slow, keep safe, to run with the traffic and watch the shadows gather ahead, beneath the slowly reddening sky.

I had to face it. I was fond of the girl, as fond as I could be of anybody. All this time some kind of feeling had been building up, creeping through all my neat defences, where I'd thought every chink had been stopped; all this time my instincts had been playing me traitor. Now they were whipping me into something like a frenzy. God, what must she be suffering now? What must she be thinking? If she was still alive to think, even—

I had to help her, whatever the cost, wherever I had to go.

I knew what that would mean. I'd have to open a gate that was closed, retrace a forgotten path, recross a forbidden threshold. That way neither reason nor memory had ever opened; my instincts were the only guides I had. And from the moment that policeman laid his fat hand on my arm those same instincts had shrieked a warning. He and the authority he represented were part of a narrower world. With them or any others in tow I'd never find the way, not if I circled those dark streets forever. Where I was going was for me alone.

The way there felt interminable. I ran into snarl-up after snarl-up, and the ring-road lights seemed to blaze red every time they saw me coming. I'd have been ready enough to run them tonight, but I didn't dare be caught, for Clare's sake. Worst of all was coming down towards the roundabout, when I heard a siren somewhere behind me; but it was some ways back, and a couple of heavy trucks were blocking it from view. I wasn't too worried. It might not be me they were after; and even if it was they couldn't possibly catch me up before the turn-off. I reached the roundabout, and I was just signalling to turn when my wing-mirror suddenly filled with another car, roaring around the outside right into my path. One bump would have bounced me into the other lanes and almost inevitably caused a multiple pile-up; I flung the wheel over just in time, to a torrent of hooting and shouting from behind. All aimed at me, of course, as if they hadn't seen the real offender; I got only a glimpse of a glittering red sports car and a swarthy face, yellowish and sneering, behind the wheel, as he sailed tranquilly past and away up Harbour Walk. While I had to filter around the roundabout again to reach the turn-off, and hear the cobbles under my tyres at long last. The high walls closed around me, and the sound of the siren seemed to fade into the distance.

Except for a truck or two Danube Street was empty, and I could put my foot down. But a new doubt assailed me; would the car itself be a problem? Shouldn't I park it, and go on foot? But I'd managed all right with Jyp; and there wasn't time to risk it. A likely-looking side-street opened before me, and without stopping to wonder I turned down it, zigzagged with it around the back walls of warehouses, forbiddingly topped with rows of spikes, or embedded glass fragments that gleamed coldly in the low light. Out into another street, stared down on by the boarded windows of a derelict factory, like a blinded sentinel, and down to a junction where my instincts faltered a moment. Streets opened to either side in every direction, long shadows stretched out along them, lazy and enigmatic. I wound down the window, and smelt the sea on the wind, heard the cries of gulls; looking up, I saw them wheeling against the threatening clouds. But they gave me no clue which way to turn. Then, looking leftward, I saw the longest shadows crowned with jagged, spiny crests, a tangled interlace of thorns; and that jungle of crosstrees and rigging sprang to life in my mind. I spun the wheel, and the car seemed to fly across the cobbles. Leftward I turned, and those shadows fell across me like giant fingers. For there before me, at the street's end, the majestic forest of mastheads lifted stark against the lit horizon.

I didn't stop; I accelerated, and turned with tyres squealing right onto the wharf itself. The high dark hulls loomed over me; in the last warm daylight they seemed less daunting, less monolithic, lined and decorated with bright paintwork, and even delicate traceries of gilt. Mellow brasswork gleamed along the rails, and round the portholes in some of the sleeker, more modern-looking craft. But there was little sign of life aboard them, save a few figures in the rigging or leaning over the rails; a gaggle of men were unloading one of them, swinging bales ashore in a net dangling from the end of a boom, something I'd never seen outside a nineteenth century photograph. A horse-drawn dray stood ready to receive them; but both men and horse watched me with incurious stares as I roared past. The wharves seemed to stretch without a break as far as I could see in either direction. But on the brickwork of the central building, in bold Victorian capitals almost bleached and crumbled away by a century or more of sun and salt air — FISHER'S WHARF. And below it, even less visible, arrows pointing to left and right, and beneath them long lists of names.

Stockholm
Trinity
Melrose
Danziger
Tyre ...

I didn't stop to read the rest. It was the way I was heading. I stamped on the accelerator and surged away, bouncing and rattling across the rough stones. Four wharves down, past warehouses that rose as high and ancient as any castle walls, and as mysterious; strange savours mingled in the wind, among the stink of tar and hides and stale oils. And at last, on a wall ahead, I saw, in Gothic script, the faded legend *Danziger Wharf* and swung the car around to a screeching stop. I jumped out, ran a few steps ... and stopped.

There, for the first time in all that great phalanx of ships, there was a breach. Three berths held tall ships like all the rest; but the fourth berth stood empty, and through the gap the harbour waters rippled golden with the sunset light. From the capstans and the iron bollards at the quayside short lengths of heavy rope lay strewn like so many dead snakes across the wharf, or dangling down over the edge. I ran forward, stooped to one and saw that its end was clean, unfrayed. In deep despair I sank down, staring at the empty waters. I'd made good time; but the Wolves, in their own strange way, had been faster. They'd cut their cables, and were gone. And Clare with them ...

But how long ago? It couldn't be more than a few minutes, half an hour at most. It took time to get those huge sailing ships stirring. Surely they'd still be in sight! I sprang up.

But then, slowly, I sank again to my knees on the rough stones. It was almost an attitude of worship. I was beyond doubting my sanity any longer. I was ready for great wonders – so I thought. But nothing I had ever imagined could prepare me for the sight I saw then.

Ahead of me the harbour walls opened onto the borderless expanses of the sea, grey and forbidding as the gathering mantle of clouds above, save where the last light of sunset burned a great slashing gap. And in that gap the thin tongues of cloud, tinged with glowing fire, formed an image of radiant sunlit slopes, edged with gold, bordering a stretch of misty azure. I knew the pattern of those slopes, I remembered them all too well, though I saw them now from yet another angle. It was the archipelago among the clouds, the same as I had seen before, opening now before me above the empty sea. And down the heart of that stretch of azure, wide and blue and glittering as an estuary studded with islands, bordered with broad golden sands, I saw the high ornate stern of a great ship, its sails outspread like wings, beating up and away into the fathomless depths of the sky.

CHAPTER FIVE

AS LONG AS THAT GLORIOUS blaze of light lasted I knelt there, dumbstruck, dazzled in eye and mind, buffeted and shaken by cold gusts. Small waves lapped at the wharf, the tall ships rocked gently at their moorings with soft slow creaks and groans, like a wind-driven wood. I felt like the least leaf in it, dry and light, quivering before that autumnal wind. Only when the clouds closed like a gate above the horizon and shut the colour out of the world did it slacken and die; and I came to myself, miserable, shaken, cold, and clambered stiffly to my feet.

Dreams. Hallucinations. Delusions. Schizophrenia –

I tumbled those wretched little weasel-words over and over in my mind, and more and more they felt like sheer presumption, blind hubris. As if I thought all infinity could be encompassed in my own little brain. As if I'd glimpsed a great cathedral dome, and claimed it was the roof of my own skull. Accept what I'd seen? No question of that. A tidal wave – accept or reject it all you like, the sea rolls over you just the same and teaches you an invaluable lesson, not to overestimate your importance in the whole order of things. Not believing – that would have been the hard thing. That would have taken a lot of imagination. That could really drive a man mad.

Only last night I had been given a glimpse of infinity; but now I'd balanced upon the world's edge, and stared out into its abyss. Those depths had tugged at me, drawn me like the emptiness beyond a cliff, but a thousand times more strongly. They'd sucked my thoughts out into hazy distances, and even now, when the vision was withdrawn, it was mortally hard to force them back. Against that vast backdrop myself or any human being seemed vanishingly small, and our concerns insignificant, passing things, bubbles in an immense unending waterfall.

And yet we must matter, if only to each other, if only

to give each other that fraction more of meaning, that slight extra significance. What more could bubbles do, than cling?

I had to help Clare. I didn't want to think why any more. But into this world beyond the Danube, this borderless wilderness, I couldn't venture on my own, not far. The twilight had turned grey, and in the still air the cold sea-haze clung clammily about me; along the wharves dim yellow eyes of light were winking on. A chilly drop of rain splashed against my brow. Wearily I climbed into the car, slammed the door, twisted the key in the ignition, and turned away back along the wharves, looking for a way back out into that maze of side-roads. I had to find something first; and it might be the hardest.

But either luck was with me, for once; or I was beginning to find my way about. The rain was growing heavier, and I'd already passed by the mouths of two streets that seemed somehow too dim and unpromising under their mantle of drizzle. The third looked no different, but as I passed across its mouth a distant gleam caught my eye, a tiny spot of colour piercing the rain-curtain for an instant. I braked, swung the car bumping and bouncing across the rough wharf, into the mouth of the street. There it was still, distant, tiny, a ruby among folds of grey velvet. My feelings told me nothing, one way or another; but I'd no better sign to follow. Down the street it led me, only a little way, to pull in beneath the windows of a grim-looking building. Once, perhaps, it had been a company's offices, a commercial fortress that ruled the fates of men from here to Norway or Vladivostock. Now a modern signboard, peeling and unreadable, obscured the carved door lintel, while most of those windows were blanked off with what looked like tarpaper behind the glass. It turned them into dark mirrors; and the image that stood in one was the mouth of the lane opposite, and the light that shone at its end. I sprang out and stood blinking, peering through the rain as it bounced and splashed over the car roof; then I slammed the door behind me, and began to run. It was the signboard of the Illyrian Tavern.

At the lane's end I went splashing into a running gutter, ankle deep, at the pavementless edge of another road. Three bounds carried me across, almost sending some sorry soul on a bicycle wobbling off into the gutter, and a fourth up to the faded red door. The latch was odd, and I was still struggling with it when I felt it shift and the door swing back. Out of the gloom peered Katjka's features, foxy and astonished. '*Stefan!* Come! Come in! There's nobody about – *Agnece Boztj!* You're soaked! Come dry yourself by the fire!'

I seized her by the arms, and she slipped them playfully under mine and ran her fingers up and down my ribs. 'Something sso urgent again, *ej?*'

She drew me into the warm gloom, and nudged the door closed with a thrust of her hip. I became aware that she was only wearing some kind of white linen shift. 'Jyp!' I said hastily. 'Is he here? Or where –'

'Ach, any minute!' she said airily. 'He's always in here of an evening –'

'Doesn't he go to other places sometimes? The Mermaid?'

She shrugged, and made a face. 'Well, sometimes – but always he drops in here, sooner or later. Just to say hello! You can wait, can't you? Mmmnh?'

'*Katjka!* Damn it, this is serious –' I got no further than that. There were spices on her lips, sweet and hot, and she burned against me through the crisp linen. In my unstable state that was enough. I clutched her, felt her writhe and sank myself in her kiss as if to drown myself out of a world that had grown too vast. A great many things might have happened next if the door latch hadn't jabbed me painfully in the small of the back as it opened. We flailed wildly and grabbed the carved bannister just in time to stop ourselves tumbling downstairs.

'Well, hello young lovers!' carolled Jyp cheerfully. 'This some new routine I've not heard about, Kat? On the stairs, huh? Enterprising, I'll allow, but a mite athletic for me –'

She gestured dismissively at him, and ruined the effect by putting out her tongue as well. 'You idle sot!

And here is poor Stefan who has been looking for you in such hurry!' she lamented.

'Well, he wouldn't have found me where he was headed!' Jyp's drawl couldn't have been more laconic, but I saw the sudden alertness in his look. 'Glad you came, though. I was hoping you would. Wanted to say sorry, sort of, for the way I went and acted this night gone. So here I am, ol' buddy – what's a'brewin'?' I gathered my breath, but before I could speak he'd caught at my arm. 'Not more trouble with those mangy Wolves? Here was I just hearing they'd shipped out as if Old Nick himself was at their asses –'

'That's right!' I said. 'And they've got – a friend of mine with them! They were after me, but – Jyp, I need help! And fast!'

I heard Katjka's sharp intake of breath. Jyp nodded slowly. 'Sounds like you do,' he said. 'But if they've sailed already, an hour more or less won't make no difference.' He overrode my protests with hands uplifted. 'Hold on, hold on. Suppose you come sit down and tell me all about it – and you, girl, scare us up some eats, eh? Then come listen yourself, y'hear?' She nodded and went padding down ahead of us, disappeared into the darkness and reappeared almost at once with a bottle and three of those little flasks. Jyp took them with a nod so courtly it was almost a bow, and ushered me into a highbacked booth by the fireplace. 'Always knows what's needed, that girl. There, get that down you; one gulp, and then another. I'll be glad to have her word on this. Katjka's been around awhile, learned a lot. She's got a feeling for this kind of thing.'

He poured me my second flask of the fierce spirit, then one for himself, and sighed as he settled down opposite me, shifting his scabbard around. 'The unrighteous man findeth no place to lay his head, as my old man'd say. Truth to tell, way things've been shaping around here lately I was thinking I might sign on and ship out again awhile. In case the neighbourhood'd turn a mite hot for me, y'understand. Then I heard those bastards'd lit out, and I was coming down here to celebrate. Only now – well, spill it, Steve.'

Spill it I did, my shock dulled by the drink: the whole tale of the raid on the office and my chase down here. After a minute Katjka arrived, clumped tall steins of beer down on the table, and squeezed into the booth beside me, leaning her chin on her bony hand and gazing at me intently. As I told my tale I saw my listeners' lean faces harden. The firelight flickered in the girl's grey eyes, and the lines around her full mouth deepened. Jyp's eyes narrowed, and he seemed to stare right through me, out into horizonless distances. The thought chilled me; I shivered as I told of that final vision, and felt Katjka's arm around my back, her thigh pressed against mine, and was glad of it. She did seem to know what was needed – and more to the point, was quick to give it; what had she been trying to give me in those mad moments before Jyp walked in? What had I needed?

'That's all,' I said, and took a deep draught of my beer.

Jyp blew out his breath sharply, and looked at me askance. 'Now just what in hell were you hoping to do if you had caught up with the bastards? Take on a whole shipload of Wolves on your lonesome?'

I'd been hoping he wouldn't ask that. 'It was me the Wolves were after, I could have offered myself to them, if they'd let her go.'

Jyp spared me the laughter, just looked bleakly at me. 'They'd have taken you cheerfully and kept her. Or let her go all right, overside. Or worse. They're not nice folk, the Wolves.' Katjka snorted. 'In fact, if you want to get technical, they're not folk at all.'

Katjka spoke, slowly. 'She's yours, this girl?'

'No,' I said hastily, 'nothing like that. She works for me, that's all – I feel responsible for her – for this –'

'Well? demanded Jyp, but he was talking to Katjka, not me.

She shrugged, and from somewhere she produced what looked like a small oblong book and laid it down on the table; then she took my hand, and laid it palm-downwards on top. It felt warm, as if it had been next to her skin, and I realized it was a pack of cards. After a moment she released my hand, shuffled the cards and with flicking fingers began to deal them out on the table between us. They pattered stiffly down in neat overlapping rows, and when she had finished she motioned to me to turn one over, and then another. A little impatiently I turned over two at random; a girl I knew once had told fortunes with Tarot, a pretty tiresome girl, and I was expecting to see the same again. But these were ordinary playing cards – or not, for I had never seen anything like them. I had drawn the knave of diamonds first, and the double figure sneered up at me, swarthy, moustachioed like an Elizabethan brigand, with such malice in its glittering eyes that they shone and sparkled with the cold fire of real diamonds. Hastily I turned it back, and looked at the other; but it was the ace of hearts, and in the trembling light it seemed to swell and pulse, bright liquid red.

Katjka turned that one back. 'One more,' she said hoarsely. Reluctantly I turned over – I don't know why – the last card dealt. It was the two of spades, and there was no sign upon it except the two black pips. But suddenly that blackness seemed to deepen and grow hollow, as if the pips were really openings into emptinesses beyond. They made my eyes blur, their focus swim, so that the two swam and shimmered and merged momentarily into one, a shimmering cavernous ace. Katjka plucked the card from my fingers and with a violent gesture swept the whole pack together.

'Nothing?' demanded Jyp.

'No!' answered Katjka curtly. 'There's a shadow over this business. There were faint signs, but … nothing I can understand, *Christe pomiluj!* Nothing …'

Steps from the back of the cellar like room broke the silence, and the waft of something spicy, singing with tomatoes and peppers and frying onions, more appetising than I would have believed possible. A face rose in the gloom, round and red and wrinkled as a winter apple but sporting a majestic hawk nose and a beaming smile; it was framed by a gaudy scarf and escaping ringlets of raven-black hair. The woman who came waddling up, bearing an immense and laden tray, could have been anywhere from fifty to seventy, plump but healthy; she laid down the tray with arms brawnier than mine.

'*Dekujeti, Malinkaçul*' said Katjka. Evidently this was Myrko's wife; she bobbed me a curtsey and reeled off a great stream of chatter I couldn't understand. I rose and imitated Jyp's bow, and the old woman seized my hands and chattered again, then kissed me forcefully on both cheeks and disappeared again, still chattering.

'She was wishing you well in your ordeals,' said Katjka slowly. 'And telling you that you must eat. It's good advice; you may need strength. I wish I could help you, but I cannot; sso ...'

Jyp, already tucking into his plateful, lifted his head and met her eye. 'Le Stryge?' he asked.

'*Sztrygoiko*,' she answered.

'Damn,' he said, and went back to his food again.

At first I only picked at it, too panicky almost to force it down. I could feel the evening wearing away, that strange ship and all aboard it drawing further and further out of our reach. But the spices set water in my mouth and fire in my innards, and I began to eat as hungrily as Jyp. Even so, I was glad to see he wasn't lingering; the moment his plate was clear he stood up, took a final swig of beer and tossed down his coarse linen napkin. He raised an eyebrow at Katjka. 'Well,' he sighed. 'Time to go call on old Stryge, I guess.'

'You don't seem too eager,' I said.

'It's got dangers of its own,' Jyp told me. 'But at this hour they shouldn't be so bad.'

'Dangers?'

'He keeps odd company. Best be going; it's a walk, and we won't be wanting to take that automobile of yours. The Stryge gets kind of touchy about that sort of thing.'

Katjka walked with us to the stairs. Nobody had asked to be paid for the food or the drink, and I had an uncomfortable feeling I'd offend somebody by offering. 'You will take care of Stefan, won't you, Jyp?' she said urgently, and suddenly put her arms around me. She didn't kiss me, only touched her cheeks rapidly to mine, and let go; it seemed almost like some kind of formal embrace. Jyp nodded soberly, and motioned me up the stairs. She made no move to follow, but stood looking silently after us, tapping that pack of cards nervously against her thigh.

A cool wind slapped me in the face as I opened the door, but the rain had stopped. The skies had cleared, the clouds raced ragged across the sky. I was surprised to see how light it still was without them, a kind of greyish twilit clarity that dimmed colours and made distances deceptive. Jyp closed the door carefully behind us, and motioned me up the street. Water still pooled in the gutters and gleamed in the seams between the worn cobblestones, so that the road ahead seemed to reflect the sky, and each oblong cobble became a small stepping stone across it. Jyp seemed to be brooding, and we walked in silence awhile. He was the first to speak. 'Said I wanted to render 'count of myself for last night.'

'You don't have to.'

'Seems to me I do – after you saving my bacon maybe three times now. Guess you knew I was scared, huh? But it wasn't just for me. I'll say that. I was kicking myself good an' hard for ever letting you get involved. Feared getting you any deeper in'd only bring down worse dangers on your head.' He gave a harsh laugh. 'Should've thought of that a mite sooner, shouldn't I?' I didn't answer.

'So I thought I'd scared you off. But I got over my fright. Old Stryge, he fixed that thing good and proper, sent it wailing off in a puff of smoke – so I thought that was all right now. Next thing I heard, the Wolves have gone –'

He shook his head. 'Steve, this is all my fault. I should've warned you better, maybe bought you protection. But honest, I never dreamed anything could happen to you out there. I've never heard of Wolves striking as deep into the Core as that, not ever before. Others, sure, now and again, but Wolves never. It looks bad, Steve.'

'It's not your fault,' I told him impatiently. 'You're not responsible for those sons of bitches. Or where they decide to tear apart. Who is, come to that? Where do they come from? You said they weren't really folk – what's that supposed to mean?' I was beginning to get angry now, with the food and drink in me burning away shock and amazement. 'What's this about the Core? If these Wolf creeps are after me I should damn well know all about them, shouldn't I?'

Jyp, though, was slow to answer. 'Can't tell you exactly all,' he said, as we turned at the top of the road. 'Don't think the Wolves know it all themselves, not for sure; but I'll tell what I can. Way the story goes, their ancestors were plain men enough, though wolfish still, a batch of ragtag pirates and their doxies down Carib way in the early days. Seems they got too much even for their buddies, and one day found themselves stranded on some little pimple of an island right off the map. An ill-famed place already, by all accounts, a sacred place of the cannibal Carib Indians of old, and shunned even by them; they dared land there only to feed their heathen gods with blood. Weren't meant to survive, you see, those maroons. But survive they did, as vermin does, by forbidden flesh.'

'Forbidden – you mean, they turned cannibal too?'

'Surely, and worse, by lying with their own flesh and breeding so, kin with blood kin. Flourished, too, like the devils they were; for it wasn't only their own they ate, but took to sharking out in crude canoes to waylay small ships that strayed near, and seeking to lure larger ones onto their island's reefs. God help the poor souls who fell into their hands! It's said they kept a few and bred them, like cattle, to slaughter. I've heard tell of some who got to living that way, in Scotland long years back – Sawney Bean, if you've heard of him, and his kin? But these were worse. And they got to be worse yet.'

Suddenly the food sat heavy and sickly in me. The implications of what he was saying ... I forced them aside. 'Jyp, just how do you get any worse than that?'

He kicked idly at a shred of polythene wrapping that blew into our path. 'Well, folk who went that way almost never came back; so fewer and fewer went, till the isle was all but forgotten. Then maybe it dropped out of the way awhile, the way places do. And meanwhile they changed. Over the generations, bit by bit.'

'Evolved, you mean.'

Jyp looked blank. 'Don't know about that. Sounds like this Darwin, and I was brought up strict. They changed, that's all I know. Like as not something unhuman crept into that bloodline along the way; maybe it was just their own bad blood showin' through – and maybe there was something else on that island. Long and the short of it is, Wolves aren't human. Don't look quite like any of us. Don't think like us; surely don't smell like us! They can't breed with the line of man any more; only their own foul kind.'

I whistled. 'They're a new species? My God, it makes sense. That's how it's supposed to happen. A small isolated group, interbreeding freely, swapping genes about – a mutation sticks, and they begin to breed true. It'd explain that foul skin colour, and the size of them. But happening to humans, to *men* –' Unheard of, maybe; but now I knew why my skin crawled at the very sight of these things. It was ancestry speaking, warning me off the interloper, the intruder – and more than that. The predator ...

'And my boss thought they were just punks! If you know what those are.'

Jyp blinked. 'Sure. And I'm not surprised. Like I said back when, it's amazing how folk only see what they want to see –' He smiled wryly. 'Tell you something, Steve. The world's a lot wider place than most of them ever realize. They cling to what they know, to the firm centre where everything's dull and deadly and predictable. Where the hours slip by at just sixty seconds to the minute from your cradle to your tombstone – that's the Core. Out here, out on the Spiral, out toward the Rim. It's not like that – not always. There's a whole lot more to this world than just a mudball spinning in emptiness like the wisemen say. It's adrift, Steve, in Time and in Space as well. And there's more tides than one that ebb and flow about its shores.'

He lifted his eyes to the dimming sky. 'So one day,

maybe, for everybody, one such tide comes lapping about their feet. And most just look and draw back before more'n their toes gets wet. They look and don't understand, or won't; and they turn back into the Core again, forever.'

'But there's always a few that don't?'

'And they look out upon infinite horizons! Some bow down in fear and slink away from the truth they've seen. But others, they take a step forward into the chill wide waters.' He nodded, to himself, deep in his own inner seeing as he walked. 'And across them, eventually. From Ports like this one, often enough, where comings and goings over a thousand years and more have tied a knot in Time, to all the corners of the wide world. Lord, lord, how wide!' He looked up at me suddenly, and I saw his teeth flash in the twilight. 'You're a well-learned kind of a man, Steve. Just how many corners d'you think the world has?'

I shrugged. 'Four, as a figure of speech. But in reality –' I saw Jyp grin again, but went on and stuck my head in the trap. 'None, because it's a sphere. More or less, anyhow.'

Jyp shook his head. 'Uh-uh. Ask the mathematical men. Like I did, when I learned me my spherical navigation. Even stuck deep in the Core they know better than that. A sphere's a concept, a limiting case; so they don't say no corners, they say it's got an infinite number. And Steve, know what? Every which one of those corners is a place. Places that were, that will be, that never were save that the minds of men gave them life. Lurking like shadows cast behind the real places in that reality of yours, shadows of their past, their legends and their lore, of what they might have been and may yet be; touching and mingling with every place at many points. And you can search your life long and never find a trace of them, yet once you learn you may pass between them in the drawing of a breath. But are they the shadows, Steve – or is your reality theirs?'

I stared, speechless, but Jyp went on, talking in a soft sing-song almost to himself, like somebody mulling over something he has known all his life, and still amazed by it. 'There, west of the sunset, east of the moonrise, there lies the Sargasso Sea and Fiddler's Green, there's the Elephant's Graveyard, there's El Dorado's kingdom and the empire of Prester John –'

'Huy Brazeal?' I suggested, for that strange cargo came back to mind.

'Been there; it's okay, but there's other places. There's everywhere. Riches, beauties, dangers – every damn thing within the mind and the memory of men. And more too, probably – only those paths are kind of harder to find.'

But thinking of that cargo had brought other memories, and with them freight of bitter anxiety. 'And that's where they've taken Clare?' I caught his arm. 'Then how the hell can we ever hope to find her again?'

Jyp smiled, a little wryly. 'That's what we're going to find out, Steve.'

I let go of him. Despair trickled down with the last drops of rain. 'You and your bloody step forward! Damn the day I ever took it!'

Jyp shrugged. 'Not for me; I'm here because you took it, three times over. And maybe not for you, neither.' He laid a hard hand on my shoulder. 'See, Steve, this side of town you soon learn you can't see the end of everything, where any deed's going to lead you. But one thing I've noticed, and that's that a whole lot depends on how you first came to take that step. Old Stryge, he says the same, and he's a real cunning bastard. With me it was slow, step by step you might say, an old shipmate I helped out from time to time, who showed me the ropes as his only way to repay. And me, I've done what I'd call all right – slowly. But you now, you just came barrelling in all in a moment, to help a man you didn't know and to hell with the risk to yourself. That's what I'd call a long straight step and a clear one, a good deed you shouldn't repent of, not till you see how it all pans out in the end. I'd have said you'd do right well for yourself from such a beginning, only …'

He hesitated, stopped walking and began to stare

around the street, as if looking for someone or searching out his way. But there was only one possible turn-off, on the far side ahead and to the right, and no living thing in sight except a distant dog, yellowish and skinny, probably a stray, that disappeared into some doorway or other. 'Only?' I prompted him. 'Only what?' But suddenly he set off across the empty road at a great pace, heading for the corner, and I had to trot after him; breathlessly repeating my question, and nudge him hard before he answered, slow and unwilling.

'Only ... it's with all this reaching out, reaching into the Core. Can't help wondering if ... well, if maybe the step wasn't all yours, good though it was. If, somehow you mightn't have been lured in − sucked in, you might say. And that part of it could be bad.'

We walked on in silence. I could hear Jyp breathing fast, and his brow glistened; we were walking quickly, yet I'd seen him less affected by a running fight. Once or twice he would glance back the way we had come. I looked, too, and saw nothing; but his hand was seldom far from his sword hilt. The street we turned into was wide and open, one I vaguely remembered driving down at some time or other. One side of it was still lined with the old warehouses, but the other had been mostly cleared. After a few yards the old imposing wall ended abruptly and barbed-wire fencing took over. Behind it massive corrugated iron sheds had been erected, looking far dirtier and more desolate hunched beneath that bleak sky; here and there a lot stood vacant, overgrown and rubbish-strewn. It was in front of one of these, lying between two of the larger sheds and ending in a high and ancient brick wall, that Jyp stopped. He glanced quickly around, and I saw his eyes widen momentarily. But when I looked I only glimpsed the hindquarters of a dog disappearing hastily around the corner, the same dog probably, nervous of man's eye as strays tend to be. Jyp seemed edgier than ever; he muttered something, then with sudden furious energy he flung himself at the barbed-wire and shinned straight up it to the top, agile as a monkey. I tried to follow him, impaled my palm on the first strand and dropped back to earth, swearing. Jyp nodded, set foot to one strand, hand to another, and heaved them so far apart I could easily clamber through.

The lot was like the rest, if anything more neglected. It was heavily overgrown and strewn with rubbish, everything from neat domestic piles tipped straight through the fence and black plastic sacks which all appeared to hold horribly dismembered corpses, to great loose swathes of soiled and shredded refuse, and even chunks of machinery. Rusting and anonymous, they poked up like strange growths among a sea of grasses, fireweed and purple willowherb at least five feet tall and in places higher, concealing the treacherous contours of the rubble beneath. The huge corrugated flanks of the sheds presented an interesting contrast, one in modern pastel shades on a brick foundation, the other in the bare galvanised metal of the fifties, rusting now and heavily patched, apparently decaying from the ground up. It was this one Jyp headed for, still silent I followed, sucking my palm and trying to remember my last tetanus shot. Even in that fresh wind the place stank as we passed through, but there was a worse atmosphere about it, something that Jyp evidently felt as keenly as I did. The grasses whispered like voices in the gathering dark, and looking back I saw one patch ripple against the wind, as if something was moving beneath, following closer and closer on our heels. Jyp saw it too, and I heard his breath hiss between his teeth; but he only plunged silently on.

As we reached the side of the older shed he seemed to pull himself together and walk with his usual calm swagger; too much of it, perhaps. In many places the wall patches themselves had half-rusted and been overlaid with others; here and there they'd gone on rusting, and left a gaping, jagged hole. Near one of these the grasses seemed to grow thinner, and a clear space was marked with a wide scar of ash. Here Jyp stopped, and booted the decaying wall, raising a thunderous boom.

'Up, Stryge! Up and out, you mangy old spider! There's callers in the parlour!'

For a moment nothing happened, and Jyp was just

about to kick the wall again when something stirred and scrabbled behind it, and gave a groan so dry and rusty I thought it was the metal giving way. Then out of the jagged gap, like a beast from a den, rolled a hunched-up form that I only knew was a man by his mane of white hair. His limbs began to unfold, very like a spider's, and I saw he was wrapped in an ancient and filthy-looking black coat, tied about the waist with a scrap of greasy rope, which hung down below the knees of his baggy greyish trousers. The boots beneath were ancient and cracked across both soles, the hands he dug into the earth like a mole's claws, crooked and hard. He crackled as he moved, like dry leaves, and the stench of him struck like a blow. He lifted his head slightly, squinted at us without looking up, his very posture full of furtive cunning. All in all, a tramp, a bum, as typical a no-hoper as ever I'd seen, and as pitiful. I couldn't help looking my disbelief at Jyp. *This?*

But Jyp's face was a pale mask of alarm in the dusk, and he shook his head in sharp warning. Then the old man coughed once, a terrible hacking rasp, heaved himself up on his hands with alarming energy and glared right up into my face. I was so shocked I stumbled away. Beneath the ingrained dirt the face was hard and square, deeply lined, the brow high, the nose a blade and the mouth a thin colourless slash above a jutting arrogant chin; the clear grey eyes drove into mine like a clenched fist. *Madman*, was my half-formed thought; *psychopath* —

I wanted to turn and run. But they held me as a snake holds a rabbit, those eyes, and suddenly I saw the intelligence that blazed out of them, alert, cold, malign, mercilessly perceptive. Tramp and madman faded from my mind; all I could think of was ascetic, anchorite, philosopher or high priest. But of what awful belief?

'Doesn't like the look of me,' rasped that rusty voice. Rusty, but clear, magisterial; I was less surprised than I would have been a minute ago. There was just the trace of an accent at times, though what kind was past telling. 'Get the brat out of here, pilot, and yourself after. What've I to do with him? I owe him nothing. There's no service he could owe me. What use'd I have for a pretty clothes-rack, an empty shell, a hollow man? And there's a stink on him I don't like −'

At the end of my tether, I snapped back '*That* just makes it fucking mutual, doesn't it?'

The old man sprang up with a truly frightening snarl. '*Out!* Or I'll spill his brain like a stale heeltap!'

Jyp's hand caught my arm, tightened. 'That's enough, Stryge you old shrike! You mayn't owe him anything, but you owe me, still − and I owe him, threefold! So save the insults, okay? And the spilling bit. There's plenty to Steve here, and I know it. And how about a little help?'

The old man grumbled and muttered, Jyp cajoled, pleaded, even obliquely threatened when the old man turned that alarming gaze on me again. But only obliquely, and I noticed him glance behind him after that, more than once, at the waving grass. At last the Stryge sat back on his haunches, sunk his head on one arthritic hand and growled 'Ach, have it your own way! He's been messing with Wolves, that's obvious, so he'll want to know where they are − or where something is −' He looked up and my skin crawled under the icy perception of that glance. 'Or maybe some*body*, eh? Halfway through a Wolf's bowels by now, no doubt. Go look for him up there −' Probably he read something in my reaction, because he chuckled unpleasantly. 'For *her*, then, and leave me be! D'you have anything of hers? No? Anything she gave you, then?'

'I don't think so −' We gave gifts occasionally, flowers on her birthday, a tie at Christmas, nothing more. Then I remembered the old filofax calendar I hadn't thrown away because the currency tables on the back were so useful, and produced that.

'Very romantic!' sneered the old man. 'Now do some work for once in your lives − build me a fire here! Boil me up some water from the tap there!' Jyp and I glanced around the revolting lot and exchanged dismayed glances. 'Go on!' cackled the Stryge. 'A little dirt's never killed me. There's wood by the wall, there; and paper enough!' I gathered the wood, while Jyp impaled foul bits of paper on his sword, street-cleaner style, and together we got a fire laid and lit on the ashen patch. Meanwhile the old man sat hunched over the calendar, brushing his fingers slowly against it and crooning softly. Jyp came back with an oil can full of dubious water and rested it deftly among the sticks to heat.

'If he thinks I'm going to drink any bloody potions …' I whispered to Jyp, and then jumped as he clutched my arm. Another figure stood at the edge of the firelight, and for a moment I was afraid we'd attracted attention from the road. But this was a figure as scruffy as Stryge, a much younger blond man in a torn donkey-jacket and tight ragged jeans. Lean-faced and sallow, his sparse beard pointed but unkempt, he stood surveying us with narrow, hostile eyes. Stryge looked up and grunted something, and the young man padded over and squatted down beside him, gazing up at him with a peculiar intensity. Jyp's grip tightened.

'What's he got to be here for?' he hissed at Stryge. 'I'm not staying here with him – get rid of him! Lose him –'

The yellow-haired man spat back a volley of curses in a thick Irish accent, and sprang up to face him.

'Jyp, no!' I hissed, hanging onto him. 'If he can help –'

'*Enough!*' thundered the Stryge, with a force I wouldn't have credited. 'Sit, Fynn! And you also, pilot! Upon pain of my utmost displeasure!' Jyp's knees seemed to fold under him, and he slumped to his haunches beside me. The young man ducked down, cowed, by Stryge's side. 'Fynn will do you no harm while I'm here, be assured of that.'

'He'd better not,' said Jyp between clenched teeth. Fynn sat silently, head lowered but glaring at us. There was something about him, the snarling curl of his lip, the way the hair grew back from the low widow's peak on that sloping brow – the colour of that hair. I began to feel less than well. It wasn't so long ago I'd seen that odd yellowish shade.

The water was bubbling in earnest now. The Stryge, with Fynn scrabbling at his back, came and seated himself cross-legged on the far side. He muttered and gestured over it as it seethed and spattered, slopping over the side into the fire. Wisps of steam drifted across its dark surface, like mist on the night sea. For a long time, still muttering, he stared into it, squinting from various angles. Then he picked up a shaving of wood, and tossing the calendar aside he laid the shaving lightly on the surface of the water. We all leaned forward to watch as it bobbed there, aimlessly at first. Then, abruptly, it changed direction, glided slow and straight to the edge and sat there quivering. Jyp sucked in his breath sharply. 'So that's their heading, eh? By south-south-west, a quarter ... Why, that'll be –'

'The Caribbees,' said the Stryge quietly. 'West Indies, most likely. Knew I didn't like the smell. First that *dupiah*, now this ... Ach.'

'But *why*?' I demanded. Fynn giggled, but the Stryge silenced him with a raised hand.

'Fair question. Because their main plan failed, that's why. Smuggling that deadly thing in, for some purpose or other. So they came after you.'

'*Me*? Why me?'

'Simple. You brought it upon yourself. Poking after them with your sendings like that. Your spells.'

'My–?'

'They must've been on the look-out already. They've their own ways of looking, just as you have.'

'You mean the computer? But there's nothing magical about that.'

The old man cackled suddenly, as if at some private joke. 'Anything you say, *mon enfant*. Your sendings came too close, and they traced them back. Just warned you off at first; but you would persist. Then they took a closer look. Decided they wanted you.'

'Yes, but *why*?'

The Stryge shrugged. 'How should I know? *I* would not want you in a gift, but have I the brain of a Wolf? Perhaps your sendings made them think you to blame for the plan's failure, and to excuse themselves they would take you back to whoever is behind it. When they lost you, they went for the next best.' The thin lips curled contemptuously. 'They'd checked on that, too. The person you care for most in the world – and who cares most for you.'

I stared, and only just stopped myself braying with laughter, telling him he was daft. He had to be. The whole idea was daft, utterly bloody insane. Serve me right for taking an old wino seriously. Clare? What had she meant to me, till all this blew up? Not that much. A secretary I'd have been sorry to lose – okay, a little more than that, a friend, a welcome spot of human warmth in the business day. But I'd lots of friends, hadn't I? More than most people, maybe, since part of my job was maintaining contacts. Colleagues, regular clients, and in my spare time the regulars at Nero's and Dirty Dick's, the crew down at the squash courts, the one's I'd gone rock-climbing and hang-gliding with at intervals – hell, half the Liberal Club, the half that went there because it was a nice old-fashioned place to drink. Good company, all of them – not the sort of friends you'd spew out your troubles to, maybe, but then that was what made them good company. You didn't humbug them, they didn't humbug you – one of Dave's handy West African expressions. And after all, it wasn't as if I didn't have the other sort of friends. I'd got on fine with my parents while they were alive, still did with my uncle and various aunts; though admittedly we'd lost touch a little, living so far apart. That was the trouble with my college friends, too, scattered all over the globe; how long since I'd heard from Neville? Come to that, how long since I'd seen Mike? He wasn't *that* far away.

A scrabbling unease was undermining my annoyance. But it was still ridiculous. I wasn't in love with Clare – anything but. I'd been closer, far closer to a good dozen or so girls since I left college – hadn't I? Never mind the odd pick-ups this last year or two; far closer. About Stephanie, Anne-Marie, two or three of them, I'd been serious, really serious. Begun thinking about marriage even. Not to mention ...

My teeth clenched shut. It was stupid; that was the past, wasn't it? But then it all was. And he was talking about right now. His eyes were mirrors; and mirrors have no mercy. I'd never seen myself like that before. I felt, in memory, the touch of a hand on my arm, a voice concerned, sympathetic, a brief gust of that warm perfume. It wasn't much; but there wasn't any more, not from anywhere. I'd seen to that, carefully, systematically, neatly. If she was really the closest I stood to any other human being, then where the hell did that leave me?

I couldn't answer it. Something was crumbling above my head, and suddenly I couldn't be sure of anything any more. I'd been thinking about myself – bad enough. But what about Clare? How close had she come? She'd had boyfriends in plenty; what did she feel about me?

If he'd flung the water in my face, and the can and the fire after it, that old swine could hardly have shocked me more. He knew it, too. Those eyes held me while I writhed inside, seeing every scrap of my inner turmoil and relishing it, the way a sadistic child might enjoy a squirming insect impaled on a pin. If Clare was who I cared for most, if she cared the most for me –

'What – what're they going to do with her?' I croaked. Fynn giggled again, and Jyp spat some word at him. Stryge appeared not to notice. He leaned forward, weasel-quick, grabbed my hands in his and brought them down towards the sides of the boiling billy-can. I flinched, but the grip of those arthritic claws, cold and horn-hard, was unbreakable.

'Do you want to know, or not? You will feel nothing you cannot bear!'

Wide-eyed, helpless, I let my hands be drawn out over the fire, my palms pressed slowly and carefully to the ribbed metal. I gasped involuntarily, but it was nothing like heat I felt; it was more the violent energy of the bubbling water, making the tin vibrate like a drum, like a mass of drums. Throbbing, pounding, a wild insistent rhythm, and above it, in the chatter of the bursting bubbles, in the roaring of the fire beneath, something more – a babble of voices, a chant singing. 'What is it?' I gasped. The tin quivered like a living thing under my hands, harder and harder to restrain.

'It is a rite,' said the old man darkly. 'A *ceremonie-caille*. I recognize it. A *mangé* – a sacrifice, perhaps to purge their failure in the eyes of their god, perhaps to a blacker end. That I cannot see; darkness hangs around it, a darkness hot and sweltering beneath damp leaves. But for that rite in particular there can be only one fit offering – and that must be a *cabrit sans cornes.*' He smiled sardonically. 'A goat without horns. Such a name.'

But I didn't need any translations, either literally or what it really meant. I felt my scalp tighten with the horror of it, and I sprang up, tearing away my hands. 'Then, Christ, what can we do about it? We've got to get her out –'

All Stryge did was smirk up at me in the firelight and shrug, and that was the last straw. A fury such as I'd seldom felt or given way to rolled over me like cold lightning, and I felt my hair bristle. 'Damn you!' I yelled. 'There must be something! And you're going to help me find it here and now – or I'll wring your scrawny bloody windpipe into nothing!' Jyp shouted something I was past hearing. 'By God I will! And I kicked the boiling can at the Stryge.

Somehow he must have had a hand up to deflect it. The can bounced aside, a great plume of water leaped hissing into the fire, but not a drop touched him. A huge steamcloud boiled up around me, and it smelt not dank and oily as you might have expected, but soft and salty and warm as a tropical seawind. Fynn snarled and sprang up, and I saw with a thrill of horror that even without the firelight his eyes glowed yellow as amber. At my side I heard the rasp of sword leaving scabbard – and the sharp click as it was thrust back. Jyp's hand landed on my shoulder.

'Easy, lad!' he hissed. 'Keep off the shoals! You don't know the lie of 'em! Give me the helm a minute!' He turned to Stryge. 'You said you'd help, old man, and so you have. Okay, damfino, but that's just the easy part, making sure what anyone could've guessed. Not the kind of work we need to come to Le Stryge for, that, is it? Not enough to level any scores, is it? And not at all like the great Stryge to leave a job halfway done ...'

I held my breath, as the steam dispersed into the darkness, and the old man huddled over the last embers of the fire. Fynn stood tense, ready, rigid except for the constant opening and closing of his fingers and his panting breath. He relaxed only when the old man spoke, and his tone had changed to a complaining whine. 'You young folk, never ready to show any spirit! Never ready to go out and do, want everything laid out before by us who've had to work for it! Thought better of you, pilot, but you're just like all the rest. No balls.' He glared at me. 'Though there's some with no soul, either. And precious little brain. What d'you expect me to do when they're off and away already? Why d'you think they hurried? Afraid of you?' He snorted, and blew his nose on his fingers. 'Once out of harbour, safe, and well they knew it.'

I looked aghast at Jyp, who shook his head angrily. 'Lay off it, Stryge. There's plenty that can be done so far off – and you can do it. As we both know!'

'Not without damaging your precious little bit of skirt as well. Your sweet little Clare. So otherwise it means fitting out a ship, doesn't it, and going after them! You wealthy? Hah?'

'No,' I said unhappily, thinking how much I could raise on my flat at short notice, and the car, and the sound system – though that was last year's, and unfashionable with the reviewers these days. 'How much would it cost?'

Jyp clicked his tongue. 'A lot, Steve. I'd help with my mite of savings, but it wouldn't make much odds. A decent ship, why that'd cost nigh on two thousand, with another thousand for a crew, five hundred or so on supplies.'

'Thousands of what?'

Jyp blinked. 'Why, guineas, of course.'

'Guineas? You mean, one pound five pence? In modern money?'

'What other kind is there? Money's money.'

I gaped at him an instant, and then suddenly I burst out laughing in sheer disbelief. 'Jyp, you can't be serious! I

earn more than your two thousand in a month! My savings
–'

'No kidding? Ah, but it's got to be gold,' he warned,
tapping the side of his nose knowingly, 'and it's a hell of a
poor rate you get for it when you're in a hurry –'

'Never mind the rate!' I barked. 'If I could lay hands
on that sort of money in a couple of hours, can you find
me a ship? And a crew? And how soon?'

'You mean it?' Jyp slapped his scabbard a ringing
blow. 'The best, pal! And by sunup! Starting with the best
pilot afloat if you'll have him, namely me! I was getting
kind of bored ashore, anyhow. And you're setting your
course for strange waters –'

I was nearly speechless. 'Jyp – it's far beyond
anything I've ever done for you! I'm more grateful than I
can say –'

But Jyp had already rounded on the Stryge. 'Satisfied,
you old polecat? You ready to help now? Or have we just
called your bluff?'

The old man snuffled noisily. 'Get you your ship, and
I'll come along.' Jyp blinked again; evidently he hadn't
expected that. He was just about to object when the
Stryge added 'Provided, of course, I can bring a brace of
friends –'

For the first time I saw real alarm cross Jyp's face.
'Not on any ship of mine!'

'Jyp!' I whispered.

'You don't know, Steve! He's ill enough company,
but lordy, any friends of his'll be worse –'

'Take it or leave it!' growled the old man.

'We need him, Jyp,' I said. 'You couldn't think of
anyone else.'

Jyp ground his teeth. 'But shipping out with us! He
hasn't never done such a thing that ever I've heard of!
Why now, for this? He doesn't care a fig for you, and little
more for me! So what in all the hells is the old devil really
up to?' He shivered, and then sighed. 'But if you really
believe we need him, Steve –'

'I ... I don't know. I suppose you could say I ... feel
it in my bones.'

'I just hope Fynn don't end up pickin' em.' Then he surprised me again, adding thoughtfully 'But we'll play it your way, Steve. Any feelings come to you, I'm inclined to trust.' He slapped me on the shoulder. 'So, you just hop back into your closed auto and get raising that money sharpish! If we miss the dawn-tide and the land-wind we'll needs wait till sundown, and give the Wolves a full day's lead.' He looked back over his shoulder. 'We'll sail at dawn. Be aboard well before; I'll send you word where.'

A sour chuckle floated after us. 'Save your breath, *cabôt*. I'll know.'

It was getting hazy and chill as I drove back into town. My first stop was at my flat, for a number of reasons. I wanted to change and pack, choosing the best clothes for what could be a pretty rough-and-tumble voyage. That done, I went through the rigmarole of opening my little wall safe and rummaging in it for my modest hoard of slightly illegal Krugerrands. Then I locked the place up, not without wondering whether I'd ever see it again, and set off for the Liberal Club. I knew that was one of the likeliest places to find Morry Jackman this time of night. Morry had sold me the coins, and I knew that within five minutes of finding him he'd inevitably be trying to sell me more. I liked Morry, and hoped his heart would stand the shock when this time I agreed.

'Tonight? You mean, like now this minute?' He put down his drink, and looked at me like a kindly owl. 'What're you doing, Stevie boy, flying the country?'

The truth can be best at times. 'I've got a deal going – a chance at a Caribbean charter, very cheap if it's in the ready. Guineas, yet.'

Morry nodded sagely. 'Caribbean for four grand? Don't blame you. On a night like this I'd pay pieces of eight, yet. Isn't an extra share going, is there? Ah, never mind. One more sticky and we'll go open up the shop,'

I drove back to the docks very carefully. The haze was turning to fog, and I didn't want to risk any accidents with that little bag of coinage chinking and chuckling unlawfully to itself on the seat beside me. Morry had come up with an amazing assortment, everything from quarter-angels and Jersey crowns to Austrian imperial half-thalers in modern reissues and, like the good lad he was, he had been quite ready to take my cheque for a fair five thousand pounds' worth at his untaxed prices. If the police found me with that they'd be bound to get suspicious and delay me, maybe fatally. So I contained my impatience, let the drunks go roaring past me into obscurity, and concentrated on finding my way. I made a couple of false turns at first, and began to sweat a little; the tendrils of the mist pointed this way and that like thin mocking fingers. But it was only shortly after midnight when a mellow gleam at street's end caught my eye, and I pulled up outside the Illyrian Tavern. So I was beginning to find my way around, was I? To fit in. Oddly enough, that idea made me feel almost more uncomfortable. I glanced nervously into the night as I climbed out of the car. I'd never been scared of the dark in the world I knew – but here?

There were plenty of people there, to judge by the hubbub, but the shadows hid them well. While I was still on the stairs, though, Jyp hailed me excitedly from a small booth by the fire. 'Steve! Let me present to you Captain Pierce, of the brigantine *Defiance* –'

A huge silhouette loomed up out of the booth behind him, towering over the two of us. 'Give me your hand, sir!' he thundered, and extended an arm swathed in so much lace I could hardly see his. 'Your servant, Master Stephen!' The hidden hand was ham-sized and hard as leather. His long sandy hair, curled like a spaniel's, framed a ham face, too. Below his heavy jowls layer upon layer of foaming ruffles spilled down the front of a peculiar waistcoat, its front panels heavily embroidered and extending almost to his knees. 'I'll desire your better acquaintance, sir, upon our voyage! But for now, time presses and tide awaits, and I fear we must bring our bargain to a speedy term!'

'You've got the money?' breathed Jyp.

I spilled out the bag upon the table. Panic seized me, seeing it sitting there in the firelight; had I made a fool of myself? Or misunderstood Jyp? Were values in this crazy world as different as everything else? It looked like such a pathetic little pile, compared to all the pirate hoards I'd seen in books and films. Jyp and the captain stared at it a moment without speaking, and I sweated. Then Jyp whistled softly. 'And you said you weren't rich!'

With an apologetic glance at me the captain picked up a coin at random, took a gnawing bite at it, and stared at the result. 'T'love o'God's will!' he breathed. 'Fine coin, this! Must be damn near pure!'

Shaky with relief, I realized that gold meant for use, as opposed to sitting on velvet bank trays, must almost always have been debased – ostensibly to make it harder, more likely to stretch its value. Jyp nodded with sublime complacency. 'What'd I tell you, skipper? There's your ship, your men and their vittles, and enough to buy 'em all over again. Want your trifle weighed out now?'

'The remainder,' I said decisively, before the captain could get a word out, 'is for you and your crew the moment we get Clare back safely. And as much again, upon our return. Tell them that!'

Pierce surged up, and bowed with such sweeping courtesy that I could only copy him. 'You are a very prince, sir, a prince! And by all that's holy, you shall have the maid, while there's power in our arms! Snuff with you, sir?' Anxious not to offend, I took a moderate pinch from the silver-mouthed ram's-horn he flourished, and snuffed it up as I'd seen done in films, off the back of my hand. I hoped I wouldn't sneeze. One doesn't, with a large Havana, lit, jammed up each nostril; and that's what it felt like. I was speechless, but luckily Pierce was too busy plugging his own cavernous nostrils with the lethal stuff to notice. He noticed all right, though, when Jyp scooped the gold back into the bag in one swift gesture and gave me it back.

'About that tide –' he said.

Pierce sneezed violently down his ruffles and roared for his hat and coat. Old Myrko hobbled up with a knee-length frock-coat stiff with elaborate piping and gleaming buttons. Over this Pierce buckled a broad leather belt slung with a huge rapier, jammed on a broad-brimmed felt hat with a tall plume, tucked an ivory-headed cane under his arm and remarked, 'It's but a short step to the wharf, sir! Would you go afoot, or shall we take your car?'

He didn't seem to fit my car, either physically or mentally. Jyp thought it was safer left at the tavern, anyway; they would keep an eye on it. 'Katjka specially,' he said dryly, as we climbed the stairs. 'On at me again about taking care of you, she was –'

'Is she around? I'd like to say goodbye –'

'Better we don't linger.' But I did, hovering on the last step, full of strange feelings. And somehow I saw her, right at the back of the dark room, her hair tossed back, her cat eyes watching me with expressionless intensity. She raised a hand to blow me a kiss; but it wasn't her fingers that touched her lips. It was the pack of cards.

The fog outside had changed, not thinned exactly but concentrated into banks and streamers that swirled around us on a faint chill breeze. We walked in silence, except for Pierce's cane tapping the stones and his scabbard slapping against his stiff coat. Jyp's sword was slung over his shoulder, and he seemed sunk in his own thoughts. So was I, and they were none of them comforting. I'd set off on long journeys before now, but with my destination printed fair and square on the tickets in my bag and the rites of passage common to every airport the world over; check-in, aisle seat, no smoking please, baggage checks and passport controls, security scans, adenoidal announcements and flickering departure screens. I'd never thought of them as reassuring before; but I would have welcomed them now, stepping out into a misty void of infinite possibilities. Maybe I was going to fall off the edge of the world.

'When emptiness opened before us, though, it was only the street's end, and the globes of gold light were not stars but the lanterns of the wharf. Beyond its rim shadowy masts lifted, and men were busy about it, scurrying up and down a gangplank, hefting sacks and rolling kegs. Above our heads there was a sudden creak, and a net of large barrels went swinging across on a spar, to be let down with much shouting and cursing into the shadows below. Pierce filled his lungs, and his bellow carried easily over the hubbub. '*Mister Mate! How's she stand?*'

'Well, sir!' The answer echoed up from below. 'Last loads come aboard now, and she trims nicely!' A string of technical details about loading followed, sounding surprisingly modern, and a brisk exchange of orders sent gangs of dark-clad men running this way and that. I moved to the wharfside, out of the way, and looked down.

'Well?' demanded Jyp, clapping me on the shoulder. 'How'd you like her?'

My mouth went dry with alarm. 'Jyp!' I protested. 'She's *tiny*! You can't have seen that bloody vast ship the Wolves have! She's a quarter the size –'

Jyp chortled. 'Surely, yes, but that's a great lumbering merchantman! The *Defiance* here'll have the heels of it, and draws far less; she'll outsail the *Chorazin* at every point, and go where they'd ground or founder. And if need be she can outrange them. See there, just along the tumble-home!' He pointed to a row of closed panels like upright trapdoors on the shallow incoming curve of the hull. 'There's eighteen-pounder guns behind those gunports, ten to a side, and long nine-pounders as chasers in bow and stern both. More ordnance than most ships this size'd carry, near as much as a frigate, but she was built for that, see? And to carry a larger crew than usual. The *Chorazin*'s a wallowing whale, but this, this is a shark, built for speed and snatching prey. Think I'd find you anything less? Though it was our luck Pierce had her in dock till this week, careening. It's a privateer we need, and *Defiance* – she's one of the best!'

It seemed I'd hired myself what was essentially a miniature private warship. I was all for private enterprise, but this was a bit much. I was still clutching my head at the thought when there came a sudden hail from high above, from the mist-cloaked mastheads. On deck and wharf alike all movement froze, and the clear voice sang through an expectant silence.

'*Wind's from the land! Dawn ho! Dawn is coming!*'

The very call seemed to strike through the mist,

severing its tangled streamers, flattening its billows. Through it, somewhere out in the still-hidden distance, I saw the first faint trace of light. It fell upon the faces of the men about me, and revealed them as the weirdest crew of cutthroats I could have imagined. Faces lined, faces scarred, faces that could have been carved from ancient wood, or simply formed in it by the vagaries of age; fierce, feral faces such as few men bear in this modern age, faces of every race I knew and some I didn't. Not all were men. There were several women, every bit as hard-faced and dressed much the same way – though there was little uniformity among them. And at that hail, without waiting for the bellowed order that followed, they snatched up every scrap of gear that littered the wharf and staggered, grotesquely laden, to the gangplank. Somebody coughed beside me, and I turned to find a hard-eyed little brute of a man bobbing nervously and touching his knuckles to his mahogany forehead. 'Beggin' yer pardon, master, but cap'n's compliments and may I kindly be seein' you aboard now?'

'Yes, of course –' I began, but he'd already snatched up the flight holdall that was all my luggage, seized my elbow and more or less dragged me to the gangplank. It was only three planks wide, without rails or anything at the sides, but I had no trouble till I was almost at the end. Some eager soul stepped on too vigorously and almost bounced me over; but a long hand shot out from the deck, caught my arm and more or less lifted me in.

'Losing your sea legs already, Master Stephen?' asked a husky, sardonic burr.

'Mall!' I laughed. 'You're coming along?'

She turned at a shout from the stern, but stayed to clap me on the back. 'A shame to leave the hunt half done, and me with the smell of Wolf just in my nostril! Aye, I'm shipped as quartermaster – and that's me called to the helm now!'

'Told you I'd get you the best, Steve,' grinned Jyp, appearing as she vanished. 'Scrappers all, and she a match for the whole pack of 'em.'

'Nobody I'd want more at my side in a roughhouse,' I agreed. 'Except you, maybe.'

'Me?' Jyp shook his head ruefully. 'That's rightly kind of you, Steve, but you little know. Her — well, there's not a swordsman or woman to match her in all the great Ports, nor any other kind of fighter from Cadiz to old Constantinople. Hasn't been, since before my time.'

'Before — she doesn't look so old! Younger than you, if anything.'

'Must be a heap of folk she's younger than, but I don't see so many. She's been around, Steve —'

A sudden commotion stopped him. Down the gangplank, complaining loudly, the old man called Le Stryge came limping. Two figures ragged as himself supported him on either arm. One was Fynn, vulpine as ever, and the other, to my surprise, was a young girl, skinny, pale and bare-legged beneath a ragged black dress, but by no means unattractive. Her dark hair straggled damply over her high cheekbones; they made her green eyes look immense, and gave her smile that hungry quality that refugees have in news pictures. I would have expected a tough crew like this to be wolf-whistling her, if nothing else, but instead they gave back, positively scuttled out of the way. Many of them made the jabbing-horns sign with their fingers, or whistled and spat. Fynn looked around with a horrible leer, and they stopped at once. Le Stryge halted at the gangway's end.

'Master Pilot! Three to come aboard!' He bowed. 'My humble self, Fynn whom you know, and may I present to you Peg Powler. A useful associate, I have no doubt.'

'No doubt!' muttered Jyp, and gestured towards the bow. 'You've the starboard foc'sle cabin. Best you get there and stay for now, you're upsetting the lads!'

The Stryge bowed. 'Anything to oblige, Master Pilot! Come, children!'

The strange trio hobbled off, and the bustle on the deck parted to let them pass. I was about to ask Jyp about the girl, but he checked me, caught my arm. 'There, Steve! Can't you feel it? Tide's changing. It's slack now.'

I glanced over the side. The greyish light was growing, but I could make out nothing but the mist heaving sluggishly below the gunports. 'I can't feel a thing. Are we sinking down any further?'

Jyp's laughter came easily, but there was something in it, something new that set my hair bristling as easily as the freshening breeze. 'Not the tides of water, Steve, slow and dragging! When our tide turns, when the channels are clear, and there's no danger of grounding — why then, Steve, we can sail east of the sun itself!'

Even as he spoke, the light changed, and quite suddenly the cold greyness was shot through; the high mastheads sprang into being, tipped with radiant light.

'*Cast off, bows!*' thundered Pierce astern. '*Loose heads'ls there! Hands aloft to loose tops'ls!*'

The rigging thrummed like a giant guitar under a rush of climbing feet, and over our heads a great fall of parchment-coloured canvas dropped with a crash, thrashed an instant then filled with a boom and bellied taut.

'*Hard a'starboard the wheel! Hands to heads'l sheets! Haul, you bitches' brood! Haul!*'

As the blossoming sails caught the wind they pulled the bows around, out from the wharfside.

'*Cast off astern!*' roared Pierce. '*Sheet home! Hands to braces!*'

I caught the rail as the ship surged suddenly beneath me, heeled slightly and leaped forward, urgent as a living thing.

Over the world's edge the sun climbed, and its low light played out across the sunken mist that stretched out to meet and merge with the dawning clouds, and turned it to waves of surging gold. The harbour wall slid by, the smells of tar and fish faded in the cold pure wind. I heard the water gurgling beneath us, but it seemed scarcely to exist as that limitless tide of light struck through it, turning all to misty translucency, water and air alike. Looking up I saw the topsails catch the air and fill – or was it the radiance that filled them, so strong, so fresh I seemed to breath it in and be borne aloft myself, a shimmering gust of fire?

Ahead of us the clouds opened. I no longer saw the

sun, as if it had sunk beneath our bows; but its light shone up before us, setting a stark and shadowed solidity on the clouds, and edging them with gold. Coastlines took shape there, fringed with bright beaches, peninsulas, promontories, islands darkly mountainous and tree-crowned. Vast and all-enveloping, the archipelago lay spread out beyond our bowsprit, and the azure channels opened to receive us. Our bows dipped, lifted, skipped and lifted again, higher and higher, while the mist broke across them and scattered to either side in tall plumes of slow-falling spray, and over us great seabirds wheeled and cried. In Jyp's voice I heard the same wild exultation, limitless as the horizonless blue beyond.

'Over the dawn! Over the airs of the earth! We're under way!'

CHAPTER SIX

AS A SMALL BOY I'd lain on the lawn, looking up at the clouds passing over our rooftop, imagining they were standing still and that I and the roof were surging upward among them. Now it was happening.

The channel opened before us as we scudded out, wider and wider, a blazing expanse of blue it hurt the eye to look at. Purest, infinite azure above us and below, the depthless blueness of an ideal sea, a perfect sky – if any horizon separated them, it was beyond my dazzled sight. And under the low sun's long rays the blue turned swiftly to burning gold, seamed with streaks of shimmering white; thin streamers of sunset cloud or wind-driven wavecaps, either or both, both at once – how could I tell? I was beyond caring, beyond thought. I stood rapt. It was in light we rode, light that filled our sails and rippled beneath our timbers, light we breathed, light that filled our veins and quickened our pulses. And outspread before us in hilly swathes of cloud lay the islands of the sunset archipelago.

Yet as we drew nearer they didn't lose that look, didn't fade as clouds do into shapeless, insubstantial billows. They grew sharper, firmer, more solid by the minute, seemed to materialize out of the mists of distance just as more mundane places do. Along their golden margins the swirling flecks of white became breakers crashing up wide pale sands; I could hear them, faintly, as we passed. The shadowy grey swirls of forest at their hearts resolved into the tops of tall trees, tossing their leaves in the wind; it brought me the strong slow breath of them, and, very faintly, the tang of leaves and pine-tar, bracken and damp mould, the scents of ancient forests long cleared from the lands. About their heights soared wings, not seabirds but broad-pinioned raptors gliding and stooping, osprey, hawk and proud eagles. From small islets in our path there came mournful yipping barks, and grey shapes stirred against the rocks, lifting round heads to watch us as we passed, some undulating away in alarm. Of other life I saw few signs, though once I was sure the antlers of a stag lifted in brief black outline against the blazing blue-gold; of humanity nothing. But once, as we rounded a high grey headland, there came drifting out to me from the cresting forests the reedy rise and fall of pipes. Not a sound I'd ever cared for; but it belonged here, plaintive but exulting, like a voice given to these wild shores to sing of their lonely splendour. It sang through me, and I thrilled to it, all other marvels forgotten in that low chant; I ached to land, to throw aside all my troubles on the beach and run off, free, through the rich woodlands. Mall's hand on my shoulder jolted me out of the trance. 'Best not to listen too close, good sir,' she observed quietly, 'when there is no man playing.'

'No man?' I repeated stupidly. 'That isn't the wind I hear.'

'Did I say it was so? But there are no men on that sweet isle. Much music, but no men.'

The beach beyond came into view. Just above the sealine a tall black rock loomed unnaturally upright against the bright sands; its flanks, glistening like flaked glass, were shaped, roughly but unmistakeably. Overhead the yards and rigging creaked, and the scoured planking beneath my feet tilted to a different angle; the set of the sails was changing. Orders were shouted, and men ran to the braces. I looked around; Jyp had the helm now, and he was taking us further from the shore.

'As wise a pilot as ever,' Mall commented. 'There's more ways than one to run upon a rock, hereabouts.' With a friendly clap on my shoulder she went back up to the quarterdeck to join him. Absently I rubbed the bruise and listened to a sailor singing to that eerie tune as it dwindled away astern.

There is no age there,
Nor any sorrow,
As the stars in heaven

Are the cattle in the valleys.
Great rivers wander
Through flowery plains,
Streams of milk and mead,
Streams of strong ale.
There is no hunger
And no thirst
In the Hollow Land,
In the Land of Youth.

'Belay that, you tarrarag!' growled Pierce; but the singer had already stopped. A flock of grey crows fluttered up from the hills, squawking derisively; and that was the last we heard.

The shores held my eyes still, but the cloudy isles sank away on either side, further and further, receding into misty distance once more. It took me a while to notice the little sailor at my side again. 'Cap'n's compliments, Master, and will you take wine with him and the Sailin' Master on the quarterdeck afore dinner?' '

I certainly would. After the alarms and excursions – God, was it only yesterday? – and a sleepless night I felt direly in need of a drink, preferably strong; I wondered if they shipped rum on privateers. The 'wine', though, turned out to be some kind of Madeira, smoky and lethal and served by the little old seacook in half-pint pewter beakers. By my second I was feeling no pain at all, and confident enough to copy Jyp and the captain, resting their feet on the rail and tilting their chairs with the light skipping motion of the ship, while Mall leaned on the great wheel. Something was bothering me, though, and as we got up to go below I realized what it was.

'The sun! It's almost *set!* But damn it, we set sail at dawn! And that was no more than two hours back! And *dinner?*'

Pierce let out a great guffaw, his jowls crinkling and bobbing, while an answering chuckle ran around the deck below; Jyp struggled to control his face, and failed. Only Mall did not even smile, but regarded me gravely from the helmsman's bench.

121

'Oh, go ahead, laugh,' I said resignedly. 'Don't mind the new boy around here.'

'Sorry, Steve,' grinned Jyp. 'I mind it hit me just that way the first time, and I was forewarned. East of the sun, west of the moon, remember, there's our road. So naturally it's setting behind us now, and we lose a day. No worry; we'll soon pick it up on our way home. Now let's eat.'

About the food I was a bit apprehensive, dimly remembering tales of weevil-ridden biscuit and salt pork, rock-hard and mouldy. I should have known better. The little saloon was brightly lit with swinging brass lanterns; the furniture was Queen Anne or something of the sort – I wouldn't have dared call it antique, not here – and laid with bright silver. Captain Pierce was evidently in a profitable line; at any rate he lived big. Five courses, with wines, and the *entrée* was several in itself, stews and sliced meat mostly, and little roasted game-birds, one each. All the three-star restaurants in town would have killed to get hold of them. I was a bit disconcerted to be told they were golden plovers, which sounded rare. But they did things differently here, and nothing was going to bring those birds back; I tucked in. On boats my stomach was always a bit unsure at first, but not here. The motion might be the same, but evidently it just didn't believe we were at sea.

After dinner there was coffee and brandy; Jyp lit a cigar, and the captain an enormous pipe, filled, I guessed, with the same blend of sulphur and nettles as his snuff. I managed to survive the result in that confined space for an hour or so, while the two of them vied with each other in what I sincerely hoped were enormous lies about past encounters with Wolves and other perils of the sea. I hardly dared disbelieve anything now, even Jyp's tale about what he had caught with an oxhead as bait. At last I was driven to make my excuses and retire, wheezing, to bed. Or cot, rather. The captain had offered me, as 'owner', the use of his cabin, but I'd thought it tactful to refuse. Instead I had one of the two little cubbyholes, as they called them, adjoining the saloon doors. Jyp, as sailing master, had the one on the port side. A little over six feet square, mine held only a rickety chair, a hinged wall-table and an ominously coffin-like box slung by ropes from the beams above. This was my bed, it was two inches too short for me, and I hadn't the knack of sleeping coiled up yet. Besides, all my instincts screamed at me that it was about nine in the morning, high time I was at work. The air was stuffy, and somehow it smelt too much of dinner; the single cloudy porthole that gave onto the deck I couldn't open. The drink buzzing around in my head didn't help. After a suffocating hour or two I gave up, dressed and mooched out on deck again, taking the brandy bottle Pierce had given me for a nightcap.

The night took my breath away, it was so beautiful. The sun was long gone now, the stars were out and a sweep of luminous grey cloud stretched in a great arch, a frozen wave, over a full moon that edged it with cold fire, bleached the decks and turned the sails to taut sheets of silver. A soft thunder seemed to echo through the vast dome of the night above us, rolling in time to the smooth slow heaving of the ship. The urgent hiss along the hull told of the true speed she was making, and the snapping flutter of the masthead pennants, the soft hum of the rigging. A few gulls still cried in our wake, or came to perch along the yardarms. The maindeck was empty but for the forms of sleeping hands, wrapped in their blankets. This was the deck watch, ready for any emergency, while their comrades rocked more comfortably in their hammocks below. Around the rails on quarterdeck and foredeck the lookouts paced, each to his own little beat, walking to keep awake, while at the helm Mall still stood, her long hair shot with light and her eyes gleaming star-bright. The lookouts and the master's mate in command saluted me as I appeared, and Mall jerked her head in casual invitation; I held up the bottle, and saw her teeth flash in answer.

'A fine wolves' moon!' she said as I clambered up the gangway.

'Don't spoil it!' I pleaded. 'It's too beautiful.'

'Is it not?' she agreed cheerfully. 'Come, you'll have a

123

wider view from here − though better yet from the rigging, or the mastheads −'

I'd done plenty of rock climbing; but rocks don't sway. 'Maybe later −' I was going to say something more, but it faded. I stared uneasily out over the ship's rail. Nowhere around us was there any trace of the depthless azure; it might never have been. In all directions, glittering like steel and gunmetal beneath the moon, there stretched a wide, empty expanse of rippling grey. It might, just might, have been a calm ocean, catching and mirroring the soft shades of that flowing, feathery arch so exactly as to make them seem one substance. Together they formed a wide tunnel, a cavemouth almost, towards which we were sailing, into the blue-black sky hung with moon and stars. Yet still the sounds were those of the sea, and it was a strong breeze that stiffened the sails, and riffled my hair.

Sea or not, it didn't seem to bother Mall, so I didn't let it bother me either; I was tired of playing tenderfoot. I just fumbled out my Swiss army knife and made a hash of uncorking the brandy. I wanted that first swig badly, but manners made it Mall's.

'To your good health, Master Stephen. And your ladylight'o'love's.' She wiped the neck delicately with her thumb before passing it back.

'My ... Clare's not my, er, ladylight. Just a friend.'

'What of her sweetheart, then? A laggard he must be, to leave the chase to you.'

I snorted. 'A hell of a time I'd have, trying to explain what's happened to her. But I don't think there is anyone, not at the moment.'

She gave me a considering look. 'The better man you, then, to speed so swiftly to her aid.'

I lowered the bottle, embarrassed, and shrugged. 'Not really. It's my fault she's in trouble. My own stupid fault, poking around and mishandling things. I should have known it would attract trouble.'

'Why so? To strike so deep into the Core like that, it's unheard-of; nobody who knew anything of Wolves would have looked for it, not Jyp, not I. There's no blaming you.'

I shook my head. 'Wish I could agree. Doesn't make any difference, though – my fault or not, I had to go after her. I couldn't just sit and do nothing.'

'But your wife, your own sweetheart – what of her? Should not you stay with her? Is't fair to herself to risk yourself on such a chase-devil as this?'

A sour taste rose in my throat. 'I'm not married. And there's hardly a girl who'd give a good goddamn if I never came back. Except maybe Clare, if that old bastard's to be believed.'

'The Stryge? Aye, believe him in this. Only beware of trusting him too far.' She regarded me with mischievous eyes. 'And this Clare, you've never –'

'No I bloody well haven't!' I countered sharply, and added for good measure 'What about you? Are you married? Does your daddy know you're out?'

She gave a bubbling chuckle, and tilted her long nose in the air. 'Wedded? Not I, I'm too much the rover. 'Sides, I like to lie o'both sides i'the bed.'

And while I took a moment to think over *that* one, she sniffed the air, glanced up into the rigging with the instinctive casualness of long experience, and eased off the wheel a little. 'Wind's freshening, but we shan't want to take in another reef, not yet. Speed's the essence, this night, with the fat sprat we're after.' I sat down on the helmsman's high bench, and studied her as she leaned forward to check the compass binnacle. She was no great beauty, a little too big-boned all over, but her black glossy breeches clung snugly to very feminine curves, and she moved with the grace of a woman athlete. Only that and the breadth of her bare shoulders hinted at any particular strength, let alone the tigerish force she'd displayed. Her easy manner betrayed nothing of the ferocity that drove it, either; but I couldn't forget they were there.

'Some sprat,' I said. 'But catching it's only half the problem; what do we do then? It makes me feel a lot better, having you along. I'm glad you came – and incredibly grateful. It's not your quarrel, after all.'

'Oh, 'tis mine all right,' she said softly. She looked up and out, to where stars glittered beyond the bows. Their

125

pale fire shone in her eyes, and she glared hard at things only she could see – memories, maybe, or forebodings. 'I've a quarrel with all Wolves and suchlike snapping brutes, and all the greater evils that lie behind them. And with all the wrongs the world o'erflows with. To set evil to rights wherever I may find it, so I'm sworn. And most of all where a maid's in distress –' She broke off, and remarked with dangerous coldness 'Say what you laugh at, Master Stephen, and we'll laugh together.'

'I wasn't laughing!' I assured her hastily. 'At least, not exactly – it's just ... well, I've never heard anyone talk like that before. Not like – I don't know – a knight errant? Or a – what's the bloody word? – a paladin. Least of all – if you don't mind – a hell of an attractive woman ...'

'A paladin?' She unfroze at once, and swept me a bow so deep her curls went foaming over her face. 'High praise, fair sir! Too high for my poor self. But I thank you nonetheless.' She smiled wryly. 'An all men took me so courteously I'd think better of them.'

'You probably just make them feel inadequate. I don't dare. You saved my neck, and you're helping me save Clare's. Like I said, I'm grateful, I can't resent you.' And I knew I'd better change the subject fast, before I began to. 'Least of all when I think about taking on those bloody Wolves again. You said ... something about greater evils behind them. Old Stryge was hinting along the same lines, but he couldn't say more – or wouldn't. You don't happen to –'

She shook her head, crossed her arms over the top of the wheel and leaned her chin on them thoughtfully. 'No, Stephen; naught more sure. But it's an easy guess. There's always evil behind such creatures, even if it's only what their first ancestors left in their blood. Deep in there at the centre, at the hub of the Great Wheel –'

'The Core, you mean?'

'Aye, aye, so many call it. There, anyhow, good and evil, they're well balanced, well blended, you might say. A smack of each in most things, and never more so than in men and their doings. Out here, though, east of the

126

sunrise, the measure of all things changes. There's great good to be found, aye, and great evil as well; and less mixed. Nay, no more brandy for now, I thank you; too much is a lee shore to a steersman.'

I lowered the bottle from my own lips. 'You talk about good and evil as if they were things in themselves.'

She considered. 'And so they may be, far out there at the margins of the worlds. Things absolute and pure. For certainly the farther from the Hub one fares, the purer they become.'

'Purer how? In people's minds – evil people? Or near-people like the Wolves?'

'Hard to say. Minds – oh, there's minds there all right. People ... maybe.' Her face took on that haunted look again. 'Some of them might have been, once. Black-hearted souls drawn outward to the greater evils like moths to a flame, and shedding more and more of their humanity as they went. But others, they may be those same greater evils reaching inward, and shaping themselves more human in the process; hence, maybe, the Wolves' strange blood. But out here between Hub and Rim one's as bad as t'other, and has as little in it of what we'd call men. You saw – you should remember. In the warehouse.' She must have seen me stiffen. 'And that creature, dreadful as it seemed, 'tis but a common servant to such outernesses, a sentry or scout. They're ever seeking to spread their black influence inward, like worms riddling sound timbers. Even deep within the Hub it lies behind more pain and suffering than most men ever guess.'

Somehow the night didn't seem quite so beautiful. 'And you think that something like this is behind the Wolves?'

'After that thing they smuggled in ... aye, I do. Trade is ever the subtlest means of passage, for it's the lifeblood of the wider worlds – the more so, for their endless variety, and the many ways about them that one man may pass with ease, and another, not in sympathy, find barred to him forever. Even the Wolves and other strange races trade at times. It must be shielded, that trade, and sentinels stand guard over its arteries lest infection creep along them, and darkness in its wake. It's not only for your Clare I'm doing this, Stephen. And I'd lay odds old Stryge is of the same mind. He's an unchancy bastard, but he'll brook no meddling of this measure. He and I, we've seen too much to let it pass unchallenged. That's my oath, my deepest purpose in life.'

'Sounds pretty good,' I acknowledged gloomily. 'Wish I'd one worth the name.'

The bell hung high on the stern rail chimed quietly into the darkness, marking the passage of the watch. On the deck below some of the dozing hands began throwing off their blankets and prodding others awake. The moon was falling from the zenith now, and long shadows oozed across the planks as more seamen came scrambling down from the rigging, took up the discarded blankets and stretched out in their place. Mall turned to lean against the wheel, studying me thoughtfully. 'No wife, no true love, no purpose ... Yet you have a mind, and some heart at least; neither of the worst, if I read aright. You must have dreams, sure; or have had them once. When I was a child I was used to waste my scanty pennies in the playhouses, standing and dreaming at plays where women dressed as boys for some brave purpose; but that only because boys took the women's part anyway. A fine irony; even on stage we could not be ourselves.'

There was something in what she said that made my hair prickle, but the drink was getting in the way of it. 'I had dreams once, maybe. Pretty stupid ones; they didn't add up to much of a purpose.'

'That takes time,' she said, and the bitterness in her voice startled me, making what I felt trivial. 'It took me long years, till I'd sloughed every last taint of my birth, left it lying behind me in the road. Till I was new-minted from my old metal.'

'Where were you born, Mall?' I asked gently, struggling to sort out what was taking shape.

She shrugged. 'Find me my father and mother, and ask. Neither name nor face can I put to them. My first memory's the bawdy-house where I was everybody's child and nobody's, being raised like fatstock for the coming trade. From that I fled as soon as ever I could; but it was not soon enough. For you now, though, it should not have been so ill.'

I shook my head, but in agreement. 'It shouldn't, I suppose. I wasn't born rich, but we were never short of anything. I got on with my parents, they gave me a good education, I took an okay degree and I've done well in my job. Very well, so far. And that was because I gave up dreaming early on, settled for sensible ambitions instead. I began planning it all out while I was still in college, how I'd get on in business and then maybe move on to a career in politics, Parliament maybe or the European bunch – oh, not for any particular party or anything like that. Not ideals. Just as a natural progression, running things. I took that pretty seriously – still do. And I suppose I dreamed of living comfortably, independently, and I do; that came true, too. So far I'm on target. What else counts?'

'You ask that of me?' she said amusedly. 'Many things, be you a man and not a straw-stuffed popinjay – or a Wolf. But a blind man on a blacker night than this could see you know that.'

'All right!' I admitted. 'The human side. Love, if you must call it that. I've had plenty of girl-friends, but I just haven't clicked with them – is that my fault? I've had lots of fun. I've got fond of them, serious even, but love – no, nobody. This last year or two I've been too busy, anyway; sinking myself in my job. Got to do a bit of that if you want to stay ahead. And in the long run, you know, it's more satisfying – oh, except the physical bit,' I added, seeing the look on her face. 'But I get that when I want it.'

'From whores,' she said coolly. 'Dolls, trulls, doxies

I began to get angry. 'Don't jump to bloody con-clusions! Casually, okay! So what? You think that's less honest than the dinners and gifts routine, the darling-I-love-you spiel when you both know it's bullshit? Or just plain conning some stupid girl onto her back? I don't. I've played that game; I got sick of it. But I don't pay – hell, I've never had to! Well, hardly ever,' I added, remembering business trips to Bangkok. 'But that was just ... playing tourist. Seeing the sights.'

'Men buy with more than coin,' she said quietly, when I'd petered out. 'Believe me, I know! But I'm no canting Puritan. They'll go a-whoring, your lads and lasses both; an ancient vice, and there's many more terrible – unless it's set in the place of something better. And by the Mass, Master Stephen, in you it is! You've never loved, you say? I give you the lie! For your own words do as much.'

I stared, and half laughed. 'Hey, Mall, you can think what you damn well like –'

I stopped. Her long hand had landed on my shoulder, lightly but firmly, as I'd tried to get up. 'Do you walk away from everything? From the plight of Clare you cannot. Why then from your own?'

'So what makes it your business, anyhow?' I parried, angrily.

'Nothing,' she said simply. 'I claim no right to meddle, even to care. But when I've held a life in my swordhand I cannot help an interest in it thereafter.'

'All right!' I acknowledged, trying not to be annoyed by the reminder. 'Maybe I was pretty keen on someone for a while. But no more. It wouldn't have worked out, God knows!'

'Hold, hold!' Mall released me and ruffled my hair amusedly. 'I only wish you to think, not tell me all your privy secrets. You may surprise yourself.'

'Well, I will tell you, dammit, and you can judge for yourself. I don't want you dreaming up all kinds of crap about me, really. I met her in my first year at college, she was at the art school and we hit it off. We had fun – God, she was more fun than any English girl I'd ever met. Just so different, so – I don't know. Outside all the rules. All the girls I knew – even the unconventional ones were unconventional along the same lines, if that makes any sense. She was Eurasian, by the way – half Chinese, from Singapore, pretty as hell. A beautiful body, near perfect. Like polished bronze. That was part of the trouble, in fact.' Mall had both hands on the wheel again, and her eyes on the horizon, but she nodded slowly to show she was listening. I watched the play of curves between her breast and ribs as she steered, and the hollows in her muscular thighs. Jacquie's shape was different, much smoother, more delicate – almost fragile. 'She wasn't rich. She was getting money from home, but never really enough. She used to model for life classes to earn more.'

'And you were jealous?'

'No,' I said, slightly surprised. 'Not really. I was proud of her, in a way. A bit uneasy, but proud. There was nothing dodgy about it, after all; she wasn't the type. She was so damn beautiful ...' She'd been something of a status symbol round the college, if I was honest. 'But she hated living off me, she wanted to pay her own way when we went out; she was obstinate like that, stupidly so. And, well, she went a bit far. She decided she'd earn most posing for magazines – and God, she went and did it without telling me.'

'Why should she? Was that so different?'

'Come on, there's all the difference in the world between a few student's scribbles and copies on every newstand in the country! They're permanent, photographs! They hang around! They could surface years later –'

Mall drew breath suddenly. 'Hah! And you feared they would?'

'Look, you've got to understand. I told you, I had it all planned out! And you know what it's like – you're young, you think it'll all happen tomorrow! She could have wrecked everything! I couldn't have some little hack turn up with these things – they were pretty damn broad – and slather them all over the papers when I was trying to get taken seriously as some kind of public figure! I mean, imagine it when I was fighting my first by-election, even! So –' I waved my hands helplessly.

'So you quarrelled?'

'Well, yes – a bit. But I didn't just drop her or anything like that, I wasn't that cruel. I just let it peter out naturally over the summer vac. We'd talked about going out to Singapore – but, well ... it lapsed. And come winter –' I shrugged. A gull cried out, wild and lonely,

131

and I shivered a little. 'She married somebody else the next summer, so she can't have been in that deep either. Not the type I'd have expected; one of her artists, a right talentless little sod. Last I heard he was graduated and designing soap wrappers. About her, nothing. Expect they're still married, if she hasn't wrung his scrawny neck by now. That's the nearest I've come to what you'd call love, Mall; and it can't have been that near, can it? Am I supposed to go on thinking about that?'

I don't know what response I expected, but it wasn't the mildly pitying look I got. 'Few care to remember being cozened of something precious for a false profit; still less when they've cozened themselves. But consider two things. One, she'd not need snow in her mouth to feel winter come. Two, politics once was not a craft a man openly professed. The word meant doing what was expedient, not what was right and true.'

The sting was in the tail. And luckily the glib answer that leaped to my lips never got beyond them. The falling moon laid down a first tinge of silver on the horizon, the billows caught it and spread it, glittering, in a great streak. From up above in answer came the lookout's voice, crackling with excitement into the exultant shriek of a seabird.

'*Sail ho! Sail ho!*'

'Whither away?' bawled the master's mate, through a speaking trumpet he hardly needed.

'*Hull down on the horizon, dead ahead!*' There was a general rush, and a snapping open of telescopes. '*Three masts i' the moonlight! And she's a big'un!*'

'Then begad, that may be she!' muttered the mate. 'Hold the deck, Mall! Cox'n, go rouse the Sailing Master and the Captain. By're leave, sir!'

'Only a league or two the head of us,' Mall gloated. 'Is this not a sweet speedy little bird we ride? We'll have 'em, Stephen, we'll have 'em! If it is the *Chorazin*, mind; must needs be sure first. There'll be all hell to pay if we open fire on someone's plain ordinary merchantman; and a warship so big'd blow us to matchwood for a pirate, with one broadside.'

'Open fire ...' I felt a drop of sweat trickle down my back; the hunched black shapes spaced out along the rails took on the look of sleeping cobras, poised to spit venom. The reality of what we were about to do took sudden drastic form. And whether it was the excitement or what, the dinner and the drink chose just that moment to strike, and it occurred to me there was one vital part of the ship I hadn't cottoned on to.

'Er – Mall – by the way, where're the, er, heads?' At least I'd remembered the proper shipping term.

She pointed in the general direction of the foredeck and the bowsprit beyond. 'Up there.'

'Up where? In the foc'sle?'

'No. Over the rail there, down into the forepeak and out onto the bowsprit. There's a ladder.'

'You mean ... in the open air?'

'For health's sake, aye.'

'Christ!' The picture appalled me. 'Why the acrobatics? Why not just use the rail, long as it's public anyway?'

'Cap'n Pierce wouldn't like it. And just one little flaw of wind, and like as not you get your own back.'

'I see,' I said, and stumbled off down the companionway.

It was only as I tottered across the foredeck towards the rail that she shouted after me. 'There's always another, mind – in the port foc'sle cabin. That's mine. By custom for ladies only, but if you'd wish to avail yourself, you being a well-brought-up sort of young man –'

'Listen!' I called back as I clambered clumsily over the rail. 'I appreciate the compliment, but – Here am I, stuck on a ship to nowhere, right? With a bunch of the toughest goons I ever saw in my life! And you think I'm going to go tempting fate and use the *ladies*?'

A cheer arose from the bowels of the ship.

So that is how we sped heroically into action, with myself crouched shivering on the wooden box behind the bowsprit. As a figurehead I left a lot to be desired, and my only comfort was that if we really were above the airs of earth, the earth was in for a bit of a shock.

By the time I clambered back up the watch below had been called up, and the deck was in a whirl of purposeful activity. Jyp and the captain were up and about; Jyp looked fresh as a daisy, but Pierce was in a filthy mood, and I was secretly glad to see him head hastily for the bowsprit.

'Any joy?' I demanded.

'We'll know any minute,' Jyp answered without lowering the telescope from his eye. 'T'gallants in – sail shortened for the night. We're overhauling her fast – too fast, maybe. I'd sooner come on 'em after moonset. Has anyone seen old Stryge? Someone roust him out!'

The lack of enthusiasm was so general that I offered to go myself. When I hammered on the small green door I expected anything from a frenzied bout of barking to a thunderbolt, but instead the girl Peg Powler opened the door, gathering her loose black rags about her. She said nothing, only looked at me large-eyed and was beckoning me in when Stryge's low snarl stopped her.

'I know!' he growled out of the darkness behind her, before I'd said anything. Swampy smells drifted out. 'I can hear! Tell the master he'll have what he needs – but not to attack before then! At his peril – and yours!'

'We'll have what we need?' enquired Jyp when I took the word back. He looked at Pierce, who'd reappeared. 'Damfino! Wonder what *what* happens to be?'

'He seemed to assume you'd know.'

'Him? Never! He just likes bein' cussed, that's all. But one thing I'll tell you – you won't get me attackin' before he's done, not at a cannon's gob. Now, Steve, what're we going to do with you? You can stay here on deck if you like, but the safest place is always below the waterline where the shot don't come –'

'Like hell!' I snapped, surprised and offended. 'You think I'm not coming with you?'

'No,' admitted Jyp. 'But I did promise the skipper I'd give you the chance. He ain't coming either, 'less it's with a relief party. See, Steve, this is kind of specialized stuff, boarding a ship, specially one a lot higher in the side. And

134

you're the only guy aboard who's not done it before –
'cept maybe the Stryge.'

'I'm a pretty fair climber,' I said. 'How many of your
lads would shin up an overhanging rockface?'

Jyp glanced at the captain, who shrugged. 'A fair
point, maybe. But you'll needs be armed, Master Stephen,
and I gather you're not trained to the sword. I can give
you a good pistol, but that's but two shots – *if* your
priming stays dry ... And speaking of which, we'll needs
arm soon, *volens-nolens!*' He snatched up his speaking-
trumpet and roared, '*Mastheads!* Be you buggers all
struck horn-blind up there? They'll have sight of us by
now!'

'*A moment more, sir! But a moment ...*' You could
have plucked the air on the quarterdeck like a taut steel
wire.

'There's scant science to a cutlass,' suggested Mall.
'Just lift, slash and parry, keep a firm hold and let the
weight work for you.'

'There is against Wolves,' objected Jyp. 'When
they've been handling them since their cradles, or whatever they have instead.' He snapped his fingers. 'Got it! A
boarding axe. That'll help with the climb, too. And I've
some duds for you.'

'Won't these do?' I was wearing a lightweight wind-
cheater, silk-lined, and activity trousers, expensive and
tough.

'Sure, if you want your pretty patch pockets hanging
off every nail and splinter on their hull, and yourself
arriving stark naked. No, what's best is heavy canvas like
the lads wear, or merhorse hide like me an' Mall; pricey
but strong. You and I are close on the same size; you can
have my spares.'

Merhorse hide? I peered suspiciously at what
Pierce's servant brought. It was blacker than the night,
felt softer than it looked, and faintly furry, like moleskin
only less so. It had a faint but disturbing smell, oily and
bitter.

'Try it,' Mall suggested, looking inscrutable.

Evidently there wasn't much point in being coy

135

around here, so I slid out of my clothes on the spot and tugged on the strange breeches and shirt. They turned out to be slightly elastic, so they made a very good fit, especially when topped off with a broad belt and the light running boots I'd been wearing. The sleeveless shirt left me shivering slightly in the keen night air, but I had an uncomfortable idea I'd be warming up soon. At least the boarding axe I was given turned out to be much the size and weight of an ice-axe, with the same long spike behind the head; Jyp explained this could be hooked into planks and other holds for climbing, while the blade would cut the netting strung along the rails to hinder boarding. Pierce lent me a long knife and the promised pistol, a little two-barreled flintlock affair he showed me how to cock – gingerly, because it was already loaded; it felt nothing like the pistols I'd fired on a range, and it unnerved me. Mall chipped in then, fastening an ornate brocade headband like her own round my brows.

'Thanks!' I said, thinking how I must look and beginning to feel incredibly piratical. 'Some sweatband!'

'It's a little more, maybe. You'll need what –'

'*Deck! Deck!*' Our heads shot up like chicks in a nest. '*She's a Wolf! A howlin' bloody Wolf!*'

'*Be you sure, man?*' bellowed Pierce. '*What's her flag?*'

'*No flag! But I see her lanterns!*'

Pierce snapped the trumpet back in its rack with a satisfied click, and leaned over the rail. 'Mr Mate! Clear for action! Hands to their stations!'

'Her lanterns?' I asked Jyp, peering at the distant dot that was all I could make out – no more than her mastheads, probably.

'You'll see!' he said tersely, as the decks drummed under the impact of running feet. We drew back from the rail a moment as sailors came streaming up to man the quarterdeck guns.

Pierce was glaring aggrievedly through his huge brass telescope. 'What the devil's the matter with 'em ahead there? You'd think they'd be running out their guns the moment we hove in sight, but damme if they're so much as astir!'

'Maybe they're trying to look innocent,' I suggested.

Pierce rumbled his dissent. 'I fear not, sir. If I spied any sail so hot on my slot, I'd run out my guns as a mere caution – and my conscience is less burdened than any Wolf's, I'll warrant. And see how they've shortened sail for the night! I'll wager the rascals never dreamed they'd be pursued, and they've set no more than a deck watch – not one mastheader, the idle bastards. What say you, sailing master?'

'That's it! And the lookouts half asleep by this hour, and with the lanterns in their eyes!' Jyp pounded the taffrail excitedly. 'Hell, that's the chance we need! All we've got to do is wait for the moonset before closing. If they haven't spotted us already, they won't now!'

'Very well!' said Pierce. 'But we'll leave naught to chance. Mr Mate! You may give the order to load!'

The whole ship quivered suddenly with a muted thunder. On the decks and down below the massive guns were being run in for loading, great lumps of iron or bronze a tonne or more in weight on wheeled wooden carriages festooned with ropes and chains to restrain them. Their crews skipped around them in a controlled flurry, moving with the ease of long experience, while the Master Gunner, a limping, sallow little man with a shock of black hair and dark malign eyes, ran from each to each inspecting them. 'Loaded an' ready, sir!' he shouted back.

'Very good, Mr Hands!' Pierce drummed his fingers on his thighs a moment. 'Stand ready, but don't run 'em out yet! We'll save our fire till we close, eh, sailing master?'

'Don't want to waste that first salvo!' agreed Jyp, and explained: 'While the guns are properly loaded and we've time to aim. Things get kind of sloppier when you're under fire.'

'I can imagine!' I said fervently. 'But – firing – won't that put Clare in danger?'

'No worse than she's in already. And it can't be helped. That's a big ship, we've got to hit her, clear a way for the boarding party at least – disable her if we can. Carry away enough spars, the rudder even, and we've got her.'

Pierce was shovelling snuff into his nostrils with such gusto I almost offered him a gun-rammer. 'To deal with at our – *leisure!*' The word came out as a thunderous sneeze. '*Damme!* But depend on it, they'll hold any precious prisoners below decks, and that's where the lass'll be safest. We're not out to hull them unless we've no other choice.'

'Anyway,' added Jyp encouragingly, 'we're going to be moving in close before we fire. That'll keep the shooting short. Might be they never even reach their guns!'

'Let's hope so!' I said. 'Let's bloody hope so!' A sort of chill horror was settling on me, at what I was about to do; I could have wished Jyp had been a bit more persuasive. I looked out to the moon. It was sinking fast now, almost touching the horizon; silver bled out of it across the strange ocean we sailed on, and turned it to a frosted mirror. Then for the first time I saw our enemy clearly, a little sharp-edged column of sails across the horizon, a child's toy drifting and yet heavy with menace. It was hard to believe it held Clare, Clare from another, infinitely distant life ... No; by now she was part of this one too.

'Better make ready while we've a few easy minutes remaining!' said Pierce. 'Cox'n, relieve Mistress Mall at the helm! Mister Mate, up with the arms chest! Boarding parties, muster on the maindeck!'

At the mainmast the arms chest stood open, and cutlasses and pistols were being passed out to the milling men – about thirty, besides us. Jyp scrambed up onto the step and raised his voice. 'Form into two parties as you draw your arms, by port and starboard watch! Port watch'll be under my command, and we'll board by the foremast stays! Starboards, take the mainmast, and follow Mistress Mall! Every man got his arms?'

A cheer went up, and a rattle of cutlasses.

'Swell! Then into the scuppers with you, hunker down by the railings – well down, and clear of the gun tackle! Any man raises his head above that goddam rail before the order, I'll have it off his shoulders! Okay? Hop to it, then – an' give'em hell!'

Mall laid a hand on my arm. 'You come with my

band, Stephen; the leap will be less, and the footholds better!'

'Suits me –' Mall's grip tightened suddenly; she was staring past me, to the bows. I turned, to see Stryge's cabin door open, and the old man himself shuffling out, his strange companions behind him.

He paused a moment, stared blearily at us and said 'Going to board them. Need help, don't you?'

'Depends,' said Jyp thinly. 'What'd you in mind exactly?'

'Mine. And theirs. You two!' ordered the old man briskly. 'Go with the boarding parties. Help them.'

'Hey, wait a goddam minute –' roared Jyp, as Fynn, casting him a malevolent look, scuttled to hunch down among Jyp's sailors. To a man they shrank away from him. But I was even more astonished to see the black-haired girl drift idly over to our group.

'You take them,' said the Stryge, implacable as ancient stone, 'if you want to stand a chance of coming back. Give up and go home, otherwise. Now I'll play my part. Stand ready!'

Jyp saw the looks the sailors exchanged at that, and acknowledged defeat with a sigh. I didn't know what to think. I could guess well enough what Fynn the body-guard was, a sort of poor man's werewolf, but I'd assumed the girl was along for another kind of comfort altogether. There must be more to her than that, though, if the old devil was willing to risk her, and she herself. In this weak moonlight she didn't look quite so pretty, her brow higher and more rounded under the lank hair, her eyes still larger, her chin too weak and narrow for the rest of the face; a hint of malformation, a lingering look of the foetus. The sailors shied away from her, too. Stryge paid them no attention, but went shuffling up the companion onto the foredeck and, standing there in the last moon-light, he began to whistle softly, as if to himself, and stretched out his arm to the skies.

'Now what's he on about? demanded Mall, as our party crouched down together behind the rail, uncom-fortably close to one of the guns. I couldn't suggest anything. Run in as the thing was, I was looking down its muzzle and into the ferocious grins of the crew behind, an unnerving sight; I could even smell the peppery sharpness of the powder. Mall was grinning, too.

'Best stop your ears when they fire, Stephen. And be thankful it's but an eighteen-pounder. The *Chorazin* has twenty-fours –'

'I thought Jyp said we outgunned them!'

'Aye, they've only five a side and a couple of chasers, where we've got ten. But five's still a deal, can they but bring them to bear.'

I considered that for a moment, then decided I didn't want to. There was something else that wouldn't go away, something Mall had let slip, and the more I mulled it over, the more my hair bristled. Beside us a spark swirled in the gathering dark, in slow figures of eight like a firefly on a string; I found it incredibly irritating. 'That guy – does he have to keep on waving that torch thing like that!'

'The gun captain? That's his linstock – he must do thus to keep it alight.'

'Well, I wish to hell he wasn't so casual about it – not near the cartridges!' Mall only chuckled. I seethed.

'Mall … There's something – I've just got to ask it –'

'Ask, then!' she hissed. No chuckle now; she sounded every bit as tense as I felt.

'Those plays – where boys acted the women's roles. That hasn't been done for … Mall, were those plays Shakespeare's?'

'Who? Oh, *Shakspur!*' She sounded surprised. 'Do they still play'em, then? Aye, some were. All the rage with the gentry, but too many words for my liking! Now your Middleton, your Master Dekker, now, there were playmakers indeed –' She broke off, her hand light on my shoulder. High above, against the darkening cloud-arch, came a shadow and a white flash, a shape circling down on narrow wings towards the still shadow on the foredeck – a smallish gull. Right on Le Stryge's upraised arm it landed, still flapping and fluttering nervously, and slowly he clasped it to him and bowed over it, petting it, ignoring its uneasy protests. He glanced up at the moon, and at the high sails of the Wolf merchantman, suddenly much closer. I was shocked to see how fast we were over-hauling her. Still crooning over his catch, he shuffled forward to the rail. Suddenly he held up the bird, gleam-ing in the last rays, and shouted something aloud, sharp and guttural and cruel. Somehow I understood what he was about to do; I half rose, a shout on my lips. But Mall yanked me down, even as the old man flung his arms wide and ripped the hapless bird apart, wing from body.

A low groan of revulsion arose from the sailors. But even as the blood spattered onto the deck, I saw the sails ahead jolt as if some vast hand had slapped at them, and flap empty and useless in the breeze. Then the moonlight dulled and dimmed, and in the shadow that spilled across the maindeck I heard Stryge's cackle of high-pitched laughter.

Pierce's bellow drowned it. 'Belay that, blast your eyes! Now we'll be on 'em in minutes! *Hands ready to go about! Starboard crews – run out your guns!*'

With a creak and a crash the ports flew open, and once again that drumming thunder shuddered through the ship. Beside my ear the tackle clattered, the carriage squealed as the straining crew sent that massive weight nosing out into the darkness, as if scenting its distant mark. Handspikes clattered, heaving the heavy barrel up to the right angle and elevation. I hoped the gun captains remembered their orders. There was a brief frantic clink-ing as wedges were hammered home to hold the aim, and then a silence so abrupt it was frightening. I'd tuned out the usual ship noises; all I could hear was my own breath-ing, very loud. My mouth tasted gummy and rank; I'd have drunk anything, even that damn brandy. On and on the silence went, the waiting, for what felt like hours, with nothing to do but think. That stroke of cruel magic had upset me horribly; and yet my words with Mall haunted me far worse. It set things boiling in the back of my brain, hopes and fears and odd concerns – and the truths she'd made me face.

'*Hands to braces!*' yelled Pierce suddenly. '*Helm

141

*a'lee! Headsail sheets! Mainsail! Cast off, starboard –
tail on, port! And haul! And haul, damn your arses,
haul!'*

Panic gripped me for a moment as overhead our
own sails shivered, emptied and flapped; but then the
yards creaked slowly around.

'Going about – into the wind and onto another
tack!' hissed Mall. Our canvas boomed full again, and
suddenly the *Chorazin*'s sails, still flailing, rose up from
the side, not ahead. 'For our broadside – or theirs –'

Then it came. *'Starboard guns – as you bear –
fire!'*

Barely in time I clapped my hands to my ears, and
squeezed my eyes tight shut. The thunder was here, it
spoke and the whole ship thrummed to the mighty word.
Orange fire danced through my eyelids. The deck heaved
sharply beneath me, and I was suddenly enveloped in
clouds of black smoke and stinging sparks. I was coughing
and choking, and even under my hands my ears rang; I
didn't hear the next command, but felt the rumble as the
guns were drawn back, and gingerly opened my eyes.
Through streaks of scarlet I watched the gun crew slam
the still smoking gun back against its tackle. The barrel
hissed and belched steam as it was swabbed out with one
quick thrust and twist of a wad of soaked rags on a pole.
Then – very gingerly – bags of dusty-looking cloth were
lifted from deep leather buckets and tipped into the gun
mouth; these were the powder cartridges, and one speck
still hot from the last shot could have sparked off a fearful
accident. Broad wads of coarse fibre were thrust in to
hold the charge, and rammed home with a heavy felt pad
on the original ten-foot pole. Only then was the iron ball
rolled in, looking absurdly small, wadded and rammed
home in its turn. A simple enough operation; but it was
done among suffocating smoke and hot metal, and literally in a second or two. The crew wove and skipped
around each other with an absurd grace – drilled movements repeated at every gun, so the deck looked like
some kind of weird dance, weird and deadly.

'Run out!' came Pierce's command. *'Train! Fire!'*

Again the stunning thunder, again the surge as the *Defiance* heeled, the flame and the burning smoke. Ship, sails, everything vanished in the searing cloud; I couldn't even see my own hands. And this was in the open air; the lower gundeck must be like some medieval vision of hell. Panic welled up in me, and a sudden desperate need to understand; I reached out blindly, and seized warm arms. The smoke flicked aside, and instead of Mall I found myself clutching a weird grinning urchin, her green eyes flashing in a soot-blackened face.

'*Mall!*' I shouted. 'Are you really five hundred years old?'

The whites of her eyes showed as they rolled skyward. 'Christ i'glory, man, what a time to be asking!'

'I had to ask! You're throwing away your life – and it's because of me – you're not really risking so much? Are you?'

She nodded soberly. 'Aye, indeed. Such things are.'

'God ...' I sagged.

She laughed softly. 'Did I not say the measure of all things changes? All things, even hours and distance. Time's what the Great Wheel turns on, the axle at the heart of the Hub – the stalk in the Core, if you will; men see it in many shapes. But break the bounds, fare outward, and the world grows wider. Well then, so also must its hours; for what are they but two sides of one cloth, cut to the same yardstick? As you voyage on one, so also in the other, back and forth. The farther you voyage, the less you settle, the lighter the hours' hold upon you; and a wanderer, I. Here your span's as much as you may win for yourself. And as much, maybe, as you may endure. Many fare wide and live long, yet drift back to their own in the end, trapped by a web they never quite shook off. Drift back, and forget. But not I, never!' She scowled. 'What was there for me, among the stews and the dens, the coney-catchers and cutgizzards? I wanted to live, to learn, to find better things – or bring them to be!'

With a yell from the crew and a rattle of chains the guns rumbled forward again. The gun captain snapped back the priming cover, and we both ducked and covered

143

our ears as the glowing linstock struck down into the powder. This time, as I opened my eyes, the gun crews were capering and cheering.

'Looks like we've hit something – God!' I shook my head again. 'Five hundred years already ... You could have as much, more – yet you're ready to stake it all on a damn-fool jaunt like this?'

'Why not? What's wealth, if you but hoard it and never use it? How long'd I love my life if I never staked it 'gainst a good cause? The longer you linger, the more you must risk yourself, to give your years meaning! It's you, my bawchuck, with your few scant years behind you who's risking more this night – and for the barest of friendships, it seems. If it were love now, I'd understand – but then you've never loved, have you?'

She checked, glanced up. I'd heard it too, a flat thudding sound like a nearby door slamming, very deep, and on its tail a sibilant, falling whistle; but even as I realized what it was, she threw us both to the deck. Just above our heads wood smashed and splintered, something snapped with a deep ringing twang, and the planks beneath us leaped to a rapid tattoo of appalling crashes.

'– seems we've woken them –' I heard her say in my ear, and then our guns erupted in answer, no longer in a salvo but a savage raking drumroll, firing the moment they were ready. I hardly realized what she meant. Crouched there behind the rail, juddering with every detonation, I felt strangely detached from the whole pandemonium. Half deafened, half blinded, scared stiff, but detached. Accidentally or deliberately, Mall had triggered off a worse turmoil in me.

Just why the hell was I so hot after Clare now? To rescue her, yes; but I'd hired a whole shipload of fighters who could all do the job better. Why was it so important to me to go along? I didn't want to hang back, to seem a coward in this tough company – but they wouldn't thank me for slowing them up, either. So why? What was I trying to prove? That I really could care for somebody?

I didn't drop her ... The hell I didn't. It gets hard to live a lie when you're looking down a cannon-mouth. You

144

could say it strips you. Fear flicked away my masks, peeled back the varnish. Slowly, thoroughly, *neatly*, I'd ditched Jacquie – and about as coldly and cruelly as it could be done. I'd kept up appearances, let her down gently – for her sake, I'd liked to think; but mainly for mine. Sheer bloody windowdressing ... had I always known that? I couldn't tell. But for the first time I realized she must have known; I couldn't have fooled her for a moment – any more than I'd fooled Mall. Then why on earth had Jacquie gone along with it, that pretence of a fading affair, of drifting apart?

For my sake. She'd gone on loving me, enough at least to let me keep my dignity when she could have destroyed it completely. To let me go on playing my part; because she saw how much I needed to, how empty I'd be without it. She'd loved me, all right. I'd betrayed her – and maybe also myself.

It was the past I saw glimmer through the gun-smoke, myself of the last few years. That disillusion, that creeping dishonesty I'd kept finding in my relationships, more and more often, poisoning them from within; when had I first begun to notice it? Not long after. Somehow nothing else had been the same, ever again, nothing – or no one. Till I'd shut away women in a separate compartment of my life, nice and safe and shallow. Why? Because I'd been too damn full of myself to realize what I held in the palm of my hand? Because I'd been idiot enough to cheat myself of it, to trade it away against some unspecified golden future? Dishonesty – some laugh. It'd been there all right; but it was in me.

Mall's hand on my shoulder fetched me up, crouching with the others behind the rail. Still lost in myself, I hardly noticed the heavy mist-strands entwining with the smoke, the spreading grey in the sky above the rail. High sails, shot-torn and smouldering, swelled up against it, and below them a blacker bulk that seemed to swing towards us with frightening, inexorable speed. On its high stern transom tall lanterns grinned, for they were carved in the shape of huge fantastical skulls, utterly unhuman – carved, or real? And as the black flanks towered above us I saw the huge smoking snouts of the cannon thrust out, and begin to tilt downward. From our own deck a wild chorus of yells arose and from the shadow above a fearful guttural howling – Wolves right enough. It would have scared anybody; it terrified me. But I knew what I was doing now, and it was horribly simple.

'It's all I've got left!' I yelled to Mall, and she seemed to understand. 'Not much – you're right – but I've got to defend it! I've *got* to fight –'

A chance to care about someone else. If I lost that ... No. Not *that*. Clare!

Then the flanks of the two ships came together, and all human sounds foundered in a squeal of tortured wood and a long-drawn-out grinding crash. The *Defiance* stood right in under the *Chorazin*'s tumblehome, and the swell of the merchantman's much higher side bulged right against our rail, clattering and splintering, a looming cliff in the dawn light. Sailors sprang up, swinging many-toothed iron hooks on long lines, and flung them out to catch through rail and gunport, grappling us to the looming cliff above.

'*Come, then!*' yelled Mall, and sprang up onto the rail. Then memory, remorse, everything dissolved in the thunder that shook the universe.

The Wolves had fired at point-blank range – but they'd left it too late. A blazing demonic breath seared the air, but the twenty-five pound shot that might have shattered our vulnerable hull screamed over our heads, terrifyingly close, and ploughed only through rigging and sails, without harm. Except one. The immense pine main-mast leaped in its socket and writhed like a live animal maimed, flinging at least one mastheader away and out in a great arc, past any help. Then with a long tearing sound, punctuated by sharp popping cracks, it tilted slowly over. In a tangle of torn rigging it crashed in among the *Chorazin*'s masts and was held there, swaying uneasily, as trees in a close forest support their falling companions.

It was an appalling moment. But in the clearing smoke I saw the rail empty – and Mall, her long hair smouldering, clinging spider-fashion to the *Chorazin*'s black planks, clinging and climbing. I jumped for the rail and flung myself after her, only dimly aware of the roar as the others did the same. I looked down –

The axe-spike bit into the lip of a timber and held – luckily for me. My mind wavered. I swung on the lip of chaos, feet scrabbling for a foothold like a hanged man's, struggling to clear my mind of the depths I'd glimpsed, that had scattered my thoughts like dry leaves in a blast. A vast void of swirling, scudding vapours and beyond it a blur of rushing speed, steel-gray infinity shot with shards of bitter light. It blinked among the mist and was gone in the very second of seeing, like the blind spot of an eye ...

Then my feet jammed against boltheads and lips of timber, my hand caught the edge of a gunport. With those firm holds it became an easy enough climb. I ducked as a grappling line hissed down, severed by a blow from above, then gaped as the black-haired girl forged past me, her dress hitched up over thin white thighs, her slender fingers clamping to the planks like a fly to a wall, the dark nails digging into the wood. Her hair glistened, and she looked wet, wet through as if she'd climbed straight from the sea. She didn't spare me a look; her eyes were intent, her lips set with childish determination. Another grapple twanged loose, but others flew in its place, and from above there came a sudden shout. Wolves were leaning over the rail, striking at Mall with axe and cutlass, and one, no more than five feet above, leant out to aim some kind of musket. The muzzle of one of the huge guns still protruded beside me. I stuck a foot on that, swung myself up by the huge stay tackle and hacked out with the axe. He yelled and dropped the musket, which went off into nowhere; I yelled and leaped for the rail with my shoe-sole sizzling. That gun was *hot!*

Mall was over the rail already, driving back Wolves with great roundhouse slashes to clear our way. Behind her the Stryge's girl slithered up through a shot-torn gap; instinctively I moved to help her, then almost fell back myself as she flung herself weaponless on the first of the enemy. Though not exactly weaponless; she went straight for the shock-headed brute's throat with those relentless fingers, yanked herself up and sank her little white teeth straight into his face. With a screech that cut through every other noise he tore himself free, stumbling and stamping and clutching frantically at his face. No wonder: it was covered with a ghastly black slime that spread and seethed and smoked like some foul acid. Another hurled him aside and slashed at her – and she spat like a cobra, full into his eyes. Back into his fellows he blundered, shrieking; with a yelp of dismay they fell back, and we were on them.

What happened in the next few minutes isn't too clear. None of these neat duels you see in the movies, certainly. Huge figures in strange gaudy rags ranged around us like a wall, blunt grey faces snarled like story-book trolls and long dull blades hissed and clashed till it seemed the mists themselves were hitting out at me. They never hit me; no doubt I was being protected, though I wasn't aware of it, or by whom. Desperately I dodged past them, parried and hacked out when I could, yelling god knows what at the top of my voice, and when my blows landed there was a wild exultation, the mirror-side of fear. Then suddenly there was a space open before me, and I stumbled out into it, uncomprehending, till Mall's hand shook my arm.

'Come, Steve, along with you! While the way's open!' I followed with eight or nine others, skidding in the puddles of smoking black slime spreading across the decks, jumping over the Wolves that writhed in them. Mall ran aft and in one fluid movement kicked a half-open hatchway back off its coaming and swung herself in.

'I saw some vanish down here!' she panted. 'Looking to their captive, maybe?'

From up forward somewhere Jyp's shouts rang across the deck. 'Sic'em, Defiants! That's the style! *Not one cent for friggin' tribute!*' It was good to know he'd got through too. There came a ghastly howl of agony, suddenly cut off, and a yelping bark, high and malevolent; I thought of Fynn. Hastily I plunged after Mall, cantered half out of control down the ladder and cannoned into

148

her in the pitch-blackness below. The stench caught at my throat and set me coughing.

'Hush!' she hissed, as the others came clattering after. 'To the walls, and flatten! They can see better than us in the dark – yet they'd need a little light – aha!' Metal clattered and chinked, a red spark winked and swelled to a yellowish flame, and suddenly we were gaping wide-eyed at one another in a narrow corridor of rough timbers painted a dull red all over, floor and ceiling included. Mall gestured to the various doors on either side, held her lantern high and hefted her sword as seamen kicked them open. They were all nothing but storerooms, mostly half empty and incredibly messy, and she padded quickly down towards the shadowy stairs at the end, casting monstrous shadows on the walls. Over-head the deck throbbed as the fighting swept astern again, and sounds rang suddenly through the muffled furore, that horrible bark, a falling blade singing in the planking, Jyp's voice cracking with excitement. '*Remember the Alamo! Tippecanoe an' Tyler too!*' Then we swept down after her into the dark.

Mall moved fast, but she was still on the stairs when the Wolves padded forward, swift and silent as their namesakes, out of the shadow-pool below. They caught her on the bottom step, sword-arm encumbered by the rail, and while one dared his cutlass against her long blade another swung around to the side and jabbed at my legs with a great spear-headed pole-axe. Still only a few steps down, I ducked below the deck, snatched the forgotten pistol from my belt and tried to cock the hammers with a rake of my hand as Pierce had. The springs were so stiff that the metal tips gouged right across my palms, so painfully I almost dropped the gun. But there it was, cocked; I leaned out, levelled it – and in my hurry pulled both triggers. The priming hissed and sizzled, but for an instant nothing happened; the powder had got damp. I was just about to throw the gun at the man's head instead when with a loud pop and a dazzling flash one barrel went off. The gun bucked madly and wrenched itself out of my unpractised grip, but at three feet I could hardly have missed. The Wolf's head exploded and he was flung back into the shadows, just as Mall twisted her opponent's guard around and passed her blade through his throat. She sprang down over him, slashed another across the belly and ran him through the back as he doubled over; a fat Wolf hacked at me with a cudgel and hit the sailor behind me as I dodged. Then a loud bang went off behind his feet; that damn pistol had only been hanging fire. He skipped and stumbled, I hit him clumsily with my axe and he vanished with a yell, tumbling down yet another ladder. We went rattling down after him, but he was sprawled silent at the foot.

'We're below their waterline here,' panted Mall, holding her lantern up. 'Abaft the hold. So those'll be the charge and shot magazines down here – still open, we caught 'em napping! And maybe – aye, a lazarette!'

It was a heavy door, brassbound and barred across the little window at wolf's head-height. I caught the bars and hauled myself up to peer in. There was another door with a wider window, and as Mall held up the lantern –

'*Clare!*'

There she was, blonde hair straggling and face smudged, smart office blouse hanging in strips, crouched away on a narrow cot and staring at me with utter horror. Then her jaw dropped and her voice came out as a dry croak.

'St–*Steve?*'

'Hold on!' I shouted, trying to fight down a weird hysterical play of feelings. Seeing her there like that, so familiar from my ordinary, everyday life, filled me with a shocking sense of dreaming, of unreality, so strong that the solid timbers around me seemed to turn misty, the threat they contained to lose all meaning. The temptation to ride with the dream was overwhelming, to just let things happen and wait to wake up. But I reached out to her, and could not come. Whatever was between us, door or dream, was all too real.

'Hold on! We'll get you out!' And dropping down I began to swing at the door with my axe. One of the sailors, a huge round-shouldered ape of a man, snatched up a Wolf's axe and joined me with great swings that sent chips and splinters flying. On either side of the lock we struck, and deep gashes were opening up when a louder crash resounded from behind us, and a sullen yellow lantern-light flooded in. The sailor's stroke faltered. Behind us another door had been flung wide, presumably leading from the hold. Wolves were crowding through it, and at their head the biggest I'd ever seen, a stubble-bearded sunken-eyed brute dressed in a filthy red frock-coat, embroidered breeches – even filthier – and a battered cocked hat with a red bandanna beneath. Round his neck hung a net of gold chains, and on one of them a heavy key. Beneath his breeches his feet were bare, and I saw why Wolves wore such massive boots; each elephantine toe was tipped, not with a human nail, but a narrow yellowish claw.

'*Off, swine-spunk!*' he roared, barely understandable. '*Stand'ee back o'there!*'

'Keep at it!' hissed Mall urgently, and skipped lightly back. The hulking creature growled something and behind him a dozen muskets were levelled. Mall laughed aloud, and flung wide the first door she'd tried. 'Thou'd let fire down here? Go to, my buckie! Best lock thy magazine ere thou play'st so! One bullet there and we'll to the angels, thou to thy black masters! Art in such haste for Hell?'

Even before she'd finished the Wolf gave one savage hiss of frustration in that horrible voice, and the muskets sank.

'*I larn thee meddling, man-bitch! I lay thy stinkin' lights open and feed'em thee!*' He snatched out an ornate broadsword as long as Mall's. '*Take 'em!*' He charged. With a baying yell the rest followed. Mall elbowed past me and met him, caught his blow on her blade, but even she stumbled under the force of that rush. Then the whole howling pack of them crashed into us, drove us reeling back into a crush so tight that only the giant and Mall could use their weapons freely, swinging and hewing at each other over our heads as the mêlée separated them. I clung desperately to the door-frame so as not to be

151

swept away, tearing at the shattered wood with my fingers; a minute more and it would surely give –

But more Wolves were pouring in from the hold, and the little corridor became a slow, struggling scrum. Sheer strength told, and inch by inch we were forced back towards the stairs. I felt my feet leave the floor, I couldn't breath under the pressure and my hold tore free. I struggled frantically to get back, but a wolf slipped across it, blocking me, and I was borne away, still struggling, with the rest.

'*Away!*' shouted Mall. 'Away back up! We'll do no more good here –'

'No!' I yelled desperately. 'Jesus, we can't leave her! Not now –'

The edge of the stair caught me painfully across the calves; my legs slipped from under me and I slid down right into that deadly trampling crush. A hand grabbed my shirt and hauled me up onto the step.

'Don't be daft!' panted Mall, shaking me. 'What shall we do else? We've found her now, there's small gain in getting gutted! An it go well on deck we may gather and sweep this rat's nest clean i'seconds –'

'*Clare!*' I yelled. '*Hang on, girl! Hang on!*'

'*Steve!*' I heard her shout. '*Steve! Don't –*'

'We're coming back! You hear? We'll get you out –' I was choked off, literally. With a howl of rage the giant Wolf plunged forward, hacked down one of his own kind who couldn't clear the way, and struck over at Mall. Trapped at an awkward angle in the stair, she was slammed back into me, but she managed to get her arm up to block the blow and hold it a moment, no more. I decided fair play wasn't exactly the burning issue round here, and with every bit of two-handed muscle I could manage I lunged out over her shoulder and brought the boarding axe down on the Wolf's head. I half expected the blade to break; it didn't. It split that fancy hat right down the middle and thumped into the skull beneath with a noise like split kindling, and stuck there. He screamed, a high shrilling sound, his sword dropped from convulsing fingers and he whirled about, wrenching the axe from my hands, and sagged down, gaping. I think he died there; but in the crush he couldn't fall.

'A very palpable hit!' whooped Mall, as the dismayed Wolves swayed back an instant. Left weaponless, I snatched at his sword as it slithered over their pinioned shoulders and whacked at them with it; to my surprise I found it more manoeuvrable than the axe, and they gave back again. Our last man living reached the stair and ducked past us, and Mall and I backed slowly up, her sword defending the narrow way and mine faking it. But the moment we reached the top Mall ran, hauling me after her, and the long-delayed fusillade came whistling at our heels, striking splinters from the timbers as we bolted for the deck.

But it wasn't going well there, at all. We emerged into thickening mists yellowed with powder smoke, and a fearful yelling furore, a wall of clashing figures surging this way and that. Out of it burst Jyp, and all but grabbed us as we slammed-to the hatch and dogged it down. 'No more?' he rasped, hoarse with shouting and smoke. 'Okay, let's get the lead out, let's be movin' –'

'*Where?*'

'Back to the brig, whaddya think?'

'*No!*' I yelled. 'We found her, she's there! Another few minutes – more men –'

'Like hell!' he yelled back. 'We're losin'em by the minute already!'

'Listen, we're bloody well not just *leaving* her –'

'We can't do anything else! See sense, Steve! We were holding this end t'give you folks below time, but we can't last out! There's just too goddam many of 'em, boiling out of every crack like cockroaches! Must've been packed in tighter'n a Portugee slaver!'

'Pierce – the rescue party –'

'They're cutting loose that goddam mast! Now will you kindly –' But I never got the choice. From out of the mists came a sudden roar and a single anguished shout of '*They come!*', and then the line shattered suddenly into little struggling knots of men.

'*Hold together, Defiants!*' howled Jyp. '*Don't get*

encircled! Group, and cut your way to the side! Quick as you can! Damn the goddam torpedoes!'

Then the Wolves were on us too, and we were fighting for our lives. With only that enormous sword I might have been in trouble, but there was no room here for science, it was stick together and hack and slash with a vengeance at any Wolf that got in the way, yelling incoherent insults and spitting when those ran out. It took a century or so to reach that rail, and left us a pack of gorecrows, our blades and our limbs sticky with carrion. All along the side our men and women were spilling back to the *Defiance,* and we didn't stand on ceremony but swung ourselves off that gloomy flank and back down with the rest. I didn't see too clearly, the smoke maybe, but I think I was crying as my feet slapped back on our deck.

It wasn't over, though. 'That goddam mast —' shouted Jyp.

'Almost away!' roared Pierce, as axes thumped into the tangle of cordage amidships. 'All hands to fend off, and lively! *All hands!'* Men were still leaping back off the *Chorazin,* while pistol shots cracked and whined above our heads, keeping the Wolves back from the rail. I saw the Stryge's girl caught by one arm, turn and rake her nails across the Wolf's ham features, leaving gouges that smoked like flung vitriol; she leaped free and landed lightly, running to the Stryge's side, where Fynn already squatted in his human shape. Then there was a sudden explosive fizz and a sullen, thudding bang, and the broken mast, blown free, swung violently, tore through the *Chorazin*'s rigging and went crashing down in havoc on its deck. 'Fend off!' Pierce bellowed, and the crew rushed to the side and snatched up anything they could, from boathooks to handspikes and fallen muskets. I got one of the ten-foot gun rammers, and as Pierce shouted '*Heave!'* we all strained against the black timbers above. Quite suddenly, with a rattle and crash of falling debris, they slid away, and the heavy mists leaped like spray between us, tinged suddenly with gold.

I stood there numbly watching it, forgetting the

154

shouts and shots that still flew between us. But it wasn't over yet. '*Guns!*' yelled Jyp's voice through the boiling mist. 'To the guns, all hands! Load and run up, port and starboard both! We've got to keep 'em off!' Before I knew it I was heaving on tackle with other smoky scarecrows, leaping aside as the gun came trundling back, and snatching up the rammer again, thankful I'd got some idea what to do watching them earlier. Thrusting those wads in was harder than it looked, but at last the shot was home, I plucked out the pole and threw my weight on the tackle with the rest as the gun ran up. From out in the fog came an echoing splash, and I saw the ghastly lanterns swing slowly around.

'She's cleared our spars, sir!' shouted the mate, leaping down from the rigging. 'Coming about —'

'Port guns!' shouted Pierce before he'd finished. 'Fire as you bear!'

We jumped back, hands to ears, as the broadside erupted, and we were so close that we heard the smash of timbers as the shot struck, and saw one of the lanterns dissolve to fragments. But just as quickly we ducked down as an answering thunder shook the mist. Shattered spars and blazing canvas came raining down on our heads, and the foretopmast snapped in half. 'Chop that wreckage loose! Gun crews, back and load!' screamed Jyp. 'Fast! Faster, or they'll have us! We've gotta keep 'em off! Teach 'em it's not worth their time!'

Again and again, with relentless rhythm, we ran those guns back and loaded, until my weary arms would hardly lift the rammer — how often I don't know, or how long it took. Only minutes, probably; but I was past telling. Gunsmoke thickened the mists around us, flame and sparks blinded us, the constant jarring explosions left us quivering and numb.

'Pound'em, lads, pound'em!' howled Pierce as we sprang to reload, but when he suddenly hesitated, and then bellowed '*Cease firing!*' we hardly understood. Some crews went on reloading almost automatically, faltered and ran down, peering in bewilderment. The wreathed gunsmoke seemed to gather and rear up, and then a sharp cool gust tore through it, parted the fog to reveal a dazzling dawn, the air clear and fresh and thrilling with light, the sky blue and bright and hard-edged as glass, fringed with flecks of cloud like ermine; beneath it, only ocean.

Real ocean, blue-green sea, rolled gently beneath us, its long, slow swell lifting us almost apologetically, its whitecaps spilling softly along our hull. Then Jyp, on the quarterdeck above, gave a shout, and pointed. Far away, halfway to the horizon, a dark shape rode, and it seemed to my exhausted eyes that some mists still clung about it like a shielding hand. A weary cheer went up from the crew; I couldn't blame them, for it must seem to them that, even if they hadn't beaten their unexpectedly strong enemy, they'd sent the Wolves running with their tails between their legs. But I knew better, and so, by their faces, did the others on the quarterdeck as I climbed unsteadily up.

'Why should they risk a longer fight?' Jyp was saying. 'We came too close that time already. They've got their prize, and they're safeguarding it. We're left dismasted, doubly, and helpless as a baby.'

Pierce snorted. 'Ach, never despair! We'll jury-rig some repair, to be sure –'

'And then?' I demanded.

It was Mall who answered, heavily. 'Limp to the nearest port – if we're thus lucky. I'm sorry, Stephen. There's no more we can do.'

CHAPTER SEVEN

UNBELIEVING, I LOOKED FROM HER to the

receding wisps of mist that trailed like a wake in the air
towards the empty horizon.

'You don't – you can't mean –' Dry sand clogged my
mouth, choked me. I stared wildly around the quarterdeck. On the companionway below Stryge sat hunched,
Fynn and the dark girl beside him, gazing up at him, their
heads laid doglike upon his unclean knees; his gloved
fingers, still spotted with darkening blood, idly stroked
their hair. The thought of that cruel magic revolted me,
but I fought down my qualms.

'You! You stopped them just now – can't you do it
again?'

The girl who was not a girl rolled her head back
languidly and gazed up at me with opaque, sated dark
eyes.

'I'm weary,' mumbled the old man, absently continuing his caresses. 'Spent. And now they're too far –'

Pierce crossed the deck in three clumping strides.
'By're leave, Master Stephen, we don't *want* 'em stopped
again! Why, why'd you think we were pounding at 'em so,
but to make 'em cut and run? To show we'd be too costly
to polish off, and best left be! But cross 'em again,
maimed as we are, and finish us they surely will! Whatever it may cost – overrun us, or just beat about and hull
us with their guns!'

My wrist ached with the weight of the sword. I slid
it gingerly into my belt till it hung by the blunt upper
edge, and rounded on the others. 'But Christ, there must
be *something* we can do! We can't just give up like that –
abandon her –'

'Refitting needn't take so long,' said Jyp, chewing at
his lip. 'Then we can go after the *Chorazin* again. Maybe
the Stryge'll still get a line on her –'

157

'Yeah! If it isn't too late! And what's the chance of that? God damn it to hell, man −' I choked again, clenched my fists, trying hard not to scream at him.

'Be easy, Stephen,' said Mall quietly. 'We gave of our best − a good dozen at least with their lives, and who may give more? And you played the man past all expectance. No fault of yours or ours they'd so many aboard.'

I stamped on the deck, because there wasn't a damn thing better I could do. 'Christ, Jyp. I *said* we needed a bigger ship!'

Jyp shook his head. 'Wouldn't have overhauled the Wolves in anything bigger, Steve. Anyhow, there wasn't a one to be found, not armed to match them. And sure as hell not able to carry four hundred men or more − if we could've found them in time. Because that's about how many Wolves we ran into!'

'A very army, who'd have expected it?' agreed Mall, then touched finger to lips in puzzlement. 'So many? But how? They'd scarce have room for supplies!'

'Aye, I did hear they were layin' 'em in heavy while they were in port,' put in Pierce. 'For long voyaging, said they, and nobody cared − longer the better, said we!'

'While they must've been living just day-to-day,' mused Jyp. 'But on the inward voyage ... Hell, they must've been starved for days − deliberately! Starved and dry! You don't do that − even Wolves − 'less you need to cram in the most bodies possible. Like for slaves − or maybe ...' He whistled softly. 'Maybe soldiers. Maybe they were an army, right enough.'

'Soldiery?' Mall gave a little laugh. 'Don't be daft, man − for what? Looting the Port? A tenfold force wouldn't serve, not even if they'd contrived to let loose that *dupiab* ... oh!'

Hand to mouth, she stared − at me. Jyp nodded. 'The Port, no − but elsewhere? Wolves alone'd never be able to do it − but with that critter to captain them?'

I stared, 'Captain them? You mean lead them? That thing had a mind?'

'Better'n yours or mine, maybe. Sure as hell different − sure as hell. With a thing like that to do the Wolves'

158

thinking for 'em, scare them on – well they just might risk it, mightn't they? Take a real cunning mind to set up that kind of a team, cunning and nasty – which is just what I'm starting to see at work!'

'What're you saying?' I demanded.

'That maybe this foraying into the Core wasn't so wild as we thought it. Maybe that's where they were headed all along. Part of their plan.'

'But ... what could they do there? Against police – soldiers –'

'Who'd have to find them first. Anyone see those Wolves coming to your office, either time? Or headed away? They've ways. They could make all kinds of hay, striking in the right places – robbery here, murder there, maybe a full-scale attack ...'

For a moment it drove Clare from my mind, the effort to imagine it, a band of terrorists who could come and go under some cloak of invisiblity, strike with fearful savagery – and unleashed by that awful devouring thing from the warehouse. I shivered. The terror they could spread – and more than terror; there would be hardly any limits ...

'And that'd be only the beginning,' said Jyp quietly. 'A bridgehead. For a real invasion. We of the Ports, we keep an eye open most times for any little tricks like this from Outside. The Wardens keep watch, and league and guild and warehousemaster their guards; there's barriers raised, barriers you never see, yet nothing can cross without alerting them. There's other precautions, too, things I don't pretend to understand; Stryge could tell you more, if he wanted to. We don't like shadows at our backs, and damn little slips past. But with a route working, they might begin to – dark things, base and bad. Worse'n your *dupiah* by a long long chalk. You know, this all begins to look kind of big ...'

'Yeah,' I agreed. 'It does. Bigger than just saving Clare, that's what you're trying to tell me, right? Okay, it may be. But she's still the centre of it! This rite they're planning for her, it's got to be connected somehow. So it doesn't change a damn thing for us, does it – any of this?

Except to make rescuing her more important than ever. If I have to bloody well *swim* after them –'

'Bravo!' said Mall softly.

'Didn't say otherwise, did I?' said Jyp quietly. 'If all else fails. But let's try for that refit first, huh?'

Pierce was already at the rail, speaking-trumpet to mouth, directing a volley of orders at the crew. 'Up, puppies! What, d'you think – it's make-and-mend day? So you'll all sit around on your arses louse-picking, will you? What kind of order d'you call this? I've seen better on a Brazil bumboat! These decks'll be the better for a swilling and a swabbing and a lick o'holystone, and us none the worse for it either, I'm thinking ...' They took the barracking with weary good humour, perhaps because Pierce was croaking as exhaustedly as anyone. I had to swallow my bitter disappointment, and accept it; there really was nothing else to be done, and everyone was quietly getting on with it. Raging wouldn't get me anywhere.

'Well,' I sighed, turning back to Jyp. 'Just show me how I can help, then, and I'll do it –' The long sword swung between my legs and tripped me flat on the deck with a crash, ruining my gesture but luckily not much else.

'If you'd cleave to that thing, best you learn the right use of it,' Mall admonished me severely as she hoisted me to my feet. 'Else you run the risk of most grievous hurt!'

'... *and practically useless on dates*, huh?' grinned Jyp, then, more critically 'Looks well on him, though. We could teach him a trick or two, eh, Mall?'

She twitched the sword from my belt and slashed the air with graceful savagery. 'Not Wolf work, this. A fine balance, but heavy – Bavarian, maybe, by the turn of the ornament. Not easy to handle – you wielded it better than I guessed.'

'Just like playing squash,' I grinned. 'Good for the wrists.' She raised an eyebrow, and Jyp chortled.

'He means kind of a tennis game – not what you were thinking, lady. Okay, we'll teach you, Steve – and heaven help your poor hide. Meantime, though, let's us buckle to on these spars. Maybe we can salvage something …'

We did, eventually; but not much, and by then the sweat had sloughed most of the powder-burn off our faces. The day grew hotter, and men took turns to collapse in the scuppers and let the deck-pumps play over them. I lay gasping among them as the stream moved on, blinking up at the sky and feeling the thin crust of salt dry almost at once on my skin; I licked it hungrily from my lips. Where were we? It felt more tropical than anything, the air warm and the sun fierce. Overhead, on the jury-rig coupled to the mainmast stump, the single sail flapped loosely as they ran it up, giving us moments of welcome shade. After five hours solid slog in the stinking heat below it was sheer paradise; I wasn't up to the technicalities of re-rigging, but patching shotholes with planks and mallets, that I could manage. Now, though, I didn't feel able to drive a nail through tissue-paper; getting back on deck had taken my last reserves, and I was glad enough to just elbow myself up again and wait for the next glorious blast of water. Instead a shadow settled over me, almost as welcome, and lingered.

'Well, hi,' came Jyp's voice. 'Still rarin' t'go, are we?'

'Bugger off,' I croaked, blinking up at him, a silhouette edged with glowing brass. He shifted, and the sunlight clashed like a giant cymbal. I sank back with a groan. 'No stay, I need the shade. My head's ready to fall off and roll down the scuppers. Any more hammering and it probably will.'

'You'll never miss it,' he said cheerfully. 'But we're close to done now. We'll be able to tack now without shipping too much water, thanks to you guys. And the new rig takes the weight of the sail just jim-dandy.'

I took the hand he stretched out and he hauled me effortlessly to my feet. He must have been working as hard as everyone else, he looked just as hot and haggard and bristly, but it didn't seem to diminish his energy in the least. His lean face was aglow as he grinned up at the primitive lash-up made with the broken foremast. How

161

old was he, I wondered; how long ago did he come into the world, and where? There was something about him, something the same as Mall, though less strong – an aura of energy, inexhaustible strength. They seemed completely tireless, almost inhumanly so – except that they positively radiated humanity, whether in good nature and kindness, almost overwhelmingly so to me, or in the startling ferocity they let loose on their enemies. Inhuman was no way to think of them; superhuman would be nearer the mark.

Was it their age alone, or was that just incidental to another quality, another force that drove them to live so long and so intensely? Now that I came to think of it, there was something the same about Pierce, in a more stolid way, and about other faces in the crew. But in them it was not as strong or as complete, and sometimes it did look inhuman; the limping Master Gunner, Hands, seemed to crackle and glitter with malicious destructive energy, as if he burned not food but gunpowder in his guts. As if he embodied the living spirit of his guns, with no purpose except to destroy, and no care as to what.

Suddenly I felt the lack deeply, even of a one-sided passion like that; nothing of the sort burned in me. I felt rusty and ashen and empty, like the long-neglected fireplace I'd uncovered in redecorating my flat. The need to help Clare raised a glow, maybe – no, more than that. One last fierce flame in the embers; but its lonely blaze only highlighted the empty hearth. The rest was cold.

Jyp clouted me amiably on the shoulder. 'Hey, cheer up!' he said, propelling me through the incredible clutter towards the quarterdeck. 'Thought you'd like to see – we're going to bring her head around now, let the sail catch the wind a little and if the rig holds – why, we're cookin' with gas!'

'*Hands! All hands!*' came the hollow roar from the bridge trumpet. '*Man the braces! Mr Mate! We'll have that sea-anchor in!* Carry on when you're ready, Sailing Master!'

As the mate and his party hauled in the float that had kept our nose into the wind, Jyp bounded up onto the companionway. 'Aye aye, cap'n! Ready, helm? Bring her round then – handsomely, now – a point, a point – sheets –' His eyes fixed on the new rig, he gave his orders in a tense monotone, hardly a shout; but the deck fell so quiet his voice carried clearly. The crude-looking square-sail began to quiver, the yard creaked; I held my breath. The canvas thrashed once, twice, then swelled taut with a satisfying thump. The mast took the strain, creaked and quivered against its stays in the play of vast tensions, like invisible fingers – and held. The deck lost its lolling motion and rose smoothly as the ship strained sluggishly forward. A great sigh went up as everyone remembered to breathe again, as if we were trying to fill the sail ourselves.

'*Steady as she goes! That's well done, my chicks!*' The squawk of the trumpet didn't quite conceal the relief in Pierce's voice. 'Very well done! A spot of refreshment's in order, I'll warrant! Not quite noon yet, but we'll consider it so!' A hoarse cheer echoed his order. 'Up spirits, Mr Mate, and a double tot for all! Then hands to eat, by watches!'

Not quite noon? There stood the sun, all right, just off the zenith – though that might mean nothing, in this crazy world. It felt more like day's end to me, after five hours in that hellhole – but then I'd started not long after dawn. Currents were building up in the crowd on deck, and I found myself drawn into one, headed for the foot of the new mainmast where two large barrels had been set up. Before I knew it I was gulping down a pannikin full of a potent mix; I'd never much liked rum, but even cut with water that grog was the best thing I'd ever tasted. Life flowed back into me with a rush, and I found myself grinning back at the other crewmen, and probably looking just as inane. I seemed to be getting along with them as well as with the officers, or maybe better, and that pleased me absurdly. Right from my college days I'd been always a chief, never an Indian, and there was a good side to being the greenhorn again. Not that there was much social distinction aboard; here came Jyp, wiping his lips from the same pannikin, and if the sailors cleared a path for him it was good-humouredly and with real respect.

'Chow time, port watch!' he shouted, and as half the hands went clattering and tumbling below he led me up to the quarterdeck for ours. He peered unenthusiastically under the covers of the elegant silver dishes Pierce's steward had laid out on a folding table. 'Just ships' ordinary, I guess – beans, salt pork, German sausage, biscuit – and all cold, dammit. The galley stove went out in the last exchange.'

'It takes five hours to relight?'

'Out with a twenty-five pound shot, I meant – right out through the side.'

'Umm. You know, this is just the weather one *prefers* a cold luncheon, don't you think?'

'By the most amazing coincidence' ... grinned Jyp. 'Still, there's rum to wash it down.'

Rum there was, in enormous tumblers, but I only managed one. Jyp swore I slid nose-down into my plate of beans, but he was exaggerating as usual; no way could I ever have flaked out before I'd finished the last one.

It was falling on me. I knew it, I could see it and I couldn't even move, a meteor streaking down the sky, glowing larger by the minute, closer, clearer, greener till it blotted out the sky, roaring down on me in flame – a vast clutching hand. The fingers closed like falling pillars and a vast explosion tore me atom from atom and scattered me to the winds. Then, just as suddenly, I was awake, staring up at the sky, stained the deep indigo of a tropical twilight. I was glad of that; my eyes didn't feel up to much else. The brighter stars gleamed like needles. Another blast shook me, and set the stars dancing in my head; I rolled over, found that was just as uncomfortable, and sat up with a groan. Now I was awake I knew that sound, and I fumbled confusedly for my sword.

'Slept your fill, Master Stephen?' inquired a familiar voice, mildly sardonic, from the direction of the helm. 'Have no fear, they're but signal guns.'

'Of course,' I mumbled, or something of the sort,

164

fighting to unstick my tongue from the roof of my mouth. 'Nice uv yuh t'let m'sleep. Nice soft deck ...'

A boot tapped musically against wood. 'Your cabin's yet unrepaired, or we'd have stowed you there. There's water in the butt here, should you wish it.'

I downed a pannikin practically in one gulp, and felt a lot better. 'Could I have another? Is there enough?'

'To soak your head in, an it'll not fall off!' grinned Mall. I followed her advice, as far as my face anyhow; the water was tepid and brackish, but incredibly refreshing all the same. 'Take all you will, there's no lack. See, we're in sight of land.'

'Uh?' I jerked my head up, spluttering and streaming. 'What? Where?' But I saw it even as she pointed, a dark streak between the sea and a strangely luminous skyline.

'We've run up a signal for aid. That's what purpose the guns serve, to call attention to it – and a'looks as though we've snared our hare!'

I wiped my streaming eyes and peered out; something was there, something like a glowing coal across the low swell, and growing slowly larger. The hands were lining the sides, laughing and pointing. I shivered, though the night was warm; it looked uncomfortably close to my dream. But when it rolled a little closer, and Pierce hailed it, I laughed myself. It was a little steamship, craziest-looking thing I'd ever seen with its immense crowned smokestack, tethered by stays just like a mast, and huge uncovered paddlewheels at either side of the little wheel-house that was all its superstructure. When it tooted its whistle and hove-to alongside I'd have expected Mickey Mouse to look out. Instead a vision of white whiskers and brass buttons appeared with a megaphone, rubbing his hands, and greeted Pierce with the cheerful sympathy of a man about to profit from his neighbour's problem. They began a spirited negotiation, only about half intelligible – which was probably just as well, given the half I could make out; terms like 'raggedy-ass lime-juice freebooter' and 'pinch-penny tea-kettle sailor' were flying back and forth quite freely. Unless I was much mistaken, each challenged the other to a duel at one point. But all at once they came to a friendly accord, and the steamboat began chugging laboriously around, paddles churning in opposite directions. Pierce and Jyp came striding aft, sounding very cheerful.

'A stroke of high fortune, by Jove!' the captain rumbled. 'A steam tug for our tow, and at a most reasonable rate.'

'That's so,' agreed Jyp placidly. 'Last one, I recall you solemnly vowed if he didn't come down two bits a mile you'd rape his wife and burn his house down. *And* shoot his dog. Okay, Mall, I'll relieve you now; this river's an old friend of mine. There's sandbars and mudbanks aplenty right up the river, and I know all their first names.'

'And whom they wedded, I've no doubt. The wheel's to yourself, pilot! I've a mind to rest me awhile.' With a friendly wave she trotted lightly down to the maindeck. Seeing the spring in her stride as she threaded her way through the growing snarl-up there, you wouldn't have thought she needed any rest at all. The mate was struggling to organize the reefing of the makeshift mainsail; without proper rigging this was a murderously difficult job, and even these hardened sailors were so tired they were tripping over and tangling lines everywhere you looked. Pierce glared and seized his speaking trumpet. 'Deck, there! Belay, all! One fall at a time! Haul by turns, you pox 'spital outsweepings!' They stared up stupidly, and he began to thump time on the rail, '*Haul,* one! Then *haul* two!'

A clear musical note picked up the rhythm of his shout and wove it into a mocking little rise-and-fall tune. Laughter rippled, and one of the women sang along with the line.

... Ranzo, Reuben Ranzo!

The men picked up the song, hoarse as corncrakes but with reviving energy. Order seemed to flow across the deck, and they threw their weight on the falls in time to the repeated lines.

166

They gave him lashes thirty –
Ranzo! Ranzo!
Because he was so dirty!
Ranzo, Reuben Ranzo!

Miracle of miracles, the snarl-up was beginning to clear, and men could shin up the makeshift mast and out on the yard – gingerly, since there wasn't any footrope.

I glanced round for the source of the music, and was astonished to see Mall appear at the door of her cabin, a violin at her shoulder, swaying with each bold sweep of her bow. Out into the tangle she stepped, skipping over snags and kicking stray ends of rope aside without missing a note, and perched herself nimbly upon the rail. As they finished hauling she shifted almost imperceptibly to another tune, a strange sad reflective melody with an oddly Elizabethan sound – or not so oddly, when you thought about it. It was incredibly calm and beautiful.

'Great little fiddler, isn't she?' said Jyp softly.

'The best – not that I'm any expert. Doesn't she ever sleep?'

'Not often. I've seen her, once or twice. Never for long.'

'Do you?'

Jyp chuckled softly. 'Now and again.'

The tug hooted impatiently, and a cloud of smutty soot from its stack blew across the deck, inspiring Pierce to further inspired cursing; a line was flung from its stern to our bows, and there made fast. The little tug tooted again and turned clumsily away, paddles stirring the dark water to a froth. The line took the strain, hummed taut, the *Defiance* wallowed horribly under us a moment and then surged forward in a new rhythm, bobbing and bucking across the waves. I turned to Jyp. 'You called this a river? With only that streak of land in sight? Looks more like the sea, still.'

'Sure is, in a sense.' He spoke a little absently, his eyes fixed on the water ahead. 'But it's a big river, this, strong current carrying a mighty load of silt and flowing right out against the sea to dump it. Delta here sticks out

167

a long way, and the current's building the banks all the time. We're steering down the main drag already; can't see it, but it's there – hallo!' A soft, almost subliminal judder seemed to pass through the ship. 'Baby's grown a mite. Ah, well, it scrapes the copper clean. Man can't be too careful round here.'

And I realized with a sudden thrill that even while we'd talked the waves around us had been growing slower, heavier, flatter, as if the water itself was turning somehow thicker; a shadow seemed to be spreading beneath. At last they began to break over the hidden solidity and their voices changed to the resigned hiss of surf – too near, all too near to come from that far-off streak of land. Slowly, almost shyly, hummocked silhouettes rose on either side in the starlight, and before long I saw them topped with scrubby grass and clumps of bushes. The ship's motion was changing, growing steadier, the thudding pulse of the surf already behind us and dying away. It was as if, in the blackness beyond the light of our lanterns, the land had reached out to meet us.

So it went on, hours into the night. Clouds hid the moon, and the starlight showed us only the barest outlines of the bank; our lanterns couldn't reach. Ahead of us blazed the open door of the tug's firebox, an angry guiding star in the blackness with the insistent, relentless chuffing of its engine. I did my best to doze, lying or sitting leaning against the transom, but without the combined effects of rum and exhaustion the discomfort of the deck kept on waking me every hour or so. Once something sang uncomfortably in my ear, and I sat up sharply and stared around. The banks had changed a little, not necessarily for the better. There were trees there now, oddly stunted and growing in swampland, to judge by what drifted out to us on the warm breeze – the smells, and the incessant chorus of chirps, croaks and whistles. And the mosquitoes; I slapped and swore, but they didn't seem to bother Jyp.

'They go off watch a little later,' he said, poised easily at the wheel. I was about to say something about them getting their tot of blood first, when a sound between a boom and a coughing roar echoed out across the night, followed by a heavy splash. 'Gator,' remarked Jyp. 'Havin' bad dreams, maybe.'

'My heart bleeds.' I sank my head in my arms to save my eyelids from the mosquitoes and drifted back in and out of my own unhappy musings. I'd meant to ask where we were going, but I was almost too weary to care. Two or three times more I remember waking in dim unease, but not what woke me. The last time was clearer. Drums thudded in my head, there was the smell of lightning on the air, and on a wall shadows glided back and forth ...

Quite abruptly, as if somebody had shaken me, I was awake, sitting up, tense and breathing hard. Nothing had changed, that I could see; yet something had. The air was cooler, for one thing, and the smells were different. The moon was out now, though very low in the sky, and stretching long shadows across the deck. But Jyp stood at the helm still, unperturbed. He nodded as I hauled myself stiffly up, yawned, stretched till my muscles cracked, and wished I hadn't eaten all those beans. I wasn't feeling conversational, so I leaned on the rail and gazed out over the river. It looked as wide and as dark as ever, but the banks were changing. The odd trees were still there – some kind of cypress, I thought, seeing them more clearly – but mingled with other kinds as the banks rose higher. And in among them I thought I saw little sparkles now and again, far-off lights. I blamed them on my eyes at first, till the sound of singing drifted out through the darkness – voices in harmony, women's mostly. It sounded like some kind of blues, slow and mournful as the turbid river.

I was about to mention it to Jyp and ask him where we were supposed to be going when another shape materialized out of the shadows in the river beside us, a tall three-masted bulk even bigger than the *Chorazin*, lolling heavily at anchor in the channel. Its immense bowsprit seemed to scorn our shattered rig as we slunk by. Beyond it other much smaller boats were moored, and others, little better than canoes, drawn up on the muddy bank. Then came trees again, but more and more cleared gaps were appearing; there were buildings here, almost to

169

the water's edge, and more voices, raucous this time. I looked over to the other bank, but it was sunk in unbroken darkness. Out in the river, though, the moonlight glinted sullenly on another big ship at anchor, a lean long shark-shape riding strangely low in the water. Its flat decks were capped with dark rounded humps, their long snouts shrouded in draped tarpaulins; a broad stubby smokestack rose up between them, only a little higher. Unmistakably it was a warship, and with turreted cannon that had to be far more modern than our muzzle-loaders. Beyond it the trees vanished, and a phalanx of big ugly buildings fringed the sky, spiked here and there with tall thin factory chimneys. A broad jetty lanced out into the river and back along the banks into the night till only its faint lights marked it, and the shadowy foliage of mastheads ranged alongside, much the same as I'd seen over the Danube Street rooftops. But among them, standing out like the broad pillared trunks of a southern rain forest, were pair after pair of smokestacks. Crowned with fantastical rondels, stellar points, even Corinthian capitals, they capped the high-sided hulls beneath as if they were the factories' floating spawn. As we drew nearer I saw the huge cylinders, stepped and flanged, at their sterns. I leaned on the rail and held my head.

Jyp made an enquiring noise. 'It's this clash of times,' I groaned. 'It's making me giddy. Do times always get jumbled together like this?'

Jyp shook his head. 'No jumble. Square-riggers, sternwheelers, tin-plate monitors even – round about the 1850s, 1860s, you'd find 'em all moored along here together.'

I nodded, considering Jyp carefully. 'Remember that, do you? From when you were young?'

'Me?' He smiled. 'Hell, no! I'm not that old. They'd all gone by the time I was born, 'cept maybe a few sternwheelers. Never saw one, anyhow, nor any kind of ship where I was raised; not a drop of sea. The grain, with its waves, mile on mile, they said that was like the ocean; what'd they know? They'd never seen it any more'n I had. Till I ran away to the coast; then I saw, and I've never left it since. Even though I got me my master's tickets just in time for the war, and the U-boats.'

I was startled the other way now; Jyp hardly seemed modern enough to have sailed against U-boats. Tunisian corsairs, yes; U-boats, no. It made his ageless look oddly more outrageous than Mall's. 'Sounds rough. What were you on? The North Atlantic run? The Murmansk Convoys?'

'Yes, to both. But I was born back before the turn of the century, in Kansas. I was maybe sixteen when I ran off; it was World War One I was talking about.' He jerked his head. 'I stuck around, that's all. In the shadows, just like those ships out there. Just like everything we're seeing – those songs from the old slave barracoons, the little fishing villages, the whole damn river under us. All part of what formed this place, its character, its image. Its shadow. It's not gone, not yet. Outside the Core it lingers on, clinging round this place. Felt maybe but never seen, though you lived a whole life long here – not 'less one day you happened to turn the right corner.'

'Which place –' I tried to ask. But the screech of the tug's whistle drowned me out, and the sudden explosion of activity around us on the deck. Jyp yelled out orders and spun the wheel; Pierce came trumpeting up from below, and turned out both watches. We had come to an empty berth along the crowded dock, and the *Defiance* had to be worked in. Which left me about the only useless person on board – except perhaps the eerie little trio huddled in that foc'sle cabin, and they hardly counted as human. I thought of taking to my half-collapsed cubbyhole, but there was no clear way off the quarterdeck. Lines were being hauled in dripping from the tug and others flung to shadowy figures along the quay. I was doing my best to dodge between them when Mall's best steam-whistle tones nearly got me hanged in a stray loop. 'Hoi, beauteous Ganymede! Sliding off like a shovelboard shilling? We'll warp her in – come lend the weight of your arm! *Hands to the capstan!*'

I couldn't quite remember who the hell Ganymede was and I wasn't sure I wanted to; but at least it was something I could do. We heaved the long bars from their

171

racks, thrust them through the slots and bent our backs to them.

Mall kicked back the pawl and hopped neatly out of our way, onto the capstan's scarred top. 'Heave, my sweet roarers! Heave, my ruddy rufflers! Heave your ways to the booze-ken! Bend your backs to the wapping-shop! What, sweat so o'er a feather? Man-milliners all, the best of you! Scarce fit to poke a shag-ruff!' She unslung the violin from her shoulder and scraped a swinging tune that was obviously a local favourite.

> *Oh once I 'ad a German girl,*
> *But she was fat an' lazy –*
> *Way haul away, we'll haul away, Joe!*
> *Then I 'ad a Yankee girl,*
> *She damn near drove me crazy!*
> *Way haul away, we'll haul away, Joe!*

As the shantymen – and women – worked their way down some national characteristics I'd never have suspected, the crippled *Defiance* was drawn in alongside the wharf. I bent my back with the rest, but once the fenders boomed against the side, the ropes were made fast and the gangplanks crashed into place, that was the end of my usefulness. The flurry of activity redoubled; everyone was either shouting orders or obeying them, or both. Nobody actually told me to get lost; but somehow I couldn't seem to find a spot of the deck where somebody didn't have a really good urgent reason for apologetically but firmly elbowing me out of the way.

I couldn't resent it, either. I knew I was lucky the crew were still so intent on the chase, after the bloody rebuff we'd suffered – whether it was revenge, or general hatred for Wolves, or the money I'd offered that drove them. It occurred to me then that these half-immortals must have a strange attitude to money. They could never be sure they had enough. They'd know it was almost inevitable they'd run out of it, sooner or later – and equally, that there was no point in lingering too long in one place to earn a lot, because that would shorten their lives, drag them back towards the Core or whatever they called it. No wonder they were so keen on trade! And so eager to earn large amounts quickly, even in ways as dangerous as this.

But I hadn't any of those drives. There was nothing I could do, and I was stiff, sticky, dirty and depressed. If I wanted some privacy and peace of mind I'd either to retreat to what was left of my cabin, or escape down the gangplank to the wharfside. I chose the latter, but my foot had no sooner touched *terra firma* than the mate and a party of seamen came clattering after me, barged me — very apologetically — aside, scrambled up on a long flatbed wagon drawn by a team of four immense horses, and trundled off into the shadows of the wharfside buildings. These were nothing like the grim walls of stone and brick I'd left behind. Just as decrepit, though — clapboard mostly, painted in what the lanterns told me were faded pastel colours, plastered with illegible shreds of posters. The windows were mostly boarded or broken, and grass grew around their stone steps. I was just about to sit down on one when a party of sailors came struggling ashore with huge sausages of canvas, evidently what sails had been salvaged, and began to spread them out across the cobbles, right to the foot of my step. Where they elbowed me — very apologetically, of course — aside. Never mind peace of mind; I wasn't even getting to rest the other end.

Leaving the sailmakers to whistle and swear over the shot-damage, I wandered away down the wharf and peered around the first corner I came to. It was a street, like any other dockside street I'd seen, but less well lit. God alone knew what the two lamps visible were burning; it wasn't gas or electricity — with that dim little flame it could be anything from colza oil to blubber. It told me nothing at all about where we were, or what kind of town it was; I was wondering if I dared look a little further when I noticed the figure standing hunched and abject under one of the lamps. Indistinct in the warm hazy air, and yet oddly familiar; somebody I'd seen before, somebody I recognized by their stance alone — and there couldn't be many of those.

I took a step forward. It gave a great start, as if it had seen me, and ran a few steps out into the road, towards me. Then it hesitated, half turned as if called away, and stood irresolute in the middle of the dim road. I hesitated too, not sure who or what I was seeing; but I was still within earshot of the dock. One good shout would bring folk running; and the bare sword that tapped my calf at every step was a strange primitive comfort. Also, as I came nearer I could see that whoever it was wasn't very big; not a Wolf. A woman, more likely, from the flowing outline of the clothes; and the impression of familiarity was getting very strong. Maybe I was just following some dockside tart – though after Katjka I'd be slow to take even one of them for granted. This one was shorter than her, though; more of a height with ...

With Clare? I shook off the thought. A couple of steps more and I'd see more clearly – but then the figure gave another great start. It looked wildly down a narrow side-street to the right, then threw up its hands and waved me frantically back. I stopped, clutched at my sword and saw the figure whip this way and that like an animal caged within high walls. Then it whirled as if despairing and bolted towards the mouth of the side street. I called out. It glanced around, caught its foot on the curb and sprawled headlong – not exactly suspicious or threatening. I ran towards it as it picked itself painfully up, and for an instant I caught a glimpse of swinging hair, long hair. I couldn't see the colour – but it was the length of Clare's, at least. But with another panicky gesture whoever it was limped off into the shadowy street, and as I reached the corner I heard hobbling steps slapping away along the pavement.

Not being a total idiot, I didn't rush in after it. Carefully I drew my sword, and stopped to let my eyes adjust. They did, and there was nobody lurking, nowhere for them to lurk against high concrete walls featureless as a jail. The road was uneven, puddled with glinting water, the long pavements were clear of everything except garbage – quite a lot of that – and those painful steps went on, with just a hint of gasping breath. I ran, leaping the puddles, skirting the softly-blowing shreds of paper and plastic, and in the gleam of a brighter lamp at streets' end I glimpsed the figure again – slim, slight, limping desperately along with arms akimbo and hair flying. Not Clare; she was less delicate, more solidly built. But still that unnerving hint of the familiar, infuriating me, under-mining all my cautious instincts with the desperate need to see. Where was the sun? We'd been all night on the river; surely it must be rising soon?

Left around corners limped my shadow-hare, left, left and right again. I darted after it, swinging round the lamp-posts like a child for speed. Then a new street opened onto a sudden brightness I found blinding; all I could make out at first were the rows of white lights that seemed to hang unsupported like stars in the hazy air, and among them, above a mass of glittering reflections, tall shafts of shimmering movement. My dazzled eyes rebelled at those dancing, glassy columns; the sound alone told me it was a fountain. Beyond it, beneath a shadowy row of arches, its reflections danced – and across them that shadow flickered, slipping from arch to arch. It was some kind of piazza, lined with shop windows dark and empty now; what shops I didn't stay to see. My running footfalls rang echoes from the roof. We were in a city square, the hare and I, brightly lit by the white globes gleaming down from elegant wrought-iron lamp-holders on the high stone walls, from ornately fluted standards ringing the railings of the garden at its heart. And down its pathways, clipped and civic, the dark figure glided, beneath the hooves of a rearing statue and beyond, towards a white wall that towered over the far side of the square, higher than all the rest. Three sharp towers loomed out of the night, the middle one tallest – no, those were crosses on top. Three spires. It was some kind of church, or cathedral more likely; but odd, outlandish with its stacked columns and narrow-arched windows, and in the midst of them all a clock. Like places I'd seen in Spain or Italy, the kind they called romanesque – and come to think of it, the rest of the square had the same sort of look. We might have been somewhere in Spain – only not quite. So where the hell was I? Correction – plain where. They wouldn't have cathedrals in hell.

Flagpoles stood stark and empty. Signs were too far for me to read without turning aside. And there in the gloom by the great barred door lurked my quarry, hesitant, fleeting, poised as if to dart inside – why? To seek sanctuary – from me?

I slowed down, walked evenly, lightly towards it, closer and closer. Till I might have lunged forward and grabbed it. But I stopped, hesitant; and the moment it saw that the figure gestured again, desperately, and backed away towards the shadowy mouth of the narrow street behind. I'd come close enough to catch a gleam of dark eyes, a flash of a parchment-colored cheek, no other detail. Who had I known with any such coloring? Except ...

The figure whirled about and ducked around the corner. I sprang after it; and found it there, standing, its back to me, as if gazing at the sky. A sky filling with light now, so that the surrounding rooftops stood out in sharp silhouette – but the light was white, and it didn't drown the stars. My hair bristled. The sun rising when the moon should have, that was bad enough. But the moon in place of the sun – a new night, in place of a dawn and an end of deep shadows – That was far worse. I took two short steps forward, caught the figure by the shoulder, and felt a loose light cloak, almost a shawl, fall from the head. It turned sharply.

'I'm sorry.' I stammered idiotically, like anyone who's accosted the wrong person, blinking hastily around for the real shadow. The face beneath the long hair was a man's, lined and bony and sickly sallow, the livid lips set thin and hard. 'I thought –'

Then the eyes met mine. The malevolent glitter in them lanced into me, diamond-hard, chilling – the triumphant eyes of the knave-card. And I *had* seen that face before! Where? A fleeting glimpse – a red car, madly driven ... The thin lips split in a soundless crow of laughter, mocking, horrible. Instinctively I flung my sword up between us, as if to ward off a blow; but the shadow-

176

man only skipped back and fled. I bolted after him, furious now, fury fed on fear. This time there was no dodging, and no limp; the street was straight and he ran, fast, one block and across a road against lights, then another, with me never more than a sword's length from his heels. Until, in the middle of the third block – he was not there. I skidded stumbling to a halt, stared wildly around, slashed at the air, at nothing. Then I gagged at a brief whiff of a horrible smell, like vomit. And that was it; I was alone.

Had he meant to lose me, whoever he was? He could damn well think again. I'd been ready for that. I'd kept track of every turn. I knew just which way we'd come, and where the river must be from here. Wherever here was ...

I slid the sword back into my belt, and glanced around. High old walls, some of them stone, small barred windows – it looked strangely familiar somehow. Yes; these were warehouses, mostly Victorian by the look of them and pretty decrepit. But here and there ornate signs stretched out across walls cleaner than the rest, window-frames newly painted; there was even a flash of pink neon. Another disco? Just the same sort of area, trendy *chic* creeping like a naked hermit crab into the shells of old solid commerce. But where? The neon sign spelt out *Praliné's* – French-sounding, which meant precisely nothing; cafés in Moscow have French names. Anyhow, this didn't smell like France – or Moscow either, some-how; there was a big-city sourness in the warm humid air, an unholy blend of traffic fumes and junk-food frying and aromatic plants that was wholly new to me. These were backstreets, with nobody about to ask. But just ahead there was more light, and the distant hum of traffic. I was curious; I went to look.

The street I emerged into was startling. No more warehouses; it was wide and well-lit and lined with houses, terraces of tall dignified houses in reddish brick. They had that elusive European look about them again, especially along their upper frontage, where a kind of continuous gallery ran, forming deep balconies under the common roof. Houseplants and large bushes grew there in tubs, bays and mimosas and others I didn't know at all, exotic, elegant, airily graceful, trailing their foliage down over the ornate ironwork railings. But these houses had been restored, too; most of them were shopfronts, now, or cafés – some open. I strolled towards the nearest, and the warm night air rose up and hit me with the rich aromas of coffee and frying onions and hot pastry, and the blare of taped jazz. And suddenly I was so hungry I could have wept.

Hungry for more than food, too; it was a glimpse of civilization, of sanity – or at least of the kind of madness I knew. But would they take my kind of money here? I felt in my pockets. In an inner pocket were a few small coins, very heavy – gold pieces, of some kind I hadn't seen, decorated with peculiar writing and elephants; they must be Jyp's. All my ordinary money was in the pockets of my own clothes, on shipboard; and I began to feel very uneasy. I ought to be getting back. But I couldn't resist peering in the window, seeing what kind of people were there. They were my own kind, exactly my own kind; they could have come from any country in the world, just about – mostly young, mostly Caucasian, but a good few blacks and Orientals too, a cheerful cosmopolitan crowd shouting so loudly over the jazz that I couldn't make out the language. There was a menu, but the window was so steamed over I couldn't make it out. And the café's sign read *Au Barataria*. Which was where, exactly?

A young couple came out, and feeling a complete idiot I stepped up to them. The girl's face, flushed and pretty, twisted; the boy's darkened and he pulled her sharply aside. I shrugged, and let them pass; nice manners they had here. I strolled down the road. Here was a bookshop window still lit, and all the titles in English, by God! Only one gaggle of bestsellers looks pretty much like another to me. What I buy is *Time* and *The Economist*; so that didn't tell me too much either. Next came a men's boutique full of black leather and called, if you'll believe it, *Goebbels*. That only went to prove that really bad taste is universal. And after that, a video shop, with just two or three cases on view; the titles were English, all right, but a little specialized – *Pretty Peaches, Pussy Talk, Body Shop*. Well, yes. Where the hell was this, the Costa Brava? The food smelt too appetizing for that.

Here came somebody else to ask, a hefty black man; but before I so much as opened my mouth I almost got a fist in it. The last day or so hadn't exactly taught me to turn the other cheek, but I restrained myself; starting trouble now might be just the wrong thing. A more respectable citizen, middle-aged and fat, was hurrying down the far pavement; I strode over to intercept him, but before I got beyond the 'Excuse me, sir –' he thrust something into my hands and scuttled off at a rate he wasn't built for. I gaped after him, then down at my hand. A few silvery coins; I picked up the two largest, and saw the eagle on each, soft-edged with wear. Quarters; twenty-five cents; hot damn, I was in America.

I stood there giggling helplessly to myself. In a night and a day – most of the latter spent drifting – I'd managed to cross the Atlantic. If I ever got the hang of how, I could play hob with the export business, that was for sure.

Or ... how long had it actually taken me? Things had been happening with time. And suddenly childhood fairy tales came back to me, about the king who'd returned from under the hill – and this, after all, was the land of Rip van Winkle ...

Suddenly I wasn't giggling any more. For all the warmth of the night I felt pinched and cold like a returning ghost, a pathetic shadow in the twilight peering in at the warmth of life it had been shut out from for so long. Now I had to know when I was, as well as where. I glanced hungrily at a café, and stifled the thought; fifty cents wouldn't buy the water in my coffee, if this was anything like New York. A squat blue bin across the street was a newspaper vending machine; that would help! I hurried back across the street – and stopped dead in the middle. Now I knew why people were shying away from me.

Just the way I'd shied away from lurches, drunks and dropouts. There I was, reflected in a dress-shop window, a grotesque ghost hovering over the stilted dummies inside. A gaping thug, wild-haired, soot-smeared, unshaven, dressed in skin-tight leather that bared arms seamed with small burns and scars, a gaudy braid band like gang colours around my forehead, and a four-foot sword dangling along my leg – God knows, *I* would've run away. Maybe Jyp was right and the sword, at least, they wouldn't notice; but what was true for him might not be for me. I was too much a part of all this.

Then a truck came roaring down on me without even trying to brake, and I leaped for the sidewalk like an electrified frog. I flipped the driver a gesture, then remembered and stuck up the single finger they understood over here. Not that I altogether blamed him, though, any more than the touchy black character. I looked barking mad and dangerous as hell. I hurried to the machine, thumbed my coins and thrust them in. Just enough – I yanked out the paper and stared. The *New Orleans States-Item*, published the fourth –

The day after I'd left. New Orleans. A day and a night – right. That was all there was to it. I felt my legs begin to tremble under me. It was true, then … I let the paper fall, turned and ran back the way I'd come, away from lights and cafés and Creole cooking odours and iron balconies, ran like hell for the river and the wharf.

Back to the square I raced, sure of every turn, and came out just by the cathedral, crossed the gardens at full tilt – astonishing some late-night strollers – and ducked panting into the street I'd left. From there it was easy, round every turn just as I'd remembered it, and my memory didn't so much as falter once. It was easier on foot, this kind of thing, when you could take your time spotting landmarks, when you didn't have to make snap decisions where to turn. Not that I didn't give one great sigh of relief, though, when I finally turned into the road where that lying apparition had first hooked me, and saw the broad river gleaming like dull copper under the hazy moon. The Mississippi, no less. Well, I'd something to ask Le Stryge about, at any rate.

From there on in I strolled quietly, getting my breath

back. I couldn't hear any noise of hammering; maybe they'd stopped work for the night. I couldn't blame them; two in a row was a bit much for anyone. I turned the corner to the wharf; and then I came to a dead halt and clutched at the side of the building, as if the running had suddenly seized my legs and turned them to water under me.

It wasn't the same building. It was no clapboard shack; there were none, not up or down the broad concrete wharves that stretched out along the river on either side. It was a modern wall of corrugated alumin- ium, just like all the others I could see, up and down. Beside some there were ships, all right – big cargo carriers with never a mast or smokestack between them, flanked by modern container cranes or grain or mineral hoppers whose banks of floodlights carved out little wedges in the night. Of the *Defiance*, of all or anything that had brought me here, there was no sign at all.

I could have gone rampaging up and down those wharves, looking; I didn't. I knew too damn well what had happened. I'd feared it from the moment I saw that paper, that date – though maybe it was already too late by then. Maybe it had been since that moon rose. My assumptions, my Core-bred basic instincts, had tangled with the reality that had brought me here. I'd pushed on too deep, gone back into the Core, seen too much of it that didn't want to let go its grip. As, no doubt, the Knave meant to happen. And some deeper part of me, despairing of fulfill- ing the purpose that had driven me so far, so fast, had retreated into what it knew best and shut out the rest. In a foreign country, without papers, passport, money or even a good explanation why I was here, it had stranded me, left me high and dry on a desolate shore. From the *Defiance*, from Mall and Jyp, from all hope of help, it had cut me off.

There'd been no dawn. Maybe there never would be, any more. There was nothing before me but streets, a cityful of corners to turn, hoping that around one, or the next ... hoping against hope. How long would that take? Empty and sick, I gripped the warehouse wall, staring up at the blank little windows high above, eyes as blind as mine to what I most needed to see. It was behind them somewhere, beneath all this modern overlay, the past sheathed in sheet steel – or coffined?

'Hey!' roared a hoarse angry voice. '*Hey you!* Whatcha doin' there? C'mon, beat it!' I almost drew on him, but remembered in time that in these parts even nightwatchmen would carry a gun; better not call attention to the sword, anyhow. A wavering flashlight tracked me like a spotlight as I stalked away, around the first corner that opened and into the shadows of unlit alleys. Darkness closed on me like a vast fist, and the shadows flooded into my head. Lost, alone, I stumbled blindly through stinking puddles, deeper and deeper into night.

At first I still tried to remember where I was going, turning this way and that, seeking another way back through the darkened ways to the river and the docks. But soon enough my tired mind lost track, and soon after that I forgot the very direction of the docks; but I kept walking, because there was nowhere to stop. Now and again I struggled to think. What did any marooned tourist do? Go see the British consul – with a convenient case of amnesia? I'd be flown home, then. With a lot of explaining to do; about here, about gold, about ... what had happened to Clare. I'd be lucky to stay out of Broadmoor. And with her on my conscience, maybe I wouldn't want to ...

After a while I found myself wandering out of the unlit maze into wider streets again, with lights and lit windows; but which streets and where I no longer cared. Some were like the elegant old brick houses I'd seen; others were garishly new, lined with blazing shop windows and neon signs – but all empty, all bare, all dead. I barged into – I didn't know what; lamp standards, trash cans, street litter. I heard voices, angry voices, didn't know where they came from. Perhaps there were people on those sidewalks, then; but if there were, I wasn't seeing them. Only the cars moved, hissing past, featureless, driverless blurs of light and noise. Sometimes, suddenly, they'd come at me with howling horns, from all directions it seemed, and I'd have to dodge and weave my way through, and stagger off before they could come around again.

My sight dimmed. My sense of isolation got worse. The noise, the colours around me, everything my senses told me, seemed to make less and less sense, to add up to nothing, no coherent picture. I felt I had to keep moving at all costs, so this horrible inchoate world couldn't close in around me and cut me off forever. But I was very tired now, and under my feet from time to time the ground would lurch suddenly and make me stumble. From overhead came a sound I knew, the whine of a circling jet; but I saw only a pattern of beating lights gliding over emptiness, and hid my eyes. Shadow and quiet drew me, and somehow, after hours, maybe, I found myself drifting along lesser ways, suburban streets lined with houses, more homely, less hostile. Yet the lit windows glared down balefully at me, and the cars still hissed by.

Until, with electrifying suddenness, one of them screeched in behind me, right to the sidewalk's edge. I swung about in sudden fright, and grabbed at my sword – then froze, half-crouching, as a blue-white light flicked across my eyes. I saw nobody, but I heard the voices, hard and harsh.

'*That's him! We got him!*'

'*Station? Contact at – yah, goin' after him now!*'

'*Watch it, watch it – he's a big one – keep it friendly* – hey, feller!'

I started and jumped back as doors slammed hollowly.

'Jesus, what's that? Machete?' I looked down. Instinctively I'd half-drawn the sword, and it spat back the blue light like icy fire.

'*Hallo? Suspect is armed, repeat armed –*'

'Hey feller! We jes' wanna word, nobody's goin'get hurt! So you put that stickah 'way now, hear?'

I backed off, kept on backing. My head was horribly clear all of a sudden. There was no way I'd get to the docks from a police cell – or a madhouse. I could see the policeman now, a burly middle-aged black man with fierce grizzled whiskers; he was trying to sound reassuring, but his fat hand hovered near the unclipped flap of his holster. The other one would be covering him from the car, no doubt. I looked around desperately, and again it was darkness and shade that caught my eye; across the road a gap opened between the houses, its sagging wire fence overhung by spreading trees. I edged back some more, then relaxed a little, bowed my head, heard the fat man's sigh of relief – and swept the sword right out of its scabbard in a hissing arc. I wasn't as well in control of it as I thought; it must have nearly parted those whiskers. He leaped backward with a startled yell, tripped over a hydrant and sprawled on his back. That opened my way for a flying leap, right over him, onto the bonnet of the squad car and out into the road, luckily empty. I reached the grass strip in a couple of bounds, narrowly stopped myself running out into the path of a highly decorated van, then ran anyway because a bullet had just gone whistling past. The van screeched around in a tyre-stripping arc, horn blaring, onto the grass between me and the squad car. I reached the fence, vaulted over it and landed ankle-deep in litter-strewn grass before I realized that – in a manner of speaking – I wasn't alone.

If I'd known more about the city I might have been less surprised at landing in a graveyard – and at the aspect of it, vast stretches of huge and imposing tombs, vandalized, neglected and overgrown. Right now they didn't worry me in the least. This ruined city of the dead looked like the safest place to hide I could imagine. I went belting off among the graves like someone desperate to get back to his own. Some way behind me I heard the sound of somebody else trying to vault the fence, and failing dismally. My conscience shrivelled again; I'd nothing at all against those cops. I didn't like doing this one bit – but no way were they going to stop me now.

I wove and dodged among the ranks of the dead, ducking from path to path, turning and turning till I lost track of time and direction. Now and again I slipped in among half-fallen models of Greek and Roman temples, gasping for breath in the heavy air, to listen for pursuit till

I was sure there wasn't any. Nothing stirred, not even a breath of wind. I didn't blame them for giving up; you could have played hide-and-seek all night in that place, and the weed-grown gravel paths didn't show tracks. Come to think of it, I wasn't too sure which way I'd come myself. I looked around. Tombs, tombs, tombs as far as I could see, a skyline of crosses and wreaths and sculpted angels and other less probable things. Nothing stirred, not even a breath of wind in this leaden air; no sign that there was a city of the living anywhere out there. It gave the cemetery a timeless, suspended feeling. I must be right in the heart of the place. At least it was pretty much flat. I set out, heading what I guessed was away from the way I'd come in. Nothing to do but walk till I hit a wall –

I shivered suddenly, though the night was warm. The chill that shot through me was so acute it was like an electric shock. I'd brushed against something, not grass, not stone –

I almost laughed. It was just a little scarecrow, no higher than my waist, a battered old hat and weather-bleached tailcoat hung on crossed poles, bulked out by the weeds that had grown up beneath it. Almost laughed; but the chill had caught my breath too strongly, and my heart was thudding wildly. I looked wildly around, but there was nothing else, nothing except a warm wind stirring the trees; nothing different about this particular little knot of tombs. Broken down, broken into, sprayed with graffitti like the rest; unusual, though, these whorls and spirals and scratchy circles. As if they'd been put on with luminous paint, or attacked by some kind of decay. I'd seen something like them somewhere before, but not so clear. Here, in the deepest darkness, a faint green phosphoresence seemed to hang around them – not so faint, either. Once your eyes got used to it you could practically see by it ...

A faint scraping scrabble startled me. I whirled around with visions of some vengeful and trigger-happy cop creeping up on me; but this was too small for that. Beneath one defaced stone the rich grass was twitching; some little animal I'd disturbed, then. What did they have here? Possums, garter snakes ... I bent down to look.

Then I sprang back with a shriek that must have split the air across the cemetery. The scrawled mandala-shape on the stone blazed out fire-bright, and against it waved the hand that had thrust out of the earth, right at my face. The earth heaved under me, almost tipping me onto it, but I kept my balance, staggering, and turned to run. The gravel swelled and hummocked in front of me as if some huge worm-thing tunnelled beneath, throwing me back. I fell; the sword in one hand, I flung out the other to catch myself and dug my fingers into the gravel to steady me – then snatched them away, barely in time. Beneath the pebbles something shut with a click, like a fish snapping after a fly. The ground convulsed again. Bushes wavered wildly and fell, first one headstone then another tipped over with a flat crump, others shuddered and crumbled. The simpering head of a marble angel toppled, bounced and rolled almost to my feet. All around me the soil was lifting, fingers clawing, an arm thrusting upward like a plant growing in a stop-motion film ...

And behind me there was a nasty little tittering sound.

I spun around. The little scarecrow had grown as well, until it towered over me, a huge thin figure barring my passage – and lifting one of those empty sleeves. Weeds rustled within it, weeds with long downreaching roots, weeds grown fat on rich food. A single finger, skinny and gnarled – twig or bone? – crooked at my face. The ancient hat tilted slightly, and a sound rustled at my ears, hissing and tickling like a close-up whisper – only in both ears at once. A voice. Like dead leaves one minute, the next liquid, gargling, horrible.

Bas 'genoux, fi' de malheu'! Fai'e moa honneu'!

It was almost worse to realize it made sense. It was some kind of bastard French or pidgin dialect, like none I'd ever heard, thickly accented; but I could understand. Telling me to bow down and worship –

Li es' royaume moan –
Li est moa qui 'regne 'ci!
Ne pas passer par' li
Sans hommage 'rendu –

Whose kingdom? Homage to who? I couldn't move. Sheer panic, like a gust from an open window, whipped up my thoughts and scattered them every which way. With a sudden squeaky rustle the finger jabbed out, right into the centre of my forehead. It struck the sweatband. Something like a high-voltage spark or a soundless explosion went off, a glare of light behind my eyes instead of in front.

'Like hell!' I bayed. Too scared to think. I slashed out. It was with luck and instinct and not much else that I used my swordhand. It was like cutting a hedge. The derby flew up, an end of stick went whipping away and the ragged tailcoat collapsed in a boneless flurry of arms. Thick stalks whipped free, oozing stinking sap; pollen sprayed into my face like ancient gravedust and set me sneezing. Something – briarstems, maybe – clawed at my ankles. I yelled again, leaped free of them and bolted for my life – or maybe something more. Right now that cop with his gun would have been the sweetest sight I could imagine – or, failing that, some real light. There almost seemed to be some, there ahead of me; a warm hazy glow, high above the shadows of the grave, infinitely warm and secure-looking. I hared off that way, fast as I could. Whatever it was, right then I wanted it, badly. I was sacred it would just slip away and leave me to the darkness rustling at my heels.

It didn't slip away. It shone steady, and grew till the trees stood out against it, a broad beacon of normality – street lights, maybe. All I could hear was my blood and breath, labouring both; steel bands squeezed at my chest and head. But the tombstones were thinning, opening out; there was a wall here, and beyond it more fence, less dilapidated than the rest. Without breaking stride I sprang up onto one of the stones ranged against the wall, from that to the wall and clutched at the wires. Fortunately they weren't electrified or barbed, and with my last burning breath I swung myself up, over, crashed down among rough weeds some twelve feet below and ran, ran until I tripped over something hard and fell sobbing to my knees at the margins of the light.

Then I cowered down, shrank back, as the ground quivered. With a rushing, hissing rumble and clack and a lonely, hooting cry something vast went flicking across my sight, an endless phalanx of speeding shadows, blotting out the light, the world.

When the thunder passed and the light was clear again, some fragment of my wits came slinking back. I looked up, gasping, and began to pick myself up, rather shamefaced. Pure luck that freight train hadn't come up this track instead of the other; next time it might. I'd blundered into some kind of marshalling yard, well lit but no safe place to wander. Miles better than that damn cemetery, though. Part of my mind was threshing furiously, fighting to rationalize what I'd just seen, to explain it away – an earth tremor, overheated imagination, anything. I ignored it. I was just too glad to be out of it. Then I froze; I heard a voice, not close, not far, clear and vehement in the still night.

'*I tell you, you go fuck around in that theah boneyard all you like, but you doan' get me –*' There, a few hundreds yards away down the track by the fence, sat a squad car with its lights flashing. And I realized the sickening inevitability of it, that they wouldn't have given up at all, just called up other cars to cover the likely exits. And this one, of all the luck, was mine; I knew that voice, and I sympathized. Staying on all fours, I began to inch forward.

'*Scared? Just you lissen a'me one damn minute, peckerhead – Hey!*'

I knew what that meant; I was off even before the doors slammed, the lights swung around towards me, the siren came on. I heard the tyres crunch across the gravel, and it was time to bolt again before I'd even got my breath.

I couldn't run much longer, but nothing would get

me back into that graveyard. Somewhere in the yard another train was coming. I limped across the tracks, into the shadow of some standing freight cars; I thought of getting into one, if only to grab a few minutes' rest, but they were very securely chained up, and the shadow seemed like no shelter at all. I ducked over the coupling and through, landed right in the path of the oncoming train and found a new turn of speed; behind me I heard gravel spray as the squad car swerved aside. Across more tracks I ran, between stolid lines of silent cars, until suddenly I was at another fence — and not more than a hundred yards up, an open gate. Wouldn't the cops head for it? I took the chance, there weren't any others. I made it, and suddenly I was free of all fences, running like a madman through an empty street; but behind me the siren was getting louder. And was that another ahead, around the corner of this tall building? I could turn this way — or that. Towards the sound — or away. That was no siren. I made my choice, and turned the corner.

I could have laughed, if my aching lungs had let me. The street was wide, glistening in the night-haze as if from recent rains; tall buildings, featureless in the night, loomed over it like chasm walls. In one narrow side door-way an old man stood, the only living soul in all that great gorge of a place, a black man in a shabby overcoat, playing a mournful trumpet; and that was the sound. I ran down towards him, and saw the heavy dark glasses he wore, the placard in front of him, the tin cup. He stopped playing suddenly, lowered his trumpet, and I swerved wide so as not to frighten him, wishing I could call out to him. But he called out to me instead.

'*Son!* Hey, sonny! Which way de fi-ah?'

Almost instinctively I came to a halt; it was a start-ling voice, deep and commanding, to come from that stooped old frame. He had an odd sing-song accent, too, not at all American. I gasped, tried to answer and couldn't; he didn't wait for one. 'You run 'way from de man? De poleece? Uh-huh, that's what I hear, those 'larums.' The wrinkled old face creased up in a wide grin, over chipped teeth. 'We fix dat. You just hunkah down behin' me heah, boy – in de doorway, okay? Oh-kay! You all snug now?' And without waiting for another answer he lifted his trumpet and began to play again. I knew the tune – 'Saint James Infirmary', mournful as hell and too horribly appropriate. I squatted down in the doorway, shivering and wheezing, struggling to get my breath back. I peering up at the old man's back, shabby and bent but surprisingly broad, and the square of sky framed in the door arch above.

> Well, I went down to the Saint James
>   Infirmary,
> I saw my baby there,
> She was layin' on a cold marble table,
> So pale, so cold, so fair ...

My mind filled in the words, and I wished it wouldn't. One of the old original blues, so old you could trace its roots back to ancient folksongs –

A siren wailed discords along the high walls, then cut them short in a screech of brakes; blue light pulsed through the door arch. 'Hey, pops!' yelled a voice, not the same one now. 'You see a big guy come runnin' this way? White boy, wavin' a machete or sumpn' – a real crazy –'

'Son,' chuckled the old trumpet player. 'It's maybe twenny yeahs gone since I saw anythin' wuth a good goddam! Or I wouldn't be standin' roun' on dis heah chilly stoop, believe me-ee!'

'Oh,' said the cop, sounding slightly abashed. 'Right, yah. Uh, you hear anyone, then? A couple of minutes back?'

The old man shrugged. 'Someone runnin', five minutes back. 'Long Decatur Street way, maybe. I wuz playin' mah horn –'

'Okay, pops!' A coin jingled into the cup. 'Better get out of the wet, hear? Somebody might take a shine to your cup, this hour o'the morning!' The siren came on again, and the light slid away from the doorway; I sagged with relief. The old man took up where he'd left off, till the siren had died away completely, then rounded out the

190

tune with a cheeky little flourish and began to shake the spit out of his trumpet.

'Nice 'nuff boys – but dey're not makin'em any bright-ah!' He turned and grinned at me, and I had the odd feeling he could see me very well. But he fumbled about just the same for the card at his feet, and I picked it up and handed it to him. It carried an incredibly ancient-looking religious print, showing a 'Black Heaven' like something out of *Green Pastures*, and beneath it in crude lettering *The Opener of the Ways*. He tucked it carefully away in the doorway, and sat carefully down beside me.

'Look,' I began, 'you got me out of one hell of a hole – I haven't done anything, but – damn, I just don't know how to thank you –' Then I realized I did. I fumbled in my pocket for Jyp's coins; I could pay him back later. I pressed two into the old man's palm, and he nodded and grinned again. 'Now mind,' I warned him. 'Those are gold. You can't spend it straight away, but you can sell it – it's not stolen or anything. Take them to a proper coin-shop if you can, not just a bank or a jeweller or a pawnbroker. Should be worth more than the weight of the gold alone.'

The old man listened gravely. 'Thank you, my good frien'. Dat's Christian kindness. Like this Saint James dey name de hospital fo', huh? Saint-Jacques, dey call him in de real ol' days – or Santiago …'

I chuckled. 'That's right, the Spanish founded the place, didn't they? You know your history.'

The old man laughed, pleased. 'Me? I jes' seen a lot, dat's all. And doan' forget. So many mem'ries, mah old cold back bends under de load!'

'Well, you could warm it up a bit now – get yourself a new coat, for a start.'

I hadn't meant it to sound patronizing, but it came out that way. The old man wagged his head amiably. 'Son, I thank you for the good advice! But I've learned some better. I give you it freely – when yo' very balls is freezin', rum's the only juice!'

'I'll bear that in mind,' I promised solemnly. 'Thanks again. But I'd better be off. The cops might come back, and I've got to get to the riverfront – to the docks – er, you

191

couldn't give me directions from here?'

He cackled, and heaved himself up before I could lift a hand to help. 'The docks, uh?' Again the glasses flashed at me with a peculiarly penetrating air. 'Dat's easily done, son. Easy.' He nodded casually down the street. 'A good Christian tune soon set you on yoah way!'

And before I could say a word, he clapped the battered trumpet to his lips and launched into a tune I recognized. '*Gospel Ship*' – a revivalist song, hardly jazz at all, but he made it swing. The trumpet wasn't mournful any more but sharp, a blade of blue notes slicing through the blackness. Its bright bell winked suddenly with reddish light, and mirrored, distorted, a web of black threads. Startled, I looked over my shoulder and saw the wedge of sky between the chasm walls turning paler, flooding with red in a tidal wave of dawn. And against that rising glow, like a winter treeline, a spiky tracery of masts stood silhouetted. Down the gloomy length of the street shone a single faint streak of gold, and danced in fire upon the bobbing trumpet.

I gaped a moment in wonder and fear, and then, forgetting everything, I began to run along that bright path. All around those gloomy walls the tune echoed, beat upon those blind windows –

> *I have good news to bring*
> *And that is why I sing –*
> *All my joys with you I'll share!*
> *I'm gonna take a trip*
> *On that ol' Gospel ship,*
> *And go sailin' through the air!*

The Last Trump should sound like that, maybe

> *I'm gonna take a trip*
> *On that ol' Gospel ship,*
> *I'm going' far beyond the sky,*
> *I'm gonna shout an' sing,*
> *Until the bell done ring,*
> *When I bid this world goodbye!*

192

I bounded along that silent stream of dawn light like a child splashing through puddles. Then I remembered I hadn't said goodbye to the old man, if man he was, and turned to wave. But his back was turned to me already, shuffling along towards Decatur or wherever, still playing, his card tucked tightly under his arm. I waved, anyway; I guessed he had more ways than one to see. And then from the docks I heard the shrill whistle of a steam-tug, and my heart missed a beat. Amid the forest of masts something was stirring, sliding past them, out into the stream; tall masts, not smokestacks. I ran like mad for the river.

No way could I have reached it in time, but I ran anyway. They might still be in hailing range – or I might get another boat to follow them ...

I found my feet slipping on dawn-slick cobbles as I reached the wharf, steadied myself on the wall at the corner and felt the paint on the warped clapboard crackle and peel under my hand. The Core had lost its hold, and I was back. But I felt no exaltation, only amazement. For the shape that slid away down the gold-tracked waters, like a shadow of night slinking off before the dawn, had three tall masts, not two, and its high transom loomed level with the capitals of the smokestacks. I gaped up and down the dock, guessed at my way and began to run again.

The guess was right. It was no more than twenty minutes later I bounded up the springy gangplank and collapsed wheezing onto the deck, newly smooth and smelling richly of tar and linseed and sappy wood. From the quarterdeck came a stampede, Jyp and the others practically tumbling down the companionway, with old Stryge wavering excitedly after them. A man and a woman of the deck watch more or less scooped me up and sat me on the hold grating, but I had hardly enough breath to speak.

'They – here –'

'Aye, aye, 'tis known!' said Mall soothingly. 'Spare your words till the wind's back i'your sail. You're not hurt otherwise? A mercy, better far than we'd feared.'

'That's so, shipmate,' remarked Jyp, shaking his head with laconic relief. 'Glad to have you back live and whole, never more so. Moment we missed you we sic'd old Stryge on your tail – and when he ups and says you've been drawn off by a sending, lured back into the Core – and into a trap – well ... He said he'd sent out a call on your behalf, and that was the best he could do.' He spat over the rail at the dockside. 'Hell, we maybe should've guessed there might be trouble. One of the old slave trade centres, here – it's still lousy with *obeah*, voodoo, you name it; part of the legacy. But why should some local *bocor* beat the drums for us? That's what I don't get. We haven't trodden on anyone's toes here – hell, how'd they even get to hear about us?'

'From the *Chorazin!*' I wheezed.

'*What?*'

'That's what I was trying to tell you,' I croaked. 'It's been docked here, too, all the time – about a mile down-river on the far bank – I saw it pulling out, not long back –'

Pierce seized my shoulder. 'You're sure, lad – I mean, Master?'

'Yes, I'm sure – damn it, I was sent to see it –'

'*Masthead!*' bellowed Pierce.

The Stryge thrust his granite face unpleasantly close to mine. 'Sent? By whom? How?'

'A-an old black man, a busker – a street musician, *you* know –'

'*Deck! A smoking teakettle with a soot-black merchantman a'tow! A good league downriver!*'

'*All hands!*' roared Pierce. 'Mr Mate! Ashore with you and roust out that old tarrarag of a tugmaster! *All hands!* We must have hit her worse than we thought, she pulled in for repairs – and saw us come by – *hah!* How's *that* for defiance, my fine buckoes?'

Stryge's eye glittered frighteningly. 'What old man? Who answered? Who came?'

'A-an old busker, like I said – played the trumpet – he had a-a card, called himself the – *Opener of the Ways*, that was it –'

Stryge jerked back, Jyp whistled and choked on it, and Mall ran her hands through her hair. 'Faith, a pretty company to be keeping!'

'Look, he was kind, whoever he was! He hid me from the cops – he showed me the way back, the *Chorazin* – he saved my hide! My mind, too, maybe – after that thing in the cemetery I thought I was going off my trolley! Maybe he was the answer to that call of yours –'

'What thing?' demanded the Stryge, but in nothing like his normal snarl. I thought I saw a flicker of real feeling cross the stonily malevolent mask; something I might have welcomed, if it hadn't looked like fear. So I told him, and watched his face crumple. Jyp went ashen, and Mall, to my astonishment, sank to her haunches beside me and hugged me bruisingly hard.

'The Baron!' said Stryge with a high shaky cackle. 'And Legba! The imbecile boy escapes the Baron, meets Legba and calls him a blind old man! As if *he'd* come to my call, hah!'

'But who's to say he didn't?' rebuked Jyp softly. 'This – it's taking a shape I feared. More at stake than just a raid into the Core – or a girl getting shanghaied – much, much more. There's strong forces at play here, if the Invisibles are taking a hand.'

'More than a hand!' said Mall shrilly. 'D'you not see? It's sides they take – and when ever did they do thus? With Stephen here caught in the middle!'

Jyp clenched his fists. 'And good or bad, they're ill meddlers with men! Hoy, Mister Mate – what of the tug?'

'None to be had!' cried the breathless mate, scorning the plank and swinging himself aboard by the new mainstays. 'There was three fired up – but two spiked overnight, a' purpose! A mercy their boilers didn't blow to blazes! And the last the Wolves took, with pistol's point as fee! We'll needs wait hours!'

Pierce threw down his hat and stamped upon it. 'By Beelzebub's burning balls! And miss the dawn? Never! *Hands to the braces!* We'll after them under sail alone! We caught the bastards before and by hell's thunders we'll do it again, if it's up Satan's arsegut they flee us! *Topmen aloft! Leap to it, rum-rotted whoreson bitch-spawn you be –*'

The mate's leathery face rumpled uneasily. 'But cap'n – how'll we know their course to follow? We've no way –'

'Ah, but we have!' said Mall grimly. 'The Stryge may check it if he wills, but I doubt his divination will fare better. A contention's in hand among the Invisibles, t'would seem. So where else would the *Chorazin* be bound in such case, but to the island that's their home?'

Jyp smacked hand into palm. 'That's it! Well, skipper – for Hispaniola?'

'Aye, set your course,' muttered Pierce, the rage drained from him. 'Hispaniola! Hayti! There's a lee shore for the soul, a shoal of shadow all a-slather with blood and black arts. But if it must be, it must. Quartermaster, to the helm! And pray God that we are in time!'

CHAPTER EIGHT

THE DARK GREEN WALLS loomed above us, brooding, impenetrable, seething beneath a thunderous sky. Emerald fire flashed from the swords as they rang together. Mine was swatted aside like an annoying fly; the broadsword sizzled by an inch from my left armpit. Somehow I parried, jumped back, lifted my guard again, gasping. Several cuts had opened, and I winced as the sweat ran into them. We circled each other, feinting. Mall grinned; it wasn't the most reassuring sight. She was swaying hypnotically, like a cobra, picking her time and place to strike.

It'd been like that all the way from New Orleans, and I had the scars to prove it. Our frantic departure seemed to be paying off, at first. We fairly flew down that great river on the wings of the morning. Le Stryge claimed credit for the unexpectedly fresh wind in our sails, which went a long way to nullify the advantage of the Wolves' steam tow; but I was more inclined to credit Jyp's unfailing pilotage. I had the odd idea, watching him at the wheel, that that calm gaze of his was seeing through the veils of time and space, choosing some invisible thread of destiny and steering a straight course between its tortuous coils, sliding from one to another. I made the mistake of mentioning it to Mall as we snatched a bite of breakfast together on the foredeck.

'Not so odd a fancy, indeed,' was her reply. 'Each one has his inborn qualities, 'tis thought; yet few live long enough to bring them to their fullest flower. Fast within the Hub, men like him are but clever navigators; yet out upon the Wheel they'll soon learn to sight you on a star through every twist and turn of shifting time. Only here does the true power blossom from within the skill and the learning that are its swaddlings. You, my friend, you might be a mighty trader in time, perhaps; though you

197

would needs first fill that void in you, feed your starved spirit that it may grow. 'Tis more than passion you lack. Men need a cause in living, lest others find it for them.' She dunked the last crust of bread in her coffee-bowl and drained it to the grounds. 'And, since we're turned the idle philosopher, Stephen my lad, high time I kept my word and opened to you something of my own peculiar mystery. My lectures are curt, but my reasonings cut deep! Up, then, and a'guard!'

So my lessons began, in swordsmanship and in other things also, perhaps. Right from the start, from the stance, they were severely practical; we fenced with naked edge and unbarred point, which soon teaches you respect for what you're messing with. At first, on our way downriver, Mall only marked each touch by landing light playful taps with the flat of her blade. It was almost a compliment when she began to deal out real stinging slaps.

By then we were at sea. We'd made such a quick passage I'd begun to hope we might find the black ship's sails still in sight when we left the delta, or get her last heading from the tug as it returned. Instead we passed its smoking remains on a sandbank.

'What do we do now?' repeated Jyp disgustedly, when I told him there was nobody left alive in the wreck. 'We'll set a good swift course for Hispaniola, that's what. But not the swiftest. We've got to overhaul the Wolves before they get there, if we can. There'll be some help awaiting them, you can depend on that; help we may not like. So, all along the way we search. We search like hell!'

And so by day and night we beat back and forth along the course, sweeping as wide as we dared; by day, over an ocean of dazzling blue, a vast sphere of sapphire, it seemed, upon which nothing stirred save schools of dolphin racing to play in our bow-wave, and great sleeting shoals of flying fish. By night –

But what lay beneath our hull by night was a question I only asked once. Jyp gazed out into infinity, and smiled. 'The seas east of the sun, west of the moon,' he said quietly. 'Between the Straits of the Night and the Sound of Morning they lie, beyond the Gates of Noon. The waves that break beneath charmed casements, beneath cloud-castle towers. There's others might give you plainer answers, but I tell it you straight, you wouldn't thank 'em. Some things're best seen for yourself – and one day, maybe, if you're in luck, you will.'

Which effectively silenced me. I never plucked up the nerve to ask anyone else. I was more than a little afraid what might happen if I couldn't believe the answer. But I kept being reminded of what I'd seen once, on a lonely night-flight back from some joyless business in France. Then, our small plane climbed between two layers of cloud, the one beneath level and rolling like a steel-blue sea, the one above heavier, craggier, foreboding as grey granite; one lone slash of pallid orange defined a horizon that would otherwise have been lost in trackless infinity. If I'd looked down, looked longer, would I have glimpsed tall masts above those cloudcrests, broad sails gliding towards that last distant light?

East-southeast that course led us, towards the Dry Tortugas and from there southeast again, between Great Bahama Bank and the haunted Havanaise coast to Windward Passage. In all that time we sighted few other sails, and none were black; nor, when we hailed them, had they sighted any. It didn't take us long to guess the Wolves were taking an eccentric course to avoid us – flattering, after a fashion. But it left Le Stryge as our main hope, and nobody liked that. He kept to his cabin, from which strange sounds and even stranger odours seeped, and emerged from time to time only to confirm that our quarry was ahead of us somewhere on more or less this bearing. Each time he seemed greyer and more exhausted. 'They grow harder to follow,' he growled, more than once. 'Something new reaches out to them, something that seeks to shield them from my sight. But it is not strong enough. Not yet.'

Meanwhile Mall systematically beat me black and blue. Did I land any back? Don't ask. At the end of a long day's swordplay I felt almost too stiff to walk. Not that I was complaining. If she was taking the time to give me a crash course in staying alive it was because she was afraid

I'd need it. And I knew how lucky I was to have such a exciting hellion of a teacher, able to make the air crackle yet never forgetting what it was like to be an awkward beginner. I remembered reading once that was a mark of true greatness in almost any field. When in our third day's lessons she suddenly started leaving delicate slices like paper cuts, that itched rather than hurt – at least till the sweat got at them – I began to feel like some kind of fighting man.

Also like some kind of masochist. But at least she knew where to stop. Just.

One bright noon – it might have been the fourth – the mastheads hailed their warnings, and we dropped everything and ran to the railings. But it was not black sails that lifted above the horizon. It was the jagged green fangs of a mountainous island, and for us they were emblems of failure. If Hispaniola was in sight, the chances were that we'd missed our foes, and that they were already there.

'And Clare –' I couldn't finish.

Jyp shook his head. 'Easy, man. Whatever they mean with her, it's some kind of ... of ritual; and they have their appointed places and times, all. Chances are it's not yet, they could hardly time their arrival so close – not after their little brush with us. And if they hadn't harmed her already, chances are they won't till then.'

'If the whole bloody business hasn't frightened her out of her mind already!'

'I doubt that,' said Mall, draping an amiable arm about my shoulder. 'We're harder than you'd gauge us, Stephen, our sex. She'll think herself snared in a nightmare, sure; but she's had a glimpse of hope. Not to lose heart, and fulfil it – that's your part. Play it to the hilts!'

On the last long tack south into Port-au-Prince the atmosphere aboard was electric. An unpleasant surprise could very well be waiting. Soon after sunrise we came sweeping into the mountain-ringed bay under full sail, guns primed and crews crouched ready behind closed ports, eyeing with deep suspicion every little isle and inlet big enough to mask a ship. But as the island's main port rose – or rather sprawled – ahead of us at bay's end, it was immediately obvious that no ship remotely large enough to be our Wolfish quarry was docked there.

In a spirit of glum anticlimax we brought the *Defiance* alongside a rickety wooden dock by a decrepit timber yard at the far end of the town. Le Stryge, complaining bitterly of exhaustion, was cajoled into trying his divination again. Meanwhile we sent parties ashore to poke about discreetly after any news. After the last little incident I, of course, wasn't allowed to go. They left me sitting on the rail, nursing my bruises, chewing my nails and glaring out at this city that was supposed to be too dangerous for me.

It didn't look it. It was nothing like approaching New Orleans up the dark Mississippi, night-bound and mysterious. The air was clear, cool, transparent, the freshening light striking every detail with stinging clarity. Not dangerous, or sinister – lazy, if anything, stretched out like a drowsy slut all across the flat shoreline, straggling back up the forested mountain slopes behind. Even along the seafront patches of untamed trees appeared between walls of white stone and sun-bleached planking, warped and salt-whitened, between elegant old villas in French or Spanish styles and dilapidated docks. In places the trees thinned out into patches of scrubby wasteland where yellowish oxen browsed, shaking their heads at the first flies. On the higher slopes clumps of the same thick greenery mingled randomly among clutches of sun-bleached buildings. Which was encroaching on which, the houses or the jungle? I couldn't say for sure. The twentieth century hadn't touched this place. There was no hum of motor traffic to be heard. Belated cockcrows drifted out to us, among the screams of flocking parrots; otherwise it was very quiet nearby. I couldn't even hear children's voices, about the most universal sound there is. All I could make out now and again was a constant dull pulsing, and chanting, perhaps, or wailing. It was the only unsettling note in the whole placid scene. Nothing dangerous about it; and yet the longer I watched and listened, the more the feeling grew on me that there was

201

something wrong, something hellishly wrong.

The twentieth century ...

Wait a minute. I'd read a lot about Port-au-Prince, hadn't I? A year or so back, when I'd been briefing one of Barry's pet clients on Caribbean trade conditions. All that stuff in the Department of Trade reports about how up-to-date the place was compared with most third-world capitals. Almost offensively so, given the state the rest of the country was in. Offices, hotels, neoned nightclubs, glaring casinos; docks that could take small cruise liners – where were they? Broad boulevards, tall towers of concrete and glass, a skyline that should have taken the sun like a forest of mirrors – where the hell were they hiding? Not a sign, however carefully I scanned the scene. Once or twice there seemed to be a glassy glitter in the air at the edge of sight. But always when I looked again, shading my eyes, it resolved into a tall white church spire, a row of white thatches on the hill, or just some fleeting trick of the light. There was nothing more.

And these forested hills ... The island had a terrible deforestation problem. I'd read that too. It didn't look like it from here; still less like it from the sea.

For a moment I had the panicky idea that it was some trick of the Wolves, some disguise of the kind they'd used to spirit Clare away. They could even be moored near us now, hidden by it. But Le Stryge would surely have sussed that out.

The true explanation crept over me by slow degrees, like a chill coming on. And with about the same feeling.

Shadows. I was seeing shadows. Shadows in broad daylight, shadows at high noon. Shadows of the city, of the eighteenth or nineteenth centuries, maybe, or a blend of both; the same shadows that lay behind Canal Street in New Orleans, behind Danube Street back home. Long images of their past, their spirit, cast deep into the time-less world beyond the Core. But these shadows were strong, not images in darkness but stronger than the daylight. The whole island must be haunted by them, not lurking at the edges of the night but right beneath the living day, ready to show through. Strong enough even at high noon to swamp what had taken their place – at least for those who moved in shadows already. Even for those who didn't, they must be a tangible, almost oppressive presence – a ghost forever at their heels, behind every step they took. Their bright modern world must seem like nothing more than a shimmer of light upon dark waters. From the right angle you could look straight through, into the fathomless deeps below.

As I'd done; as I was doing even now. I shivered. It was noon now; but night would fall. If they were so strong even in the light, those shadows, what dominion must darkness bring them?

Suddenly I was very damn glad I hadn't gone ashore.

When the others came trooping back on board, dusty and footsore, they agreed; they had good reason to. They'd found a spell of fear upon the whole dockside quarter, and few willing to answer aloud what they asked; for the *Chorazin* had indeed come in, only hours before the dawn, riding before a storm that seemed to crack the heavens, only to set sail again before light. And it was whispered that strange shapes had come stalking through the streets to meet it, and that those who crossed their paths had not returned.

'Half of the folk still squatting in their shacks shaking!' said Jyp grimly, sipping gratefully at the goblet of cool sherry Pierce's steward handed him. 'Or rushing to their *houngans* for exorcisms and *traitements*. But the *houngans* are just as jumpy; hell, you can hear the drums from here!'

'Aye, and the singing!' Mall had added, no less sombre. 'But it's whispered that there's some of the heathen priests – those they think are secret *bocors*, that they guess serve with both hands, as t'were, the bright powers and the dark – that went a'purpose to meet the black ship. That all their gear's gone from their shrines, all, as if packed for some great festival elsewhere –'

Even she jumped; we all did. Pierce's crystal goblet shattered in his great paw. The door of the great cabin flew open with a crash and Le Stryge in all his squalor came storming in, more or less dragging the girl-creature along by her wrist.

'Mists!' snarled the old man. 'Vapours! Think they'll pull those over my eyes, do they? *Tiens*, they may think again!'

'What?' roared Pierce, licking sherry off his fingers. 'You have them, sirrah? Upon which heading?'

'South – east – they follow the coast – you have but to do likewise! Go, follow while you can! That veil grows thicker as they near its source! I had to resort to desperate measures.' He wheezed exhaustedly and sank down among Pierce's silken cushions. 'Or would you stand about arguing while they pick the bones of the precious, the expensive Clare?'

Pierce and Jyp were already out of their chairs, pushing past Stryge's companion without a glance. But I saw with a shudder that though her face remained blank and unmoved, from below her left eye a thin straight thread of blood ran down, like a tear. Overhead the big brass bell jangled the crew from their rest, and the cabin floor quivered as men thumped from their hammocks below. Le Stryge sagged like a disjointed doll.

'Nearer its source?' I demanded. 'What source, then?'

'Idiot boy – how should I tell? But unless the Stryge is a fool, which he is not, they are heading for some secret anchorage. Leave me now, I am exhausted! If you want to know any more you can look with your own damned sheeps' eyes!'

And so I'd been doing, intently scanning sea and land in the few short minutes Mall would spare me from her savage exercise. She seemed more determined than ever to drive some skill into me, and more and more often I found myself facing the point as well as the edge of that unforgiving sword. I might have to face the real thing soon enough, of course; but I suspected that she was really trying to keep me too busy to worry. I found myself thinking lightheadedly what a squash partner Mall would have made, whirling around me, lunging, feinting, cutting with fluid grace while I clumped heavily after her across the heaving deck. It was evening now, and my legs felt like lead, and ready to melt at that.

A swift ripple ran through the forested coast above.

A land breeze like a long slow sigh played about us – not cool but hot, languorous, heavy with strange scents of musk and spice and smoke, and an eerie babble of bird-calls. I was distracted – and Mall lunged. With a wild effort I managed to parry, bind and swing the swords about. I meant to drive hers back against her as she'd taught me. Somehow, though, the swords kept on swinging, right up to the vertical. Mine was the one pushed back. We met, hissing fiercely, forehead to forehead. Sweat ran down our faces. Mine; Mall was hardly even warm. At least I'd held her –

Then somehow her blade rolled lazily over, and steel sizzled wickedly as it shot right past mine. Something licked at the side of my neck with cold catlike delicacy. It left the faintest icy tickle. Then a hot welling wetness brought a sharper pain – right over my jugular.

I yelped and shied like a fly-stung horse. Of course she'd set the whole move up with scalpel accuracy, damn her! The ship heaved gently at a sudden sultry gust. The bind collapsed, our swords clattered to the deck and I overbalanced against her; we clutched at each other to steady ourselves –

One sting after another. Suddenly I was acutely aware of her bare arms against mine, the touch of smooth suntanned skin, the cool silky flow of her hair on my throat – so intensely female, so close. She tried to jerk back, but faltered, and only ground her hips more heavily against me. The strength of my reaction startled me; I pulled her sharply closer and kissed her. And, wonder of wonders, she responded. Her hips shifted against me. Her lips pressed hard against mine. Then for one luxurious moment her teeth parted on salty warmth and a langorous, twining tongue.

One moment. Till the silence crashed around us, and the needling awareness that every eye in the whole damn ship was goggling at the pair of us. Mall's pale eyes blazed open. She snaked irresistibly out of my grip and recoiled explosively, panting, spitting, rubbing her forearm across her lips. A wave of laughter rocked the ship, and I had the uncomfortable feeling I wasn't going to live this one down in a hurry. Assuming I lived at all. Mall was standing, staring down at her sword. Hastily I ducked and scooped up mine. I had a definite case of the shakes – and so, by God, did she. You'd think that things had gone a whole lot further than one quick squeeze.

Peacemaking? It seemed like the natural thing to try, till I saw the way her fists were clenching and unclenching. The last natural thing I'd tried hadn't turned out too well. I glanced around quickly. On the quarterdeck Jyp was grinning sardonically and Pierce was tactfully doubled up, his face as purple as his port-stained waistcoat. No use taking refuge in respectable company, there wasn't any. The shadow of the foremast shrouds fell over me, and it occurred to me that I'd never been up the rigging yet, and there was – after all – no time like the present.

Easily, without undue haste, I slid my sword into my belt, reached up as I'd seen the sailors do and swung myself over the rail. I felt a lot more at home on shipboard now, or so I told myself. And as far as risks went, the one I'd just run looked a lot bigger. I looked down at Mall, and she looked back at me, her face expressionless but flaming. I dug my feet into the ratlines and began to climb.

I even quite enjoyed the challenge, at first. Rock-climbing had quelled any great fear of heights; and I needn't go all the way, after all, just up to the top platform. The taut shrouds weren't much harder to climb than a ladder, but the step-like ratlines flexed slightly under my hands at every movement of the ship, strangely alive. I'd never felt so keenly aware of the *Defiance* as a living thing before, the sailors' sense; it was like scaling the mane of some immense sea-beast. Almost as frightening, too. This wasn't like a rockface; it swayed, casually, unpredictably, as if it had a mind of its own. And the higher you got, the wider the swing. The first time I looked down the deck seemed miles distant already, Mall not more than a speck staring up at me, blonde fluff blowing. She couldn't be thinking of coming after me, could she? I found myself hurrying to reach the top; but when I got there, it was almost scarier to sit on that bare platform in the whistling wind with no rail or anything else to hold onto. Only the masthead, with its crow's-nest for the look-out, offered any kind of security. I didn't want to go slinking down again so soon, even if Mall had cooled off a bit in the meantime. I stepped into the topmast shrouds and began to climb.

This time I carefully didn't look down, and it seemed to help. I reached the foretop quite quickly, though the ropes raised blisters and the sweat was stinging my cuts. The crow's-nest was nothing like those nice secure tubs you see in films – just another bare platform, but with iron loops set at waist height on either side of the mast, and allow rail to slip your toes under. The look-out, a picklefaced she-pirate with the build of a Russian trawler captain, showed me how to fasten my belt to the loops, cackling all the while.

'You and Mistress Mall, heh-heh! Saw you from atop here! A fine disarmin' stroke you have on you. Go try't on a Wolf! But ware the return thrust, heh-heh-heh!' Busy finding my footing, I ignored all that till she thrust her leathery face into mine, more serious now. 'Twas a fell time in these parts to be tryin' such jinks, young sir! Best not, when the *souffle Erzulie*'s a-blowin'! Or there's no tellin' what the end might be!'

'The what?'

'The landwind – did you not feel't? Aye, well, that's what they calls the sigh of Erzulie down this-a-way, the warm airs blowin' from the land at even. Aye, and a wicked hot wench she is, to be sure! Sets fire in the blood without reck'nin' how it'll burn, or who.'

I grinned. 'She doesn't sound so bad. I could use a little fire in mine, maybe.'

'There's fire that warms and fire that burns, hah? And when she's Erzulie Blood-i'the-Eye, *Gé-Rouge*, then 'ware all that's young and open; for she'll run madness in their reins! Might've brought you a sword in the heart, she might, that riggish mistress! For is not seven such the sign of her – heh? It's not for nothin' they've another name for that wind, down Jamaicey way – the Undertaker,

so they call it. Sweeps the last breath of the dyin' away!'
And with a final cackle she plunged over the edge of
the platform.

'*Hey!*' I protested, or something equally sensible –
and looked down after her.

That really was a mistake.

Emptiness roared up into my face. It was like looking
off a cliff – and having it whipped out from under you.
There was nothing directly beneath me. No deck, no ship
– nothing but the churning ocean an impossible distance
below, and the waves heaving greedily up towards me,
dropping away with sickening suddenness. My fingers
clamped tight to the loop, but the sweat made them slip.
My toes were dug in under the rail, but my legs were
shaking. I had to turn my head to see the *Defiance*, almost
hidden behind the bulging sails; she looked like a toy boat
at the end of a supple stick, bounced and buffeted this
way and that by the sea she rode on. And at this height
every little movement of that heeling deck became a
lurch, a wild whipping sway ...

After eternity or thereabouts I managed to force my
eyes away, to those inscrutable hills. Against their softly
tossing treetops the sway was less noticeable, and I began
to ride with the rhythm of it. After a while I was able to
turn my mind to the job I seemed to have got stuck with,
and risk a careful scan around the darkening horizon. I
saw no more than we'd seen since we left the Mississippi;
the sun, angry at its fall, and nothing new under it. No
other ship; no turn in our luck.

I shifted uneasily on my windblown perch. Look
with your own damned sheep's eyes, Le Stryge had said;
and I'd ended up doing exactly that. Just coincidence, of
course. It had damn well better be coincidence. But then
you couldn't be sure of *anything* around here.

Such as exactly what I was supposed to be looking
for. Anything capable of defeating Le Stryge's unpleasant
ways of seeing ought to be able to play hob with my plain
two eyes. Unless, of course, it only had power over
sorcery. But it wouldn't take much magic to hide things
among these lushly overgrown hills. For long hours we'd

seen no sign of life bigger than birds and giant butterflies, flutters of flashy colour against the green, and the occasional white thread of smoke rising from a distant clearing, or a patch of leafy thatches. We'd put in at several of these little settlements along the shore. We'd hove to and questioned fishermen in their boats, we'd sent ashore to ask villagers, always the same question – *un grand navire noir aux trois mats, orné aux lanternes comme des cranes grotesques, on l'a vu, hein? Ils viennent d'enlever une fillette* –

And always a veil fell between us. They were plain, lean peasant people for the most part, very simply dressed, looking more African than the West Indians I knew. All but the youngest had that look of premature age that goes with gruelling work and poor food. Their faces, old and young, ran to high bones and hard lines, well made to be inscrutable; their downcast eyes gave nothing away. Even the children, meant to be happy and laughing, would fall silent and scuff their toes in the dust when we spoke to them, and all the cajoling in the world would not move them. You couldn't blame them; the word that something was brewing must have spread, and they'd no more reason to trust us than the Wolves. In one or two places the very sight of us landing sent villagers bolting screaming into the jungle; in another somebody even shot at us, winging a crewman. Not badly; it was crude bird-shot, fired more in fright than in malice. It wasn't even worth trying to find whoever fired it among that shadowy tangle. We left them in peace, and went back to using our own eyes.

Mine, now; sweeping this way and that over land and sea and sky, bleak and empty all.

We rounded a promontory, crossed yet another empty bay; no village, no smoke, nothing but trees to the water's rim. Out ahead, beyond the far headland, the sun was a blazing copper dome sinking into the sea, the clouds like plumes of exploding steam. I thought of Atlantis; was it, too, out here somewhere? In the shadows were all things, it seemed. This ship itself was part of shadow, a lingerer beyond the Core – and I? I had ridden on it, east of the sunrise; for better or worse I was part of it. I had begun to see with different eyes. So where, now, did I belong? The sunset burned the headland ahead into stark silhouette, its fringe of trees bending and tossing in that mocking, stifling breeze.

Except that some weren't bending or tossing. Only swaying a little, stiffly, leafless. One – two – three –

We were not far off the point. I gathered my nerve and my breath together, leant over and shouted, but it was no use. I hadn't the knack of hailing; the wind whipped away my words. Any louder, too, and it might be heard elsewhere, give someone the extra minute to run out those enormous guns. Quickly, trying not to fumble, I unclipped my belt and swung down through the open trap – called the 'lubber's hole', suitably enough – and into the shrouds again. It was just like rock climbing – getting down was the hard part. In one piece, anyhow. My legs were shaking; I was going too slowly. Desperately I looked around, and saw, just below me, one of the back-stays meet the mast – a heavy cable taut as a piano-wire, angling steeply away towards the rail. With abseil gear – but I didn't have any. Too bad.

Slinging my sword well back, I reached out, wrapped an arm, then a leg, monkey-fashion, about the cable and swung myself across. Hand over hand, that was how to slide down – only I didn't get the chance. I was sliding already, too fast, the cable skidding through my sweaty hands. I clung like the original monkey on a stick, whimpering, and dug my shoe soles into the rope like brake pads. They juddered across the ridged coils so hard they almost jolted me right off; then they bit. I arrived at the deck green and gasping, my arm streaked with scarlet rope-burns – but in time to wheeze out my message.

It flung the ship into a flurry of action, but noise-lessly. Pierce's one hissed order, as eloquent as his usual bellow, was enough to send the hands scampering to the braces. The slap of their feet on the deck was about the loudest man-made sound. With the embroidered gloves he persisted in clutching, even in this heat, Pierce sketched a sharp line in the air, right to left. The mate lifted his cane in answer; there was one loud creak and rumble as the larboard ports flew open and the guns ran out, and that was all. We were as ready as we could be. In breathless silence, we bucked and dipped through the turbulent seas around the point.

Gradually the lee flank of the headland came into view, as steep and tree-clad as the other, wrapped in deeper twilight. From here the sun was hidden; the only light came from the sunset sky, reflected in the waters of the sheltered bay. And there, in towards the shore, riding easily above the clouds mirrored in that glass-calm pool, was the unmistakeable silhouette of the *Chorazin.*

The linstocks stopped whirling. The gun-captains held them poised above the touch-holes, ready to rake the Wolves' ship with yet another terrible barrage. If Clare had escaped our last broadsides, could she still survive this? The mate looked anxiously up to the quarterdeck; we were still sweeping by, across the bay. Already the ideal moment to fire was past. But Pierce stood still, fingering his chin, while Jyp whistled softly between his teeth. There lay our formidable quarry, ports closed, sails furled tight, moored peacefully by bow and stern and showing no light anywhere, nor any other sign of life. And just how likely was that?

'Head and stern, d'you see?' whispered Pierce suddenly. Why was he asking me? 'She's moored head and stern. Head only, why, she might swing around on a spring, might she not? Bring her guns to bear thus. But now she can't. God's wounds! It's worth the candle! We'll in and look her over!' He gestured again, Jyp spun the helm and in the same uncanny silence the deck hands flung themselves on the falls and hauled, taking the strain with a single hissing breath. Even the bosun and his mates dimmed their ritual abuse to a few hoarse whispers, and the mate stood cracking his cane into his palm to set the hauling pace. The sails shifted, the deck dipped; in a fierce, tense hush *Defiance* swung her nose around and stood in towards the land.

Pierce never took his eyes from the black ship. His brief nod to the mate sent the topmen streaming up the shrouds and along the yardarms with a nonchalance that made me feel slightly sick. Their control was daunting; with hardly a word spoken or a movement wasted the sails were taken in, and *Defiance* slowed to a stately glide. It brought home to me, with a slight shiver, how old the people I was watching really were. These complex, dangerous evolutions came to them as easily, as automatically as breathing now. They could almost have gone about and shortened sail in their sleep; and why not? They'd been doing it, some of them, for three or four lifetimes. Or more.

Suddenly Pierce flipped up his gloves again, held them high for a second, another – and then brought them sharply down to his side. With its capstan pawl thrown the anchor was trailed down with scarcely a splash to disturb the still waters, and in a second or so *Defiance* strained gently to a halt. I goggled. With just those two seconds of calculation Pierce had managed to position us neatly at an ideal angle to the black merchantman. Few of her guns could reach us here, but our broadside could rake the stern off her if need be. He'd taken this for granted; the moment the anchor touched water he'd turned away and whispered a barrage of orders. Jyp was already down on the maindeck pulling together a boarding party. I was on my way to muscle in when Mall appeared, hustling along a sick-looking Stryge. She didn't even glance at me.

'Well, sorcerer?' rumbled Pierce.

Stryge scowled at him. The old man really did look exhausted. He coughed raspingly, spat copiously on Pierce's clean deck and traced a complex figure in the phlegm with his toe. He watched it settle, and sighed. 'There is little I can tell you. The cloud still hangs about the ship. But if she is not aboard ...' He nodded to the island. 'Try there.'

'Some guess!' I snapped. 'You're supposed to be such a powerful sorcerer, and that's all you can tell me?'

'I'm spent!' muttered Stryge. Disdainfully he sniffed the rich, dank odours from the land. 'And how should I achieve more in this place? I belong to the North. Give me a frosty night air that smells of resin and sharp wood-smoke. Take me back to the pines on the Brocken, where the dark powers meet –'

'You can't have been there lately,' I told him. 'There aren't any. The East Germans cut down all the forest and stuck up a damn great concrete blockhouse, like the Berlin Wall –'

Stryge leered. 'Where the dark powers meet, as I said. Such a stage of human folly suits the sabbats just as well. Or better.' He seemed to cheer up, and stared again at the shapeless smear of mucus. 'High up, maybe. Up hills. That's the best I can do. Now tell this bitch to let me sleep!'

From near sea level the *Chorazin* looked ten times the size, looming over the longboats as we rowed nearer. It was hard to remember I'd scaled those bulging flanks only days before, and under fire. The two musketeers in our bows kept nervously sweeping their weapons along the high rail; Jyp didn't stop them. We reached the side without being challenged. Boarding axes hooked quietly on to the blackened planks, and under the watchful eyes of the musketeers in Mall's longboat the sailors swarmed up the wooden steps as easily as a broad staircase. As for me, I was so much dreading what I'd find that I was at the deck before I knew it, and swinging myself over the rail.

The deck boomed deafeningly under my feet; but there was no watch to be alerted. No sign of anyone, in fact. The high-pitched creak that made everyone jump was just a door swinging in the breeze. As we spread out to search the ship I made for the aft companionway, and with Jyp at my heels hissing caution I swung myself down onto the gloomy stairs.

He could have saved himself the trouble. The moment my head went below the hatchway I knew there was nobody there. I didn't need to be a warlock or anything. I just knew. It may have been the stillness of the foul air, or something in the way the sounds echoed, our footfalls, the slap and swirl of the water in the bilges; but that ship felt empty. All the way down, deck to deck, it was the same; dark, stinking, still. I tried not to think what it must have been like for Clare, days of it down here among these sewer stenches. But if only she could still be there ... Somehow. The lazarette door was locked. I looked at Jyp, shrugged, and blew the lock out with a shot. But as Jyp ripped it open my heart sank; the inner door stood ajar. I knew there'd be nobody inside, but I looked all the same. On the heap of rags meant for a bed lay something dark; I picked it up – and horrified myself by bursting into tears.

'Her skirt?' said Jyp. 'Hey, look, it's got torn, that's why she couldn't keep it on, it'd just fall down. Doesn't mean she's not still okay –'

I didn't explain. It wasn't just that. It was everything I'd left behind, my ordered office world, my carefully structured little normality, my scrupulously sexless intimacy – or was it *our* world, *our* intimacy? The sight of that once-trim skirt brought it all rushing back to me in a flood of emotion I couldn't even recognize, let alone control. I wanted to hide my head and howl. But I had that much control left, at least; instead I think I said just about every swearword I knew. Even then I spoke four languages, so it must have been quite a lot. Then I rolled the skirt up and thrust it into my belt.

Jyp nodded in judicious agreement. 'Let's amscray. See if anyone else's turned up anything yet.'

But, as we both expected, nobody had. The ship looked bare – not stripped, ready for sea, but bare. And all her boats were gone. That had one obvious answer. Jyp's sharp order sent our boat's crew streaming back over the side. 'Might as well have your boys finish the search,' he told Mall as we clambered onto the ladder. 'Follow on in when you're done. But signal the ship, will you, and have 'em cover us?'

'Aye, at once!' she said. 'But have a care of yourselves!'

She wasted no time. As we pulled away from the shot-scarred flank the *Defiance*, drawn by her spring cables, was already swinging ponderously at her mooring. It was under the comforting cover of her guns that we rowed for the long crescent of beach. The curtain of jungle-like forest overhanging the dunes was unnerving. It could have hidden an army of snipers, and I expected it to erupt any moment. The moment our keel crunched in the pale sand we flung ourselves into the shallows and streamed up the beach, dropping down behind sandhills, rocks, palm roots, any cover that offered. But nothing came from beneath the ominous darkness of the trees except an amazing chatter of bird-calls.

Jyp lifted his head and peered anxiously up and down the beach. 'Course, there's no guaranteeing they did come ashore here; might've rowed round to the next bay, or the last. But Stryge, he – *hey!* See there!'

All I could make out was an odd fan-shaped patch in the dampish sand just above the tideline.

'Yeah, that's what I meant! They landed here, okay – then tried to brush out their tracks and keelmarks; nearly always leave a trace if you try that in a hurry. They'll have stowed the boats somewhere near. Okay, boys!' he snapped. 'Up, and get looking! Their boats, their tracks, anything! Before we lose the light!'

We found the boats quickly enough, sunk in the wide pool of a creek at the forest's edge, with stones and sand providing both weight and camouflage. From there our trackers followed faint traces to an impenetrable-looking thicket of wild maguey and aloes. Trouble had been taken not to disturb it, but close to the ground bent twigs and bruised leaves still bled sap, enough to show that a whole party had passed through only a few hours since. And beyond it you could see the beginnings of a narrow trail, leading away uphill.

Jyp looked at me. 'Uphill, eh? Never does to ignore that old bastard.' He plucked out his pocket telescope, and we scanned the slopes above. From here they looked immense, and full of folds and convolutions. High on the hills sunlight still lingered, but it was faint and uncertain.

'I can't see a damn thing except treetops,' I complained.

'Me neither,' admitted Jyp. 'Unless – what d'you make of that?' He passed me the telescope. 'Not on this slope, the one beyond, just on this side of the hill.

Wouldn't see it from the ship. Where there's a sort of shelf before the crest.'

Tropical twilights are short. It took me almost too long to spot it. But a gust of wind ruffled the trees apart just long enough to show a flash of white, and after that the outlines were clear. 'Got it!'

'Yeah. Quite something, ain't it?'

It was a castle. Or rather it was a mansion in unmistakeably Spanish style, a huge relic of the old colonial days; but the elegant white-walled terraces around it were topped with crenellations and embrasures for cannon. 'Somebody must've been afraid of something.'

'You bet! Way they treated the blacks, those Spaniards, they were always scared crazy 'bout revolt. Wasn't a wall high enough to save 'em when it came, though.'

'What d'you make of it?'

'A day and a night's march is what I make of it.'

'That much? It's not so far.'

'On foot? Up this hill, down into the next valley or two, then up that slope – and through heavy forest, near as dammit jungle. Far enough, huh? We'll need supplies. Look, you better hotfoot it back to the beach and meet Mall and her boys. Have 'em fetch up all the boat rations.'

'How about reinforcements? They've emptied their ship. Our sixty against their three hundred or more?'

'Better odds than we had in the boarding. Even if we stripped *Defiance* – which we don't dare do – we still couldn't match them man for man.'

'Stryge, then! No, he's half-dead. But his creatures –'

'*No!* We've better Wolfbane along. You haven't seen Mall in action yet, not really. She's ... an experience. But it's not a thing she can summon up to order, not often.' He smiled wryly. 'Yet. A moment back there, I thought you'd maybe found the trick. Anyhow, there isn't time to fetch more men. Our main hope's surprise – and speed. Remember, it was only hours back they passed that bush. They may be heading for the castle, sure – but they're not there yet!'

Night fell, and most of the wind with it; the air hung

216

hot and breathless. The surf's soft roar grew muted. In the rippling sky the stars danced around an angry moon. Mall's boat was heading in; I strolled along the shore to meet it, enjoying the darting antics of the fiddler crabs that scuttled around the tideline. I noticed a disturbance in the sand, and squatted down beside the sagging crater of a turtle's nest, now mostly hatched. Looking around, I saw only one of the tiny hatchlings, coated in sand, struggling gamely almost down to the water. I stood up and went to help him, but a crab dashed in ahead of me, snapped up the little creature in its oversized claw and bore him off flapping to a burrow. I kicked sand into it, feeling futile, but stopped myself; all part of the process of nature, wasn't it? Great. Tell that to the turtle.

The incoming boat left a wake of cool fire in the still waters; phosphoresence dripped from the oars, swirled around our ankles as we pulled it in. Mall sprang out, and I touched her arm as she stalked past me. 'Listen – I'm sorry if I offended you! Really sorry! But ... Let people think that was just horseplay, Mall. It meant something to me. To you, too.'

She smouldered and walked quickly away from the others. 'Then let something stand for all, for there'll be no more! Go, follow me not, go brag of your manhood among your fellow-men! None will doubt it now! But I pray you, pick some other to practise't on!'

It was my turn to be stung. 'That's bloody unfair! Just what in hell gives you the right to assume I'd show off like that? Any more than you would! I like you! I admire you – I owe you my life! Can't I even love you a little?'

She sat down in the sand with a bump. 'Five centuries!' she said hoarsely, and laughed a little. It sent shivers down my spine; it didn't sound like human laughter at all. 'And still I drag the chains! Ah, a nice irony – loved by one I daren't rebuff, lest I kill what shreds of feeling he's left himself.' I was about to reach out; I didn't realize it, but she did. 'Nay, never paw me! I've scant use for stallions!' Then, relenting a little, she rubbed her hand awkwardly on my knee. 'Even ones of some mettle. Come, sirrah!' she said softly. 'I'll not lie with you; but an I live another thousand year I'll not forget you.' Her finger and thumb tweaked the sensitive leg nerves with a force that shot me yelping to my feet. 'Not altogether. Will thus much serve?'

'It's a hell of a lot,' I said humbly.

'Not Hell!' she exclaimed, very seriously. 'Heaven, man! Heaven!'

Under the shadow of the branches, the jungle seemed an eerie, claustrophobic place. The air hung hotter, heavier, incredibly humid, like one vast exhaled breath – bad breath, because it stank. It throbbed with the metallic *chir* of cicadas and the morbid croaking of tree-frogs. Our few lanterns did little except attract assorted blundering nightlife. My pack seemed to snag in every twig I passed. I was beginning to see Le Stryge's point about the south, and we weren't even through the thicket yet.

Cutlasses slashed at the spiny mass, their short weighty blades more use here than broadswords. We didn't mind leaving a track behind us; quite the opposite. Small birds flew up in a startled twittering as we hacked our way through. 'Bananaquits, maybe,' grinned Jyp. 'Bright little fellers. Only I wish they weren't so loud.'

I knew what he meant. No point in letting the Wolves hear us coming. Or see us; once we were through the thicket, one by one the lanterns were blown out. The trail was narrow, and the Wolves deliberately hadn't cleared it much. Between tall ferns it led us, under looping vines invisible in the dark and only too eager to hang us, into the gloomy shadow of royal palms and mango trees, the ground squishy with their overripe fruit. The chatter of small streams surrounded us. Every so often one would cross the path, and we would slip and splash and curse across the mud, sending small frogs scattering. When the moon rose high enough to slip its light between the trees it seemed to help; but also it threw strange shadows, dappled, ambiguous, half alive, into which we couldn't help poking our swords as we passed.

Time went by, and with it we toiled upward, sweating and sore. The air grew purer, full of sweet heady smells. A grateful breeze freshened the forest's dank whispers with the rush of surf. Owl cries, more like the hooting *whit-tu-whu!* than any I'd heard back home, bounced back and forth. Some of the other noises that came floating out were scary in the extreme, shrill shrieks and demented gibbering laughter. It was silent things, though, impossible to avoid, that worried me more. The trail was steep; I found myself envying a Wolf's clawed feet when the soft loam crumbled and slithered away beneath me. The brush on the upper slopes was thinner but tougher, mostly sisal and other spiky-leaved horrors. The sailors marched on like ageless automatons, but me, I was getting tired, very tired. At last Jyp ordered a halt, and I bumped into him before I understood. The reddening, swollen moon hung level with us beyond the nodding palm fronds ahead. We had topped the first slope. Leaving the others for a drink and a bite – biscuit and lukewarm water – we inched forward on our bellies to peer over the edge. 'Quite a view, huh?' breathed Jyp softly.

'Ace,' I agreed, squirming, wondering what was slithering about under me and did they have snakes here, or scorpions maybe? 'See anything?'

'No. Doesn't mean they're not out there, though.' It was certainly quite a sight. The valley yawned wide beneath us, lined with trees whose tops trailed faint ghost-banners of mist beneath the moon. In gaps I glimpsed a snaking band of silver, and a rush of water roared louder than the surf. From the far wall it came; from a steep false summit water skipped down a twisting stair of rocks, to fall at last as a cascading curtain into a shadowed pool. Shining vapours boiled out of it, and a deep insistent voice, and flirting among them the ragged shadows of hunting bats. Above the falls the hill rose straight and steep and thickly wooded to almost twice the height, till it touched the outermost terrace of the castle. You could see it more clearly from here, like a pale ship foundering in a dark sea, yet still dominating the hillside with stony arrogance.

Jyp glanced back. 'Not long till dawn.' The sea glimmered through the trees, our mastheads skeletal silhouettes against it, still surprisingly close. We'd mostly been travelling upwards, not away. 'Better be shifting. Eat up!'

The biscuit wasn't that sustaining, but as we filed cautiously over the summit Jyp plucked dark fruits from a tree we passed and handed me one. I saw others doing the same, dug my thumbnail in and sniffed cautiously, and got something of a shock. It was a little avocado, far more fragrant than those leathery banes of business lunches back home. The pulp was so juicy and green I hardly missed the *vinaigrette*. Further on there was an orange tree, and though the fruits were sour they were good to suck for thirst. An hour or so later the moon, mad and burning, set beyond the castle. The air grew cooler, and in the warm damp dark beneath the fading stars the jungle began to stretch and stir expectantly. Chirrups and titters rose among the undergrowth, and an eared dove began cooing in a weird little minor tone, awakening relations and neighbours along the way. By the time an orange sunrise touched the paling sky the air rang with a real dawn chorus, every call imaginable from the chipping of wren and kiskadee to the manic whoops and cackles of things Jyp called Corny-birds – I found out later the name was *corneille*. As we came downhill the trees changed; we passed through a long grove of calabash trees, and down towards the river whole thickets of mangoes, their fruit dangling disturbingly from long green cords.

'Uh-huh,' said Jyp. 'Thought so. Been cultivated, way back – plantation for the castle up there. Pity they're not ripe yet.' He shook his head. 'Though maybe they'd stick in my gullet. Any plantations here they watered with blood.'

Small parrots or parakeets popped up among the branches like live flowers, or swung upside-down to peer at us, screeching mockingly. Then they took fright at something and flew up with a rush and a flutter, and the rising sun struck flame from their plumage as they wheeled. The air swiftly grew very warm, and the cool rush of the stream drew us like a magnet; we stumbled towards it, hardly noticing the soggy half-marsh that plucked at our boots. Until, that is, the legions of flies descended in a discordantly droning cloud, and sent us bolting and slipping through the stony-bedded stream, beating ineffectually, and up onto the far slopes, steeper and drier, where they didn't follow. We flung ourselves down to rest, a miserable, muddy and bitten crew; only Mall, who'd brought up the rear, seeméd completely untouched.

'Knew we should've brought Stryge!' I sighed. 'One whiff of him and they'd have forgotten the rest of us!'

One of the foretopmen grunted. 'Aye, an' dropped darn dead t'mòment they bit 'un!'

'Or his little friends —'

'Like hell!' said Jyp with soft savagery. 'Don't even wish it!'

I was nettled. 'Okay, okay! They give me the creeps, too — but they saved some necks in the boarding, didn't they? Mine included. So what's the matter with them.'

'You don't want to know,' he said bluntly.

'Hey, come on — I've seen a few things too now, remember? The girl — I can't imagine; but Fynn's — I don't know, some kind of werewolf, isn't he?'

'No,' said Mall softly. 'He is a dog. A yellow cur of the gutters, vicious and strong, deformed by warlockery into the shape of men. Held so by the power of Stryge's will — as habitation for another mind.'

Even in the sun I shivered. 'Whose mind?'

'One dead — or one who has never lived. Either way, a force from outside. From the further regions of the Rim. A spirit.'

'And the girl? Some animal, too?'

'No. Peg Powler is an old country name, from my day, for the spirit of a river.'

'A *river?*'

Jyp growled. 'A devouring, drowning spirit. That the old fiend trapped somehow, in the body of one of its victims — a suicide, maybe, or just plain accident. Hope so. But from what little I know, he'd have had to be real close by at the exact moment she died. And well prepared.'

'Oh Christ,' I said, wishing I'd never asked. 'That slime she spouts ...'

'A *polluted* river,' spat Jyp, with an irritated glance at Mall. 'Like the one runs down to those docks of yours, maybe. C'mon, let's move!'

He drove us on uphill. The trees grew taller on this side of the valley, but on the slope they gave less shade. Many of them were towering *trompettes*, whose broad fronds like giant fig-leaves spread only from the summit. They let the sun through as it climbed towards the zenith, and it hammered down upon our sweating backs. Incessant metallic chimes rasped across the valley like its maddening voice, but they were only the calls of bellbirds. My mouth was parched, my head aching, but I knew to the last drop how little there was left in my canteen, and cursed the flies that had driven us from the river. The thick ferny mould tore down underfoot, baring the red soil like a raw wound. That was moist enough, and you could hear other streams along the hill, no doubt leading to the falls. But they were too far off our trail. It was early afternoon before we crested the false summit, more or less sliding down into the dip beyond, and sank down gratefully by the muddy little streamlet at its foot.

Something more than tiredness weighed me down; a sick inner emptiness, a chill all that heat could not disperse. Jyp had been right. I wished I'd never asked about Stryge's creatures. The idea had a special kind of horror that gripped me and shook me and wouldn't let me go – of possession, of something lurking within a body like a shell, of some other, alien, mind peering out from behind eyes that didn't belong to it, like painted shutters on an empty, crumbling house. A haunted house. A ghost in a machine; but the wrong ghost, the wrong hands on the controls ...

'Aye,' said Mall, when I let slip something of what I felt. She splashed the brownish streamlet water on her glowing cheeks. 'That's so. Possession's a thing most potent in any magic, for good or ill. Be it in spellsong of Finnmark or Bermoothes *obeah* or plain homebred warlockry, a spirit in a body doesn't belong to it, that's a terrible thing, an unnatural mingling that unleashes great powers. And if some malign spell fix it there, why then, 'tis free to walk abroad among men unhindered and turn those powers to all manner of ill. Those creatures, the Stryge hardly dares let them from his sight. Yet they are most imperfect, one an animal, the other a living corpse; neither could go undetected for long among men. And once detected, the remedy's swift and sure. So fear them, aye, but don't dwell on them; they're no harm to you.'

How could I explain it wasn't them I was afraid of, at all? It was the bare idea – the way some people are scared of spiders or cats or knives scraping plates, sheer abstract terrors. It frightened me whether it had anything to do with me or not, a horrible sense of total vulnerability. And the idea that it might – or with Clare ... Almost more than I could stand. Did phobias take living shape, too, outside the Core? I couldn't ask. I couldn't explain. I just thanked her; and when Jyp gave the word I went on.

Up here above the falls the trees were changing, growing taller still and thicker; scrubby pines of some kind at first, aromatic eucalyptus, and then tall *ormes* – Haiitian elms – and fragrant cedars. In their shade the going was easier, but the gloom made me apprehensive.

Jyp seemed to feel it, too. 'Can't be far to the castle now,' he muttered, avoiding my eye.

'Right! And they'll be there by now, won't they? And what'll they be doing with –'

'Hell, Steve, I don't know. Look, whatever they do, these ceremonies of theirs, they're always at night, right? And we'll get there before then.'

Just. He didn't say it; but the word hung in the air, like the dustmotes in the sunbeams that slanted between the trunks. They were slanting low now, though, and dark clouds were rolling in from the west. We hadn't much time, and I couldn't even see the bloody castle yet.

That's what I thought, anyhow. It turned out I'd been looking at it for a while. On this steep slope the mansion itself was hidden by the outermost terrace wall, so thoroughly overgrown that, seen from below, it blended into the tossing greenery behind. So we pushed through a really nasty thicket of spiky-leaved sisal, and it pounced. There were the terrace walls, there was the towering façade of the castle right in front of us, louring over us so suddenly we stopped dead and collided with each other like guilty children. The hands pressed close in a babble of half-voiced oaths. A cool breeze trailed across our faces. The silence that fell was devastating. If ever a place lay in ambush, that one did.

We could see it clearly now, high and stark under the dark clouds rolling swiftly in. That wasn't the least bit reassuring; it looked as if *it* could see us. There was an eyeless, gaping quality about those tall windows with their upswept architraves like devilish eyebrows, as if the darkness behind them wasn't just emptiness but in constant oily motion. But it didn't look any the less deserted. The tropics aren't kind to the works of men. Its stucco was stained and crumbling, its stonework root-cracked and rain-worn, the sinister crenellations decaying and the cruel *cheveaux-de-frise* on the inner walls half toothless with rust. Wrought-iron balconies sagged like withered tendrils; fragments of shutters drooped from half-torn hinges, and the roof gaped tileless in a dozen places. There wasn't a sign or sound of life.

Until, that is, something rattled. A slow, tormented creak split the air, and faded into a swift, juddering tattoo. In that place, beneath the black clouds rolling in, it was a ghastly sound. It made me think of some ghostly galleon, riding at anchor over the rippling treetops; or of dry bones dancing on a wind-whipped gibbet.

Mall, coming up from the rear, broke the spell. 'Fools! Asses! What is't but cane?' And so it was, a great green and yellow canebrake waving stiffly in the wind at the top of the wall, its stems colliding musically. But the nervous laughter died in our throats, for beyond the brake, at the apex of the terrace, stood a sinister vision. One I, at least, had seen before – the same scarecrow shape from the Vieux Carré graveyard, but far taller, black and stark as a withered tree against the onrushing storm. Its high-collared greatcoat trailed from crossed-stick shoulders the height of my head, its tattered hat tilted forward as if sunk in thought, brooding amidst the dry clattering cane.

'The Baron's watching his boneyard!' said Jyp acidly. But as he spoke the wind seemed to take the hat, for it turned, rolled on the shoulder and lifted as if to look out seaward. As one man we ducked down and crept by like mice beneath a watchful owl. Call us crazy if you like.

At the wall's foot we found a gateway, flanked by massive pillars; the gates that once blocked it were gone, the hinge pins rusted to stumps. The lintel, ornately carved with a religious subject – St Peter, it looked like, before cockcrow – lay shattered and half buried to one side. Beyond it a long narrow stair climbed to the terrace; its balustrade was ruinous and overgrown, its steps cracked and tilting, but it seemed to be the only way up. Quickly, keeping low, we scurried through and climbed, looking up nervously; we could hardly be more vulnerable here. At the top Jyp beckoned me forward, and together we peered cautiously over the edge. The cracked terrace flagstones stretched out before us to the inner wall, empty except for clumps of bushes and rattling cane; the largest of them hid the sinister stick figure from us – or was it the other way round? Beyond an imposing inner gate, one of whose doors still hung rotting from the hinge, stood another figure like it, but no longer clothed; minus its hat and coat the outstretched scarecrow arms looked more pathetic than sinister.

'Featherman! Taupo! Come with us!' hissed Jyp to the two sailors behind us, a big white-haired thug and a grizzled little ferret. 'No pistols, cold steel only. The rest follow when we pass the word it's safe. Mall, if we're jumped, you take command. C'mon, Steve!'

Half crouching, the four of us sped and stumbled across the uneven flags, ducking down behind every convenient bush till we reached the inner gate and hunched down behind the gatepost. We were just peering through the gap between post and sagging gate when a sudden flicker made us whirl around. A pale light spattered the mounting cloudheads above, and a soft crackle echoed between the valley walls. We looked at each other uneasily, then turned back to the gate. Between it and the looming façade of the mansion – palace, almost – lay what must once have been an elegant courtyard, flagged with decorative stones and planted here and there with shady trees in stone tubs. Now they had burst their tubs and grown tall, fastening their roots through the flags with savage vigour. Some had fallen, blown over in a hurricane perhaps, and torn up great stretches of paving in their agonies. Piles of rubble and dirt littered the rest of the court, and the empty windows and gaping door of the great house grinned mockingly down over the wreckage. As far as we could see it was completely empty. But the wide double stairs leading up to it were noticeably clear of rubbish in the middle, as if people had used them lately – a lot of people. We risked putting our heads around the gate, then stepped out swiftly, with ready swords. Except for that one stick-figure the courtyard was empty; there was no sign of any watchers at window or rooftop. Jyp and I turned to wave the others forward – and were hurled off our feet.

Flat on my back, half-winded, I saw Jyp flung back against the gatepost; little Taupo fell on top of him, his neck lolling brokenly. The Featherman was on top of me and kicking furiously at my stomach. I struggled to get out from under, but the kicking rose to a paroxysm and he fell aside, gurgling. I heaved myself up – and faced the dark fingers an instant before they clamped home on my throat. That gave me a split second to do two things – tuck in my chin and thrust up my sword, hard. I felt it sink home with a horrible meaty impact – but the spindly ironhard hands about my neck didn't so much as twitch, only closed home their appalling grip. I stabbed again, again, twisting the blade as it came out – and then a mighty flash of lightning ripped the air, and showed me my attacker's face. The exploding thunderclap drowned my scream. It wasn't monstrous, not in itself, that face. I'd seen its twin in half the little villages, high-boned, leather-hard, dusty-skinned. But not sagging, staring, a glaze-eyed skull under stretched skin. My jawbone creaked as that chill grip tightened, my throat convulsed. It was killing me, this *thing*, and it wasn't even *looking* at me –

Then came a sudden swish like the wind, and the face flew up into the darkness. The grip convulsed, but held till blades thudded into the thin stick-insect arms. No blood spurted, but they relaxed, sagged. In a flare of lightning the headless body rolled aside. Mall jabbed it with her sword, stained tarry black. Flat raindrops pattered on the flagstones.

'Jyp,' I croaked as he helped me up, 'Why're the zombies in the movies always *slow?*'

He grinned, fingering a scraped brow. 'Ever see *Frankenstein*? Karloff got it about right. Anyhow, they call 'em *corps-cadavres* here; *zombi's* what's got into them.'

'Will you stand blethering while the heavens fall?' demanded Mall, and a mighty thunderclap burst the air to punctuate her. 'Surely we've woken the watchdog! Into the castle, and quick!'

Lightnings crossed above the rooftree, thunder battered at us and the rain came sleeting around us as we bolted up the steps. But there was no way we'd rush blindly between those yawning double doors. Those of us with pistols drew and cocked them; I hoped the rain hadn't got into the priming. Then the lightning flashed again, and in its lurid glare we saw a great hall before us, high-roofed, nobly proportioned, with a dais at one end on which stood the dilapidated remains of high seats, richly carved and canopied – thrones, almost, crumbling and cobweb-shrouded now. It had been a palace, once, this place, for some wealthy noble; but it was horribly empty now. Cautiously we crowded into the doorway.

'Lanterns!' order Jyp, whispering despite the storm. 'Light 'em up, and quick!'

But either the rain had got into them, or the wind was blowing out the tinder, or there was some other cause, because there was a tremendous bother over lighting them. Mall pushed through impatiently, and managed to coax one into feeble life. Then she held it up; and we all shrank together in the middle of the floor. For by its swinging light shadows moved across those wide white walls – but there was nothing to throw them.

They were sharp, clear shadows, the shapes of men and women circling in pairs to a stately step, a minuet, maybe, or a sarabande. You could see every detail of their dress, the women's immense hoopskirts and high-piled wigs billowing out as they danced, their fans fluttering as they curtsied to the men, whose flared sleeves and ribboned queues stuck out stiffly as they bowed in return. There was no sound of their music, nothing but the sudden rush and splashing of rain. Around us they circled, their shadows swelling and blurring as they neared a light which was not ours, diminishing as the dance swept them away again. It was a dance such as this hall must once have known; but for all that it was peculiarly terrible to see. Then I heard gasps; but I'd already seen it, the darker, solitary silhouette that passed among the dancers like a cloud, dressed like the men but holding a slender cane at an elegant angle. It bowed to them as it passed, elegant as a major-domo or dancing master; and they bowed back, but didn't rise. The men faltered, folded, collapsed; the women swayed in their courtesies and sank down. The dance swept round them oblivious; but it was a dance of death, for couple after couple dropped as they turned, hands clutching desperately at each other, at the air, futile. They sank and were gone. But behind the darker shadow another pair would fall in line, heads bent, hands fallen limp, dancing no more.

Only Mall had the nerve to speak. 'The worst in these things are but shadows!' she laughed. 'They've no power to harm us! Come!' She plunged on into the hall, broadsword at the ready, towards the high arch at the rear; its great tapestry curtain had gone grey with the dust that pooled in its sagging folds. As her swordpoint touched it a good half tore and dropped with a thump in a cloud of dust and fat insect larvae. Through the archway we plunged, into a separate hall made less deep by the curving stairways at either end. To the left one of the great pictures, at least twelve feet tall, that hung above the stair had come away. Its gilded frame stood shattered across the ruined middle steps, and spiders were using it for their own delicate works. On the other side the frame still hung, but what it held had been eaten away, leaving only an obscene fungus stain on the wall behind. One look showed nobody had passed either way for centuries – at least no body material; both stairs were curtained thick with dust-caked webs. But between those stairs in the far wall were other doors. They were mostly warped shut, but the central one hung ajar from one hinge, and the splintered wood was recent.

When Mall and I peered in, we found it was a stair, wide but functional; and the darkness it led down into seemed to well up at us. We looked at each, shrugged, and waved the others after us. They obeyed, but not too eagerly – and that was the first time I'd noticed any real hesitation on this whole crazy voyage. Well, I couldn't blame them. I'd no choice, and Mall and Jyp had made theirs for their own reasons. But even someone who loves gold and hates Wolves can be forgiven for not wanting to walk into such an obvious trap.

Yet walk they did, all the same, as cautiously as us, shuffling down with backs to the walls, pistols at the ready, never sure what the next step would bring, or whether it would be there at all. The air was still, but the lantern-flame cowered and trembled as if a slow breath played upon it; I somehow felt that if anyone but Mall carried it, it wouldn't have stayed alight. Not that it was much help; but it made more difference than you could imagine. The atmosphere of the place was like a physical weight pressing down on our shoulders, and even when the light caught the edge of a tall vaulted stone arch and we felt the stairwell open out into a wider ambience, the claustrophobia didn't let up. The storm was no more than a distant rumble. It was quiet as the grave – most graves, anyway; but no way were we alone.

Then, just at the edge of the lamplight there came a sudden flurry and rush of motion. Jyp's pistol and mine went off together. There was a dazzling flash, and a single high-pitched scream that chilled my heart. That was no Wolf's cry – who had my panicky shot hit? Then, as my sight cleared, I sagged with relief. On the steps below lay the gory remains of two fat black rats, one cut completely in two, the other, a foreleg blown away, kicking into death. Jyp and I exchanged shamefaced grins.

'Nice shootin', pal!' he said.

'Some shooting! There must have been a hundred there!'

'That few?'

Mall held up the lantern, and as they caught the light her long curls flared golden and seemed to redouble it; her pale eyes flashed. Overhead a roughly vaulted ceiling appeared, and to left and right dim outlined alcoves, and the sense of oppression eased a little.

'Where they stored their wines, maybe!' whispered Jyp, when it became clear nothing was going to leap out at us just immediately. 'Sure looks like –'

Something crunched softly under his foot, and he looked down. 'Maize flour? Well, vittles too, maybe –'

Then the light touched the back of an alcove. 'Uh,' he remarked. 'Not a wine cellar, then.'

'Not unless they kept a cask of amontillado,' I whispered back, looking at the row of dangling chains and fetters, and he smiled wryly.

Mall tossed her curls angrily, and the flames leaped as the lantern swung. Along the wall the row of alcoves stood out, and the rusting remains of iron cages swinging from the roof, that a man might crouch in, but neither sit nor stand. In the centre of the floor opened a brick-built hearth, like a blacksmith's; but the long-handled irons still standing in its ashen charcoal I knew were not for working metal.

Mall spat like a cat. 'Those damned dog-Dagoes! May the Devil fry 'em in's warming-pan! A dungeon! A dungeon for helpless slaves! And a place of torment! Stir you, hell, and swallow it whole to set its bitch-gotten masters in!'

She wasn't whispering. Her curse shivered the air with its force, and the steel of her voice set pins and needles in my skin. The shadows leaped in panic as she brandished the lantern, and the light flared high and clear. Even the rusty cages creaked and swung, and I shuddered as I saw dangling from one the yellowed bones of a handless arm. Rats had gnawed them, by the look of it. They seemed almost to be pointing, down at the floor. And the new light did indeed show up something there, tracks and swirls and spirals traced out in mounds of yellowish dust. Shapes that reminded me of something, something definitely unpleasant; but all I could think of was how odd it was that they hadn't gone mouldy, that the rats hadn't eaten them ...

Jyp snapped his fingers. '*Vevers!* In maize flour, of course!'

I remembered then. 'Jyp, what – these – these are the shapes they smeared all over my office!'

'I'll just bet they are! Crests, signs of the *loa!* There've been rites held here, and not by the Spaniards neither! Sort of heraldry – you make the sign, you invoke 'em – see there, like a ship with a sail, that's the sea-god Agwé! And just in front of us here, like the compass-rose, that –' His voice faltered a moment. 'That's a friend of yours, that's Papa Legba – and there, that heart with the swirls around it? They're swords piercing it –'

'*For is not seven such the sign of her!*' I repeated, astonished.

'*What?*'

'What the look-out said – I'd forgotten it – the dark woman with the leathery face – I thought she was just –'

'May Henry,' said Mall thoughtfully. 'An old Bermoothes pirate, sailed these waters so long she's crusted with their superstitions like barnacles. She's strange in mind, aye, but not wandered. A shame she'd not come with us. What'd she say it of?'

'Of me – after you and I – and the wind, she said the Undertaker's wind –'

'That bears off the dying, aye! And evil sendings! And by all that's clean and holy, she was right! Erzulie, the pierced heart is her sign, the power of love! But this one, this *vever*, did you not see the shape of it, Jyp?'

'It's rough, sure. Sort of slanted; distorted, almost ... Oh-oh. You mean this is Erzulie Gé-Rouge?'

'Aye – Erzulie of the left-hand path, the love of pain

and anger! The love that breeds destruction! Erzulie in the thrall of Petro! Don Petro, the *loa* who warps all the rest, who wrenches them to his own fell purpose! Who twists the good in them to savagery!' Mall glared at me, panting. 'Just as it twisted you, Stephen, and I – to set us against one another! A sending rode that wind, a sending of love twisted, love made into a snare and a tripwire ...' She paused, sweat trickling down between her heaving breasts. 'I was meant to strike you down! Or at least quarrel, aid you no more! To leave you and yours at sorest need! I – *I*! See, see, they're all twisted, all turned – all captive – all save his, that heads the rest!' She stepped forward and swung the lantern high over the largest shape of all, stretching from wall to wall, a great scolloped circle around a cruelly-barbed cross. In sudden fury she kicked at it, savagely, and a choking flurry of dust exploded up into the light. Then, as it fell in thin plumes around her, she froze, and her sword levelled.

'*What was that?*'

Out of the obscurity, clear but faint, it came, a haunting echo of a sound that must practically be graven into the very stones about us – a sudden clink of chain, and a short cry, half stifled sob, half scream.

After the shadow-dance, it was almost too much. The hands backed away hastily towards the stair, halfway to panic – and me? I was right there with them. I'd have felt more ashamed of that if Jyp hadn't reacted the same way, sidestepping hastily over the *vevers* as he backed off. Only Mall stood her ground, straight and shining in the gloom, and cried aloud '*Who speaks?*'

The curtain of dust swirled before her with impossible energies, but no answer came. But the very ring of that voice, mellow and fearless, drove back the tide of fear that threatened to wash over our minds. And to me above all it brought a sudden realization of what that sound might be. '*Clare!*' I yelled. '*Clare! Is it you?*'

And this time the answer came – just one word, but it sent me bounding back past Mall, snatching the lantern, and straight through the swirling dust. It was my name.

'*Steve!*'

It came from the last alcove along the right-hand wall. So like the rest that we hadn't even looked into it – and there in the dark, kneeling, her ash-blonde hair straggling and slick about her stained face, was Clare.

Her arms outflung, she was fighting to tear her wrists free of the rusty iron cuffs bolted about them, straining against the massive chain that ran between them through thick staples set in the stone. But at the sight of me she shrank back, then repeated my name slowly, disbelievingly.

'Steve ... *Steve?* I ... Those shots ... I couldn't see ... just that awful giant of a woman ... and then I heard ... I heard ... *Steve!*' But by then she was babbling, wavering on her knees – and I flung myself at her just in time to catch her as she flopped forward; she felt light and fragile as a bubble, after Mall.

Not quite a classic faint, but nearly. Her eyes were open, but wild, and she writhed in sudden panic as Mall strode up behind me. Small wonder; I was half-afraid she'd heard Clare call her a giant, which she certainly wasn't. But she did look it then, looming over the lantern like a statue of Fury. The lamplight glittered on her face as it flushed first red then deadly white, anger itself coursing like a living light beneath her clear skin. She left no doubt why, though, when she snatched up the chain and tugged at it.

Clare's eyes flew open, and widened in sudden horror; she shrank back. '*Steve! Look out!*'

Mall shook her head reassuringly, reaching for Clare's hands. 'Soft, soft, my mistress, I'm no Wolf. We'll straightway pluck the gyves from off these white wrists of yours –'

A harsh, rasping laugh rang through the cellar. '*But to fasten 'em about thine own, thou barren bitch! Leave the doxy be, or stay in her stead till thou starv'st!*'

We swung around as one, and saw what only Clare had seen. Jyp's voice filled the silence. 'Ah – *crap!*' And that about seemed to sum it up.

We weren't total fools. Jyp had set a watch on door and stairs. And where the single huge Wolf who now

233

stood on the middle steps had come from, I couldn't imagine – short of walking through the wall. But there he was, queasily resplendent in a frock-coat of scarlet and filthy lace, with a bell-mouthed pistol levelled at us all. Evidently he was some sort of commander or captain. He stood taller and thinner than the usual run of them, and his hair was left lank and black about his shoulders, but powdered with what looked like gold-dust; his beard was trimmed to a Vandyke point, with sneering moustachios. And though he stood alone, he had an air of unshakeable confidence. Then I saw why, and why no watch at all could have done us any good – except possibly Stryge's. Around his bare feet the rats were scampering, a whole flood of them pattering down the stairs. And as they gathered around him they sat up swiftly – and on up, rising and swelling as fast as blown flames to manheight and above, tall Wolves riffling their gaudy plumes and stretching with luxurious relief. There could have been a hundred and fifty or more, jostling there on the stairs.

For a long moment nobody said anything; and then Jyp shook his head sadly. 'From rat to Wolf – piss-poor progress. I call it. Me, I liked you better as you were.'

Mall gave a slight cool chuckle. And it was the same laughter I had heard from her on the beach, the same strange sound; deep and dark and echoing, almost, before it left her throat. She hefted her sword lightly, still chuckling. The Wolf stiffened in alarm, and levelled his gun. She shrugged, opened her hand and let it fall; and the Wolf relaxed. But even as the blade clanged once on the stones she whirled about, turning her back on the Wolves, seized Clare's chain in both hands – and in a shower of sparks, with one sharp wrench, she shattered chain and staples together. Bits of metal pattered across the flagstones, and smoke curled from the cracked stone around their roots.

She scooped up her sword then and turned back to us, left staring, with a deep satisfied breath and a slow unearthly smile; and it came to me with a slight shiver that somehow she did look taller. Then she looked at the stunned Wolves, threw back her head and laughed again, more loudly, a sound that rang as ordinary laughter might in a bronze bell, or a whole chime of bells, striking strange resonances and harmonies off each other. It was a daunting sound to me, and to the Wolf more terrible still; for he threw up his hands like a man attacked, and fired. Mall's sword flashed at a speed I couldn't believe, there was a bang louder than the shot, and the Wolves crowding the stairs ducked away in panic from the spitting sing of a ricochet. She had turned the shot in mid-flight.

The lantern toppled unheeded at her feet, but the light did not falter, it grew, it swelled, for it really was coming from her, shining in radiance from her clear skin, glinting among her hair as it streamed out in some immortal wind. And I, kneeling at her feet with Claire, felt that light blaze through me as if I were a bubble of thin glass, understood at last what had so strongly drawn me to her. Then she cried aloud, once, and stretched out her sword. Light flashed from it, clear and fierce as her gaze, merciless to the shadows it chased. The sword hissed through the air, the Wolves bayed and blinked – and with one laughing shout of '*At them, Defiants!*' she sprang towards them. We could no more have resisted a whirlwind; dazed and dazzled, we were snatched up, borne along in a comet's train. Even Clare at my side was shouting with her, and laughing wildly at the flash and bang of my pistols as I fired them into the mass on the stairs, and flung them after. Then with an almost solid crash we were on them, and the killing began.

The mêlée was terrible, swirling this way and that; for the Wolves, though daunted by the sight of Mall transfigured, did not turn tail as they might have – as I would have, or any normal man. They were huge, and had more than twice our numbers; and without Mall we would have been lost. Something drove them as she led us, something dark that devoured light even as she radiated it. We saw it in their maddened eyes as they threw themselves at us, tearing at us with their terrifying strength even as we cut them down, forcing their way down the weapons that thrust through them to reach the wielders. But where she came they could not stand, and she leaped to the aid of men borne down, straddling them like a tower of flame. I clung to Clare and hewed out where I could, and in a sudden swirl of men Jyp caught hold of us both and thrust us towards the stairs where the fight was clearest. A Wolf leaped in my way. I hacked at him as Mall had shown me, he went down and I lunged at the last one in my way. But even as my sword ran through his throat I was bowled aside in a flash of scarlet, and slammed winded against the wall. I heard Clare shriek once, and reeling away, struggling not to fall back into the mass, I saw the scarlet-clad Wolf captain, menacing me with his cutlass, dragging her off up the stair. I swung at him, we crossed blades, but another Wolf brandishing a great Spanish poniard sprang in my way and aimed a stab I couldn't parry. A flash and a bang scorched my ear, the Wolf's face convulsed, and he doubled over; looking around, dazed, I saw Jyp below, gesticulating with his pistol. 'Hey, don't just stand there!' he screamed. 'Get after her!'

Bouncing off the walls like a drunkard, I staggered to the top and out, gulping the cold air in to clear my head. The hall was empty, but a muffled cry and a crash came from the stairs to one side; lightning flared, and the Wolf captain was hobbling along the landing above, lugging a cobwebbed and struggling Clare after him. I ran to the rickety stair and up through the track they'd left, leaping from step to step, hearing many collapse behind me. The boards of the landing were rotten, too, and more than once both the Wolf captain and I were sunk to our ankles in powdering wood, cursing ourselves free. At the landings' end there was another stair, and though Claire kicked and thrashed at him as he dragged her up it, she delayed him not in the least; and he was fast. He reached the top long before me, and made straight for a wide door; but by a great mercy it was stuck, and he had to hammer at it and finally, as I reached the top, hurl his great weight bodily against it. And with that, as the doors flew open, I was on him.

He rounded on me, pistol in hand, and I ducked frantically. The shot whizzed wide, and I aimed a slash that should have opened him from chest to crotch. It was parried so strongly I was hurled back out onto the landing. I charged back at him. He parried again and skipped aside. I skidded on the rain-soaked floor, collided with a railing behind him, felt it shatter – and go flying out into empty space. I barely stopped myself at the edge, seeing the broken wood dwindle away into the dark below me – then rolled aside just in time as the cutlass crashed into the floor beside me. If I hadn't been up that mast the black abyss would have held me one moment longer, and my head would have followed the railing. As it was I jabbed viciously, and he sprang back with a growl and a curse, blood welling from his side. That gave me time to scramble up, and I saw where we were: on a gallery running just below the roof, which was mostly open, with little waterfalls of rain pouring down. That emptiness beneath us must be the great hall. Almost certainly he was trying to get to the far side of the house, to some back stair and escape.

But he wasn't going anywhere now. He was coming for me, letting Clare lie where he'd dropped her, confident he could clear me out of his way first; it showed. Breathing hard, wishing I had just a little more puff left, I levelled my sword.

He sneered – and lunged so quickly I yelped in panic and hopped away. But that overextended him, and he had to drop and duck aside from my own wide slash, right to the fragile rail. There he parried, twisted his blade and slashed at my ankles; I skipped and chopped at him, he caught it and rose to one knee, sending me staggering. I hacked two-handed at his head, he flicked up his cutlass and turned my blow against the rail, smashing it through. Then while my sword was entangled he sprang up and swung a cut. I got free and met it with another and we chopped at each in a flurry of fast blows, back and forth, high and low, with the lightning flickering overhead. I held him off; but three days, even of Mall's training, doesn't make a master swordsman – only one who can see the end coming. In this straight slogging match he was bound to win. He had height and strength and reach over me, and whatever nasty experience could make him captain of the *Chorazin* –

Agony spiked up my leg, and I yelled. His huge foot had stamped down on my shoe – and his clawed toenails pinned it to the spot. His heavy blade sang down on my head. I flung up my own, two-handed, and stopped it – just. But my head only came up to his chest, and he was stronger than me anyway. He leaned, and slowly but inexorably he forced my sword back down onto me. Effort twisted his face into a snarling grin, and threads of slaver dripped from his yellowed tusks.

Then I saw Clare stir and look up, her eyes wide; and suddenly I was back in the office, reading – reading the *Chorazin*'s database entry ...

I caught his eye and winked, though my arms were creaking and it hurt to breathe. 'Hey, captain – recognize anything?'

He started, stared, his cat-eyes glinting. '*That sword! So 'twas thou slew Diego my first mate!*' There was laughter in the appalling voice. '*Vaunt thyself not o'ermuch! Serviceable be was, a most valiant rogue, a lovely bully – but no match for me!*'

'Nor me – was he? And are you so sure you are? Your warehouse raid cocked up – what about that? Your lousy green light put out – the wind knocked out of your sails – how's about that, Rooke? Or should I call you Azazael?'

That caught him! With a sudden deafening roar he forced me down on my knees, and loomed over me, spitting. '*How cam'st thou by that name, swine's stale?*'

I'd remembered it from the database entry. 'Oh – that's *my* magic – don't you remember?' It's hard to sound sarcastic when you're fighting for breath. 'You traced it back – sent your goons after me – all they got their paws on – a helpless girl! Too stupid – whole pack of you – too frigging thick to catch up with me – *me!*'

I hadn't expected that to have the effect it did, the flicker of alarm in the yellow eyes, the sudden relaxing of the pressure. But it did the trick. There was a sudden, sickeningly meaty thump, and he jerked upright, rigid. Any man would have doubled up in helpless agony, but though his slatey face writhed and his cat-eyes bulged he held me still and hewed at me – too late. I'd seen what was coming, and he hadn't; I ducked under the stroke, and clamping both hands on the hilt I thrust upward. I needn't have. He gave a horrible gargling yell as the point took him just under the breastbone, but it was the rush of his own blow that drove him onto it and lifted him, impaled, kicking, over my shoulder. A gush of stinking blood burned my arm as he slid off the blade, toppled onto the railing in a shower of splinters – and over, out into emptiness. A terrible dwindling wail ended, abruptly in a splintering crash. Thunder detonated overhead, shaking the roof and showering us with rattling fragments of tile.

I didn't look after him. I turned to Clare, hopping on one leg clutching the bare foot she'd applied where it mattered, and plunged for the landing. Rotten wood popped and crackled under us; I was afraid we'd fall right through any minute. We ran for the other stairs; there wasn't enough left of the ones we'd come up. From the inner hall below a sudden uproar arose, and men spilled out across the floor; the crew had fought free of the cellar. Through the fighting Mall streamed like a comet, and where she passed the Wolves hid their eyes and bolted, or died.

'Grand, Steve, grand!' she shouted as she saw us. 'Out, out, away and a'haste! Some other sending comes!'

In an avalanche of disintegrating wood we more or less fell the last flight. As we dashed out into the outer hall after the others the floor shook beneath us, and by the lightning that sizzled around the windows I saw the Wolf captain's corpse sprawled on the shattered remains of the high thrones. Tremors ran through the ceiling; plaster fell, and the stone walls seemed to quiver and blur with the vibration. In the doorway stood Jyp, frantically waving the men out past him, his other arm hanging limp and darkened. Beside him Mall burned like a white-hot casting, her eyes too bright to look at, her hair rising in wreaths like smoke. Her outstretched sword-arm seemed to fence with the plunging shadows, and keep the tremors at bay. As we passed, last of all, she danced in behind us, backing away, swinging her sword in great hissing sweeps. On the floor a few wounded Wolves writhed or crawled; what others remained were spilling out of the windows in screaming panic, with no heed to us. Out we staggered onto the terrace, Jyp gasping as each step jarred his wounded arm; the rain came flailing down on us and he slipped and fell. I stooped to help, still supporting Claire – and stared in sheer horror.

The lightning was flashing almost constantly now, like a gigantic strobelight; and in its pulsing glare a strange change had come over the frontage of the mansion, some shifting overlay of shadows that formed a sinister image. The tall windows above the door seemed to change shape, to merge into two great dark ovals. It was as if a face had settled on the house, or became visible through it, a face with heavy sunshades resting above cheekbones undershot and fleshless, the door its stretched, screaming gape of a mouth – a mocking deathshead of a face. And even as we stared that face contorted; the whole housefront seemed to soften and swell, the mouth to work, the heavy stone lintel and pillars of the doorway flexing like lips, the rain-slickened stair a curling, glistening tongue reaching out hungrily towards us as we struggled in the rain. Suddenly Mall stood over us, aglow no more, her face grey and drawn, her hair plastered limp about her cheeks by the rain. But she stooped and seized Jyp as if he weighed nothing at all, drew his good arm up over her shoulder and dragged him away across the flags, out of the baleful shadow of the door.

'Come!' she panted. 'I cannot face Ghedé now, and he may have others to rally, Wolves or worse –'

Even as she spoke, I saw the wind catch the stick-image at the terrace's end and strip the clothes from it. The stick-frame toppled forward with a crash; the hat went bowling skyward, but the coat swooped down on us like a vast flapping raven, arms outstretched. Mall's sword and mine lashed out in the same second and slashed into it; it swirled up and flapped away over the brink of the terrace, riding the blast. The crewmen rallied around us then, taking Jyp from Mall; but I held tight to Clare.

'Not down the steps!' she ordered. 'The way we came is marked! Fly, all! By the back of the terrace – into the jungle! Fly for your lives – and souls!'

CHAPTER NINE

IT WAS THE SAME SUN we'd spent all yesterday cursing, but we cheered it when it rose. Over the hill it came, just like the cavalry, flashing its golden sabres between the trees to warm our spirits and thrust back the pursuing dark. Now Jyp and Clare and I stretched and sighed, basking like lizards on a long slab of rock. The rest of the party lay scattered on other warm spots round about. Nobody moved, except to grunt and shift as a wound twinged, or to throw an arm over their eyes to blot out the feverish swirling behind their lids. After nightlong hours of terrified blundering through tangles that whipped and slashed and strangled with an almost human malice, just lying here and not moving was everything we could want, lulled by the soft thunder of the nearby falls. We'd done it; we were away, we were safe, and we could be back at the ship by nightfall.

And we'd got Clare. It felt almost unreal. Here she was, flaked out on the rock shelf beside me, just as if we were back sunbathing on the office roof at lunchtime. We'd got her out, got her away. She could go back to her old everyday life now ...

She, and I. That started up all sorts of odd thoughts. I clenched my eyelids tight in a vain attempt to shut them out. I wished I could sleep, but the events of last night still ramped and roared through my mind, untameable. That wild flight through the jungle, with the storm and God alone knew what else baying on our heels, seemed almost an anticlimax after what had gone before. Somehow we'd held together —

No, not somehow. I knew how. None of us, not the bravest among us, would have dared lose sight or sound of Mall, if they'd had to tear off a limb to keep up. Mall had held us together, though herself drained and shaken, leading us in a great arc around the slopes away from the

242

castle and the deadly paths to it, and down, down towards the far end of the little valley that led to the falls. As the first greyness showed in the sky we reached it, the first light that showed each man his neighbour's face, and scored upon it the same haggard terrors and utter exhaustion he himself had felt. All except me; for nearest me, warm in the crook of my arm, was Clare, and on her face was only a wide-eyed wonder and delight.

That had come as something of a shock. After all she'd been through, God alone knew what I'd expected – probably to find her shattered, stunned, an uncomprehending wreck. I'd a fair idea I would have been. At best I was praying the effects wouldn't be too lasting, that she'd be able to get back to something like her old crisp confident self again. I certainly hadn't expected to find this new Clare, relaxed, accepting, apparently blissfully happy in my company and asking no explanations, not even a word about going home. It occurred to me that after days of dark and terror and rough handling even the bloodshed and horror, the manic flight, must have spelt revenge and exhilarating freedom. This rest and peace probably felt like paradise. But I'd have to watch her, later, in case some reaction set in.

A shame, really. I felt oddly relaxed with her myself, in a way I never had back at the office. If it hadn't been so unnatural I might almost have preferred her like this.

I rolled over on my side again, and swung an arm out to her; but it only flopped over the edge of the shelf. A sharp qualm of alarm faded; I remembered her saying that the moment she could get back on her feet she'd go down to the pool to bathe, which she certainly needed. Days in the Wolves' tender care – though mercifully she seemed to think there'd only been one – had left her ragged and filthy, and she'd added a fair quota of gore helping Mall tend our wounds. Probably she'd assumed I was asleep, and wandered off without disturbing me. She wasn't worried, and nor was I, not really; there were sentries posted, but under this clear sun our impromptu camp felt safe enough anyway. It was realizing I stank to high heaven in the heat, too, that brought me to my feet. Just the thought set me itching; having Clare around was reviving civilized ideas. Cool water and clean sleek skin glided through my mind. One or two other ideas darted about like teasing fish, but I let them slip away. I wasn't the sort to take advantage – no way. But all the same ...

All the same, it might be as well if I kept an eye on things. I stretched, a little stiffly, no more; there were a few twinges from misused muscles and cuts half-healed, but otherwise I felt startlingly fit. Jyp stirred as my shadow fell across him, winced as he jarred his arm a little, then sank mumbling back into sleep. There was no disturbing him, anyhow; or any of the others I could see. The camp slept; only the sentries stirred at their stations in the shade. I clambered off down the rocky slope towards the falls.

The trees grew high around them, the undergrowth greener. As I pushed through, shreds of colour on a crisp-leaved succulent bush caught my eye. Strands of pastel fabric, very ragged and shapeless, translucent with damp; the remnants of Clare's clothes, set out to dry. I hesitated, feeling awkward; but I could still feel her clinging to me in the long night, still see her, bruised and breathless, dragging herself painfully up against the wall to plant that sharp kick just where the Wolf captain felt it. The way she'd kept hold of her sanity, her strength of mind, all through this nightmare I'd accidentally wished on her – she was one hell of a special person. Even when she was just my ideal secretary, smart, efficient, loyal, I'd felt a sort of admiration for her, cool but strong, a touch protective, maybe. I'd never lost sight of how big a help she was to my career; I'd have looked after her, too. But that admiration welled up far more powerfully now; and something else with it, like the first sharp thrust of a seedling through its shell, raw and wet and unconfined, searching for shape and purpose. I saw something new in her – something of Mall ...

I drew a deep unsteady breath. The air was cool and fragrant with blossoms. Maybe I'd always wanted her; but unconsciously felt I had her, in the ways that mattered.

Was it just protective, that admiration, or possessive? And she – she'd felt something for me, all right; enough to get her kidnapped. Could that be why her various boyfriends never stuck around long? Because it was really me …?

Beyond the bushes there was a brief swirl of water, and in my mind she turned, basking, the sun gleaming on her flank, her outstretched arms. All those teasing ideas leaped up at the thought; old ideas, highly traditional ideas. To the victor, the spoils; none but the brave deserve the fair; that kind of thing. Not that I'd go forcing myself on her. Perhaps I wouldn't even need to say anything; it would all just fall together. It'd be natural enough, after all, something fitting, something right. Something I'd earned; or we both had. The hell with sense; the hell with holding back. Maybe she'd been right, Mall; maybe I had been cheating myself of … something. Quietly, unhurriedly, I parted the bushes and stepped through onto the sandy fringe of the pool.

Clare was there, but not alone. With her, beneath the glassy fringes of the fall, Mall stood, naked as she was, thigh-deep in the foaming water. She stooped over Clare, arms around her, hands across her back clasping her close as Clare clasped her, her parted lips fastened on Clare's in a deep, searching kiss. Neither woman moved; they might have been statues in a fountain, their tangling hair carved in one flowing mass of ashy gold. Neither saw me. Without the faintest idea why I took a single step forward, and my feet tangled in Mall's clothes, shed carelessly on the sand. I turned numbly and went back into the bushes again.

Still dazed, I made my way back to my perch on the rock, and sat down with a bump. I slumped there for I don't know how long, till I felt a shadow lean over between me and the sun. Cool hands rested lightly on my shoulders, as they often had at the office, lingering to massage away tension. Affronted, shocked, I shrugged them away, and looked up angrily as I heard Clare's cool giggle. She met my glare with wide, amused eyes, bit gently on her knuckle and stood contemplating me for a moment, swaying lightly from foot to foot. Then when it was obvious I wasn't going to say anything she shrugged, smiled and drifted away down the slope to another vacant patch of rock. She caught my eye as she stretched out, and smiled again. I looked away, only to find Jyp awake and regarding me with his clear eyes.

'You're all mad at her of a sudden. How come?'

I growled. 'Angry? Me? Why should I be? I'm just ... Jesus, I'm worried, if you must know! Still worried – about her! Drifting about like that – doing things she'd never even bloody dream of, not ... Not normally.'

'You so sure? What kind of things?'

'Christ Jesus, man! Isn't it obvious? I mean, look at her! Wandering about just – *draping* herself round everyone, giggling like a bubblehead – that's not the Clare I know! As if she doesn't give a damn – as if she thinks this is just some sort of dream or fantasy!'

'I'd bet that's just exactly what she does think,' murmured Jyp.

'Hey, come off it! She doesn't exactly need to pinch herself – not after booting that Wolf in the ghoolies! If she doesn't know she's awake, she's off her bloody rocker!'

Jyp heaved himself up painfully. 'Number of times I've seen this happen – Steve, listen! She's far more deeply rooted in the Core than ever you were. And also, I guess, she's more used to using her imagination. You had some time to get used to all this, to shape what goes on for yourself. You're sure it's real 'cause you don't have strong fantasies or more likely you've sat on them. But nobody's told her. She knows she's awake, sure – but in no world she understands. She's adrift. So, are you surprised she finds it easier writing this off as some kind of a fever dream, a delirium? Where the path of least resistance is the smoothest. Where it's best to just take things as they come, to follow as her instincts lead her. It's one hell of a lot better than being driven right off her trolley – and believe me, if she'd been a tad less stable –'

'Great!' I snarled. 'So she just thinks she's in some kind of neverland – where she can get up to all sorts of things she'd never normally do, and it doesn't matter! Like, well ... fantasies.'

Jyp chuckled. 'So? Does it?'

A huge yellow butterfly came to perch on my knee. Irritably I brushed it away. 'Okay! But what about when she finds it's no dream?'

'Will she? Steve, I guarantee you, maybe two days after we get her home that's just exactly what it'll seem like. She'll remember there was some sort of fracas at the office, that you and some friends got her away from some thugs and that she's very, very grateful to them – but mostly to you, 'cause you'll still be there. That's all. And in time even that'll blur.'

'Yes – but the others there –'

'I'd be damn surprised if they remember that much. Memories rooted outside the Core, they don't last too well, not if they're not reinforced. How much did you believe, that first morning after?' I was still digesting that one when he added, 'And isn't that just as well? That all she's gone through won't leave its mark on her?'

I thought. I felt so much to blame for what had happened to Clare. I'd almost been afraid to face her, at first; but if it wasn't going to haunt her so much ... 'That's a point, I suppose.'

'Sure it is. So where's the harm?'

I boiled. 'The harm? Jesus! Just because she won't remember – does that make it right for her to go throwing herself about – so anyone can take advantage –'

'Oh? Like whoever gets a sudden urge for a swim?' His tolerant grin took the sting out of the comment; most of it, anyhow. I remembered my nice little line in self-deception, and shrivelled. Something of Mall, eh?

Nobody likes feeling a bloody fool. I bit my lip angrily. 'Listen, there wasn't any harm in that! It needn't have come to anything – and so what if it did, anyhow? She's had boyfriends; it'd be normal enough! There's a vast bloody difference between me and Mall –' I stopped dead, grating my teeth in embarrassment. But Jyp only opened his eyes wide in understanding, and his grin turned a little wry.

247

'Uh-huh. Maybe. Maybe. You sound kind of shocked.'

'Shocked? Of course I'm bloody shocked! I know Clare, remember? I've known her for years –'

'Steve, most people don't even know themselves that well! Not till something strips the surface back – dreams, maybe, or great danger – and what's underneath comes through. Dreams, and danger! And she's wrapped up in both!'

'But Clare! Clare, of all people! She's just a nice normal girl! It's not the sort of thing she'd ever –' I petered out again.

'Well no, or it wouldn't be under the surface, would it? It's still part of her. Some of the things you did last night, you'd never dreamt you could – but they're part of you, too. Along with a lot that's less creditable. Smile – you're human. You, me, Clare – we're no goddam plaster saints. Once in a while we slip. And if we don't overdo it, it can even be fun.'

'*Fun?* Jesus! I mean, look, I'm as sophisticated as the next man – but Clare ... Clare of all people! *Why?*' Jyp didn't say anything, and I brooded, shivering in the sun. 'Christ, it's not as if I can't understand the ... the magnetism of the woman, I've felt it. Fluttering around the same bloody candle myself – you know that. Only it took a little unfriendly help. It bloody well would, wouldn't it? For me.' I spat out the bitterness. 'And I just got burned. *To the victor* ... Only some are more victorious than others, aren't they? Naturally!'

Jyp shook his head sympathetically. 'Mall, Clare – lord sakes, boy, you just don't know which one you're more jealous of, do you?'

'Sod that!'

'Whatever you say. So it's Mall you're truly mad at?'

'Yeah! Flaming mad! What the bloody hell d'you expect me to be, dancing for fucking joy?' But the words tasted false; and after a moment I closed my eyes and let my head sag. 'No. No. Ah, crap. Can't be, can I? Not even jealous. Not allowed.'

Jyp's eyes were searching. ''Fraid you'd seem a mite ungrateful?'

'Well, yes! The most ungrateful s.o.b. this side of the sunset; but –' I brushed that aside. 'It's more than that – isn't it? Her kind; it's in their nature, right? To love pretty much as it takes them.'

Jyp chewed on nothing a moment, considering. 'So you do understand. Never would've expected it, Steve. You're full of surprises.'

'After the castle – yes, I understand. Some of it, anyhow. You told me, didn't you? About people who move outward, towards the Rim, one way or another. Who change and grow – towards evil, or towards good. And Mall's one of them. Immortals, I mean. Or what would you call them? Goddesses. Demi-goddesses, anyhow.'

'Just beginning to be, yeah. You don't often see it, that fit coming on her. Guess it's got to be there under the surface all the time, though; what makes her such a hell-fighter. Then something wakes it up, and – *whiz-bang!* Though, jehosaphat! I tell you straight, I never saw her like last night before, never quite, and for whole minutes at a time. That's a big step she took. Some day, maybe, a long time from now, that'll break through forever, and in the end she'll just slough off the surface like ragged ol' slops and blaze pure. But till then she's got her feelings and her weaknesses like the rest of us – maybe more so. When it passes, then she's at her weakest, all over. Then she really backslides. She needs ...' He frowned. 'I don't know. Love, comfort. A lot of it. She reaches out where she can.' He considered me again for a moment, 'Not still mad?'

I sighed. 'No. Maybe not. It's just ... well, the ancient Greeks – with all those randy gods and goddesses around ...'

'Yeah?'

'No wonder they turned out philosophical, that's all.'

He laughed softly. 'I've been there. Believe me!'

But he didn't elaborate. It was my turn to weigh him up. 'How about you, Jyp? You on your way to becoming a god, too?

'Me?' I expected him to laugh again, but he looked

249

mildly appalled at the prospect, like the office junior offered a vice-presidency. 'No! I'm barely past my first century yet. Got a long way to go – if I want to. But I doubt I ever will. Guess I'll just go on going around in circles, long as I'm spared – but at least they won't be ever-decreasing ones. Keep moving, keep living, keep the blood flowing and the vices polished up till one day the meter runs out – that's how most of us keep going. But some, some with a real passion, a real spirit, they start losing the taste for anything else. They narrow down, they fine out, they grind themselves down to needle points. More and more they become that passion; you can see it in 'em.'

'Like Hands!'

'Sure, like Israel Hands. If he lived long enough and he'd half a brain he'd burn right down to a mind of fire and sparks and flying iron. He'd maybe become somebody's gun-god, somewhere in time, and be whistled up at their ceremonials to cast new cannon, or have gunners sacrifice to him for better aim. Maybe when the storms go trampling 'cross the skies men somewhere say to their children "*Hark! There's ol' Israel's cannons, scaring up the stars!*" ' We chuckled, though I still tasted bitter bile. 'But Mall now,' he mused. 'She's harder to nail. Justice, that's a part of her passion; but so's a good fight, and music. And a kind of wisdom, insight, when she's least troubled ...'

I nodded, thinking back to that starry night by the wheel, when she'd drawn my life out of me as few others could have. He pressed on.

'It's mostly the ones like that who make it, they say. Who reach the Rim, cross it maybe – who knows? – and come back transfigured. Come back somewhere, anyhow; time means less, the further Rimward you get. Maybe she already has come back. Maybe it's Minerva we're shipped with, Steve boy; or Diana. Or some hunting goddess of our first forefathers, squatting in caves among the Great Ice. Or some power only the future'll know, when all those clever little boxes of yours have crumbled back to the silica beaches they came from. I don't know. Nobody does. But it sure can happen.'

It was a sobering thought; and when Mall came back from the pool a little later I was ready to look at her with new eyes. But she had never seemed more ordinary, pale even, with her curls plastered damp around her face, rawboned and ungainly instead of sleekly graceful. She looked like a autumn wood wind-stripped of its leaves, and she avoided meeting my glance – or, I noticed, Clare's. It came to me then that maybe last night had put her through an experience more shattering than any of ours. 'Bide but ten minutes idling!' she announced flatly. 'Then up straitly and to the ship!' A chorus of groans and complaints arose, but she rounded on us stridently. 'You witless pack of puling whipjacks! D'you fancy another Bedlam night i'the woods, then? We'll scarce be to the beach by sunset!'

That did it. Nobody claimed their extra ten minutes, and my urge for a swim vanished mysteriously. Suddenly we were all hopping and hobbling, buckling belts, priming pistols and loosening swords in scabbard. As we moved off Clare fell in beside me and took my hand, quite naturally; then, spotting Mall, she reached out the other to her. Mall hovered, obviously a little nonplussed, till I waved her over impatiently. It didn't take much effort. Clare pushed her in between us, and I felt Mall's hand clasp mine and clutch at it like a handhold on a cliff. My resentment was fading fast. Her fate might be the loneliest of anybody's – and if she really would remember me a thousand years, better it wasn't bitterly.

The trail soon grew steep and narrow, forcing us apart; and we had to help Jyp. Since he couldn't hang on to the branches and the outcrops he slipped a lot, and every jolt was agony to his arm. He made it worse by continually looking around sharply at everything except his footing. Wounds had been treated with what was to hand – my powder-burned hands with juice of bitter aloes, for one; but he had nothing to stem the pain, except alternately and colourfully cursing the Wolf who shot him, and his own stupidity.

'At least he didn't hit the bone,' Clare encouraged him. 'Or just chipped it, anyway. An inch over and he'd really have broken your arm –'

'He'd ha' blown it clean off,' said Mall sombrely. She seemed as edgy as Jyp, continually looking back over her shoulder.

Clare winced in sympathy. 'Oh god! Well, you're lucky he didn't have an automatic, at least.'

I looked at her sharply, but she just smiled. It was just as Jyp had said; she was moving in a dream, almost, accepting, not questioning. Not thinking through the implications of what she'd said. And yet still the old Clare, all right. Unconsciously or not, she'd made a pretty good point.

They were such all-round stinkers, those Wolves, I couldn't imagine them missing a chance to spread that bit more mayhem. Why didn't any of them have modern weapons? They could surely get them easily enough. Why not tommy-guns or M-16s instead of cutlasses? Why not, for that matter, naval guns instead of muzzle-loading cannon, fast pursuit boats instead of sailing ships? It had never occurred to me to ask. But in one of our brief halts, at noon under the spreading shade of a vast star-apple tree, Jyp was ready enough to talk — I suspect because it kept his mind off the pain, or other things.

'Sure, they could use 'em. So could we. Once in a while some Mutt'n'Jeff does get his mitts on what you and I'd call a modern gun, and raises plenty ruckus — mostly till he jams it, or his ammo runs out. Then what? Chances are he ruins it trying to repair it. And for ammo, he could just about handcast .45 shells, I guess; hand-turn new cases, maybe, or save spent ones. Stuff 'em with black powder or gun-cotton, at half the power — but making the firing caps, fulminate of mercury or some such stuff, that's tough work. Hard as handcrafting a whole new musket, even hand-rifling it — one he'd have not rouble loading. But he manages — and then maybe his second or third homemade shell blows in the breech and takes his hand off. See?'

'I begin to,' I said, wondering. 'They've never heard of industry out here — of mass-production —'

Jyp gestured airily. 'Oh, heard, sure. But industry's big; it binds folk together, ties 'em down. And you need a

252

whole chain of industries to make your modern weapons, or ships, or anything else. Men don't settle too long out here, or sooner or later the Core'll suck them in once again. So who refines the gas for your fast boats? Who turns out the plugs and cams and piston-rings? Or trues the steam-cylinders, even? Not many places'll run to more'n a shipyard or two – and the workers come and go. There's no call for more; we don't miss it. Out here a man can live and sail and fight any way takes his fancy, all the ways we've ever done –'

'Up until the Industrial Revolution,' said Clare thoughtfully, rolling her head around. 'Like a barrier ...'

'The what?' Jyp looked at her dubiously. 'Not one of those Wobbly types, are you, lady? Skip it. Me, I'm glad they went and gave you the vote, but –'

I interrupted hastily. 'What she means is, out here you can't ever go the way the Core has. And a lot of people there do think it was a mistake. Not me! Though I'll admit you seem to live better than I'd have expected without progress – in medicine, for one thing ...'

Jyp forgot himself, started to shrug and winced heavily. 'Ah, we're short on progress all right; but we've got other advantages ...'

Clare lifted her head from my knee, and grinned. 'You mean disadvantages, don't you?'

'Lady, I mean what I say. You've only seen the rough side of it, so far. We've other things going for us. Other forces, other wisdom.'

'Magic?'

'A word. It covers one hell of a lot of things. Like something that'll knit up my arm for me in a few hours when we get back aboard *Defiance* – and it can't be too soon. How much further now?'

'A few miles – maybe four. Mostly downhill. We've skirted the ridge, we'll come onto the beach from further around the bay.'

'A few miles!' he echoed, and glanced quickly up at the sun, and the hillside behind us. 'You'll be dragging me by my boots, then.'

'You'll manage,' I told him firmly. 'Saving your lousy

neck got me into this. You don't think I'm going to waste it all now?'

I didn't say anything about it, not while Clare was within earshot; but it was then, remembering those first mad moments on the misty wharf, that something else began to worry me. All through the march back it nagged at me, and more than once I caught Clare looking at me, evidently wondering why I'd gone so silent and pre-occupied. But I wanted to wait till I could get Jyp alone, and my chance didn't come for hours. We were clamber-ing down the last slope then, pushing nervously between thickets of cutlass-bladed aloes. What little sky we could see between the trees was reddening fast; but at least we knew we'd make it in time, when the men in front hailed and pointed excitedly. A faint streak of light was showing at the bottom of the slope, the distant beach shining through the forest's fringe. You could feel the immediate relief, the infectious lightening of everyone's mood, even the wounded; all except Mall and Jyp. She was grim, silent, vigilant, snapping the head off anyone who spoke to her. He had fallen uncharacteristically silent, moody even, so jumpy he started at every odd noise; and in that twilit forest there were plenty.

'Well,' I ventured sympathetically, helping him sit up after a really bad fall, 'you're having a rough time, but at least we're not dragging you yet –'

'Rough!' he agreed, tight-lipped, cradling his arm. 'Ah hell, could've been a whole lot worse.' He looked back upslope, listened a moment, then shook his head. 'Should've been, when you think about it.'

'Glutton for punishment, aren't you?'

'Hell, no! We got off lightly, that's all. Maybe too lightly. How many Wolves did they sic on us last night – a hundred and fifty? No more. Okay, that leaves more'n half the shipload unaccounted for – where were they when the lights went out?'

I began helping him get up. 'That's what's spooking you? They must have been covering the trail, surely. Lying in wait. They didn't expect us to take to the tall timber – I didn't, I can tell you! With any luck they're still blunder-ing about up there now –'

'Aye, with any luck!' Mall called up sourly from below. 'But a'nightfall things may change. Enough lingering; it stays for no man!'

'He can't stand!' I told her angrily, but Jyp brushed me aside and staggered up.

'She's right! Me, I'll not feel safe till I set my feet fair on old *Defiance*'s planks again!'

That brought back my own troubles. 'Yes – and what then?'

'Then?' The thought cheered him. 'Home 'n beauty, and a great weight off your mind – mostly in gold!'

'God knows, you've all earned it! But what about me?'

He glanced at me, considered a joky answer, and visibly changed his mind. 'Okay, what about you?'

'You've said Clare ... won't really remember any of this. But me? What about me? Am I just going to forget it all?'

Jyp stumbled past me down the muddy slope, into the heavy-scented tangles of hibiscus ahead. 'Depends,' he flung back over his shoulder. He caught a branch with his good arm and began picking his unsteady way down.

'What on?' I repeated the question as I skidded after him. 'Jyp, I want to know! It matters, damn it!'

'Steve –' he grated between his teeth, 'it's not so simple – if I could tell you – I would – okay?'

Our boots skidded and slipped, bruising the bright hibiscus blossoms, and they bled glossy black sap onto the earth. I didn't ask any more.

Among the trees down below I saw the leading sailors break into a run, and Mall do nothing to hold them back, only stop and wave us impatiently on. Clare came skipping back to help, and a long low ray of sunset set a flush on her bare limbs and jewels of fire in her hair. With the other stragglers we came stumbling down into long grass, hissing in the soft wind. Through the last curtain of trees I saw the grey-blue champaign of the ocean, and the sun's rim blazing its furious last against the stifling clouds.

The sea shimmered a moment the colour of fresh blood; the light dimmed. We emerged into the first rosy

255

flush of island twilight. There lay the ships, a mile or so away in the sheltered arm of the bay. Faint windrows riffled across the calm water, like smoke across a mirror. And there on the shore were the boats, luring even the wounded to hurry on, forgetting their pain, eager to get free of even the shadow of that forest. The fit hands held back to help them with nervy patience, casting black looks up at the treeline as the uneven column straggled along the beach. We weren't under the cover of the *Defiance*'s guns yet, and twitched like kittens at every rustle. Orders were passed down the line in hoarse whispers. Pistols were clicked to half-cock, swords drawn; every bird that fluttered up risked a dozen deaths, though fortunately nobody was actually fool enough to fire. When we came near enough we waved frantically at the ship – we didn't dare hail them aloud – and got a laconic reply. It seemed like the first tangible link between us and safety, however weak – the thread that pulls over the lifeline. We all felt our spirits lift and leap like the boats, coming alive under our hands as we ran them down into the light surf.

It seemed almost like an anticlimax as we bundled into them, unopposed. I even heard some of the madder hands wishing the Wolves had come down after us, so they could have shown them what for. When the castle came briefly into view as the first boat bounced out through the shallows, a great baying call of mockery and defiance went up. I remembered the jarring, meaty thump as my sword ran through the great Wolf captain, and ground my teeth in exultation, forgetting how starkly terrified I'd been. I caught Claire about the shoulders and hugged her tight. She looked up at me and laughed, and we watched the hateful shore fall further behind at every stroke.

Only Mall seemed not to share the feeling, and perhaps also Jyp. She sat hunched and still in the bows of the other boat, her hand near her sword, constantly looking from ship to shore as if measuring the distance some unknown menace might travel in our wake. Jyp was slumped exhausted in the stern of ours, but his eyes flickered across the same course, ship to shore and back again; and after a few minutes he began to force his injured arm to flex, trying to stop it stiffening.

'Stop it, you berk!' I told him. 'You'll start it bleeding again!'

'Sure, but at least I'll have the use of it!' he answered quietly. 'Like I said – not till I set my feet on that deck ... And maybe not even then. We're getting off too lightly.'

'Twelve dead and eighteen wounded is light?'

'Well, no. And may be Mall put the fear of ... Mall into them! But odds are they'd not give up so easily – not the Invisibles. They're planning more hell yet. Maybe it's already here.' His pain-reddened eyes rested on Clare for an instant. 'Something we're carrying with us, maybe.'

She huddled back against me. 'What's he saying?'

'Nothing. He's feverish. Can it, Jyp. This is just Clare, right?'

He nodded, perspiring as he flexed his arm. 'Right. I trust your feelings, Steve. Wanted to be sure, that's all.' He leaned back and closed his eyes. I found myself swaying away from Clare a little, looking her up and down, meeting her gaze hard.

'Just Clare,' I repeated, and, rather hesitantly, she smiled.

Even so, it was a moment of deep relief as we came under the lee of the *Defiance* and saw the mate in the bows waving us in. The derricks creaked out, and I noticed May Henry, muffled up in a bright bandanna, among the sleepy hands who shuffled up to tip rope ladders down to us.

'And a sling and chair for the wounded!' yelled Mall impatiently. 'Shift your idle scuts!'

With a last glance back at the shore she drove her men up the ladders, helping such of the wounded as could climb. I was already helping Jyp up, with Clare beneath us; Mall came shinning up the boarding steps past us, swearing at the slowness of the hands above. Together, straddling the rail, we bundled Jyp up and over. Hearing his feet thump decisively on the deck, I was about to chaff him about his definition of safety when I saw the look on his face. I looked up sharply – and stiffened.

As we were meant to. The horror of the sight held us just long enough. Rising in the rigging, bobbing in the breeze by the noose about its throat, the grotesquely twisted corpse of a yellow dog –

The flung nets exploded over us, caught Clare opening her mouth to scream, Mall swinging her leg over the rail and reaching for her sword, me turning to shout a warning. We were jerked violently back, toppling over the rail and crashing in a tangled heap on the planks. All in silence; but a sudden hoarse shout went up.

I tore at the net, only entangling myself further – but freed Jyp, nearest its edge. He scrabbled up and swung himself onto the rail. Heavy boots boomed across the deck after him, but I saw him launch himself away in a creditable swallow dive, his injured arm outflung. From below came shouts and splashes as sailors, warned by the struggle, flung themselves off the ladders and out of the boats. A ghastly baying of Wolf voices arose, the crackle of pistols and the flatter bang of muskets. My sword was snagged under me; I struggled for it, flopping and twisting like a landed fish, with Mall clawing and snarling above me. Then, planting her knee in my stomach, she heaved herself up and caught two great handfuls of the net, about to tear it apart; and she might have managed, even with her inner fires dulled. But May Henry loomed above her, dough-faced, glassy-eyed, and struck down viciously with a belaying pin; Mall fell kicking on top of me, clutching her head, and I felt her jerk as the pin sang against her skull a second time.

With the force of that blow the bandanna slipped – and Clare, trapped beneath Mall and myself, screamed in horror. From beneath it gaped a great jagged gouge in the she-pirate's throat, a black bloodless trench, bare to a gleam of spine-bone. I surged up with a yell, throwing Mall off me, and grabbed Clare. With the net still tangled around us I hurled myself at the quarterdeck ladder, and by some access of strength I almost made it. Till my foot slipped in a pool of tarry slime, and I came crashing down almost on top of something horrible that lay in the door of the foc'sle cabin. A firescorched mass, surrounded by a great star of charred timber, only vaguely human in outline; but by a hank of long hair and a scrap of ragged black that had escaped at one edge I knew it must be the girl Le Stryge had called Peg Powler. They had come prepared this time; and polluted water had not put out their flame.

My hair was seized, my head jerked back. I stared up into Wolf eyes and others, dark eyes narrowed in exultant, gloating faces. Not handsome faces; their silhouettes were odder than the Wolves'. Their earlobes drooped low, their lips were scarred, their brows oddly flattened and narrowed, and the whole was covered in lacy traceries of black, paint or tattoo that all but hid the coppery yellow shade beneath. Against the glowing sky something swung up, fell. A burst of agonizing light —

I don't know whether I went out entirely, or for how long. I seemed to feel myself being turned over, my head bumping sickeningly on the deck, the blood-stopping bite of thongs; and I do remember being hoisted bodily, trussed like a hog, by hands that were deadly cold. Yet perhaps I was already ashore by then, the swaying motion that of the pole I was slung from, the soft sighing rush the wind in the leaves again. My first clear memory was the deadly sickness, the rush of vomit in my throat, the coughing panic as it almost choked me. I managed to turn my head to clear it, just; and after that, though my skull seemed to swell and contract at every throbbing heartbeat, I felt a bit more alive and aware. Very shaken and light-headed, though, and utterly exhausted; unsure whether what I could see of the procession that bore me was real or a fever dream, flaring and flickering like the torch-flames, stuttering like the drums and the low droning voices. Long Wolf-limbs strode and shuffled, half-dancing to the dull beat. Shorter ones stalked beside them, naked and covered in that same black tracery; the red torchlight and the shifting muscles gave it a horrible animation, like a grating into hell. Only the feet that carried me didn't dance, but plodded along, leaden and stolid as any laden ox. They paid no heed to any obstacles, branch or jutting rock, but blundered into them and past, and swung me against them just as carelessly. Battered, bruised, scratched and sickened, I lost all sense of time till I was flung bodily down among soft grasses, with the pole on top of me. The jar made my head swim again. I barely caught the hoarse whisper from the dark beside me.

'Howdy.'

At first I couldn't speak. 'Oh – hi, Jyp. Didn't make it, eh?'

'Caught me in the shallows. This goddam arm. Not the Wolves, the Caribs – not nice guys. Held my head under a few times for sport – God knows why they didn't just finish the job.'

Fear crawled. 'The others? Mall – Clare –'

'I've seen Clare. Zombies dumped her up there a ways – awake and okay, so far. Mall I didn't see …'

'She – they hit her pretty hard, Jyp.' I didn't want to say more; nor he to hear it.

He was silent awhile, against the background of jabbering Wolf voices. 'Skipper's here, anyhow, and what's left of the crew.'

'Jyp – did you see? May Henry –'

'And the mate – and Gray Coll, Lousy MacIlwine, Dickon Merret – yeah, I saw. Lord, that was a neat trick they pulled. There was I half afraid the ship'd been hit first – right from the moment I saw the castle was a trap. It made sense – but when I saw them all waving, natural as kiss my ass … There's more'n Wolves behind this, or these Injuns. There's a brain.'

I shivered in the chill breeze. 'The Indians – who are they, anyhow?'

'Amerinds. Caribs – what the dagoes named the sea for. After wiping them out, mostly, or enslaving them. They're regular guys enough, the ones left; but this isn't them.'

'You mean – these are the originals? Another hangover in time?'

'Kind of looks that way.' He fell silent as footsteps approached, stopped a moment, then hurried on. 'You said – they hit Mall real hard?'

'She — she may be dead, Jyp.'

'That could be the worst mistake they ever made,' he said at last — thoughtfully, not vengefully. 'She —' I heard him choke and gasp at the thud of a boot. I got the same treatment next, not hard but right in the kidneys. Writhing, I was only dimly aware of being untied from the pole. My hands and legs still bound, I was dragged bodily through the grass till it vanished abruptly on bare rocky ground, where I was dropped. I lay blinking, thinking how bright the torchlight seemed; then a hand in my hair hauled me to my knees, and I saw the two tall fires, and the white stones between, and the dark silhouettes passing to and fro.

More than that I didn't make of them, just then, because chains rattled suddenly, and ice-cold iron snapped around my throat, pinching the flesh painfully. I pulled away instinctively — and found I wasn't alone. Clare and all the rest of the crew, Pierce and Hands and the crabbed little steward among them, were slumped in rows on the cold ground beside me, fastened together with what looked like old slave collars. And next to me, uncomfortably close, sat the Stryge himself. He curled his lip in something like a sarcastic greeting, but I paid him no more attention, because next in line sat Mall. Alive; but her head hung, she was deadly pale, and a thick clot of blood caked her curls at the forehead. Her lowered eyes were dull and glazed, and my heart sank; I saw concussion there, if not a fractured skull. A biker had looked like that, after a pile-up I witnessed; and he'd died in the ambulance.

Stifled cursing told me Jyp had been dumped just behind me. 'So what's this?' he demanded. 'We in line for service, or what?'

'Undoubtedly,' grated Stryge through his stained teeth. 'Though I should be in no haste about it, if I were you.'

I knew what he meant. My eyes were adjusting to the light, and the more I saw of the crowd that was gathering the less I liked it. Apart from the Wolves there were ordinary men and women both among them, more

261

than a few evidently Haitians. Not all were the dark-skinned villager types, though, and those looked better fed and complacent. The rest were mulattoes, Haiti's powerful aristocracy – well-groomed creatures who could have jetted in from London or New York. Gold gleamed around their necks and their fingers, jewels flashed in the firelight; some wore elegant powdered wigs and carried quizzing-glasses, but others sported hornrims and chunky Rolexes on their wrists. The heavy robes they all wore looked well cut, and the *vevers* and other strange symbols swirling about them shone with sequins and gold bullion. These elegant creatures mingled grotesquely with the naked Caribs in their war-tracery, and yet they jangled with ornaments just as valuable; not only brass bangles and spirals about arm and neck and ankle, but rings of pure soft gold weighing down their distorted ear-lobes, plugs of gold through lips and nose catching the fire redly. Here and there, too, white faces gleamed among the crowd, white of all shades, sallow as old parchment or bleached albino-pale; many of them, too, wore heavy ear-rings and ornaments in styles long forgotten, others unmistakeably modern hairstyles, glasses even. One blue-rinsed matron had upswept *diamanté* frames, pure Palm Beach chic that looked incredibly grotesque and sinister here. I had the odd feeling I was watching a gathering from far away, from long years apart in the island's terrible history; and I knew it could be true.

But whatever their origins, swaying, jostling to that soft sinuous beat, they all looked alike, horribly alike. If ever I doubted the brotherhood of man, I saw it paraded before me that night – at its worst and darkest. Kinship is a terrible thing when it lies in cold, devouring looks, merciless, ruthless, utterly selfish or actively malign, weighing us up like prospects for a show. I could imagine Romans looking that way at captives in the arena, or predatory Western tourists at some of the nastier Bangkok cabarets, more with cruelty and delight in degradation than plain old lust. It had less effect on me than it might; I was too worried about Mall and Clare. But it did cross my mind momentarily that there were worse ways to be than

262

empty. If my life had been hollow, fuelled by nothing but ambition, at least it hadn't been filled with that sort of feeling, driven by those drives. At least emptiness was neutral – not a good thing maybe, but not a bad one either, depriving nobody but myself. Or was it?

It was as blinding in its way as that crack on the head, the sudden shock of recognition. They might have been ambitious, too, these people, just as I was. They sure as hell looked it; they looked just like the types I knew. They might have cut everything else out of their lives, just as I had; got what they wanted, where they wanted – and what then? A plateau. Nowhere else to go; or a long, long wait. And what could they do then? I'd been sensing it already, that emptiness in my life, that gnawing discontent – right from that moment at the traffic lights. Sheer ambition – casual sex – they'd been growing less enjoyable all the time, these sterile pleasures of mine. When they finally waned, what then? What would I have gone looking for, to fill up my hollow life? What short-cuts to rewards I felt I deserved, to fulfilments I felt cheated of? What else, that I mightn't have known was evil, because I hadn't left myself enough feeling, enough empathy, to judge? Suppose I came across something like this ... Would I have woken up, one bright morning, and seen that look in my shaving mirror?

Back and forth they swirled, chattering, drinking, reaching up a hand to caress the tall white stones as they passed them. The stone was stained and scarred with what looked like firesmoke; it highlighted some sort of markings on them, rough crude scratchings hardly worth being claimed even as primitive art. They looked childish, moronic almost, and yet this elegant, excited crew was greeting them with an almost sensuous reverence.

'Take me out to the ballgame!' remarked Jyp laconically. 'What's the big attraction, old man? This is some sort of *boumfor*, right?'

Stryge sneered. 'More than that, infant! Can you read the signs on those stones? I thought not! That is the work of these red savages, these *Caribal* apes, carved before other men came to these islands. This is a *sobagui*, an altar, one of their ancient shrines – and their cult, you will remember, was amusing.'

'Wait a minute,' I said, with a sudden sinking feeling. 'It's not only the sea that's named for them, is it? Caribals ... *Cannibals?*'

'You got it,' said Jyp. 'Can't you just see it, them and the Wolves squabbling over our chitlings? Me, I'd sooner feed the Caribs – any day.'

'Would you?' Stryge spat in the dust. His voice was venomous with contempt. 'When they slashed open your sides while you still lived, to stuff you with herbs and peppers for the spit? They worshipped cruel gods, that tribe, preying on their hapless neighbours to feed their observances. When slaves mingled with them, raised in cruelty, shaped with the lash and the brand – oh, they understood such worship all right. Some took it, mingled it with their own Congo witchcraft and the brutalities their masters taught them. They worshipped a new god then, one who set himself above the rest, whose rite could bind and bend them to his will. A cult of wrath and anger and revenge, drawing its strength from all things common men call vile.'

He turned to me, his gaunt face working with strange emotions. 'You, boy – do you hear those drums? Do you? You who would not leave well enough alone, you who would meddle in the affairs of forces past the scope of your empty dreaming! They are the drums I made you hear, far away, beyond the ocean and the sunset, the *tambours maringuin*. They speak a name, softly yet; soon, more loudly, till the hillsides throb with the beat, and all in town or village tremble and bar their doors, clasp their charms tight against *loup-garous* and *mangeurs moun*. For this is the cult of Petro, the dark way of *ouanga*, the leftward path of *vodun* that can twist and deform even the Invisibles themselves into shapes of vicious evil. And this, tonight at these ancient stones, this is its ancestral *tonnelle*, the temple where it was first proclaimed.'

I felt deadly cold; but I was running with sweat. 'You mean – that it was a ceremony like this? In the boiling water? That they were going to sacrifice —'

'Triple idiot!' raged the old man. '*Crétin*, can you not listen to a word I say? It was not some such ceremony! It was *this* ceremony! Here! Tonight, child of misfortune! A rite of sacrifice — and something more! And all your fool's labours have served only to lead us to it! Not only she you sought to snatch back — all of us! To share her fate!'

He spoke loud enough for Clare to hear. I looked up in alarm and met her eyes, wide and wild with fright — and yet searching, I could tell, for some word to say. 'You tried!' she choked. 'You tried — that's what matters —'

But the others were silent, even Jyp; and Strgye laughed coldly. 'You may think little enough of yourself to say that, child! But a chit's life, or this hollow shell that calls itself a man, what are they to mine? I for one did not live in the worlds so long to be turned out of them on such a fool's errand, and left to wander my own way back again!'

'Then do something about it!' barked Jyp. 'Or go choke on your own forked tongue, you old copperhead —'

'Stay!' said Le Stryge, very sharply, and the fire gleamed on his greasy coat as he leaned forward, listening. Or was he listening? He seemed intent on some sense; but it was not one I shared. Then, very coldly, he laughed. 'Do? What can I do, fettered in cold iron? No strength in me will pass it. Find me a force from outside, now ... But for that, even could it be done, it is too late. Something comes, some other approaches ...' Suddenly the sweat stood out on his high brow and he cried out softly. 'Evil is here! A strength — an evil ancient and strong. Not of my kind —'

He rounded on me, wild-eyed and panting, so hard he almost pulled Mall over. 'You! You starver of your soul, you waverer between good and evil, taster of neither — you worshipper of emptiness, of gauds and trinkets! This is your doing, this you have brought on us! It draws nearer ... nearer ...'

CHAPTER TEN

I TWISTED MY HEAD away from the old man's spitting vehemence, like a cobra's venom. I could have felt ashamed, or angry, I suppose; in fact I felt almost nothing. A little nervousness, a little queasy uncertainty – but at the heart of it all an absence of feeling, a numbness. It was like looking out of a window into a deep black pit. An awareness of failure, maybe; I didn't know. I wasn't used to it.

But the poisonous old voice dropped suddenly to a whisper and fell silent. The drums, too, sank to a shuddering mutter, the jabbering commotion of the crowd collapsed into an awed murmur, the sounds merging into a soft, uneasy threnody. Even the flames seemed to bend and dwindle, though the dank air was still and cool. Then the crowd parted suddenly, men and women scuttling hastily aside, clearing a path to the fires and the stone beyond. For a moment it stood empty; then something moved across the flames. Along the barren ground towards us a long shadow fell. What cast it was no more than a shape, a dark silhouette like the outline of a man swathed in hooded robes, like a medieval monk almost; or a leper. Along its own shadow it came gliding towards us, black and impenetrable, as if no more than a deeper shadow itself. It halted smoothly a few feet in front of us – in front of me. And then in one fluid movement it bowed.

Bowed from the waist, with a dancer's grace, almost to the ground. For a nicely calculated instant it remained poised, steadying itself on a tall slender black cane; then it rose unhurriedly upright, and brushed back the shadowing cowl. Bright dark eyes glittered into mine, with an impact that was almost physical – a shock so sharp I didn't immediately see there was any face around them. Let alone a face I'd seen before.

266

Not a Wolf's face, or a native's. A European face; but naturally swarthy, deeply tanned, and tinged with an unpleasant yellow, jaundiced and unhealthy, nothing like the golden-skinned Caribs. The high brow was deeply furrowed, the face unlined save for the deep channels that flanked the narrow hooked nose and shaped the black moustachios like fangs around the thin dark lips and jutting, arrogant chin. Black hair only slightly tinged with grey swept back from that frowning forehead to ripple elegantly about the neck. Blacker still were the eyes it hooded, curiously empty despite their glitter, as if some vast void lurked behind their bright lenses; and the whites were yellowed and unhealthy. All in all, a strange, striking face, now I saw it clearly. Proud as a king's, almost – and yet too marked with concern, cunning, malice to look royal. A statesman's face, a politician's – a Talleyrand, not a Napoleon. And with a hint of sickliness that I hadn't noticed, in that New Orleans street, leading me astray; or behind the wheel of that car nobody but me seemed to see. Or on Katjka's cards ...

Not a king, then – a knave.

For an instant he seemed to hesitate. Then long fingers rippled in an elegant salute, gems flashing in the firelight; and he spoke.

'*¡Muy estimado señores y señoritas!*' Softly, deferentially; and mainly to me. 'I beg your most gracious forgiveness that I am forced to receive you in such a fashion, without announcement or proper introduction. Such, however, are the circumstances of the hour.' Sometime around the eighteenth century they must have made a big fuss about his perfect English. To me, with his lisping accent, it was heavy going. 'May I therefore take the liberty of presenting myself? I have the honour to be the Don Pedro Argote Luis-Maria de Gomez y Zaldivar, Hidalgo of the most Royal Order of ... But a mere recitation of honours would no doubt weary folk of your station! To these our poor observances let me bid you a most sincere welcome.'

Nobody said anything. The Knave seemed to be waiting.

'You know who we are,' I growled. 'All of us, if you're the man behind all this. Are you?'

'In a sense, *señor,* you oblige me to admit that I am.' He bowed again, less deeply. The cloak parted to reveal a costume not unlike Pierce's but about ten times as florid – an outburst of ruffles at the throat, a long waistcoat embroidered with what looked like pearls and other stones, breeches with a satiny sheen and gilded shoes. It was the sort of costume you see in the Prado, going dusty in portraits of long-forgotten grandees. 'In another sense, however, the one "behind all this", as you so amusingly put it, is *you, Señor* Esteban.'

'*Me?*'

He spread his hands wide. 'Why, of a certainty. For it was you yourself, *señor,* that we have been seeking. All this so very great effort was expended for the sole purpose of attracting you to this island; or to a lesser place within our reach. But the island was best.'

'I knew it!' exploded Jyp. 'I damn well knew it! I was right to chase you away! Shouldn't ever have let you come back again –'

A courteous hand was lifted, and Jyp shut up at once. 'Ah, *Señor* Pilot, I must ask your forgiveness for having so unfortunately misled you. Of our original intention the *Señor* Esteban formed no part; how could he, when we were not then aware even of his existence? Only when he began – you will forgive me? – to interfere, and moreover to take an interest in us, using his own most curious magical devices, to a gravely unhealthy extent; only then did he call himself to our attention. Yet the creature you call the *dupiah,* had it been released successfully from its hiding-place, would have had as its ultimate and most difficult task to ensnare just such a man as he.'

'And just what the hell d'you mean by that?' I demanded.

He gave a slightly surprised shrug. 'Why, a man of some small standing within the Inner World, *señor.* A young man, no doubt, yet one who had already achieved much success, whose undoubted gifts carried the promise of far greater advancement still. But a man of hollowness, an empty soul.'

It was my turn to explode. 'You primping little son-of-a-bitch —'

Again the hand lifted. Courteously; but the very gesture hit me like a vicious slap in the open mouth, jarring my teeth, stiffening my tongue. I strangled on my words.

'But *señor*, an expression merely — a figure of speech, no more!' There was no trace of mockery in the level tones. 'I beg you most earnestly to accept that I intended not the slightest insult.' The long fingers waved deprecatingly. 'After all, was I not once just such a man myself?'

I gaped, and then a sort of horrible laughter welled up in me. '*You?* You're putting me on a level with —'

The snigger was politely deprecating. 'Oh, hardly, *señor*, hardly! After all, was I not born a *hidalgo*, the lord of wide plantations, even some silver mines, and many strong slaves to work them? Whereas yourself ... But I was constrained to grow up very much alone, there being no other child within easy reach fit for me to associate with. It was perhaps inevitable that, dwelling alone among mean and lesser men, so far from the civilized company of my peers, I should grow somewhat ... apart from them.'

He turned for a moment to survey the silent crowd behind him, and they avoided his look. Wolf and human alike. For the first time I felt an openly sardonic edge to his voice, and something else, something more deeply disturbing.

'What use had I for them, after all? What could they show me but the mirror of myself, the follies of love and hate alike? Upon reaching manhood I was sent into society for a while — and there they presumed to reject me. They — I! Those strutting popinjays the men! Those lovely women, who should have been flattered to uncover the fires they kindled! They laughed foolishly behind their fans and passed on. Bored — jaded — and have you not felt as much, *señor?* — I sank myself in my work, my ambition I drove my slaves with fear and pain to labour to their miserable limit, I grew incomparably rich as the world measures riches; yet I valued wealth only as an emblem of success – a banner I could brandish in the face of the world. As, *señor*, I am sure you understand.'

I'd never been anything like rich – and yet, though part of me revolted violently at the idea, I found myself nodding automatically. I *did* understand. Somehow that unsettling note in his voice, part pleading, part persuading, and still somehow dominating, compelled me to face up to it, to admit how alike we were. And yet …

I couldn't help protesting. 'But I've never done anything like … like you! Never wanted to! I had ambitions, yes. A career – politics, maybe, one day … But the feeling of achievement, I didn't really want more than that. Knowing I was succeeding … showing it –' Success – the successful man's image – that's what it was. A badge, a seal of approval to prove how much I mattered, how important I was. To drive home my status in other people's eyes. To shield me from their questions, their doubts – and from my own. *You can't argue with success* …

He saw my hesitation, and nodded benignly; he forgave me. 'Ah, I might have been thus content, *señor*, in my turn. For what else remains to those the world will not give their due? Were it not for a most fortunate turn in my affairs … Though I admit it did not seem so at the time; as your present situation, perhaps, does not to you. There came an outbreak of the *vomito negro*, that you call the Yellow Jack fever, and I was infected. It took that. It took weeks of fever and delirium and spectral visions, of lying close to death and weeping lest it claim me still young, before I had found out what it was to live. It took so much to lift me out of my narrow sphere to that which my talents truly deserved.' He smiled.

'As it has taken all this for you, I doubt not. For in my delirium I walked strange paths, saw visions, understood for the first time that there must be worlds beyond the limits of our own. And I saw myself. It was at the very crisis of that mortal distemper that the truth came to me – that it was death itself that gave life meaning. That one

270

never lives so intensely, or clings so keenly to life, but in death's presence. Then, *señor*, then I understood; it was the driving of slaves that truly fulfilled me, and not the result. And never more so than in the dealing out of life and death, the slow or sudden tipping of the scale.'

The Knave smiled faintly. 'I had of course already become acquainted with the many and curious varieties of religious practice my purchased creatures had brought with them from their African homelands. Many, naturally, benign and insipid, or mere crude raucous release. But others were more promising. And among the Maundangues, from that region you call by the barbarous name *Cangau*, I now discovered beliefs and techniques which though unrefined were quite peculiarly to my taste. So the elect few who knew of them I spared and studied — oh, in a spirit of simple amusement, at first, I assure you! Until I began to perceive that within these bloody barbarian games there were real forces at work, and greater gains to be had than mere diversion. Then I set myself to learn. I sat at the feet of those who bore my fetters, even embraced them as brothers in blood — I, a grandee of Spain!' He tapped the ground with his cane, twice; and the chill of it seemed to flow up into me, numbing my heart. 'But only by such abasements is enlightenment attained. Regard, if you please, these inconveniences you now suffer in that light; for from them, believe me, I intend that you shall gain! Every bit as much as I did. And that was great.'

His voice had dropped, yet I hung upon his every word. 'For I became a *houngan* priest, in touch with the Invisibles. But that was only a first step, a shallow one. The true depths are dark, and to darkness I turned, to the most wicked and corrupt among that servile race. I learned from them the arts of malice and compulsion, of sorcery and necromancy; I became a *bocor*, an adept of the dark. And within a short time, my inborn mastery asserting itself, I became the greatest among those who had taught me, and cast them down to tremble and suffer with the rest of their kind.'

A sudden image swirled before me, like paint in

water. Myself, in the white robes of the men around us, plastered with painted markings ... 'And that's what you mean for me?' I couldn't stifle another manic attack of giggles. 'You want to make me into a bloody witch-doctor?'

He seemed more amused than offended. 'Oh, no indeed, *señor*! You misjudge me. That dreary and wasteful time I would spare you. So many false turnings, so many foolish seekings after fulfilment – so many terrible regrets! I did not then realize they were but one step on a quest longer than I could have dreamt – save perhaps in my fevers. Such squalor, such mere savagery – these were mere beginnings I have long surpassed.' He gazed down at me with a look of delight and wonder, almost childish, the way a single-minded scientist might contemplate his rarest and most precious specimen. 'As you will, *señor*, in your turn.'

I stared. That was about all I could do. 'I don't understand,' I stammered. 'What're you talking about? What *are* you offering me?'

He laughed. 'Things you cannot yet imagine! Power beyond your dreams! But for now, only to begin with – power as you would understand it, dominion in your world. Men will follow you, men, aye, and women – a few at first, then a party – a city – a region – a nation! You will deal with them at your whim, the more so, the more they will flock to you! And you will draw sustenance from them as I did, and live on as they die, untouched by years! What do I offer you? That, *señor!* That but for a beginning!'

I stared. The tirade had left me literally speechless, my thoughts whirling like a sputtering firework. I'd seen the soul of a man laid bare – or more than a man, or less. And why? Because this Don Pedro thought I was another of his kind. That I'd hardly be anything less than eager to leap at what he offered, if only I could be made to understand. Not a scientist, or a child; a lonely monster, maybe hoping he'd found a friend?

And how wrong was he? He'd gone looking for – call it love; human warmth, at least. Denied it, he'd channelled his frustration into ambition, sadism, god knows what. But me – I'd had love, hadn't I? And I'd thrown it away. I'd taken that same ambition and stuck it up on an altar, deliberately sacrificed love to it. If anything, that sounded worse. God above, maybe he was right! Maybe I *would* like what he offered. Maybe he was what I'd come to, anyway, in the end.

There was the image again. Myself as – what was the name? A *bocor*, mumbo-jumboing over the embers of a dying fire, drawing *vevers* with my fingers ...

No! It was too damn ridiculous. I was about to burst out laughing again when I felt the gritty maize flour turn to computer keys beneath my fingertips. That brought back, sharp as a tang of spices, the familiar thrill of calling up information, juggling it, manipulating it. The way I felt getting to grips with a really difficult deal, tying up a knotty contract in a watertight package of agreements, provisos, penalties ...

Only here, somehow, I knew I was dealing a whole order of magnitude higher. The flows of world trade, the checks and balances of high commerce, the economies of nations – all the forces that dictate the life of every man, from the Amazon Indian in his grass hut to the Chairman of the Supreme Soviet. And they would become one man's to command. They would obey these flowing fingers, the face reflected in the borders of the screen. A handsome face in its way, hard but magnetic, strongly lined, white-haired but crackling with youthful vigour – and still unarguably mine.

I fought to blink away the vision. There was a fierce directness to it that shot right past consciousness and common sense, as wholesale a grab at my instincts as a Pirelli calendar – or a religious experience. My words slurred over my tongue. 'Why ...'

'*Why?*' Again that possessive, gloating smile. 'Because, *señor*, I have need of you! Because to gain my end I had to sacrifice all that I had amassed. In my quest I was forced to leave the Inner World behind me, to slough off all that was worldly about me. So now I must have an agent within it – clever instrument of my designs, trusted sharer in their rich rewards! And in you I find the fabric, the fallow soil fit for the plough, the fine clay for the turning – and the firing!' He wrung his hands in sheer pleasure. 'And soon, swiftly! Without the long years I cast away on gratifying childish fancies – on trifling, tentative essays of my will. All that I have, I shall share with you! All that I am, I shall make you! And all you can reach out and grasp shall be yours!'

I was spellbound; I couldn't protest, I didn't want to. Through my hands, through my commanding mind the world's commerce poured like a shining river, to be diverted this way and that, settling its gold-dust sediments wheresoever I chose. But still something didn't quite belong there, some factor that kept bobbing up in the torrents of my mind and wouldn't sink ...

'The others!' I choked. 'Okay, I'm here! What d'you need them for, now? Clare – you don't have any use for her any more! Let her go! Let them all go!'

I don't know what reaction I expected. Anything, perhaps, except the ghastly flicker of fury that crossed the sallow face, clear as lightning in a sulphurous sky. The nostrils pinched tight, the dark eyes narrowed to slits, the livid lips crumpled; blood rose beneath the high cheek-bones, then drained as swiftly from the papery skin. It fell inward as if sucked, flat against the bone, leathery and wrinkled; the teeth bared in a horrible grin, the muscles shrank, the tendons stood out like rope. Only the eyes remained full beneath their parchment lids, but their lustre dulled like drying ink.

Sweep a torch around a dry crypt or catacomb and a face like that might leap out at you; or as I'd done, in one of those Neapolitan mausoleums with glass-panelled coffins, I'd seen hands, too, with nails that had gone on growing, yellowed and ridged and curling; and though his never touched me, I felt the bite of them as my face was slapped sharply, from side to side. Still fuming, he bowed again, very stiffly.

'Desolated as I am to contradict the *señor*, not for anything in the world would I have these your friends miss the occasion! Indeed, their absence would severely hinder the whole proceedings!'

274

Stryge let out a horrible sneering caw of laughter, and his breath rolled over me like sewer gas. 'Call yourself one who binds Immortals, do you? And you can't even spell this empty thing's mind off his friends! You – bah! I've met the like of you before – spiders in your ceiling! What man dares hold Their kind in thrall?'

Don Pedro bowed deeply once again, and when he rose the face was clear and composed as before. 'I defer to a colleague of rare distinction; a pity he must share the fate of his inferiors. True, no man could humble Them so. But I have long since ceased to be only a man.'

Stryge gargled and spat. 'That error's common enough – the cure swift and final! What are you but a petty Caligula who's learned a bit of hedge-wizardry? Enjoy your delusions while you may, man; they only mock you, biding Their time to strip them from you! Yes, and all else besides!'

'Caligula?' The dark man seemed amused. 'Hardly; for he was but a mortal who dreamed himself a god. Whereas I –' He looked at me again. 'At first, I assure you, I had no such thoughts. I sought only to enhance an existence grown burdensome, to find ... satisfactions beyond the conventional.' He chuckled slightly, as a man might at some naïve childhood memory. 'With the wealth my creatures made me I bought ever more, and devised me ingenious amusements. Some I sent to deaths swift and painful. Others I spared to tread a narrow line, loosening little by little their holds on life, watching them cling all the faster to the dwindling, deluding shreds left them. From that death in life I gave them, fast or slow, I learned to draw new life to refresh me, and that was much; yet even that paled. For once I held the race of slaves in the palm of my hand, once I as both master and *bocor* could lash not only their cringing bodies but their thoughts, their dreams, their hearts – then the strength I could draw from their torments grew thin. Even then I had come to depend on it, to sustain my very being. Even then blood was the wine I drank, anguish the air I breathed. I must needs cast around for some new source. But as yet I lacked the courage and the vision to seek the Absolute.

So, limited as I still was, I turned – as a man must, must he not? – to my own people.'

The Knave smiled. 'Not that it was altogether without satisfaction. Poor fools! Their cruelties had been almost as great as mine, but idly practised, without purpose. The island seethed beneath them, yet still they drifted fecklessly through their masques and levées and futile festivals. Upon them I unleashed plagues and poxes and contentions unnumbered, and filled their graveyards. And then out of them I awoke some of them, those who had most offended me, and the loveliest. Them I led through many a rout of my own devising.' He shook his head with nostalgic indulgence. 'It is said memories of some still linger among the walls of my old home – you saw, perhaps? Even so. That was satisfying, of course; yet some artistic touch seemed called for, to cap the jest. So I took my hold over the slaves, and turned it into a stronger whip than their masters'. A cult of blood and revenge – with rites of such enormities that they left those who took part stripped of restraint or fear; for they had already done the worst. I became as a god among them, almost one of the Invisibles myself; and I lashed them into savage and merciless revolt. Triple irony!' He tittered faintly. 'That I, their tormentor, should win them their freedom! Though of course I saw to it that the aftermath was suitably bloody, that little peace has come to them down the years. A greater irony still, then, that they by their worship should set my faltering feet on the path to power.'

All this time nobody had spoken; it wasn't hard to guess why. But at that, abruptly, a head lifted, and a voice croaked '*Thou*? Their most bestial of tormentors they've worshipped as their liberator? The Petro rites, the living spirit of the slave-folk's vengeance – the cult of anger, the bloody offerings – all *thine*?'

To my astonishment – and by the look of the man, to his – it was Mall who had managed to speak. Bedraggled, blood-streaked, wan – but alive and awake. My heart almost literally leapt at the sight of her. The man whom she had called Don Pedro seemed to feel very differently. His dark glance flicked over her like a snake's tongue, and he bowed, stiffly this time, almost guardedly.

'The *señorita* is correct,' he said. 'Mine, all of them. The mob embrace him who will pour out blood before them, and fail to see it is their own. Was it not ever so, with liberators?'

She said nothing more, only struggled to hold her wavering gaze on him. He turned away from her in a billow of cloak, and to me once again. 'I am Don Pedro, whom they name Petro; and as one of the Invisibles themselves have I become, and into my hand their powers are given.' He clenched it, solemnly, slowly. 'I had lived many centuries, when at last I took the great step. I had brought my inner purpose to blossom, come into my true strength. And yet next to the Invisibles I was still as nothing. To be feared, to be obeyed is much; yet those who obeyed were but the poor folk of a wretched island, easily cowed and driven. And god though they thought me, still I was no more than an intermediary, able in subtle ways to call upon the powers of the Invisibles, but wielding little that was mine. The powers of the Invisibles! They did but remind me more fully of my emptiness. The want of them burned within me, reduced my most refined joys to ashes. The agonies of a very race seemed too cheap a gift to console me for what I did not have! So I probed constantly, I summoned, questioned, bargained – till at last I understood that to gain my greater end I must first lose all I had. So I took the last step, the greatest. I loosed my bonds. I set the Inner World behind me, and cast myself adrift upon the currents of Time, in constant quest of some still closer, deeper, more fulfilling union with Death. I sought – and I found! Among the Invisibles themselves I found One forever hungry for dominion over the rest, and over a wider world – over all the worlds that might be, in the end. Yet even He could not assert it, not alone. Infinitely beyond mine was His strength; but my driving intelligence – that He lacked! Till He came to me and joined with me, poured himself into my hollow heart! I found – and for the first time in all my long life I tasted fulfilment! From the heights to the depths I was filled, I was complete and more than complete!'

He pressed his hand to his chest. 'Thus blended, we became a greater One – greater than His fellows, and master among them. Able to bend their strengths to my will, to torment not merely mortal men but higher forces, and draw out their strength for my own. To put blood in Erzulie's eye, searing fire in her thighs! To drive Agwé to a storming frenzy, to have Damballah shake the Earth within his coils! All must obey me when my drums beat, when my rite is chanted – when over my stone the life-blood streams!'

The fires crackled and flared suddenly, and though he stood with his back almost squarely to them an answering gleam seemed to leap and flicker in his eyes. 'I attained the highest power I sought – and in that timeless hour I first tasted true joy. And that, *señor* Esteban – all that is what I offer you – and you *dare* to hesitate?'

'What –' I was croaking. 'What are you going to do?'

The long fingers rippled like descending rain. 'Tonight our rites shall call down the *loas* – and they will come. Come to you! But not in their bland natural forms, no, to make bestial festival with fools. They shall come as I will them, in the power and the terror that we shall unleash upon that unsuspecting Inner World, you and I! And through it, all the infinite universes, all the time and times which spiral out from it! They will be our wine-press, in which we tread the hearts of men and higher forces alike, tread them out to the bitter lees! From the agonies of a single child to worlds that go down in slow fire!'

He must have caught the look on my face. He made a deprecating gesture. 'Of course, these are but mysteries to you now. You do not yet appreciate them – how could you? But I expected more – ambition, shall we say? Less mired in the passing fates of others. Still, I assure you, all will be clear to you, soon, soon. When you in turn are fulfilled. When the *loa* takes his place within you, when you are no longer the shell you have left yourself – then you will understand. Reach out, *Señor* Esteban, accept with joy the cup that is offered you! It is a great honour;

but one which, if you are wise, you will not refuse.' His voice faded to a soft crooning whisper. 'Indeed, in all conscience I could not allow you to.'

The courtesies were an open mockery now. To begin with he'd been weaving a web around me, a net of meanings behind his words, charged with some power to persuade me, snare me into eager submission. Now it blew in the wind like ragged cobwebs. He would not take me by subtlety now; which meant, I guessed, he was going to rely on force. What kind, I couldn't guess; but I was horribly afraid. The idea of not being me – I was shaking, and my bruises hurt. Idiotically, knowing how useless it was, I strained and kicked against my bonds; but the iron neckring clattered. It had held the strongest slaves once; and what had he done to them? I fought to stifle a whimper, and was deadly ashamed when I couldn't.

Slowly the Knave shook his head. Again the cane tapped the ground. The numbing chill was spreading through all my limbs now; a leaden, languorous feeling that was not entirely unpleasant, as soft and relentless as that quiet voice. 'Struggle, if you will; you but pain yourself to no purpose. In such as you, *señor*, there is no power to resist what comes. The door stands open, there is none within to bar it. And as for your friends, let me reassure you. Only be patient, and you will see their worries also come to an end! And now, I trust you will excuse me. Our solemn rite must not be delayed!'

Once, twice, he bobbed deep bows to me, then whirled around in a billow of cloak and strode away –

Or did he? He seemed to be walking; but he passed over the rough ground too smoothly and too fast, gliding like a wind-spun leaf. A deadly shiver shook me, a chill deeper than the ground. I'd thwarted him, somehow; and in anger and disappointment, as one does, he was letting appearances slip. 'What the hell *is* he?' I breathed.

Le Stryge let out a great spraying wheeze of a chuckle. 'But of course, yes, you were pleading with him! So touching; but a trace too late – a century or two, maybe! How did you not see at once? From the eyes, boy, the eyes! A creature gnawed away from within, like a grub with a parasite, a walking shell. Nothing left of him but habits and memories, the real man eaten up long since. From such as that let a man keep his distance, if he wants to stay a man! Small use pleading with it!'

'What else can I do?' I demanded, feeling the blood sink out of my face. Don Pedro had been trying to persuade me I could go the way he went – and still stay human. What would it really be like? Being worked like a puppet from within?

Or would I even know about it? Would thoughts come to me just the way my own did? Ideas to act on, that seemed like my own most of the time – and yet, just now and again, there might be this creeping, helpless doubt. And all the time there'd be less and less that was really mine, until ...

I saw only too clearly what Le Stryge had meant. In school biology class I'd kept caterpillars. Some died suddenly; and I'd found that the growing wasp larva within had eaten them away to a mere bag of skin, a living mask of flesh. And all the while they'd kept moving, kept on feeding just the same as ever, so I'd never noticed the difference.

'I don't want to become like him!'

'You won't be able to help it,' Stryge told me evenly. 'It is as he says. You also are empty, though you are not so aware. Less empty than he, maybe, since you show some concern for others; but the spirit within you is small and shrivelled. You know neither great love nor great hate, great good or great evil. You have starved your life of what life is, and there is too much space within. Such people are most easily possessed; and often, despite what they think, they welcome it.'

'So you say!' I snarled. 'So you bloody well keep saying! Who the hell are you to condemn me? You're damn near as creepy as he is! If you're a full man I'd sooner be empty.'

Stryge's smile was suddenly frightening, and in his eyes I seemed to see the orange firelight flickering among the rubbish-strewn scrub-grass of his vacant lot. 'I am full,

I contain multitudes ... Most of it you would neither like nor understand. But at least it is all of my own choosing. It serves me, not I it.'

I shivered. 'And me? What's he need me for so badly, anyhow?'

The old man snorted. 'What? Is it not obvious? This Don Pedro, for all his power, left the Core long centuries ago, having dwelt nowhere beyond this isle; and for that we may be thankful. Of this world he wishes to rule he knows little – whereas you, boy that you are, are adept at manipulating it. With you as their instrument they'll have all your skills at their disposal. They would not need such clumsy plots as the one you and the Pilot foiled; trying to sneak a *dupiah* and a Wolf-pack past our barriers to seek power by brigandage in the Core. They could smuggle in whatever they liked, by ways we of the Ports cannot touch. And they may aim higher, intending to have you rise to a position of power. What could one such *homme d'affaires* not achieve with the might of the Invisibles behind him, wielded subtly and ruthlessly? You would unleash their domain throughout all the circles of the World –'

'Stop it! *Stop it!*' It was as if Clare's voice broke the bonds her limbs couldn't. 'Don't just *gloat* over him, you smelly old bastard! It's not his fault!'

A sudden roll and surge of the drums gave weight to her words, a thunderous crash that faded suddenly to silence. The crowd swayed and split, and for a moment I glimpsed the drums themselves, dark cylinders the height of ordinary men, grouped in threes with their tall Wolf drummers poised over them, their elephantine skins gleaming with oil and sweat, their dyed parrot-crests brushing the ceremonial *tonnelle* roof.

'There's truly nothing you may do?' Mall demanded thickly, over that instant of tense quiet. 'However desperate – nothing?'

Stryge snuffled scornfully. 'If there were, I'd not have waited on your word! The ceremony begins. First the *mangés mineurs*, the lesser sacrifices to lure down the Invisibles among the worshippers. Then the *mangés majeurs*, the great sacrifices, that will bend them to Don Pedro's will. Then – it will be too late. They'll bring their power to bear on our empty-headed friend here, and he must fall. Not that we'll be there to see it! If any hope remains –' He jerked his head in my direction; and for the first time I saw fear flicker faintly in that ancient, flinty gaze. 'Then let it lie with him.'

'With *me?*'

I almost screamed aloud at the cruelty of it. Lay all this on *me?*

Fingers stroked the drumheads and they sang, a low humming note that swelled and grew. Another note blended with it, a soft droning chant that fell oddly off the beat, a lurching, distorted music. There were words in it, but I couldn't make them out. Then the stretched hides bellowed and roared as bone sticks and open palms fell on them, a roll that rose and fell like surf and stuttered into a kind of march. From behind the drums figures appeared, half-swaying, half-strutting, with the solemn slowness of a ritual procession. Slowly, very slowly, they wove towards the fire, towards the high white stones. A tall Wolf, robed in ragged black, led the way, shaking a huge gourd hung about with what looked like knuckle-bones, and white ivory beads that gleamed in the red light – or were they teeth? On either side of him, dwarfed, two haughty-looking mulatto women swung tall thin staves topped with red banners, embroidered with complex *vever* signs. Behind them marched two Carib men, holding up naked cutlasses on their tattooed palms and trailing in their wake men and women of all the motley races there, rattling bone-gourds, shuffling their bare feet on the ground. I saw some tread on sharp-looking stones, on still-glowing fragments spat from sappy logs, but they didn't seem to notice. Others drifted out from the crowd as they passed, while the rest took up the chant and swayed to it, stretching their arms wide, rolling their heads from side to side. Around the flames they wheeled, still chanting, and shuffled to a halt before the altar-stone.

Abruptly, without any signal that I could see, the toneless chant broke off. The whole procession sank down as one, the crowd sagged like collapsing canvas. Wolf and human alike crouched huddled with arms above their heads. Only one was left standing, at the rear of the gathering, one I knew damn well hadn't been there a moment ago. With the unhurried movement of a ritual the cowled figure glided forward over the backs of his prostrate followers and stepped delicately up onto the flat fire-scarred rock. The drums stammered and yelped, the arms stretched out and the cowl fell back. Like the moon glinting from behind black cloud the cold sallow face of Don Pedro gazed down upon his followers.

I could see him clearly, still with that faint half-smile. An instant of breathless silence was shattered by a burst of animal noise, a deep rebellious lowing that set off a cacophony of other calls. Chickens squawked, something bleated – sheep or goats, maybe – and at least two dogs were yelping. It didn't sound one little bit absurd; it was unnerving as hell. If they were what I thought they were …

Don Pedro spread his hands and snapped his fingers once, explosively. In a flurry of robes the leading Wolf scuttled up to join him on the altar, and others behind him, Caribs and whites and blacks, almost all towering over the little figure. It was he, though, outlined in the light, who seemd like the one fixed point, and they as insubstantial as their shadows on the stone, hunched and shivering. He sang out, in that lisping voice of his

> *Coté solei' levé?*
> *Li levé lans l'est!*
> *Cotée solei' couché?*
> *Li couché lans Guinée!*

Yet it sounded harsher, more powerful than the thunderous, ecstatic whisper of the crowd's response.

> *Li nans Guinée,*
> *Grands, ouvri'chemin pour moins!*

Then slowly at first, in a peculiar throbbing rhythm,

they began to clap, growing stronger, faster till they drowned out the drums. 'The *battérie maconnique*,' murmured the Stryge softly. 'The Knocking on the Door –'

'Party gettin' under way, huh?' said Jyp tautly.

Don Pedro closed his eyes an instant, as if in anticipation. Then he took a tall pitcher from one of his acolytes, and turning to face the front, the fires and finally the rock behind, he lifted it and shook it gently in salutation – to the compass points, it looked like. Then abruptly he yelled something, and dashed a stream of what the pitcher held against the white stone. It looked like blood, flushing red-brown; but then, leaning unconcerned out over the flames, he tipped a stream into the left-hand fire and swung it around into the right. An arc of blue fire hissed up across the front of the altar. He raised the pitcher to us – and hurled it, spraying, through the flames. We ducked aside as it fell and shattered amongst us, leaving a comet's trail of droplets that blazed and stung. The crowd roared, the drums rolled in celebration, and the cries of the startled animals rang louder than ever. A sickly stink filled the air; it was rum he'd burned, and pretty powerful stuff.

The drumbeat quickened. On the altar the acolytes bobbed and hopped around their god-figure, flinging out libations of rum and flour and what looked like wine. The crowd clustered forward, holding up their hands in the supplication of the starving for the symbolic food, barging and trampling, twisting this way and that like snakes following the charmer's pipe. Among the crowd a woman screeched, a frightful tearing sound that was something more than protest, and sprang out before the altar, whirling, leaping to the beat, cavorting in the tangle of her robes till she looked no longer human in the firelight, more like some wind-tossed bird. Suddenly a tall black man was dancing, flinging himself against the stone at Don Pedro's feet. Behind him a shorter white man swayed like a withy, graceless and boneless, lank hair streaming. Wolves bayed in their horrible voices and joined the dance, their heavy boots shaking the ground; and once they were in the whole crowd began to seethe and swirl like a heating pot. Only our Carib guards stayed aloof at the edge of the clearing, shuffling and circling in slower circles of their own, shaking their heads and tapping the ground with their spears. But as the dance swirled past one shrieked aloud, ducked down and came stamping forward, tattooed legs splayed, spear outthrust in a menacing, posturing mime. The drums yammered frenzy at him as he hopped and stabbed, and his fellow Caribs began to quiver and jerk and shudder like the rest. Bottles gleamed in the hands of the dancers, tilted high, passed from hand to hand indiscriminately and, near empty, were flung to crash against the white stone. The acolytes had to dodge them, but Don Pedro only smiled and stood, arms outstretched like a priest's in blessing – or like a puppet master with many strings.

Then he gestured, a strange circular movement slashed sharply across – once – twice. The crowd fell back, still dancing. An acolyte sprang down and tipped maize flour from a bowl on the ground before the stone, and as he poured his shuffling feet traced the same design, a circle quartered by two lines.

Men and women burst out of the crowd swinging fluttering bundles – chickens, dangling helpless by their feet. Up towards the stone they held the birds, swinging them in time to the dance; and suddenly a long blade caught the firelight in Don Pedro's lean yellow hand. Across, back it licked, and with an exultant yell the acolytes flung the headless bodies, still flapping and struggling and spattering blood, high in the air to crash in their death-throes into the quartered circle. Don Pedro flung his arms above his head and sang out

Carrefour! Me gleau! Me manger! Carrefour!

The crowd howled and swung forward, Carib, Wolf, white and all, dancing and reeling from side to side. A young black woman seized one of the headless thrashing things and tearing open her robe sprayed its blood down her naked front; then she pressed it to her breasts, swaying

285

and singing. And in her high clear voice I began to catch words I knew

> *Mait' Carrefour – ouvrir barrière pour moins!*
> *Papa Legba – coté p'tits ou?*
> *Mait' Carrefour – ou ouvre yo!*
> *Papa Legba – ouvri barrière pour li passer!*
> *Ouvri! Ouvri! Carrefour!*

Carrefour – that was crossroads in French. And *Legba* – My fists clenched. Not a French word – a name, one I'd heard before. With a shout like breathless laughter the crowd drew back, pointing. In the open space before the blood-spattered design two or three figures limped and hobbled on sticks they plucked from the fire. One, a plump middle-aged mulatto, came lurching past us, leering and blinking with rheumy eyes. But as mine met them I felt a cold thrill of excitement. There was no real resemblance – it was more like an expression that flickered across that wholly different face, and a strange one at that. A grimace, twisted, distorted almost beyond recognition – but all the same it was unmistakable. It was the look of the old musician from the New Orleans street corner – from the crossroads. And *Legba* was the name Le Stryge had given him ...

Desperately I called it after him. The man hesitated, glanced back at me, and I couldn't be sure whether I still saw that look about him or not. Dry-throated, I raised my tethered hands to him. But then Don Pedro cried out *Carrefour!* again, and the crowd echoed the name like thunder. The dancers stiffened, straightened, no longer leant on their sticks. Rising to their full height and onto their toes, they spread their arms in great sweeping gestures of blocking and defiance, their faces settling into a mode of grim negation. The crowd crowed in welcome.

The man before me laughed a horrible bubbling laugh that seemed entirely his own, took a vast swig of rum – and spewed it out over the still-glowing stick at me.

Fire showered down on me like a rush of stinging hornets; I thrashed and yelled in my bonds. Stryge caught

286

some, and snarled his anger. The man just laughed again, vindictively. *'Pou' faire chauffer les grains, blanc!'* he spat, and shuffled back to the dance. To warm up my – ? My balls. Nice of him. But momentarily, as he'd turned away, I could have sworn I'd seen his face twist, as if in the throes of some terrible doubt or agony – and there was that Legba look again! Something more than malice had flashed into that slack malevolent face, something different – as if *he* were pleading to *me*?

Me again – always me. What did they want of me? What could I give?

'Calling on him?' muttered Stryge darkly. 'You might have saved your damned fool's breath.'

'He helped me in New Orleans!' I protested.

'Maybe! Though how or why –' Stryge wagged his head grimly. His voice rattled like the *açon* gourds. 'But here he will not. He cannot. The *haut chant* was fed with living blood. He could not resist. It called his shadow-self, his distorted form – the Dark Guardian. Carrefour. Not the Opener of the Ways, but the Watcher at the Crossroads. And Carrefour is no man's friend.' He hunched his head down into his shoulders. 'Now the ways stand open. And the Others must follow, when it's blood that calls ...'

Lines of maize flour traced out another, more complex *vever* pattern. The drums boomed and stuttered, the crowd swayed – and suddenly another hellish libation of rum flared over the fires. Men and women in the crowd dragged a few goats forward, and others some dogs – miserable skinny mongrels, but pitiful in the way they wagged their tails uncertainly and snuffled about. Don Pedro's reedy howl rose high again.

> *Damballah! Damballah Oueddo!*
> *Ou Coulevre moins!*
> *Ou Coulevre!*

The crowd flung the name back to him.

> *Damballah!*
> *Nous p'vini!*

'Voodoo rites,' muttered Jyp. 'I've seen a few – but nothing like this one, not ever! It takes the goddam cake! The prayers are the same – the words, anyhow – but the whole tone's wrong! They're not praying to the *loas*, they're damn well *ordering* 'em!'

'Ordering indeed!' Stryge said huskily. 'Power is abroad here. This is Don Pedro's own *tonnelle*, the heart of his cult. This is the rite of which the other Petro rites are shadows, echoes, imitations half understood – the central rite. Blood draws the Invisibles, living blood, and his power ensnares them. Their natures are fluid, he cannot change and his power ensnares them. Their natures are fluid, he cannot change them – but he can bind them in a form governed by their worst aspects. Damballah is a force of sky, of rain and weather, but they make him the Coulevre, the Devouring Serpent – a thing of storm and flood –'

He stopped, or more likely was drowned out by Clare's scream. With brutal dispatch the goat was flung up to the altar, spreadeagled and bleating desperately. Don Pedro's sword made one slow lopping slice down the hindquarters. The trussed beast jerked and shrieked and the worshippers yelled; my stomach heaved. It seemed like an eternity before the blade struck again. Blood fountained up, and the yelling crowd leaped to catch it and taste it, sucking at their hands, their robes or those of their neighbours for the least spot more. The headless body, still kicking, was flung down among them, but they trampled it carelessly in their rush to see the next one sacrificed.

The ritual was the same each time – the two cuts, one to castrate, the other, after a savoured moment, to behead. I shrivelled at every thud of the blade. This was how he would work along the pathetic line of victims, driven frantic now by the chanting and the shrieking and the reek of blood. And when they were gone it was how he'd offer up his *cabrits sans cornes*, his special goats without horns – Clare, and Mall, and Jyp, and Le Stryge, and all the others. But not me, it seemed. For me he had something really special in mind.

All I'd have to do was sit and watch.

I saw horrible things done. When he killed the dogs it seemed worst of all – illogical, maybe, but that's how it felt. And each time we saw the sacrifice's legs kicking and fresh blood spurting and steaming down the runnels in the stone, we thought he'd start on us next. At each new round, as each new *vever* was traced in the paste of maize flour and blood and trampled soil, new libations were poured, new names shrieked to the skies, new rhythms battered from the drums; the dancers, humans and Wolves alike, flung themselves into new frenzies, and the barren earth shivered under their pounding feet.

Against the pulsating firelight their threshing shapes, milling like a shattered anthill, really did look like a vision of hell. So far most of the dancers hadn't done anything significant, just scream and sing and stamp with the rest. But it came as no surprise when some of them began to run amok altogether, cavorting and gibbering and falling down in fits. Others ran this way and that in transports of ecstasy, or exploded into screaming hysterics so violent that their neighbours were forced to grab them and pin them down. But the fits soon passed; and more and more of the crowd began to change. Just as the first few had mimicked old men, they took on attitudes as they danced; they chanted in hoarse assumed voices, strutted and capered with peculiar gestures, almost ritualized. They looked like actors auditioning for the same roles. It was as if some other identity had settled over them like a veil, hiding their own.

Disturbing enough in itself, the sight unnerved me horribly. This was possession – the possession I dreaded so much, the distorted *loas* descending to mount their followers. But they seemed to court it, to embrace it. One or two of the acolytes around the stone snatched up a few props laid ready, as if they knew already what other self would seize upon them. Some of the crowd, too, stayed in the same guise, dancing in the same way, even smearing their faces into improvised masks with charcoal, blood or the spilled flour. But most of the dancers let each new name, each new god's descent, wash over them like breaking waves of emotion. In the blink of an eye they'd shift from one mood to another, wild whooping wrath or serpentine grace, in a kind of shivering exaltation, half hysterical, half sexual, that burst all everyday bounds of behaviour.

One minute, as the chant of *Ghedé!* went up, they jerked and ground their thighs in crude spasmodic mimicry, ritualistic, robotic – like disjointed skeletons mocking the movements of the flesh. The next, to the cry of *Zandor!*, they trenched the stony soil with their feet, like ploughs – then, crouching, spilled their guts and trampled it in. When the name *Marinette!* was called from the altar, the dancers stalked and rolled their eyes in grotesquely seductive attitudes, posturing before the altar, each other, even us where we lay bound. A Wolf woman strutted and cavorted up and down before us in her rags, flinging her straggling purple hair against her long limbs, mocking us with gestures, movements, tearing her robes; others came to join her, women and men, either sex flinging and flaunting themselves carelessly in our faces. The things they did were just crude in themselves – no worse than a whore's show or a lover's game, even. But to us they were aggressive, meant to deride us, to humiliate us – and that made them really brutally obscene.

Another minute, another name – and the dancers forgot us and flung themselves at their neighbours, snatching, clawing, mouthing at each other, mounting. But though some of it turned to sex, it took a vicious, nauseating turn, and they shrieked with laughter at the blood that flowed. It was an orgy without passion, without a trace of real lust, even. It turned my stomach. And the moment the little man shrieked out the name *Agwé!* they forgot, fell apart, rolled and swept their limbs as if swimming over the filthy soil.

I was swimming, too, fighting to stay afloat. Struggling to keep thinking, to work out what Stryge could possibly expect of me – something I could still do and he, with his strange powers, couldn't. But the drums pounded my thoughts to pulp, my head ached and my concentration shredded. The flickering of dance and flame became hypnotic. I couldn't force my eyes away from twisted rituals acted out before me. Hours and minutes had no meaning; there was only an endless bloody blur of night, alive with the roar and reek of the seething, manic crowd, doing mad things at a madman's command. I tried to prove Le Stryge was wrong; I tried to pray. But what could I say? And who to? So much else was out here I'd never believed in, maybe gods were, too – some, any, all, maybe. But what had I to say to any of them?

My mind wandered. Again and again I caught myself swaying in time to the fearful music of drums and voices. I sank my teeth into my lip in a frantic attempt to keep awake, to keep thinking – at least to resist, somehow. But it kept on happening, and I couldn't find the energy. Sitting on the cold ground like this was numbing me, slowing my circulation. A low voice kept distracting me, mumbling words I half understood. I tried to yell at whoever it was – and only then realized it was me. I thought I was cracking up, at first; then I knew the truth, and that was worse.

I flailed in panic. It was happening already. The thing I dreaded – it was coming over me, softly, insidiously, even as I sat there. Trying to resist that? I hadn't a dog's chance.

Frantically I bit down on my disobedient tongue, chomped hard to restrain it. That gave me a better point of pain to concentrate on – and then I knew that the Stryge had been right. There was one thing I could still do. One way I could thwart this Don Pedro, one way of escaping the destiny the little bastard was planning for me. But I also knew why he hadn't told me what it was.

I could bite through my tongue, choke on the blood, and die.

Easy to think about; not so easy to do. I'd heard of people managing it, prisoners under torture, madmen in straitjackets. And I told myself I ought to have at least as much of a motive as they did, surely. Not that dying would save my friends – but it might save a lot of others. And it would save me from something worse; from being a puppet and a prisoner in my own body, the hollow shell of some predatory horror I could hardly imagine. So I tried. Oh yes, I tried, all right, clamped my teeth down on the thick heart of the muscle till the pain was appalling and the veins stood out – and no further. I couldn't; I was ready, I had the strength ... and I just couldn't.

Call it cowardice, call it subconscious resistance – but I could no more do it than fly out of the chains that held me. I kept on trying, I bit sharply, I shook my head about; but nothing I could think of would force my jaws to close.

So much for playing hero; and all this time I could feel my control slipping. I knew something was affecting me – the drums, the cold, the chanting, the foul air, the twisted little parade of cruelties at the altar. That was what I thought at first. Soon I knew better. They helped, yes; they trampled around in my thoughts and muddied them. But it was something else, something behind them, that was at work; something greater than their ghastly sum. With every new waft of presence it grew stronger, like hands tugging at me, light but implacable. They pressured my thoughts this way and that, like loosening a tooth in its socket.

It was no illusion; I was beginning to see things. Figures, many times manheight, that leaped and wheeled and capered behind the dancers, mimicking them like giant shadows cast upon the sky. Every minute I saw them more clearly, whirling over me, and what was around me grew hazier. Voices spoke in my brain, little tickling whispers, deep thunderous tones. I felt flashes of thoughts and memories that weren't mine, that couldn't be any man's, that left only confusion in their wake, so far were they from any experience I could identify.

If I could have been any more terrified than I was, I should have been. It wasn't like that at all. Every minute now I felt easier, more wondering. A distant door ajar, and coming from behind it warm light, the smell of wholesome cooking, the sound of familiar voices – that, to a child lost and hungry on an icy night, might be some shadow of what I felt. All the trappings of an absolute security, of a happiness I'd never known, of a richness I'd been longing for all my life yet never knew I lacked – the remotest taste of these things came to me, the promise that they lay ahead and were getting nearer. It didn't bother me at all that my body seemed to be growing light, numb – until suddenly I felt my limbs twitch sharply, once, twice, without my having tried to move them. As if they were coming under the control of some other will –

I jolted awake, shivering and sweating. My head had nodded, my chin sunk down on my chest. It was like struggling to stay awake when I was working late. Except that in the warm blackness behind my eyelids *Something* was waiting …

I fought desperately to regain control. Somewhere, somewhere far away, there was a new clangour in the drumming, a sharp metallic dinging like the incarnation of a headache. And there were voices – Stryge's, as harsh and desolate as ever I'd heard it. '– beating the *ogan* iron – can't you hear? That's it – that's the end. The last – the greatest. If they can command Him –'

Something he'd said caught my attention – some memory. Some shreds of my will began to reassert themselves. I concentrated feverishly on whatever still bound me to earth – the pain in my tongue, the dull sting of the burns, the ache in my buttocks from the cold ground, and colder still the iron of the collar and chains. *Ogan* – that was the word I'd caught; now where had I heard something like that before? I smiled; Frederick, of course. It was good to think of him now. Old Frederick with his muttonchop whiskers, puffing with honest outrage, as belligerent as his picture of St James – '*Think, man! What will you tell the Invisibles? You can't argue with Ogoun!*'

Courage came late to us both, he and I; well, better late than never. This had to stop here, now. Death, extinction – I had to hold onto something. Better them than fall for that sickly-sweet seduction, that happiness that wouldn't let me be myself. Stryge had accused me of worshipping nothing; but he'd been wrong. Once before

293

I'd thrown my happiness away – and that was because I worshipped success. Not its trappings – not what it could bring me. Just the satisfaction of achievement, the accomplishment, the abstract thing Itself. And by whatever god it represented, if I could sacrifice myself to it then, I should damn well be able to do the same now. Anything less –

Its opposite. Its ultimate negation, its Antichrist. Failure. The ultimate Failure of all …

You can't argue with success …

You can't argue with …

You can't argue with …

Ogoun …

I drew a breath so deep it howled in my ears, threw my head back and slamming my chin down hard on my chest I bit –

And just for one instant the shadows flew back from me, and left me gasping on the ground, pouring blood from my mouth. My tongue hurt horribly, but all I'd done was bite the side of it. I was in no danger of choking. I saw Jyp staring at me, and Mall's glazed eyes, and at the line's end Clare, wide-eyed with horror; that I couldn't bear.

'S'okay!' I mumbled thickly, trying fuzzily to find a reassuring reason for threshing about like that. 'S'nothing. Just like the bastard said – my balls *are* freezing! I could …'

I was stunned at the way they reacted. Even Le Stryge pulled away from me in sheer fright, jerking me half off the ground by my collar, which was not the nicest way; and the others shrank back with expressions I couldn't read.

'Hey!' I said, struggling to speak more clearly as I spat out the gore. 'S'okay! I was just saying I could use some of that bloody rum now, because my –'

'Yeah!' croaked Jyp. I'd only once seen his face that pale, and that was after the *dupiah*. 'But how come you said it in Creole?'

'In Creole?' My turn to be astonished. 'I don't speak Creole! A bit of French, but –' I tried to say it again. And I

294

actually heard my own voice change, felt the muscles in my throat slacken and change, and the sound they formed go impossibly deep and gravelly, felt the tongue that shaped it form new sounds, new shades of tone – another word, another language, another voice altogether.

'*Graine moaine 'fret! Don'moa d'rhum!*'

And by damn, it was Creole all right.

The shadows swayed before me, and just as suddenly my throat tightened and I knew my voice would be my own again.

But before I could force out a word Le Stryge, staring at me, suddenly hissed 'Go on! *Go on!* Don't fight it!' And with his bound legs he began to thrash about in the spilled meal-flour that by now covered the whole ground before us, grunting with his efforts, struggling to form a shape. A complex one – no wonder he struggled; like a fantastic piece of wrought ironwork, a hatched portcullis or gate ...

Without warning the beating of the iron rose in a crescendo, the drums thundered madly to keep up – and broke off on the off-beat. The sudden lack of sound was worse than just silence. More like a pistol hanging fire, a match poised above a fuse. I looked up – and across the space I met the distant eyes of Don Pedro, unreadable as the gaze of Night itself. With the dripping sword he gestured, and two of his *bokor* acolytes sprang down off the altar and strode towards us. In their hands were rope halters, that must have come from the animals. The drumbeat began again, a slow solemn roll. As they walked they began to chant in time with it, intoning the words with businesslike, confident urgency.

> *Si ou mander poule, me bai ou.*
> *Si ou mander cabrit, me bai ou.*
> *Si ou mander chien, me bai ou.*
> *Si ou mander bef, me bai ou ...*

I was startled to find I understood them – only too well.

I just bet they could. The crowd parted before them, then fell in behind. One or two began to jeer and howl, waving their bottles, but most joined the chant. Their twisted faces showed a strange inhuman mix of greed and awe.

> *Si ou mander cabrit sans cor*
> *Coté me pren'pr bai ou?*
> *Ou a mangé viande moins,*
> *Ou à quitter zos pour demain?*

> *If you ask me for a goat without horns,*
> *Where do I go for that?*
> *Will you eat the meat off me,*
> *And leave the bones for tomorrow?*

This was it, at last. The minor sacrifices – the animals, those were done. The *loas* were here in the persons of their riders. And I hadn't given in the easy way. Now, as Le Stryge had predicted, Don Pedro would have to bend them to his will, make them take me by force. That would need more blood, stronger blood – *mangés majeurs*. Human blood. Ours.

They were coming to this end of the line, starting with Stryge himself probably. He paid them no attention, just went on scraping with his heels in the mud and soggy flour, gasping to himself with the effort. I realized suddenly that he was chanting too, to the same drumbeat – a stranger, spikier invocation of his own.

> *Par pouvoir St. Jacques Majeur,*
> *Ogoun Ferraille, negre fer, negre feraille,*
> *negre tagnifer tago,*
> *Ogoun Badagris,*
> *negre Baguido Bago,*
> *Ogoun Batala . . .*

The rhythm seemed to drive the words home into

my head like so many nails. I *felt* them, with a force that went beyond understanding. And I felt something more, something that made me forget danger, humiliation and everything else besides. I needed —

I needed a drink — badly. In the worst possible way. I didn't like bottles, but the thirst had me gulping greedily for the sickly bite of it. The dancers milled around us now, catcalling, spitting; but all I could see were those bloody bottles. Them swigging and spilling it like that when I didn't have any, that made me suddenly furious. I yelled at them, and when they only howled and jeered all the louder I felt myself boil up like a kettle. In red rage I demanded my share, I pounded on the ground with my bound fists and roared out *'Rhum, merd'e'chienne! D'rhum —'*

I was a bit startled at how it came out, so loudly it drowned out crowd and drums together. I saw the advancing acolytes hesitate, the crowd sway back.

There went the rum!

I snatched out after the nearest bottle, and found that somehow my wrists had come free, though the broken bindings still dangled from them. My feet were still tied — I couldn't think why, so I kicked them free with a joyous whoop, tried a flying grab for that bottle — and fell sprawling on my face in the mud.

Of course! There was this bloody iron collar and chain round my neck — and the others, too! What were we — spaniels or something?

I tapped the iron indignantly. I heard myself demand in aggrieved tones why my old friend, my faithful old servant was treating me like this. Didn't it know me? Didn't it recognize its master? I caressed the worn old surface agreeably — and felt the joy that leaped and shivered in the living iron, like an eager dog greeting its master. I heard the bolt squeal in delight as it squirmed and wormed its way to freedom, and the singing clang of wild liberation as the collar burst from my neck.

The laughter faltered. With one great gasping breath the crowd shrank back. I leapt up into a tense crouch, like a cat ready to spring. Beside me Le Stryge kicked violently at his diagram, then with an exhausted groan he collapsed. One acolyte caught sight of it, and his eyes bulged. He jabbed a finger and shrilled out '*Li vever! Ogoun! Ogoun Ferraille!*'

Something in me leaped to that name, something billowed like a banner of bright scarlet in the wind, something sang like trumpets. I felt a wild whirl of exaltation, a madly singing, strutting, capering joy. I was the Boss, I was the Man in Charge, I gave the orders round here – and don't You forget it!

These *bokor* bastards! They'd thought –

They'd had the nerve to think –

They'd dared to believe they could ride the Invisibles as the Invisibles rode men.

They'd dared try to compel me to help them! Me!

Me –

Me –

Me –

Me –

Me –

Me –

Me!

They'd thought they could sacrifice my friends –

My friends –

To shackle them in iron –

My iron!

And they'd dared to deny Me rum!

RUM!

The rum that was My right. My sign. My life-blood – they *DARED* –

I roared. This time I really roared. And the sound went crackling out across the darkness, the guttural thunder of a stalking lion. The flames bent before it. The crowd shrieked, the acolytes dropped their halters and scuttled back, one snatching awkwardly at a cutlass in his belt. The drums stuttered, faltered, failed. They didn't start again.

My heart was pounding so hard I shook with every beat. Like a tidal wave a red haze swept down on the night – and I went for the nearest Wolf. He lashed out at me barehanded. I caught the arm, wrenched it, seized the bottle from his other hand and hurled him aside. He sprang up, spitting blue murder, and caught me by the throat. With my free hand I seized his wrist, but it was huge – my grip slipped. Something else faltered, something inside. Then behind me I heard Le Stryge rasping out

> *Ogoun vini caille nous!*
> *Li gran' gout, li grangran soif!*
> *Grand me'ci, Ogoun Badagris!*
> *Manger! Bueh! Sat'!*

I heard. *I heard –*

> *Ogoun come to where we are!*
> *You're very hungry, very dry!*
> *Great thanks to you, Ogoun Badagris!*
> *Come eat! Come drink! Be filled!*

Very right and proper, too. With a great shout I tilted the bottle to my lips and drained it in one glugging draught. The Wolf boggled. The hot spirit seemed to burst straight from my throat into my veins and suffuse them in a flash, threading my body with tiny lines of tingling fire. I clamped my fingers down on that huge wrist, and felt the squeak and crack of bone. The Wolf yelled, gaped – then crossed his green eyes as I brought the empty bottle smashing down on his half-shaven pate. More Wolves raced at me, maybe three. I threw him sprawling at one, punched another's nose into pulp and kicked the last in the stomach, because he had a bottle. He whooped and folded, I caught it in mid-air and swigged at it – almost full! I laughed for sheer joy, loud and thunderous, a laugh of liberation. The chains laughed with me and leaped in the air. With an answering chatter all the other shackles flew apart. Jyp and the others fell sprawling, but Le Stryge, still bound, shuffled himself to his knees, hair wild, eyes blazing.

The crowd was a churning mess, the ones at the

front trying to get back, the ones at the back pressing forward to see what the fuss was. The Carib guards couldn't get near us. Through the milling figures the acolyte burst, swinging a cutlass at my head. I chirruped a greeting. The steel blade jerked to a stop in the air before it touched me. The man's jaw dropped, and I caught his outstretched wrist, shook him like a whipcrack and flung him away in a cartwheel of limbs. He hit a stone and crumpled. Jyp shouted to me; the Caribs were circling around, forcing a way through the crush. I reached down, hoisted him to his feet and tore the ropes off his wrist. A Wolf lunged at me, dirk in hand, bottle in his waistband; he met my own empty coming the other way. I swigged at his, vaguely aware of Jyp seizing the dirk and cutting his feet free, then turning to the rest.

There had to be more rum somewhere –

I saw a bottle and went for whoever was holding it; but a gaggle of Wolves ploughed through panicking humans and barged in on me, trying to snatch me, stab me and generally getting in my way. I damned their nerve, and whistled to the discarded chains. Leaping and nuzzling up to my hands they came, and I grabbed them in my fists and swung them in great loops around my head. Up went the chains with a whistle and whirr, whirling about like a circular saw, scattering my attackers left and right as I advanced. A spear arced over my head, touched that spinning curtain and shattered to matchwood. Those bloody Caribs! I lashed out an arm. The chain went humming off like a *bolas* and whipped around the leaders, scything the legs from them and catching them up into a screaming tangle of limbs. The others tripped over them, and with a shout Jyp and the men he'd freed were on them, snatching their spears and clubs and returning them with interest.

They were obviously managing, so I looked around hopefully for more rum. And something else I didn't have, something I couldn't quite remember – but it was preying on my mind, like an itch I couldn't scratch. Meanwhile I wanted rum. Most of the humans in the crowd were unarmed, or had only light weapons, and after I felled a few who pulled knives they were only too ready to get out of my way. One tugged a long-barreled pistol out of his robe, got the hammer snagged for a second and didn't live to regret it. But up on the altar a high thin voice was shrieking out orders or invocations or both, calling his real fighters to heel. Against the fires I saw Wolves mustering there in answer, handing round swords and other weapons they must have had laid by in case of trouble.

Swords! *That's* what the itch was! My fingers clamped shut where a hilt had been. Of course! Those lousy bastards – they'd taken it! Chained me in iron – rum denied me – stolen my sword – *my sword* – I'd show them, the scumbags!

I took one howling breath, and smelt on it the special savour of the steel. I blew the breath out in a shivering, blasting whistle, thin and sharp as starlight. The flames blew flat, the air quivered, men threw themselves down and clutched their ears – and up above the altar something leaped high into the blackness, with a bejewelled hand snatching vainly after it, Don Pedro's. In the night it hung, spinning madly about its axis like some crazy airscrew, growing larger – larger – closer – until there was the stinging smack of the shark-skin grip in my palm, and the sudden glorious weight. I held it up and howled with delight – till I saw the gore that caked it. That little prick! Slaughtering his foul *mangés* with my sword –

Mine –

Mine –

Mine –

I howled again. Not with delight, this time. The main group of Wolves were beginning to press through the crowd, but it stopped them in their tracks. Behind me I was vaguely aware of Jyp protesting to Stryge as he cut him loose 'What the hell's *happened* to him? What've you done? You get him back, you hear, you goddam' old vulture? Or if Don Pedro don't settle your hash I swear to God I will!'

'I did nothing!' brayed the old man contemptuously.

'He did it himself! The one thing Don Pedro wouldn't have bargained for – that the idiot boy had belly enough left to try and kill himself! As I meant him to! Only he tried it at the right time – when they were calling down a *loa!* Spilling the blood of others – but he was spilling his own! And to help others, not himself! There's no sacrifice stronger than that – no offering you can make greater than yourself!'

'You mean –'

'I mean the *loa* came, fool! But to him! Him alone! And free of Don Pedro! And what a *loa!* All I did was complete the *débâtment* – hold Him fast! Now get me out of here! Get us all out! Do you want to be caught in what's coming? Don't you know who That is?'

All very interesting, but what were those Wolves hanging around for? Don Pedro was shrilling at them, but they didn't seem too eager to budge.

'It's Ogoun, you idiot!' screamed Stryge, in answer to something I hadn't heard. 'The one *loa* who'd root most gladly in such a mind as his! Ogoun Feraille the Iron-master, Lord of Smiths – and so of industry, commerce, all that dross! Of politics, even! Ogoun the Giver of Profit! Ogoun the Giver of Success!'

'Wait a minute!' breathed Jyp, in tones of awe and horror. '*Ogoun?* That's not all he is –'

'No! He's more!' Le Stryge crackled. 'Shall I turn Him loose, invoke His other aspect? Do you want to be caught in range when I do? Forget the boy – get me out of here! Save yourself!'

I turned to look at them. Jyp stepped back a pace, nothing more. Stryge snarled with laughter. 'So be it, then! At least it'll be amusing!' He dug his fingers into the design, and chanted

> *Ogoun Badagris, ou général sanglant!*
> *Ou saizi clé z'orage;*
> *Ou scell'orage;*
> *Ou fais kataou z'eclai'!*
>
> *Ogoun Badagris, you bloody general!*

You grasp the keys of the storm;
You hold it locked;
You unleash the thunder and lightning!

I looked down, panting. With swift strokes he was adding something to that *vever*, a flourish, a great crest – what looked like a sword, flanked by two banners, backed with stars ...

Something stirred in me – like something vast moving under the earth, or an insect shaping in its chrysalis. But not yet ready to burst out ...

I was caught, snared in some inner turmoil, suddenly unsure of myself. I looked around. The Wolves were stirring now, getting ready to charge in earnest. Stryge shook his head wildly, redoubled his chant – until a harsher laugh cut through it. It was Mall, her bonds cut, with Clare trying to support her. But she couldn't stand, and fell to her knees at the edge of the design. She managed a brief glance of contempt at Stryge. 'Thou'rt not all-wise, old man!' she croaked. 'Hast forgotten aught? But then thou wouldst – the godless sorcerer thou art!' Dark blood was trickling from her head-wound again, but she stretched out trembling fingers, rubbed raw by her bonds, and with a vast effort began tracing lines that cut the banners across.

'Let me!' said Clare quickly. 'What d'you want? Crosses? Christian crosses?'

'Aye, so!' whispered Mall. 'Crusader crosses! For they've lent this One a Christian name, too! A saint's name!' Her breath rattled in her throat as she watched Clare complete the design. Something shifted, balanced on a brink – and slid down solidly into place. 'And let Don Pedro hear it now, and tremble! For 'tis the battle cry of his own folk, whom he betrayed! Saint-Jaques, Saint James the Great –'

'*Santiago!*' The shout burst unbidden from my lips, in the sheer glory of battle. I was a sword, a flame, a winged horseman, I was the print in Frederick's window; I was edged iron and all the work that it could do, and I wasn't disposed to wait. Gleefully I crooked a beckoning finger at the advancing Wolves. '*Vin' donc, foutues!*' I screamed. '*Loup-garous dépouillés, écouillés!* Come on, you sons of bitches! Shift ass! Come and lick my sword clean! *Come on, you crap-haired cowardly sheep-shaggers!*'

That last one did the trick. The Wolves were on me, and as they burst through the crowd I cracked the remaining chain-length like a steel whip over their heads, so close the shameful collars whistled through their rainbow hair. Then I let it snake back around my arm, and flung myself at them. They'd no time to form any kind of line. The first, the leader, I caught with a great slash at midriff height and cut him in two, and while his limbs still tottered my return stroke swept the heads from two behind. One raised a buckler to me and I pounded down on it, once, twice, three times, so fast he couldn't raise a counterstroke and was hammered down to the ground like a nail. On the fourth stroke the shield split, and so did the Wolf beneath it. I kicked him under the feet of his fellows and growled with delight, then laid right on into the real meat. Swords shattered before they'd touch me, axes broke without daring to bite upon me, and bits of weapon and Wolf flew everywhere.

Behind me Stryge, like a man demented, was shrieking out, over and over.

Ogoun Badagris, ou général sanglant!

I laughed louder than ever as I sent the Wolves spilling from my path, left and right and over my shoulder on my sword's point, kicked one in the belly and vaulted over him as he doubled up, aimed a great slash at another, lunged, hewed, thrust. There was a loud crash, and something whistled near me. One of the worshippers was kneeling, steadying a revolver of some kind on his arm. I wheeled and ran straight at him. He pulled the trigger once more, but the hammer stayed where it was; and then I was on him. Blued steel is still iron at heart.

Noise erupted behind me. Some Wolves had circled round and attacked the crew as the last of them were getting cut loose. As I turned one of them hurled an axe at my head; I reached out, caught it and went for him with it, and they all fell over themselves avoiding me. Pierce rolled at my feet, entangled with a monster of a Wolf who was trying to throttle him. I pressed the axe into Pierce's flailing hand, sprang over him and went for the rest with great two-handed slashes. Now they fell back at every dart I made, but I was faster. The ones in front fell against the ones behind, and I carved at them like a solid mass, driving them back, back among the terrified crowd, pressing on towards that stinking altar. How long it lasted, I don't know, the mad music of hewing metal, the shouts, the screams and the hacking, jarring impacts; but suddenly I'd run out of enemies. The Wolf ranks broke. They fled like mad in all directions, and the remaining worshippers bolted with them – back towards the altar, seeking their master's shadow, or just out into the night. I shouted after them, I don't know what. The fouled ground before me seethed with shapes that groaned or kicked or twitched their way down into stillness, and I chuckled deep in my throat to see them, mocking the insistent cries that came from the altar. A few more disciplined Wolves were trying to turn the rout by the simple means of felling anyone, Wolf or human, who tried to push past. A terrified free-for-all developed, Wolf against Wolf with the humans caught bloodily in the middle, tearing each other to shreds like rabbits with a ferret loose in their burrows. I drank deep of the reeking air, and was just about to press on after them when a cry turned me in my tracks, as perhaps no other could.

It was Clare's voice, from where she knelt. Stretched out across the *vever* Mall lay sprawled, unmoving, limbs outflung, blood from her head seeping along the wide gouged lines. Slowly, very slowly. Two strides took me to Clare's side. I looked down. Mall's eyes were half-open, but rolled back so the pupils had disappeared. Clare sobbed. Something within me sang a high steely tone of recognition, of acknowledgement, and without quite knowing what I was doing I knelt slowly down, reached out and touched my middle finger right to the centre of Mall's forehead.

Her eyes closed. The whole night seemed to tremble

with a growing vibration, the clear singing note of an infinite violin string that swelled louder than the silenced drums. It blew through us like a great wind, shaking us. I felt it whip my hair about my face, send hers billowing and streaming out like smoke. Whether it was in her or me, I couldn't tell – but as her eyes snapped open again a spark flashed between us, and light leaped up within the very heart of her, so bright that the skull blazed out beneath the flesh. Clare gave a high-pitched shriek, then clapped her hands in laughing delight. The gouts of clotted blood about Mall's head dried, crumbled, blew away. The bruised flesh paled and cleared; the depressed gouge left across her temple by the Carib club swelled and filled. She convulsed with the force of it, then sagged back with a deep breath of infinite relief. 'My thanks, my lord! But i'the name of all hates ill, stay not! Go settle the viper, and I –' She swung her legs under her, and rose smoothly, unhurriedly to her feet. 'By thy grace, I'll shield those here for now!' Her eyes flamed with alarm. '*Go! Go now!*'

I turned –

Clambering high on the white rock behind the altar, casting about, I saw Don Pedro. In the same instant he saw me, and across that space our gazes locked. A card turned in the air – a two of spades merged to become an ace, a pool of infinite blackness drawing me on – in – and down. Falling. Falling ...

My elbow slipped sideways, my head jerked; I stopped it barely an instant before my nose hit the keyboard of my terminal and scrambled everything on the screen. My coffee-cup, untouched, teetered on the edge of the desk, and I retrieved it hastily; we'd had enough mess and breakages round here lately. Dozing off at my desk! Serve me right for spending half the week-end in discos, and not getting enough sleep. Some daydream! Some damn daydream! It'd left me still ringing with the violence of it. I struggled to pull myself together. I jumped when the intercom buzzed.

'*Steve?*' inquired Clare's voice.

'Y ... yes?'

'*You sound a bit funny, You're all right?*'

'Sure. Just ... wrapped up in something, that's all.'

'*You shouldn't overdo it, really. Your four o'clock appointment, remember? Mr Peters is in Reception.*'

I shook my head, swallowed a sip of the cold coffee and straightened my tie. 'Well, then. Show him in!'

CHAPTER ELEVEN

I STOOD UP AUTOMATICALLY as the door opened. The man who stepped through looked like most of the clients I saw – no, like the cream of them, the ones who usually arrived via Barry's office, suitably stoked with hospitality and charm. His dark three-piece suit was cut like an Armani diamond, his white shirt crisp and smooth, its collar tailored precisely to his throat, his ruler-straight tie as silkily iridescent as a grey opal. The sheer sleek perfection of the ensemble, down to his finely tooled dark shoes and soft glove-leather attaché case, created an air of the exotic, the foreign which exactly fitted his face – high-browed, hook-nosed, sallow, with a slender drooping moustache and eyes like sunken inkwells. Foreign clients almost always meant serious money.

'Mr Peters,' I said, and his thin lips curved in a smile. He held out a long hand, and I reached out –

Blackness. Noise.

I jerked back my hand, without the least idea why. It'd been the weirdest feeling. Like the time I nodded off in my first big meeting, lulled by the heat and the monotonous droning voices – and then snapped awake, flushing with guilt and adrenalin, wondering how long I'd been out for, if anyone had noticed – like that. Only here I'd been dipping down into a nightmare, hellishly vivid – like that damn daydream again. Dark, firelight, screaming and shouting, and one voice, much nearer, speaking words I couldn't quite make out. It left me shaken, just when I didn't want to be. Peters' smile didn't change, but somehow it left me in no doubt at all that he'd noticed; bad start. I hastily tried to cover up my embarrassment by waving him to a chair.

'Er – won't you sit down? If you'd like some coffee – or a drink, perhaps? Sherry? An excellent *fino*, cooled –' Sherry seemed to go with that face, though I felt the urge for something a lot stronger myself.

'No; no, I thank you. You are most kind, but I regret I have very little time. I would prefer, if you will forgive me the discourtesy, to proceed to our most urgent business.'

I relaxed, though his voice gave me the crawls. His English had the same exaggerated perfection as his suit. Exotic, all right, with that accent; and yet – dammit, I knew it. I knew *him*, somehow – God alone knew where from. And I didn't like him one little bit. It was a struggle not to let it show. I couldn't remember the exact details of my daydream, but he'd have fitted into it rather nicely – the voice especially. Maybe I'd dreamed it up around that voice.

'Well,' I said, just a trace stiffly, 'we're here to be of service. As I understand the situation from our conversation earlier, Mr Peters, you want us to take responsibility for handling a consignment of a highly confidential nature, from the Caribbean area. We're more than willing to do this, naturally, at conditions you'll find competitive and with the highest standards of care. Provided –' I tapped the desk gently with my ruler. 'Always provided we ourselves know the nature of it, its origin, content and destination, and are free to inspect it at any time. In total confidence, it goes without saying. Confidence is the lynch-pin of our business –'

Peters held up a hand in deferential interruption. 'I regret not having more fully informed you sooner,' he smirked. 'But it is not one consignment that is involved, but many. A continuous contract, in fact. The commercial forces I represent aim to become a significant force in the trade from this area – and, confidentially, to dominate it within a very short time.' He stabbed the air gently with a black lacquer ballpoint.

The cane-tip lifted.

I blinked. What had I just –? A flicker of movement. Something I'd recognized momentarily – yet not now, somehow ...

'Understand,' he added, 'this is no idle ambition. It is a project in which you personally would do very well to become involved.'

309

Great. Was I seeing things? And I couldn't quite believe what I was hearing, either. I clasped the ruler in steepled fingers, and stared down at my bare desktop, trying to formulate a reply.

A spouting of yellow fire – God, a fireball! Racing across the barren ground – swelling – a swathe of his own people caught in it – fragmented silhouettes capering, blazing, falling – scythed down like smouldering grass – filling my sight –

And as if that wasn't enough –

'Go on!' I said to myself. Literally. I knew my own voice when I heard it. 'Answer him! Just as you would normally. This is where it's all happening!'

I smiled. A bit sickly, maybe, but it wasn't too much of an effort. Seeing things, hearing things I might be, but here at least I was on firm familiar ground.

'You must understand, Mr Peters – in this I have to consider the interests of the company before my own. Neither on their behalf, nor on mine, have I any interest in breaching the law or the established ethics of the trade, even passively.'

I flung up my sword against the blast –

'And however great the profit. That is our settled policy, and I agree with it wholeheartedly. We manage well by our own methods. We don't need to change. We don't want to.'

Scorching smell in my nostrils –

I looked down hastily at my terminal in case it was overheating.

Spots dancing before my eyes – burning colours – the fireball broken. Dust cascading.

'Nice one!' said myself to me.

I found I was panting, perspiring, my throat dry; I had the damndest urge for a drink. But Peters, appearing not to notice, spread his arms wide, waving the pen expressively. 'That is regrettable. Deeply regrettable. Consider the interests of your firm, then, if you will. We have most substantial backing – and we will not hesitate to make use of the resources at our disposal. If need be, globally.'

*The cane turned – pointed, twirled like a wand in a
sweeping, luminous arc –*

'I must be frank. If, after all, we cannot make use of
you, we must – how shall I put this? – replace you. You
suit us admirably, but there are, after all, other agencies,
other young men of your qualifications and bright
prospects. If we with our influence chose to favour one
such instead of you, it would inevitably blight your career,
your success – would it not?'

Not at me, but at the left-hand fire.

'Would it? Forgive me, Mr Peters, I don't see how.'

Or to put it another way – are you threatening me
personally, you little jerk?

'My dear sir, English expresses it admirably: there is
only room for one at the top. In our hands such a person,
and the agency he must one day come to head, would be
placed in a position of high advantage – favoured, for
example, by official sources, by departments of government, by government itself. Not only in the Caribbean
area, but at this end also, in this country. The rise of such
an agency would be – how shall I put it? Meteoric.'

*The tip moved – the fire lifted, logs, twigs, coals and
all – a roaring pillar of flame – crazies bolting in all
directions –*

God. Was this what a breakdown was like? Or a
touch of that stress paranoia I'd heard about in high-
pressure jobs. Just get me through this one meeting, that's
all; this next half-hour. Then I can rush down and sneak
Gemma's valium. All of it.

'Quite meteoric. Its competitors would find themselves at its mercy, to be … taken over if they had the
sense to allow it, or otherwise – simply overwhelmed.'

I blinked, and flexed the ruler thoughtfully in my
hands. Somehow or other, quite suddenly, the panic had
subsided. Was I seeing things – or just dramatizing what
he was threatening me with? A touch of stress, maybe –
but the threats were real enough, to me, to the company.
A good company, a lot of good people with careers sunk
in it. Surely I was getting way out of my depth here, I
ought to be passing this little tick on to higher authority.

311

This kind of tough talking was Barry's territory, if anybody's. And yet, somehow, I felt that I did have authority behind me, all the damned authority I could ever need. The hell with breakdowns; if I was hearing voices, they were talking sense. A colossal confidence was welling up in me – and I was just itching to deal with this little son-of-a-bitch on my own.

The fiery pillar opening out – its summit spreading, broadening – looming, cresting, streaming flames and smoke – curling over like a tidal wave – coming thundering down over the heads of the remaining worshippers – straight at me.

Some dramatizing! I must really hate this guy; well – why not?

I chuckled, and touched the ruler to my lips. 'You've chosen a rather extreme way of putting your point, surely? This is an established agency, with a long list of satisfied and continuing customers – governments included. So we're not entirely without backing and influence ourselves, you know. The agency can cope with commercial and political pressures; it's had to before, and survived. In fact it's flourished. Otherwise why are you coming to me now?'

I spat on my swordblade, and flicked it skyward –

'That's right!' I was talking to myself again. 'That's what it's all about. You're ahead of any game he knows. Tell him that.'

'And,' I said aloud, 'to be equally frank – if I personally am half the man you think I am, then I ought to be well able to deal with any such assaults on my own account. Shouldn't I?'

I shouted with laughter – filled my cheeks – blew a loud rude rasp at the descending stream. The cascading fire touched the steel – and split. Spattered like a stream of tapwater – lost its unity – collapsed, raining a choking cloud of bright embers and hot ashes on the heads of the terrified crowd. Wild shrieking spread the panic – here and there hair and clothes burst into flames. I bellowed with thunderous triumph –

I swallowed. Jesus, that was vivid! Where the hell

312

was I getting all this! Maybe it had been creeping up on me since that mysterious call of his; maybe I'd sussed out something wrong about him them. Subconsciously, maybe – or I was developing a sixth sense. Telepathy I could just about believe in, but – No. Too many late nights with low life down at the docks, that was it. No wonder I'd dreamed up that sort of a fantasy round him, kept seeing it every time I nodded off. Though I'd have expected my kind of mind to come up with arms dealers or drug barons, something – well, more practical. Mundane, if you like. Just went to show what a funny beast the subconscious must be. I glanced up at the office around me. The familiar, the everyday, the solid – bookcases, plants, pictures, Dave's desk (and where was *he* right now?). Usual, everyday things. Things a man would cling to – no, better than that. Things I could set my feet in firmly, and brace myself against whatever the world threw at me. Real things; or were they?

These weird visions, these sudden plunges into blackness, assaulting all the senses at once, consistently – could *they* be real? God knows, they felt it while they lasted. The old quibble – is the philosopher dreaming he's a butterfly, or the butterfly dreaming he's a philosopher?

The new twist being that here the answer mattered.

Whatever my counterstroke really was, Peters hadn't liked it one bit – that was obvious. He shifted awkwardly in his chair and smoothed back his grey-streaked black hair. Where was I going to get stood on? Where was the real battle being fought? I tensed. He leaned forward and tapped the pen sharply on the arm of his chair.

'Your confidence is admirable, but, I fear, based on insufficient experience. One might almost say ignorance. A crude frontal assault, possibly – but suppose it were simply too broadly based to resist? The devastation of your clientele – a flood of traffic at compelling rates that would simply swamp all available shipping …'

Already the cane was moving again – with it the right-hand fire. Not lifting but slithering, snaking forward – wider than a man's reach, spreading – the

313

coarse bushes bursting into flame as it passed –
worshippers who can't move fast enough caught in its
path stumbling, falling, vanishing with a hiss and a
shriek into its blazing maw –

'Watch him!' said my inner voice. 'Don't just defend
yourself! Bat it right back at him!'

You again! How can I? When I don't know where I
am, what battle I'm really fighting? When I can't trust my
own senses? My mind –

'What's it matter?' said my voice, far too calmly.

What d'you mean, what's it matter?

'Real – unreal – it's the same fight, isn't it? In either
world you ought to have the edge on him! Look for it in
the one you know best. Find it, and the other will follow
– then you'll know!'

Right. Well, I had the answer to that quibble now.
Stand on the butterfly, and see what happens next. If it
dies, it's real. But in the world I knew best, there was a
way to deal with Peters.

I rubbed my hands. 'Well then. In that case, I'd bring
in more shipping of our own – and more backing, if need
be. There's no shortage of either, Mr Peters, elsewhere in
the world – not for people who've a trustworthy track
record. And we can play a wider gambit too; political
dirty tricks won't shift us, not with our competitors to
help. Agencies stand together against this kind of badger
game, and the banks behind them. We've helped beat it in
the past – and others would help us beat you! I'd turn
your own damned tactics right back against you –'

*Somewhere behind me – a vast impossible distance
– a voice croaking urgently*

Ou fais kataou z'eclat'!

I ignored it. I knew already what I had to do. I found
I was clutching the metal ruler tightly, and –

*I thrust my sword in my belt – clapped my hands,
hard. Stooping – snatching up the chains again – whirling them, one in each hand – hear them sing!*

A whistle – on the same notes – loud – louder –

*A mighty crackle filled the air, and they stuck out,
stiff as rods, every link, every collar quivering – not at*

the onrolling flames, but high above them. The field flashing alight with a wild blue glare –

My summons obeyed.

Mine –

Mine –

Mine –

The black night crashed in around me. A drumroll of thunder split the clouds. Blue sparks sizzled in a wild corona from every collar as the lightning's fearful charge coursed through me and along the chains and lanced out like a jagged crack in the night itself, straight at Don Pedro.

The iron chains melted in my hands as that surge of power passed through them. They fell in sizzling, spattering beads, to sink gratefully back into the earth they'd been torn from. But the power in him also was daunting; Don Pedro was not blasted, not consumed. Only the bolt struck his outstretched cane, with its silver mountings, and drove it leaping backward in his hand.

And, as he had commanded, the fire followed it.

It rose like a cobra, coiling back on itself, and struck. Over the apex of the high stone it splashed, and I saw him as it fell, saw him lose his balance under the torrent of blazing debris, slide forward and down, tumbling among that crashing avalanche of fire down onto his own altar. The crowd howled and fell back; but I rushed up to the very edge of the stone, eager to be sure of my triumph ...

And stopped. On the altar all was blazing ruin, a heap of shattered wood still flaming, the shed blood sizzling and blackening around its edge, hissing as the first drops of rain began to fall. Yet at the centre of it, suddenly, there was a thrusting upward, a spilling aside – and Don Pedro stood there. His robes hung ragged and smouldering, his cane was gone, his face scorched, his hair and beard a halo of fire; yet he did not seem to notice. He glided towards me, right to the edge of the stone above me – and I saw that his very eyebrows were aflame; yet the darkness beyond them was deeper than ever as it fastened upon me ...

*

Peters shook his head, with all the sad wisdom of age and experience. 'I see that to have any hope of convincing you I must place my cards on the table,' he sighed, 'and reveal the full extent of our operation.' He snapped the silver-worked catches on his attaché case, opened it, and held it out with both hands. 'The documentation speaks for itself ...'

Instinctively I rose and leaned forward. But something in my memory rose up and clawed at me. Cards on the table? Katjka's cards – Ace of Hearts, the Two of Spades – two empty pools of blackness that became one. And the Knave with the cold dark eyes ...

My hesitation saved me. Out of the open case – *his cupped hands* – a blade of yellow flame spat upwards. As if to impale a star – right where, if I hadn't hesitated, my eyes would have been. With a snarl of anger I snatched up the first thing to hand – the ruler – and sprang up, vaulted right across the desk, and went for him.

Blackness roared –

Light again. His chair tipped back, we crashed over – snapping and champing like animals, both of us – rolling about this way, that way. My hand on his throat – his cane holding back my sword – his free hand scrabbling for my eyes – Christ, he was strong! All the noise we must be making, why didn't somebody come in –

Searing heat –

What the hell? Something burnt – my hair smouldering – we'd rolled into the fire. What fire? The light glaring – the floor hot –

On and off – light to dark – back and forth – two worlds flickering around us as we tumbled back and forth. I'd been right, my other voice!

'Right! Right! Doesn't bloody matter! Here or there, you lousy little sod – I'll wring you till your bloody pips squeak –'

'*Hijo de la puta adiva* –' choked the small man.

Peters – Pedro struggling to twist his cane around to strike me – tearing my sword from my hand. I put a little more effort into it – and both cane and sword tore free, fell aside. Our hands shot straight for each other's throats –

316

My arms were longer – my grip caught, tightened – harder – tighter. Into the vacuum of his eyes a green spark leaped, exploding upwards. Threads of green fire crackled and coursed along his sleeves as they met mine – and spurting sparks of red sprang up in answer. His eyes weren't black any longer, they were shimmering green mirrors, and I could see myself in them. A self I hardly recognized – a snarling, ferocious mask with eyes of blazing red –

Tighter.

Tighter –

His grip loosened. One hand fell from my throat – and though he couldn't have seen where the cane lay, flew straight to it, snatched it up and struck at my head. But somehow my sword was under my open fingers, and as he surged up I closed both hands around the hilt and lashed out.

A classic forehand smash. It caught him right on the sleek crown of his head, knocked him flying, flat on his back on his own altar. The sword rang in my fingers as if I'd struck solid stone. He lay groaning, writhing, kicking feebly, fingers scrabbling at the dark trenched gash. A wound like that should be fatal – but this was no ordinary man. Panting, I staggered forward, bent over him, lifting the sword to strike again. His mouth opened –

I sprang back with a yell of disgust. Just in time to avoid the fountain of blackness he vomited out.

'You filthy bastard –' I gargled, about to hack wildly at him, I think. Somebody caught my arm, though, and I looked around, into Jyp's face. It was only about then my memory really began to reassert itself.

'No,' said Jyp wearily. 'Don't go near him. That wasn't any attack. He won't attack again.'

'But –'

'No buts. You whipped him. You met him out here on the Spiral, where he gained all his power, and you beat the bejasus out of him. Fought him, spell for spell –'

I shook my head, confused. 'Spell? It – it wasn't like that. I wasn't using any magic. Something was happening here, but I wasn't … in control of that. He had me

317

thinking we – were just talking business, till the end. In my office – just sparring over a deal –'

'Your kind of knowledge. Your kind of magic. Oh, the power behind it, that was ... someone else's, sure. But the using of it, the will – that was all yours. You had to make the moves. Don Pedro, he must've seen what had happened, thought you were the weak link in the partnership, that he could beat you on that level. So that's how you saw it; but you turned it against him. And what you did there you were doing here too, I guess. Didn't matter how you beat him – you did, and that's what counts. Smashed his power, broke his body. And now he's tried to escape from you. To run.'

'Running? But he's –'

'In time. Fled away out of this wider world, where he was beaten. Fled blindly! Panicked like a wounded animal. Remember how I said some folk just break and bolt when the Spiral gets too much for them – back to the moment they first entered it? And look where that's taken him. Back to his sick-bed. He's dying of *vomito negro* – Yellow Jack. Just like he should've done all along.'

And as I stared at the writhing form of my enemy I saw that there was some subtle change around him, that the white stones behind him did take on something of the look of high stucco'd walls, the fitful light of the dying flames flickering across them like a single guttering lamp – or a sick man's image of the fever consuming him. The rich robes his hands clenched and tore in their delirious agony spread out like embroidered coverlets, the stained altar-stone the soiled sheets of a lordly sick-bed. Nausea welled up in me, and a terrible unexpected pity, and I could only stand there, without speaking.

'You are wrong in one thing only, Master Pilot,' said Mall softly. 'Aye, he has the yellow fever. But 'tis not that which kills him. See, the blackened and bloated tongue that near chokes him! Too often I've seen men die thus. Helpless in his derangement he cannot look to himself, and he has none loves him enough to risk coming near. Sooner than court infection, they leave him to perish most miserably – of thirst.'

Another voice beside us broke the brief silence. 'Well! Hope he enjoys it, the little bastard! I'd say that's just about up to his own standards of amusement – wouldn't you?' Clare's mouth set hard as she contemplated the writhing figure. 'Oh, don't look so shocked! When they chained me up in that dungeon of his, with the cage and the bones and everything – they were laughing, those Wolves. Then they took the light away. I'd a few hours to think about his kind of fun.'

'I just bet you did,' said Jyp sympathetically. 'But that's done with now. And by the look of it, so's he.'

Once again, though, he was mistaken. Racked by the last throes of his delirium, Don Pedro shrieked and sat upright, clutching at the headwound, his fingers scrabbling in agony, tearing like claws, tearing away the very flesh. Until suddenly it ripped – and slid away and sank, the sallow face sagging like crumpled linen ...

There was no blood. There was no white bone laid bare beneath. No skull. Nothing but a shape, a mould, a form of the same solid darkness that lay behind his eyes, shining in the firelight like the blackest of opal.

The few Wolves and Caribs and worshippers who had not yet fallen or fled the field took one look. Then, with a great wailing unison howl they turned and bolted, stumbling over rocks, blundering into trees, trampling each other in their final dissolution of panic, as the hand that had held them was lifted and they looked upon its secret source. One acolyte alone I saw of the dozens there had been, a tall mulatto, backing away, his fingers knotting in his ash-stained robes; then he flung them over his eyes, and with a yell he hurled himself bodily into the still-blazing fire. The flesh slid wholly from the shape that staggered upright before me, slipping down in tatters, collapsing with the remnants of the robe.

Some thing reared up where it had been. A weird thing, a skeletal, shining shape, black against the leaping fires – a glossy chitinous beetle carapace, a tottering stick-insect caricature of a man. It stood, swaying gently, a head above me, far taller than Don Pedro. Indeed, it was stretching and straightening those distorted spider-limbs as if they had been too long cramped, as if it had to pump blood into them after bursting its chrysalis in a new birth. And like something newborn it was swaying its onyx skull of a head this way and that and making low uncertain chittering noises, as if peering around with anxious timidity at what might be a hostile world.

It looked grotesque, grisly, unpleasant – but not in the least bit menacing. Pitiful, almost, as I circled around it, sword ready, and snatched a burning stick from the altar. I advanced, and it hunched its limbs protectively, cheeped and chittered and backed away in great bounding strides. It looked so miserable, this thing of fear stripped of all its disguising, that it was almost hilarious. I couldn't help it; I began to laugh, great gusty whole-hearted laughter that boomed across the air like the thunder overhead. And at my side I heard Mall suddenly laugh, as she had laughed in the castle. Her high clear tones blended with mine and together we shook the skies, like the laughter of the gods from cloud-wreathed Olympus.

Jyp was laughing; I could see it, though I couldn't hear him. Clare staggered up to us, picking her barefoot way across the stony ground, and hung on our shoulders, doubled-up and helpless. Pierce threw down his bloody axe and guffawed himself scarlet, and all the surviving crew with him, mocking, pointing, mopping and mowing and making rude gestures at the quivering thing that hopped from foot to foot before us. Hands the gunner sniggered and pointed and spat – and even Le Stryge, arms folded over his filthy coat, gave a frosty smile and snorted. At last, less in attack than in dismissal, I hefted the brand and flung it. It bounced off that black skull with no more than a musical clonk, quite harmless; but the dark thing shrilled in panic, and whirling about fled chittering away into the darkness with great bounds of its long legs, and faded utterly into the drizzling night.

Our laughter pursued it, but faltered at last. A great silence fell over that field, with its ghastly harvest of burned bodies, scattered, smouldering, steaming as the soft rain touched them. Slowly I thrust my sword back into my belt. I kicked at the rum bottles that lay around, but most had shattered or spilled. Jyp picked up a full one, still corked, and tossed it to me. I looked to the silent drums where they lay in the wrecked *tonnelle*, overturned and broken, their decorated skins pierced; and as I strode over to them a robe of rich scarlet, torn and abandoned, tangled about my foot. I picked it up, draped it around over my shoulder, tied it round me like a sash. From beside the drums I scooped up the *ogan*, the iron gong, and the hammer that had played it. I tapped once, in an experimental sort of way, a quieter, more lilting rhythm than it had played before – then I broke off a moment, put the rum to my lips, drew the cork with my teeth and spat it flying at the altar. I took a great swig, and let the sweet aromatic fire gurgle down my throat. Then I drew a deep breath, and began to play the rhythm again, and, lifting my feet, I danced. A warrior's dance, a dance of rejoicing but a solemn one, a noble *bransle*. I snapped my fingers, and thunder beat a vast slow roll. I turned to Mall, took her hand and she danced with me, whirling together under the pattering rain. Jyp danced with Clare, the men and women of the crew in a weaving, wavering line, our eyes laughing one to another in a sort of solemn frenzy of deliverance. A richness and a joy welled up in me that I felt I'd never known. In this my hour of triumph the world – even the wider world, the Spiral and all the worlds within it – seemed too narrow a place for my embrace, for the vast infinite love that was mine to give. And while the thunder and the iron played we swept slowly away from that place of barrenness and ruin towards the forest's edge.

The storm-wind stirred the green leaves till they flew like banners above us; and as we passed beneath their shelter I looked back once, and out of the iron-clad confidence within me I shouted a command. Before the first echo died a blue finger of lightning pressed down, once, twice, three times to the solemn beat of the dance. The altar flew into fragments, the white stones tumbled; the barren hill-crown was blasted clean. Still dancing, I turned away, and holding Mall's hand – who held Jyp's, who held Clare's

321

who held Pierce's – we paced away, without breaking our dance, down into the darkling jungle towards the sea.

How long we danced for, to the beating of the iron and the crashing in the heavens, I've no idea. All the way down to the beach, perhaps; for it was on the sand I woke up, face pillowed in my arms, as the first grey foretaste of dawn touched me. The first thing I decided was that I'd been eating the sand, because my mouth seemed full of it, and my body was weighed down, my guts leaden; I couldn't so much as move, even though I heard voices beside me. Stryge was holding forth, sardonic as ever.

'You did not recognize the thing? You surprise me. I knew at once; and if I had not been sure, I would have when I remembered the castle's guardians – the coat and hat figures, the zombie, the rats. That was Baron Samedi, guardian of the underworld, the graveyard god – personification of death. That was the *loa* with which Don Pedro was so proud to have allied himself.'

'Sounds natural,' muttered Jyp. 'One as evil as the other –'

'Hardly!' said Le Stryge with all his usual contempt. 'Samedi is not evil – he has his honoured place among the Invisibles, he is essential to the natural order. That he should seek to extend his dominion, his realm, is only natural to him, by whatever means imbecile mankind may give him – murder, famine, war. The evil in that is not his; he would not understand it. Did you see any in him, when he stood revealed? In their partnership it was all Don Pedro's – and so it was only his evil nature that endured, in the end, beyond his normal span. Whatever else there might once have been in the man, Samedi had already devoured. So, when the shell perished, there was only naked Death remaining. And we were well equipped, just then, to laugh at the fear of Him.'

With a low devastated moan I managed to roll over. My own head seemed to be full of black rocks. Through gummy eyes I saw Clare bending over me, and behind her Jyp. 'How do you feel?' she asked softly, passing a cool hand over my brow.

'Terrible ...' I croaked. 'Mouth like the docks at low tide. Like the worst hangover I ever had – and worse again, much worse –'

'Yeah, well, that's not surprising,' chuckled Jyp gently. 'Guess you don't know it, but you're lucky you're not waking up slightly dead. You put away nigh on five quarts of high-proof hooch in about the space of half an hour last night.'

'Yes,' I gargled, feeling the acid rise at the back of my throat. 'I remember. But Somebody else got most of the benefit. That wasn't entirely me –'

'You remember?' barked Le Stryge, pushing the others aside and hauling me up by the scarlet sash I still wore. 'You *remember?*' He barked in my face. 'That's unheard-of. You can't do that –'

'Well, I can,' I mumbled, thrusting him back from me so sharply he sat down hard on the sand, 'all about it, so piss off. No offence intended.'

I scrambled unsteadily to my feet. Le Stryge's breath had finished off what the acid had begun. The sea was nearer than the bushes, so I staggered to the water's edge and proceeded to heave the entire contents of my stomach into the tide. After that I sat down heavily, a lot better but weaker, only half aware of Le Stryge still rabbiting on behind me.

'– but that – that is impossible! The one ridden by the *loa* is the merest instrument – a vessel, a vehicle for the Invisible. After such possession – such total domination of the self – the conscious mind cannot recall anything of what happened when the *loa* was in command.'

'Zat so?' demanded Jyp sceptically. 'And yet you heard me talking to him just after the whole shebang broke – didn't you? Listen, that was Steve there, and nobody else – not that I could see, anyhow. What about Don P? You were saying that was kind of a fifty-fifty partnership.'

'Indeed – but that was no mere possession. *That* was more like a conscious alliance, of a kind that could only come about with a being of vast potential. Not such an

323

empty commonplace shadow of a creature as this boy –'
The hard, creaking voice tailed off. Suddenly I had the
sensation of keen eyes on the back of my neck, that I was
being studied with a new and suspicious intensity.

I didn't turn round. I hardly cared. Empty, a shadow,
that was exactly how I felt – like a discarded garment
forgotten on the ground. I thought of Don Pedro's flesh
slipping away, and shuddered; little better than that. It
wasn't just the hangover, it was worse, far worse. It was
the memory of having been suddenly full, full to over-
flowing with a furious joy in life. I had been given a
glimpse, a taste of what it was I most lacked – and it had
all gone in fighting, all save those last few minutes. I had
had no chance to turn my thoughts to anything else. I had
tasted fullness, and had it snatched from my mouth.

But then Clare, who had held back while I was being
sick, came to put a comforting arm about my shoulder,
and that didn't feel bad at all. And only a minute later
came Pierce's cheerful hail.

'Ahoy there, my gentle lords and ladies! The boats
are readied, the wind is from the land. Let us make all
haste aboard, that we may be quit of this demon-haunted
place with the first light of dawning!'

That fetched us. We scrambled up and half-staggered
along to where the captain and Mall stood waiting by the
boats. There rode the two ships at anchor in the mirroring bay, just as we had left them; but no ill shapes hung
from the rigging now. 'Aye, we've been aboard,' said Mall,
following my gaze. 'While you yet slept. Made all secure,
though in truth little enough was touched – unusual for
Wolves, they must have been on the tightest leash.'

'They were,' I agreed, thinking of how nothing had
been stolen from our office.

She smirked mischievously. 'Even your gold was yet
there in your cabin,' she added, and a great cheer went up
from the surviving crew. I looked at them, and thought of
all they had risked, and of those whose long existences
had found their eventual end on this quest – and I looked
at Clare; and I thought how little money that gold actually
represented, even with what more I'd promised.

'I'll double it!' I shouted. 'The whole bloody bonus! Double what I promised you!'

We were all but swept aboard shoulder-high. They nearly upset the boats. But Pierce's bellow broke up the turmoil at once; we were shorthanded, and the rush to set sail was overwhelming. Everyone had to plunge in and help, whether they knew what they were doing or not. I found myself quite blithely scrambling up the ratlines with the mastheaders Even shuffling out along the yard on the looped footrope to undo the sail-lashings wasn't too bad, since the ship wasn't heeling. And it was a great moment when the white mainsail boomed out beneath us, and seemed to fill with the very first high beam of the rising sun, a golden wind. I could even look down below and see Clare's slender limbs among the team at the capstan, hauling up the anchor; and there was Israel Hands limping along, leading a party below.

What for, I found out as we scrambled back down to the deck, and the old *Defiance* began to get under way. Pierce shouted a warning to us, then a command, and the whole ship heeled with a thunderous crash. The *Chorazin*, still in shadow, juddered at her moorings; water fountained, and bits of planking flew skyward. 'Be firing' at 'er waterline,' the topman next to me remarked sagely. Again the blast – and this time the black ship wallowed sharply, and began to turn on a broken mooring. One of the masts juddered free, and collapsed in a flailing mass of rigging.

'A pricey prize she might've been!' said another.

'Balls!' said my neighbour, and spat overside. 'Who'd buy her? Nobbut more Wolves – and I'll have their money by other means, I thank you.'

I joined Jyp and Mall on the quarterdeck, looking back as the Wolf ship settled into the shallow waters. 'There'll be scuba divers find that one day and thinking they've found the wreck of a pirate ship,' remarked Jyp dryly.

'Won't they realize it hasn't been sunk for two or three hundred years?' I enquired.

Mall grinned and rumpled my hair. 'Why, what year

325

d'you think is this?' she enquired innocently.

I put my hands to my head and groaned, while the others laughed. At least I knew better than to get into that sort of discussion now. I imagined that ship, no longer a living, travelling thing, sinking back into Time as it settled to the shallow bed, back to the era of its building and belonging; to become a haven and a shelter for small crawling things, to rot and break up, and at last be gently entombed by the pale shifting sands of the bay. I looked back at the island beyond, full of sleepy dawn sounds and the rush of surf – and, finding that I still wore the red sash, I undid it and tipped it over the stern. It spread out and floated in our wake for a moment, a scarlet stain on the blue waters of the bay; and then it folded in and sank from sight. I glanced up at the hillside, but I couldn't make out the mansion anywhere. The whole view seemed cleaner now, and that was the way to leave it.

Ahead of us, under the curve of the mainsail, long fingers of cloud stretched low along the horizon, their upper curves sun-reddening hills, their trailing edges fringed with gold – a new archipelago, beckoning us onward. And even as I saw it we passed beyond the point into the open sea, I felt our bows lift and go on lifting – and now I dared look overside and see the sun-gilded sea fall away beneath us into a deeper azure, a mist of blue and gold. Higher we rose, riding on other seas, our sails filled with the winds of many thousand dawnings, driving us out of shadow to chase the timeless morning and pass over it and beyond, homeward bound.

Sunset came soon, and it was night. The arch of cloud shone against the stars, the wind was steady and Jyp was at the helm. In the mild warm night we, officers and gentlefolk – including Le Stryge, unfortunately – sat around on the quarterdeck, under the light of the lanterns. Up in the foc'sle the crew were singing, soft distant songs and ballads long vanished from the changing years. I was sitting with my back to the deck railing, counting out the gold to Pierce, who was humming happily and plying me with most amazing old brandy in the hope I'd make just a little mistake. I hadn't the heart to remind him I was a businessman too. Clare was chatting happily to Mall, who was tuning up her fiddle with meticulous care. She twanged a couple of strings experimentally, played a note or two, then began to play along softly with the ballads the foc'sle were singing.

I sighed. The music was getting to me. 'What's the matter, Steve?' enquired Clare softly.

'I feel ... hollow. Hungry.'

She chuckled, and punched me gently in the arm. 'What, after that breakfast? You wait till we get back. You've bought me dinner once or twice, but you've never let me cook you a meal. And you're going to get the biggest, most marvellous —'

'I didn't mean that. I mean, I accept, I'll love it, I really am starving, I can hardly wait, but — that wasn't how I meant it. I'm hollow like a tooth; aching. Le Stryge was right. Don Pedro was right, Mall — all right, all of you. I was empty; I've made myself empty, in ways I never even realized till ... Till I was filled. That was wonderful. An honour, a glory; but its left me feeling like ... I don't know. An empty bottle. An unfulfilled purpose. There's a gap in me, right in the centre of my life, and somehow I've got to find ways to fill it, to live as something like a whole man again. God alone knows how.'

Clare smiled, and put her arm round my shoulders again. 'Oh, that's simple enough. Come home. Go on building up your career. You've got a great one ahead of you — take my word for it. Secretaries always know; and there isn't one in the company who doesn't think so, even Barry's Jane. Just remember there're things in life besides work, now and again.' She chuckled. 'Such as food. If you're really still starving you'll need something to soak up that brandy. I'll go raid Mr Pierce's cabin stores.'

'Eh?' said Pierce, alarmed, losing count; then he remembered he was homeward bound, and rich, and chuckled. 'Go ahead, m'dear. There's half a round of fine Stilton still there, and a case of good biscuit and some pickles — oh, bring what you may find, we'll all have a bite.'

I watched Clare trip away down the ladder and

across the deck, her hair flying, her slim legs flashing beneath the striped sailor's jumper from the siop chest that made a short dress for her. *The one who cares most for you* ...

Something was shifting inside me, the first stirrings of an injured limb after the plaster comes off or the stitches are removed, slow and painful but with the promise of eventual satisfaction That hunger of mine reached out after her, craving whatever she could give.

'You know,' commented Jyp, leaning over the wheel. 'Clare may be right, but – there's another way open to you, Steve. And me, I think it's a better way. Stay in the outer world. Stay out on the Spiral. Don't sink back into the Core. Stay with us, with Mall and me. We'll see you find your feet okay, and soon – why, there'll be no holding you back! Life out here's not always the way you've been living it. It can be like one long holiday, for as long as you want it that way. Think of the endless worlds waiting out there! And you needn't ever navigate an office desk again.'

Pierce rumbled agreement. Le Stryge just snorted. Mall, I noticed, played on.

'Jyp,' I said, 'that's flattering as hell. Thank you a million times over – damn it, I've never had friends like you and Mall. And yes, I can see there's a whole new life here. But – I don't know. I'm torn.' I looked after Clare, silhouetted a moment against the light of Pierce's cabin door. 'If I go back ... She won't remember, you say. A few days and it'll all be gone. But will I? I asked you that before. You've time to answer now.'

Jyp whistled. 'That's a great big can of worms. Like I said, it depends on a lot of things. A whole lot of things. What kind of person you are. How you change. How much you want to remember. How much you try. How much you refresh those memories, maybe.'

'By coming back, you mean? Out of the Core?'

'Sure. But I got to admit, that's got problems, too. Folk who make it a habit, well, they remember okay. It's the Core they tend to forget. Never completely, maybe – but it's liable to kind of slip away when they aren't

328

looking. Time slackens its grip on 'em, and bang! goes a year, or two years, or more, since last they set the evening at their heels. Till they linger so long that no navigation can get them right back where they were. Till, sooner than it seems, maybe, they begin to forget – and find they're forgotten.'

It seemed to me there'd been something more in his voice than his usual laconic good nature 'Is that what happened to you?'

'I'd a wife back then,' he said, neutrally. 'Sailors' wives, they get used to their men staying away; but if I'd known how long it was, maybe … Crap, maybe I did know. You can't have it both ways. You make your own choice in the end, I guess. And I'll level with you, Steve – answer what you were really asking. Yes. Yes, it's more'n likely you'll not remember. Yes, this may be the only chance to choose you get.'

'That's so,' said Mall, and went on playing.

Clare reappeared, laden with a tray of good things, and brought it up to us. I couldn't help noticing the lilt of her breasts beneath the striped jersey, the flash of thighs as she climbed to the deck, the faintest glimpse of golden hair as she stooped to put down the tray. Mall, too, was looking; and she suddenly sang a line or two from the ballad she was playing, in her mellow voice.

> *Let never a man a'wooing wend*
> *That lacked thinges thrie,*
> *A purse of gold,*
> *An open heart,*
> *And full of charitie …*

I sighed again. My heart wasn't open, and my purse was fast emptying; not that I grudged a penny of it. Clare smiled, as if acknowledging what Mall was saying, and settled down beside me. She took my arm and started feeding me some kind of paté on biscuits.

'I don't know,' I said again, when my mouth wasn't full. 'What a hell of a choice – there's no other like it. God, I'm tempted – I'm torn. Almost literally,' I added,

329

feeling Clare's grip tighten on my arm, the pressure of words unspoken. 'But the way it seems to me —'

They all leaned forward, waiting for my answer. It was amazing, a wonderful thing in itself; that I should matter to them. Come to that, they mattered to me — even that evil thing, Le Stryge, in his way. There was a debt there, if nothing more. I'd never had to feel like this before.

'It seems to me that the life I knew, the old life I had — I made a hash of that, a whole lot of mistakes. It's pure chance I didn't just go on making them, or worse. And though I've done a bit of learning, maybe, I've not finished yet. This new life I'm offered — I could make a real hash of that, too, couldn't I? Only the consequences might be worse — infinitely worse. Christ, they almost were!' I shuddered at the thought of what I might have been at this moment, so easily.

'I laid myself open to one kind of evil. I'd better make sure I'm less open to others, before I start hanging around them again. I don't want to leave you all — but, but I think I'd better. I should go back and learn to live my first life properly, and then maybe I can think about seeking out some others. I'll try and remember! I'll fight to stay in touch — and maybe I will. But if I don't — that's how it'll have to be. That's best for all of us.'

'A brave settling,' said Mall quietly, 'and, a'mine avis, the right and the true one. May't serve you better than you know now, my Stephen. I — I shall not forget.'

'Yeah, well, you've got a point, I guess,' conceded Jyp. 'There're some real ugly guys around out here. Can't have you whizzin' about like a bomb ready primed for the first comer to pick up. So — go!' He sighed. 'Forget all else if you must — but don't forget the docks, and Danube Street. And 'fore all the Tavern! Fix that in your mind. Fight for it. Then maybe the rest'll stay. And when you're good and ready, you just keep asking your way, and you'll find it in the end, if you really want to. But till then — well, I guess staying away, that's right 'nough the safest thing for you …'

Le Stryge snorted — much closer, I knew now, to a

real laugh than that evil cackle of his. Contempt must be one of his few remaining links with human feelings. 'The safest? Is it? I would not be so sure, boy. Stay away if you like, from this wider world of ours – and pray for your own sake that it stays away from you! I wonder if it will. Your destiny is uncertain, even in my eyes – do you know that? But should it chance to lie beyond the limits you once knew, that would not surprise me. And should that be so, then whatever you do to avoid it, it will surely find you out.'

I swallowed. The deck felt suddenly chill beneath me; but Clare's arm was warm on mine, and held me tight. As if she was anxious to draw me away …

I rose, and she rose with me. 'How long before we reach home?' she asked.

'Why, hours yet, m'dear,' rumbled Pierce. 'Till we cross the dawn again. At sunset – which sunset, sailing master?'

Jyp grinned. 'The sunset after the dawn we sailed. They'll hardly have had time to miss you.'

I gaped, but Mall just chuckled. 'Not for naught's he named the Pilot. Time holds few shoals for him.'

I shook my head wonderingly. Clare, accepting as ever, just chuckled, and drew me with her to the companionway. Laughing, skipping lightly to the tune of Mall's music, she led me by the hand down to the deck. I went, not looking back. But at my cabin door I hesitated, staring out into the night. Far ahead there, just above the horizon – was that faint streak of deeper darkness the first sight of land, or just a line of dark cloud? Whatever it was, it hung there like a frontier between sea and sky, or a barrier between the wider world and the narrow, between many dreams and a single cold awakening. Suddenly I was afraid of it, of crossing that dark bar once more and into the embrace of harbour walls, both sheltering and imprisoning. There I could find my firm berth again and never leave it, rooted fast to the mud. While all the seas of the world, all the infinite oceans of space and time beat between shore and shadow, only the breadth of a memory beyond my reach. I was afraid to go home.

But then, softly, Clare opened the door, and drew me in.

Why not? If she'd soon forget — if I might, also — what harm could it hold for us? We'd earned our holiday; and I, my first new lessons in living. And loving; there was time for a little of that. Time enough, till morning.

APPENDIX

From *The Consistory of London Correction Book*
for 27th January 1612 ...

Officium Domine contra Mariam Frithe

This day & place the sayd Mary appeared personally &
then & there voluntarily confessed that she had long
frequented all or most of the disorderly & licentious
places in this Cittie as namely she hath vsually in the
habite of a man resorted to alehowses Tavernes Tobacco
shops & also to play howses there to see plaies & pryses
& namely being at a playe about 3 quarters of a yeare
since at the ffortune in mans apparell & in her bootes &
with a sword by her syde ... And also sat there vppon the
stage in the publique view of all the people there
presente in mans apparell & playd vppon her lute &
sange a songe...

    & hath also vsually associated her selfe with
Ruffinly swaggering & lewd company as namely with cut
purses blasphemous drunkardes & others of bad note &
of most dissolute behaviour with whom she hath to the
great shame of her sexe often tymes (as she sayd) dranke
hard & distempered her heade with drinke

    And further confesseth ... she was since vpon Christ-
mas day at night taken in Powles Church with her peti-
coate tucked vp about her in the fashion of a man with a
mans cloake on her to the great scandal of diuers persons
who understood the same & to the disgrace of all woman-
hood...

    And then she being pressed to declare whether she
had not byn dishonest of her body & hath not also
drawne other women to lewdnes by her perswasions & by

carrying her self lyke a bawde, she absolutely denied that she was chargeable with eyther of these imputacions ... *[Mulholland, R.E.S., new series xxviii (1977), 31]*

Mary Frith, popularly known as 'Mad Mall', was remanded for further investigation, but seems to have come to no great harm – certainly not the public whipping usually reserved for 'lewdnes'. She is last heard of almost fifty years later – having reached an astonishing age for that period – and apparently still going strong.

Magic...Mystery...Revelations
Welcome to
**THE FANTASTICAL
WORLD OF AMBER!**

ROGER ZELAZNY'S
VISUAL GUIDE to
CASTLE
AMBER

by Roger Zelazny and Neil Randall

75566-1/$8.95 US/$10.95 Can

AN AVON TRADE PAPERBACK

Tour Castle Amber—
through vivid illustrations, detailed floor plans,
cutaway drawings, and page after page
of never-before-revealed information!